RESILIENCE

BOOK ONE OF THE RESILIENCE DUET

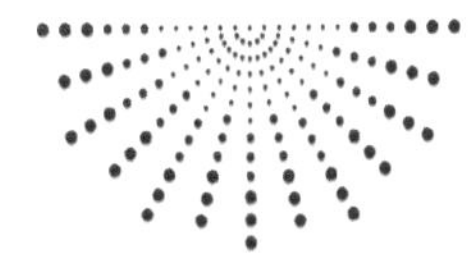

AMANDA SHELLEY

CONNECT WITH AMANDA SHELLEY

Want to be the first to know about upcoming sales and new releases? Make sure you sign up for my newsletter as well as connect with me on social media and your favorite retail store.

Website:
www.amandashelley.com
Newsletter:
https://geni.us/AmandaShelleyNL
Facebook:
https://www.facebook.com/authoramandashelley/
Instagram:
https://www.instagram.com/authoramandashelley/
Reader's Group:
https://www.facebook.com/groups/AmandasArmyofReaders/
Amazon:
http://amazon.com/author/amandashelley

Goodreads:
https://www.goodreads.com/author/show/19713563.Aman
da_Shelley
Book Bub:
https://www.bookbub.com/profile/amanda-shelley

ABOUT THE BOOK

Samantha never saw Enzo coming.

As the dust settles from her divorce, her life is full. She doesn't have time for distractions. She's too busy running her own company and checking off numerous items from her kids' demanding schedule to have a life of her own.

Then he walks into her kitchen with his breathtaking green eyes and a mischievous grin. He's there to surprise his father - her contractor, but his presence makes everything off kilter.

Enzo's perfectly content with his adventurous life as an elite rescue pilot, until a harmless prank turns on him. Instead of surprising his father, he finds his world thrown off course by the beautiful woman with a sexy smile, wicked sass and the mouthwatering ability to keep him on his toes.

With his limited time on leave, is she worth the risk to his heart?

SAMANTHA

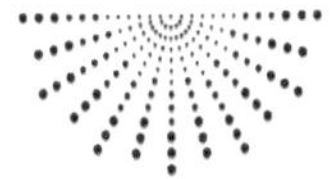

I wake by hearing the kids moving about. Glancing at my clock, I realize my alarm was never set. *Shit!* I frantically dash out of bed, grateful for the alarms in each of their bedrooms. Maddie is already dressed and eating cereal in the kitchen. I hear Declan in the shower, and Frankie is dressed and watching cartoons. The bus will arrive in thirty minutes, so I dash into the kitchen to finish putting their lunches together.

"Frankie, have you eaten breakfast?" I ask as I make my way past her.

"Yeah. I had Lucky Charms. Can I have PB&J for my lunch today?"

She always has PB&J. Does she think I'll suddenly forget? "Sure thing, sugar. Do you want an apple or a banana today?" I say in my best morning voice.

"Apple. Can you slice it? Oh, and Ava wants me to come over today after school. Can her mom take me to ballet and you pick me up?"

Ava is Frankie's best friend. Thankfully, I already planned this with Ava's mother so I could be here if my contractors are able to start the kitchen remodel this afternoon. "That's the plan, Stan. I'm going to pick you up from ballet first then we'll grab Dec and go to Maddie's match. We'll grab dinner out tonight since I don't know if we can cook at home with the contractor coming."

"Okay, Mama. Sounds good." Frankie takes her lunch and puts it into her backpack. Though she's my youngest at eight years old, Frankie has been the most resilient of my three kids. She has somehow found a way to accept our new "normal" and has adjusted to the recent changes in our family with ease.

Declan, my ten-year-old shouts from the stairs, "Hey, Mom, did you wash my practice uniform for soccer? It's not in my bag."

Crap. I must have left it in the dryer. I'm so off my routine this morning. I holler, "Check the dryer," up the stairs so he can get it himself.

"Thanks, Mom. Got it." I hear drift through the house a few seconds later.

Maddie removes her earbuds as she gets up from the table to put her dish in the sink from breakfast. "Hey, Mom, you're going to make it to my match tonight, right?" Maddie is a freshman and managed to make the varsity volleyball team. She doesn't get a lot of playing time, but I wouldn't miss it for the world.

"There's no way I'd miss it, Mads. I'm picking everyone up and we'll be there on time. Promise."

She comes over and gives me an unexpected hug. "I know,

Mom. I'm just not sure if Dad will make it, so I want to make sure you're there."

"Don't worry. Even if he can't make it, I know he'd want to be there." I glance to the clock and find they have five minutes to make it to the bus. I holler for everyone to hear, "Okay, guys, time to get going! The bus will be here any minute. Maddie, so will your ride."

I rush each of them out the door and realize I have less than an hour to get ready to meet with the contractor. One of the benefits of owning my own business is I can work from home today. I'll have to fit reviewing a manuscript in at some point. Who needs sleep, right? At least I can do most of my work with my laptop or e-reader if I'm just reading for content. I can work from just about anywhere. Before I shower, I start the coffee pot. It feels like I will need an extra dose of caffeine today.

I'm just settled at the breakfast bar with my coffee and my computer, ready to check emails and review my calendar, when I hear a knock at the door. Lorenzo Harper, my contractor, greets me. He's an older man but has kept himself in great shape over the years. His dark hair is thick and barely showing any gray, just a little around his temples. He has a warm smile on his face that lights up his green eyes.

"Morning, Samantha!" he greets me warmly. "Are ya ready to show me what needs to be done around here?"

"Thanks for coming, Lorenzo," I eagerly welcome him into my home. "I can't wait to get things started!"

Lorenzo has done some work for us in the past. He's the guy who comes out to write the bids and sets everything into motion for his crew, then manages it as the project continues, even though he may have multiple projects going on at once. He has been in business for years and is nearing retirement age, but he's not ready for that to happen anytime soon. He claims he's a people person and knows how to get the job done right. I walk Lorenzo around my kitchen, family room, and dining room, discussing the final plans for the changes being done. He verifies the timeline for how long everything will take. He's already been to my home, and we've discussed the project on the phone, so the proper permits have been filed and the renovation should begin shortly. I know when it's finished, I'll be more than happy with it.

When we're done touring, Lorenzo opens his computer and taps out a few things. A few minutes later, he stops and looks at me with a huge grin. "Well, darlin', you're in luck. One of my crews just finished a job early and we can be over here as soon as tomorrow to begin demolition. We'll start in the kitchen so we can get it back to functioning for you as soon as possible. You should only be without your appliances for about a week or so if your order comes in on time."

Relieved he can get started right away, I nearly hug him. "Sounds great. While the crew is here, I'll work from home and try not to get in your way."

Lorenzo gets up to leave. "I'll see you tomorrow morning then. You'll have to empty out those cupboards since we'll be starting there." He grins ruefully as he knows it will take me some time today to clear those out.

"It's a good thing I've bought boxes then, isn't it?" I smile back at him.

After spending the day packing up my kitchen, I pick up Frankie from ballet and Declan from soccer practice, then rush to Maddie's volleyball game. Realizing we only have about ten minutes until Maddie's match starts, I speed into the parking lot at the high school and the tires screech as I come to an abrupt stop in the first open spot I see. I quickly unload everyone and briskly walk across the parking lot, stopping dead in my tracks when I see Devin, my ex, helping a pixie-like woman out of his car. He places his hand on the small of her back and escorts her to the gymnasium. He doesn't see me at first, so I have a moment to school my features before I meet who I assume is Aubrey, his new girlfriend.

Unfortunately, I don't get much of a chance to pull myself together because Frankie notices her father immediately. She squeals, "Daddy!" as she rushes toward him. I see Devin startle, his body instantly frozen in place, but eagerly turns and scoops her up into his arms for a gigantic hug.

Our divorce has had its challenges and not all of us are as eager as Frankie to greet one another. I straighten my back, lift my chin, and make sure to have a smile on my face as I do my best to greet him warmly. Devin still wants to have an active role as a parent, so I do all I can to keep things positive. I've never been one to hold onto grudges or play into bitterness; I simply don't have time for that. Hopefully, one day I'll be able to have a real conversation with him again that doesn't feel forced.

"Hey, Devin. Maddie will be so happy you're here for her match." I somehow manage to make my voice sound smooth and unaffected by him.

An indescribable emotion flits through Devin's eyes for a moment before he replies. "Yeah, I'm glad I could make it. Aubrey and I just got back into town from a business trip." He politely smiles in my direction before gesturing to the blonde beside him and states, "Aubrey, this is Sam. Sam, this is Aubrey."

For a split second, Aubrey looks a little nervous as she looks me over, but quickly recovers by sticking out her hand and saying, "It's a pleasure to meet you. I've heard lovely things about you." A slow smile spreads across her face, as I instinctively push my hand out to meet hers.

I can't help but look at Devin to make sure my ears weren't deceiving me. Not that he makes a habit of bad mouthing me, but I have to say, I'm surprised. *Well, at least he hasn't been a complete asshat, I'll give him that. I guess things could have been much worse.* I inwardly shrug. I briefly look to Devin with a flash of surprise before I remember my manners. "Nice to meet you, too."

Aubrey then turns to Declan and asks encouragingly, "How was your soccer game last weekend? I heard you scored in the last game."

Declan quickly tries to gauge my reaction. He's very aware of my feelings and has become a bit protective of me. I give him my best supportive smile and he sighs. "Yeah... it was amazing. I scored from the backfield with only a few minutes to go. We'd been tied, so I got the winning goal." He looks pointedly at his father before adding, "Sorry you missed it." I inwardly cringe at his disappointment.

"I'm sorry, too, bud," Devin states sincerely as he ruffles Declan's wavy brown hair. "I'll be there tomorrow night. You know how things go with the business. I had to fly to New York to pitch that new ad campaign. I'm pretty sure we nailed the pitch, so I won't have to leave town again for a few more weeks." Devin puts his arm around Declan and pulls him in for a side hug.

Devin owns his own advertising firm. He's worked hard over the years and has made a name for himself. He has quite a few employees who usually do the traveling, but occasionally, there's a client for whom he needs to do the pitch. Travel was never a problem while we were married, until one day it was. He didn't meet Aubrey until after we were divorced, so I shouldn't have any animosity toward her, at least in that regard.

Before anyone can say anything else, Frankie exclaims, "Let's go watch Maddie! Dad, you can sit with us, right?" She suddenly looks at me to see if it's okay.

Great. Just what I need after a long day. I quickly remind myself that once again, this isn't about me. I refuse to be one of those parents who spars with her ex. You know, the ones who are bitter and vindictive and leave a wake of destruction in their path, caring nothing about the effects their rancor has on those they love, especially the children. My self-respect, not to mention my love for my children, won't let me behave that way.

Maddie doesn't expect to start the match, being a freshman. We find her sitting on the bench after the National Anthem is sung. But the smile that crosses her face when she realizes we've all arrived is priceless. By the way she keeps rubbing her hands up and down her legs, I can tell she's nervous since this is only their second match. She ends up getting to play during the second and the third sets, as setter, and does her best to help her team pull off a win. When she approaches us after the game, her smile is infectious.

"Hey, Mad-dog," Declan announces as she heads toward where we're seated in the bleachers. "Way to go out there!" He lifts his hand for a fist bump. He bursts with pride for his sister's success.

I can't help the way my heart flutters when I see the two of them supporting each other. Sure, they can also shriek like banshees when they really get into it, but overall, they really do care about each other. I sneak a glance at Devin who meets my eye and winks. *Yeah, we did something right.* His pride shines, too.

"Thanks for being here," Maddie says, gesturing to all of us. I can't help but notice her quick glance in my direction before hugging her dad. She knows things can still be tense between us, and having Aubrey here is new to our family dynamics.

"Amazing save out there." Aubrey smiles as she pats Maddie on the arm to congratulate her.

"Thanks. I didn't think I'd get that last dig, but somehow I managed." Maddie beams with pride for her accomplishment during the game. "Can we stop and get something to eat on the way home? I'm starving." She looks at me before glancing at her dad and Aubrey.

"Sure thing, Mads," Devin exclaims. Then he turns to me. "Want to join us, or should I drop them at the house after we get a bite to eat? I'm thinking pizza sounds amazing just about now." He rubs his stomach then beams at each of the kids before looking at Aubrey, then me for our reactions.

As awkward as this might be, I'm thankful I have the excuse of the remodel to politely decline. There's no way I want him back, but I'm just not ready to go out to dinner with Devin and his new girlfriend.

On the drive home, my mind whirls with thoughts of this evening and how far things have changed between Devin and me over the last couple of years. There wasn't just one thing that led to my decision to ask for a divorce. It was a multitude of things, compounding over time, which resulted in the demise of our marriage. The stresses of daily living, both at work and at home didn't help matters, but such is life. Everyone experiences those things; Devin and I weren't any different. The problem was when things became broken, it wasn't me to whom Devin turned. We tried to work things out, but nothing seemed to change. Eventually, when I realized how little I felt toward one act of betrayal or another, I knew it was time to pull the plug. I could no longer let the fear of the unknown keep me from doing what I knew was best. Obviously, my "give a fuck" had been broken and I no longer had any fucks left to give. Here I am at thirty-eight, starting over.

2

SAMANTHA

By the end of the next day, my kitchen is no longer recognizable. Lorenzo's crew brought in drop blankets to cover my furniture that hadn't been pushed into the garage. The walls have been stripped of the cupboards and all the appliances are gone. The carpet has been ripped out and the wall being removed is set to go in the morning. With all the banging and people moving about, it's difficult to get much of my own work done.

Tonight, the kids will be at Devin's. He saw the state of my kitchen when he picked up the kids and offered to take them tomorrow night, too, starting the weekend early since it's his time for visitation anyway. The kids are excited to be there since we can't cook here. They begrudgingly ate hot lunch today at school, but I know they're looking forward to their cold lunches for the rest of the week, courtesy of Devin. After they left, I went out and got dinner for myself, then settled in for the evening to catch up on some much-needed reading.

About noon on Thursday, Lorenzo returns to check on his crew before they break for lunch. He checks on their progress and is in the middle of a phone call for another job when an unfamiliar man walks in with a guy I recognize from the crew.

This new man immediately grabs my attention. He's well over six feet tall, with short, tousled, dark-blond hair. He's easily in his mid-thirties. He has an athletic build and a mischievous smile that makes his familiar green eyes sparkle with delight. *If I'm being honest, he is like sex on a stick. No man should look that good.* He's clearly up to something, but it's hard to tell from my vantage point in the hallway. When he notices me, he quickly motions for me to stay quiet by placing a finger over his lips and winks as he stalks up behind Lorenzo. As soon as Lorenzo ends his phone call and turns around, the stranger embraces him in a gigantic bear hug, nearly lifting Lorenzo off his feet, which is no small feat; Lorenzo is just slightly smaller than the size of this man in front of me.

"Hey, Pops!" The stranger chuckles.

The look of utter shock and then bewilderment quickly transforms Lorenzo's features. He quickly returns the hug with an UMPH and a muffled chuckle. "What the fuck are you doing here, son?" As soon as he's released, Lorenzo steps back to fully assess his son. Then without a word, pulls his son in for another tight embrace, patting him on the back like men do. "I... I... can't believe you're here." Lorenzo gathers his wits and remembers where he is, looking around the room, still in a daze.

While keeping an arm around him, Lorenzo spots me and beams. "Samantha, this is my son, Enzo. The last I knew, he was stationed in Germany, not due to come home for a few more months." Then he looks pointedly at Enzo. "Everything all right?"

"Yeah, Pops, it sure is!" Enzo beams back at his father. "I just got leave and thought I'd surprise you."

"Well, you sure as shit did!" Lorenzo chortles, still looking amazed and bewildered. "Did you see your Ma yet?"

"Yep. I stopped there first thing this morning. She told me where to find you. Need a hand?"

"Well, I might, but not today. Today, I'm going to knock off a few hours early and catch up with you... if Samantha doesn't mind." Lorenzo looks at me with a grin on his face, but a question in his voice.

Who am I to begrudge the man seeing his son. I know I would do the same. "I wouldn't want it any other way. Have fun!"

"Thank you, Samantha." Enzo looks at me with appreciation, then gives me a once-over. "I appreciate your understanding. I know Pops doesn't usually like to cut out on work." He looks around the room, assessing the project at hand. "I'll be sure to give him a hand to make up for it later."

I can't help but chuckle. "No worries. Your dad's helped me out a lot over the years. I know he'll enjoy every moment he gets to spend with you."

Before they leave, Lorenzo shows him the rest of the project. I go back to the living room and attempt to work on the manuscript I had planned to read today. For the first time in forever, I seem to be a little distracted though. I find myself reading the same paragraph over and over again, as I steal glances at Enzo. *Gaahh! Why am I letting him do this to me?* Sure, he's unbelievably gorgeous. He's muscular, but in a way that shows he's active, not a gym junkie. He has a presence about him that completely draws my attention. I have no idea the last time I felt this drawn to anyone, including Devin when we first started dating. There's just something about that man I can't get out of my mind. If I'm being honest, it's a little unnerving.

I steal glimpses of Enzo as they walk through my home. Who wouldn't look at a man like that? One time, he catches me in the act. *Crap!* He nods his head at me once, with a smile forming on his lips and a twinkle in his eye. Even though the man is breathtaking, I scold myself for staring. What the hell has gotten into me? I'm being utterly ridiculous. I'm not a schoolgirl easily distracted by the captain of the football team. I'm a grown woman, for God's sake, with kids and responsibilities. Being a single mom, I have no business getting caught up with thoughts about a stranger. It's not like he would ever be interested in me. Besides, he's going to leave, and I'll never see him again, *except in my fantasies,* but those don't count.

God, how long has it even been? Just the possibility of connecting with someone again has turned me into a bundle of nerves. Maybe I should consider dating again? But if I end up acting like this, I'm better off single.

3

ENZO

WHEN I ARRIVE AT POP'S WORKSITE, MY MIND IS ENTIRELY focused on surprising him. But I can't help but notice the sexy brunette in the hallway as I make my way to him. Her alluring smile and chestnut eyes almost distract me from my mission. But I manage to catch Pops off guard. He always was one for surprises growing up, wanting to get one in while he could, and I couldn't pass up this opportunity.

As Pops shows me around Samantha's beautiful home and explains what he has in store for it, I find myself glancing in her direction more than I should. When I catch her doing the same, a smile spreads across my lips. It's a spontaneous reaction, happening before I could put any thought into it. Pops quickly points out something else, and I'm back to having my attention focused on him.

I'm relieved to be home. I just spent thirty straight hours traveling from Germany. I had a few long layovers, then I snagged the last jump seat from New York City to Portland.

14

Being in the Air Force has its perks. Though it feels strange to let another person sit in the cockpit. Surprisingly, I managed to sleep most of that leg of my trip, so I'm still alert and ready for action.

As Pops and I make our way toward the door, I glance at Samantha one more time. She nods with a sheepish grin and tucks her shoulder-length hair behind one ear. A slight blush spreads across her face and she immediately has my full attention. *What would make her do that?* Upon further inspection, I notice she isn't wearing any jewelry, at least not on her fingers. As an airman, my life may be wild and full of adventures, but a married woman is a 'no-fly zone' no matter my level of attraction to her. Samantha has a natural beauty about her that draws my attention to her further. She's wearing little makeup, jeans and a dark-blue shirt that hug her curves perfectly. Samantha's shy demeanor and sexiness is a contradiction, making the selfish bastard in me want to get to know her further. But knowing there's an expiration date on anything that could transpire, I know there's little that can happen.

"So, what do you have in mind for today, son?" Pops pulls me from my thoughts.

"Well, I just got into town and could use some lunch," I mention, rubbing my stomach. I had surprised Ma earlier and, of course, she wanted to cook for me, but she was on her way to meet some friends for lunch, so I insisted she go with them, knowing we will have plenty of time to catch up. "Why don't we leave my rental car here and hit that diner only a few blocks away? I can come back for it later."

While we're waiting for our orders at the diner, Pops finally asks the question I've been waiting for. "So... have you decided if you're going to retire?"

He knows I need to decide within the next few months about whether I'm going to be in for four more years. I've already been in nearly twenty years and am eligible to retire, thanks to Running Start, a program which allowed me to graduate from high school with my associate's degree as well as high school diploma through a local community college. From there, I worked my ass off, when I wasn't deployed, to get through college and into flight school as soon as I possibly could.

But by the time I retire, thirty-eight still seems young and I love to fly. I could go into the private sector, but there's something to be said about flying helos for special ops, as opposed to civilians. I'm licensed to fly a variety of aircrafts, but I'm just not sure about the direction I want to go. Flying has been my life for the better part of forever, so as long as I'm airborne, I'll be a happy man.

"I'm still keeping my options open," I say with a sly grin. "That's part of the reason I'm on leave. There's a few opportunities I want to check out before I finalize my decision."

"Have you ever thought about settling down, son? I know that didn't work out for you years ago, but you're not getting any younger. I could use some more grandbabies and so could your ma," Pops teases.

I laugh. My younger brother and sister have already given them five grandkids. "Like you don't already have enough. You can't even move across the room on Christmas morning, there are so many kids under foot."

He doesn't know much about the details of my past, but I'm sure he can put two and two together. He doesn't have any expectations, but he likes to ask every now and then. I was almost married once, but while on deployment, I got a 'Dear John' letter and haven't given serious relationships much of a thought ever since. The Air Force has been my life. It's much easier to live in the moment, enjoying one day at a time. Besides, being the perpetual bachelor has had its perks. I enjoy women as much as the next guy and being a pilot hasn't left me lonely. Who am I to complain?

Pops sighs and is distracted by our meal arriving. We both dig into our BLT sandwiches and fries while Pops fills me in on what I've missed over the last few months. He updates me on my sister Erin and her two kids as well as my brother Zane, his daughter, and two boys. I feel like they're growing like weeds and I need to try to get to know them better while I'm here.

After we finish eating, we make our way across town to check in on the other sites his crews are working on. As he shows me around, I can't help but be impressed. His craftsmanship and dependability are the reasons he stays so busy. Pops isn't yet sixty years old and I can't even imagine him slowing down. My old man is still fit and in his prime. His employees, as well as clients, have nothing but compliments to give him. I aspire to be the man he is one day.

It's nearly six when Pops drops me back off at my rental car. He and Ma have tickets to a show she's been dying to see. Not wanting my surprise visit to be an imposition, I insist they continue with their plans, knowing we'll have plenty of time to catch up in the coming weeks. Since the street is full of cars,

Pops pulls in to drop me off from an open spot just down the block, so that he's not late. As it is, he'll barely have time to make it home and change before he and Ma must leave for the theater.

Just as I put my hand on the car door, I see the striking woman from earlier exit her house and lock the door. I can't help but take in her sexy curves and natural beauty. I catch her eye, and a grin spreads across my face. Without even giving it much thought, I find myself being pulled to her. By the time she makes it down to her car in the driveway, I'm only a few feet from her.

"Hey." My voice comes out thicker than expected, but I quickly recover. "Thanks again for letting Pops spend the afternoon with me. I really appreciate it."

A smile pulls at those kissable lips as she replies, "It's not a problem. Your dad would want me to spend time with my family if they'd just gotten into town." She fidgets with her keys and suddenly appears nervous, looking anywhere but at me.

"So where are ya off to?" My curiosity gets control of my mouth before I have the chance to think about it. When my brain catches up, I shake my head in disbelief. *Great. Stalker much.* I seem to be in the mindset of a teenager, rather than a man of my thirties. I've met beautiful women from all over the world, but can't figure out for the life of me, what it is about this woman that has me wanting to go out of my way to talk to her again.

"I'm on my way to grab something to eat. I think I might try the new Thai restaurant that just opened down the street." She points in the direction of the place as if I'm supposed to know where it is. "It's supposed to be good."

My mouth waters and my stomach has impeccable timing as it completely roars at the thought of my favorite food. I can't control the chuckle that escapes. "Obviously, Thai's my favorite. I'll have to try it while I'm here on leave." I can't remember when I'd last eaten decent Thai food. It doesn't help that it's been hours since Pops and I ate.

Samantha fidgets a little more with her keys. Then her head tilts to the side as if she's weighing a decision. I have no idea what's making this utterly attractive woman hesitate. Suddenly, she closes her eyes for the blink of a second, squares her shoulders, then pins me with rich mahogany eyes that nearly take my breath away and says, "Want to join me?"

4

SAMANTHA

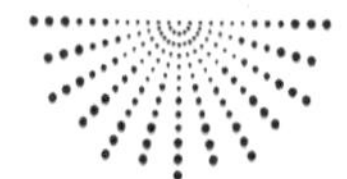

I HAVE NO IDEA WHAT JUST CAME OVER ME. I SQUEEZE MY EYES tight for just a moment so I won't have to see his immediate reaction to my utter absurdity. He appears to be the type that's used to being propositioned, but I'd just ejected out of my comfort zone and am spiraling out of my mind as I force my eyes open to await his answer.

When I open my eyes, I see complete amusement spread across his sexy, rugged face. He's developing a five o'clock shadow, and a small dimple peeks at me from his left cheek. I swoon at the devastatingly handsome man before me.

Damn, Enzo's one of the sexiest men I've ever laid eyes on. He possesses me with a gaze that's right out of the pages of a magazine. The kind only models with airbrushed faces can portray. I know. I look at the beautiful faces of said models on books I assist in publishing on a regular basis. *But God help me, it's even better in real life.* I know that look. It could mean one of two things. A, he thinks I'm a complete nut job, or B, he could be interested. *Ha! As if!* I haven't been on the receiving end of a magnificent gaze like that, in ages. So, he must think I'm out of my mind. Great! What was I thinking?!?!? I haven't asked anyone out in my entire life. Sure, I have had business meetings with attractive people, but I've never asked anyone I've just met to dinner. That's what I get for getting married in college.

I'm just about to prattle on and make some excuse for why he probably wouldn't be interested when he surprises the ever-loving hell out of me and simply states, "Sure. I'd love to."

I let out the breath I didn't know I'd been holding and shake my head in disbelief. Asking a man out, is by far, one of the most uncharacteristic things I've done. Sure, I'm confident in myself. I'm at the top of my game when it comes to getting things I want at work. I know where I stand. But, since I haven't dated much since high school, this is a little unnerving, especially since I just met the man. I'm not sure what possessed me to be so forward, but I smile at myself in awe, still a little shocked I just blurted out what was on my mind, rather than keep it as an amazing fantasy, like I usually do. I've been single for over a year, but never just put myself out there with someone I'm this attracted to. It seems as if my girly bits might just be dusting themselves off.

Suddenly, he seems to be waiting for a response of some sort, so I quickly regain the brain power I still have control over and will myself to say, "Would you like me to drive?" I jingle my keys between us.

He shrugs then looks at his car parked on the street in front of my house. "I suppose I could ride shotgun for a change." His glorious green eyes shine with mirth. There seems to be some hidden secret I'm not privy to, but based on the devious look on his face, I hope to find out more about it soon.

We fill the short ride to the restaurant with small talk, discussing what his dad is doing to remodel my house as well as how happy he was to spend the day with his father. The ride itself takes less than ten minutes before we pull into the parking lot. I'm thankful to have driving to focus on, a reprieve from ogling the ridiculously gorgeous man next to me. Surprisingly, there weren't any awkward moments or nervous gaps of silence, as I'd feared. Enzo has this natural presence that puts me at ease and I feel comfortable around him instantly. Maybe that's why I asked him to dinner in the first place. Who knows what I was thinking? I just hope I don't regret my bold move later.

As we exit the car, he immediately comes to my side and helps me with my door. When we walk toward the entrance of the restaurant, my nerves flutter even more as he places his large hand on the small of my back to lead me in. Feeling his strong warm hand causes a mixture of emotions. For as much as my nerves feel like a twitching cattail in a room full of rockers, Enzo is a calming presence as well.

As we take our seats we're handed our menus. We spend a few moments in silence perusing what the restaurant has to offer. Once I decide, I place my menu aside and look up to find his beautiful green eyes focused in my direction. A slight upturn of his lips has that ridiculously sexy dimple popping out again. *Yikes! Please God… give me coherent thoughts,* I plead internally.

"So, have you decided, Samantha?" Enzo asks in a deep

tone I can't help but be entranced by. I notice his menu is off to the side and his entire attention is now focused on me.

"It's Sam," I say hesitantly. "Only my parents call me by Samantha. I met your dad through them and never thought to correct him. But yes," getting back to what he had asked, "I'm going to have the broccoli and chicken with peanut sauce. It's one of my favorite Thai treats."

The greenish-gold specks in Enzo's eyes sparkle as the corners of his lips pull into a smile. "Well, Samantha is a beautiful name and it's quite fitting for you. I'm going with the cashew nut chicken. What would you like to drink?"

He picks up the drink menu and looks it over. When the waiter arrives, I decide on a glass of wine since the kids aren't with me tonight, and he orders a beer.

"So how long are you on leave for?" I ask, remembering bits of conversation with his dad. I know he's in the Air Force and he has been in it for quite some time.

"I actually have the next six weeks off." He takes a pull on his beer before adding, "I can't remember the last time I was home for so long. Usually, it's just a couple of weeks at a time."

The way he curves his lips around the long neck of the bottle has an interesting effect on me. One I haven't felt in forever. It may be the wine, or Enzo himself, but a sudden warmth spreads over me and makes my nerves flare all over again. *Calm down,* I chastise myself. *It's not like you've never been on a date before. But it has been a long time since you were this attracted to anyone,* my inner voice reminds me. *And he's H-O-T. When was the last time you ever felt this way about anyone, including Devin?* I ask myself. My libido has been dormant for way too long and I have no idea how to handle it.

"That's exciting for you," I add after finishing a sip of my wine, trying to keep my thoughts under control. "You seem close with your dad. Will you spend a lot of time with your family?"

He nods, but we're interrupted by the waiter bringing our delicious-smelling food. My mouth waters at the thought of tasting it. I quickly grab my fork and take a bite. My mouth explodes with flavor and I can't help myself when a little moan escapes. I glance up at Enzo and see his gaze darken. *Great, now he thinks I'm a freak.*

Suddenly embarrassed, I cover my mouth and speak when it's cleared. "Sorry. I haven't eaten since breakfast. With the construction, I forgot to eat lunch today." I wave my hand in the air, trying to dismiss my savageness.

He glances at his watch. "Do you make a habit of that?" he teases. "It's after seven. You ought to be starving by now. I ate around noon, and you heard my stomach rumble." He chuckles lightly.

"No." I motion to myself. "I obviously don't skip many meals. But with no kitchen, I just hadn't gotten around to getting out of the house yet today."

He gives me a full assessment before he adds, "You certainly don't have room to miss many more meals."

The way he says that has me squirming in my seat. I'm dumbfounded at his remark. I work out when I can, but a regular regiment isn't really on my schedule. With work, three kids, and my taxi schedule in the evenings, I'm lucky to fit any time in for myself. I usually try to fit in a jog a couple of times a week, but sometimes even then it's difficult unless I go first thing in the morning. But the way he looks at me makes me think he might appreciate the efforts I do make.

I shake my head and dismiss the comment with a laugh. He hesitates for a moment before picking up his fork to take a bite of his own food. For the next few minutes, each of us are consumed with the savory food that's before us. Eventually, Enzo breaks the silence.

"So... what do you do when you're not hanging around a remodel?"

"Well, I'm a commissioning editor for a small publishing house in Portland." Enzo looks interested, so I continue to explain my job since most don't know what it really entails. "Basically, I find books worthy of print. I work with authors and keep them on track and stay within budget. Since it's a small company, I also assist in the basics with editing from time to time when the need arises. Usually, others do the nitty-gritty of that aspect. But when a project calls to me, I sometimes like to see it to completion." I smile when I think of some of the amazing projects I have worked on over the years.

"It sounds like you love your job," Enzo observes. "I can tell by the look on your face while you're talking, it's something you're passionate about." He forks another bite into his mouth as he waits for my response.

I sigh, and a smile spreads across my features. "Yeah, I'm actually part owner of the company. My best friend Lexi and I started it after college and have built it from the ground up. We remain small because we both like to stay involved in the entire process and help undiscovered authors reach their dreams. We have quite a few full-time and part-time employees, but neither of us wants to become part of the impersonal corporate conglomerates like the bigger publishing houses. Some big names have come through our doors. Once we discover new authors, our attention to detail and the ability to match them to the right market allows us to compete with the bigger houses, but on a smaller scale."

"That's impressive," Enzo adds as he leans in and rests his forearms on the table, giving me his undivided attention. "It's nice to see people's goals pay off for them. That must be quite rewarding."

Nodding, I reply, "Yes, it certainly is, but enough about me. What is it that you do exactly?"

He nods his head and shrugs hesitantly. "Well, I don't really talk about the specifics much, but I'm actually a pilot. I mostly fly the PJs, that's the Pararescue men in and out of their missions. For the past ten years or so, I've been working with those teams." He stops for a moment then shrugs. "There isn't much I can't fly. My job is to get the teams there and back safely and I do what I can to make that happen."

His voice sounds somber at the end. For some reason, he sounds quite humble when he says this. Sure, he exudes confidence and I'm sure he has a cocky side to him as well, but it amazes me at how that side of him slipped away as he explained his job. He shows a great sense of pride in his abilities, but he isn't pretentious in the slightest. I have no idea what it specifically entails, but from the look on his face, I'm not sure if he can or should go into further detail with me. But all the same, I'm in awe of his service and skills.

"Wow, that's incredible," I whisper. "Have you been in Germany long?"

"Well, for the last couple of years, I've been based out of

Ramstein Air Force Base, but my missions have taken me all over the world. My hope is to be stateside again soon." Enzo locks his gaze upon mine before continuing. "I'm actually home this time to feel out a few offers and decide whether I'm going to stay in." He shakes his head before adding, "I'm not even sure why I've told you all of that. I haven't even mentioned it much to my family, so if you can, keep this between us while I decide?"

The way he says it makes me think I might be seeing more of him in the future. This pleases me to no end, but it's a little unnerving at the same time. I can't believe how much I'm enjoying my time with Enzo tonight. I don't remember the last time I've enjoyed a man's company like this, apart from Devin when things were happy in our marriage.

I nod in agreement, my heart full of understanding. "That definitely is a lot to consider." I find myself reaching across the table and patting his forearm. Before I can pull my hand back, Enzo grasps my hand lightly and holds it on the table. The spark of electricity that zooms through me catches me off guard. I can sense Enzo feels something as well because he holds my gaze for a long moment before saying another word.

"I've actually been in for nearly twenty years. It's kind of hard to imagine what life would be like without being a part of a unit." Enzo looks as if he's a little lost in thought at the end of this statement. I can tell it's a decision he won't make easily.

"That's truly amazing. Thank you so much for your service and dedication!" I say with sincerity.

"I don't know any other way." He grins humbly, then shakes his head as if dismissing a thought. "Over the years, there have been many stories to tell. Some worth repeating, while others are unmentionable. I've traveled the world, though not in the way you would traditionally think. Not a lot of sightseeing done on this job. But it pays off when the mission is successful, I get to help bring someone home."

"What would you do if you weren't in the Air Force?" I ask as I let go of his hand to take another sip of my wine.

"That's the million-dollar question." Enzo quirks a smile, making his dimple pop again. "I could stay in, I could go into the Air National Guard because it's based here in Portland. Or I could go into the private sector and continue with missions much like what I currently do. I have a few meetings lined up. I've already been propositioned by a couple of ops teams, but I need to see if the fit is right." Enzo gives me a knowing nod and I shake my head in agreement.

"It's always good to have options," I weigh in, not really knowing how to respond. I take another bite of my chicken and a sip of wine.

Enzo takes another bite as well before taking another pull on his beer. "Enough about work. What do you do outside of work, Sam?"

Suddenly, I think of my kids and my recent divorce. I guess I should be as straightforward with him as possible and break the news to him about my kids. I know from experience as well as what my friends have told me, that kids are sometimes a deal breaker for guys in general, especially sexy airmen like him. I might as well rip the bandage off before either of us get too invested. I love my kids and I'm proud of them. If he reacts poorly, I'd rather know up front. It's unlikely we will even see one another with him only being here temporarily *Geesh, Sam. Get a grip.*

"Well... I actually spend a lot of time being a glorified taxi to my three wonderful children." I smile and shrug dismissively. I inwardly cringe, hoping he won't react wrong because we seem to be hitting it off well. For the first time since my divorce, I want to consider a second date. However, my kids are my life, so if he doesn't respond well... he can suck it.

To my surprise, he grins sheepishly before adding, "I saw their pictures at your house. They're beautiful. What are their names and ages?" he asks as he leans forward and pats a hand on my forearm, sending a zing of electricity shooting through me.

Of course, I'm a proud Mama so I dive into telling him all about Frankie, Maddie, and Declan. I tell Enzo their interests as well as characteristics which make each of my kids unique. Enzo prods me with questions as he gets to know them better through our conversation.

After a few minutes of letting me fawn over my kids, I ask, "So what about you, do you have a family of your own?"

A dark cloud crosses his features before he shakes his head and dismissively states, "I love kids and at one point, I wanted some of my own. But it wasn't in the cards for me." He has a far-off look in his eyes, as he continues with, "Ever since I've kept my life focused on my job." He's silent for a heartbeat before his mood lightens. "Besides, that's what my nieces and nephews are for."

There seems to be a story there, but I won't push it. Maybe someday he'll tell me more, but since I just met the man, there's no way I'm going to push this issue now. Instead, I change my tone to match his and tease, "Well, you must date a lot." I eye him up and down with a grin on my face, trying to get a read on him.

He sighs, and the side of his mouth turns up as he states, "Well… I don't really date a lot, but yes, I've had relationships. Some have lasted longer than others, but nothing permanent."

I'm not really sure how to take that, but for some reason, he doesn't come across as a complete serial dater. The more we talk, the more I want to get to know him.

We spend the better part of the next hour making small talk and just enjoying each other's company. When the check comes, Enzo grabs it before I even know it's here. I try to put up an argument and attempt to pay since I asked him, but he won't hear it. He insists on paying. As we get up to leave, he once again puts his hand on the small of my back and leads me to the car. The zinging sensation I experience is almost indescribable and I'm not really ready for it to end.

"Are you okay to drive?" he asks as we approach my car.

"Yes." I appreciate his concern. I only had the one glass and had finished it at the beginning of our meal.

When we get back to my house, I feel a little awkward. As the evening went on, the dinner we shared felt more like a date than any I had been on. Since my divorce, my best friend Lexi insisted I date a few times. There were even a few orchestrated setups, but I had never been that into it. Enzo seems different. I can't put my finger on it, but everything about him seems to spark my senses.

I'm not sure what to do next as he gets out and walks me to my door. Once again, he leads me with his hand on the small of my back. His touch sends a bolt of electricity through my entire body. It's as if there's a live wire connecting us and I have no desire to shut it off.

When we get to my door, he brushes a stray strand of hair behind my ear. I gaze into those delicious green eyes and get completely lost in Enzo for a moment. In a gravelly voice, Enzo whispers, "I had a great time." His hand lingers on my cheek as he says, "If it were any other night, I'd find a way to get you to invite me in because I'm nowhere ready for my time with you to end. But..." he hesitates, like he's forcing himself to say the words, "I just got back into town today and I promised Ma and Pops I'd be home when they returned from their night out. It's the only way they'd go out this evening. Is there any way we can continue this evening another time?"

He completely entrances me with his stare. The determination shining through his green eyes to get me to agree with him not only sets me on fire but leaves a swarm of butterflies taking flight in my belly. I haven't felt this much of a pull toward someone in as long as I can remember. I'm so lost in him, I forget to respond.

He gives me his wicked grin, pulling out that lickable dimple, and rests the hand that had brushed my hair away from the base of my neck. "So... what do you say, Samantha?" Enzo whispers smoothly.

5

ENZO

I FEEL LIKE A COMPLETE ASS. I'M SO INTO SAMANTHA MY PANTS have shrunk about three sizes since she asked me to dinner in the first place. I'm sure she thinks I'm a complete tool for ending things so abruptly. *Meeting my parents?* What a dumbass thing to say. I'm thirty-seven years old and I haven't used Ma and Pops as an excuse to leave since I was in my teens. But I know, with every fiber of my being, if I were to go inside, I wouldn't be leaving anytime soon. I promised my parents I'd be there when they got home... and if there's anything redeeming about me, I'm a man of my word. Besides, she's a mom and who knows where her kids might be?

Christ, what is it about Samantha? I usually steer clear of women like her. She's the epitome of a long-term commitment in the making. *Huh? This should scare the shit out of me.* But there's something about her I'm not ready to walk away from. *Yet, anyway.*

As my hand reaches the base of her neck, it takes

everything in my power to keep from completely devouring her. I'm dying for just one taste. Which I will have before I leave as the chemistry between us is almost palpable. But first, I need her to say yes. "So, what do you say, Samantha?"

She takes in a deep breath. Her gaze locks on mine and for a moment, I have no idea what her response will be. This is so unnerving. I've never had to work to get a woman to agree to see me. Suddenly, she seems to gather her thoughts and I hear her whisper, "Sure. I'd love to."

Relief washes over me and before she can even finish her thought, I find myself pulling her face toward mine. I bend down, closing the distance between us. My lips crash onto hers, releasing some of the pent-up chemistry we've been flirting with all night. As my tongue sweeps across her lips, they part, and I feel as if I've died and gone to heaven. If she tastes this sweet, with just a kiss, I can only imagine what it'd be like to taste elsewhere. When she brings one hand to my neck and fists what little hair I have at the back of my head in her other, I feel as if she has just set off an inferno inside me. If I don't end this now, I won't be held accountable for my future actions. Something primal has been lit and there is no telling how this night will end. After a few more moments of completely devouring her delicious mouth, I pull back, attempting to regain control of myself and the situation.

"So..." I kiss her once more, soft and feathery, trying to keep my tone light. "What are your plans..." Another amazing kiss. There is no way I'll be able to wait to see her again, "... for..." quick peck, "tomorrow?"

She pulls back with a pant, looking me in the eyes. "Um... I'm working again from home. The kids are with their dad through the weekend." She leans up, brushing my lips with a kiss, seeming just as eager as I am to keep her body in contact with mine.

"Great!" I say, realizing my wait might not be as long as I'd feared. "Can I pick you up tomorrow afternoon?" Like a magnet, I'm pulled to her. Before she can answer, I sweep down across her lips, kissing her once more. Her body is addictive and I haven't had enough, but I force myself to pull back.

"Sounds good," she says breathlessly before reaching up on her toes for another kiss.

I nearly lose myself in the moment, but when she lets out a deep moan, setting my nerves on fire, I'm also brought back to reality. I need to slow things down. I pull back for good this time. I've been with my share of women, but no one, and I mean no one has *ever* made me feel the way Samantha does. I pluck her keys from her hand, then unlock and open the door for her. She steps in and I wait for her to put in a security code. I briefly kiss her once more before whispering, "Until tomorrow," in a huskier voice than I recognize. Then I turn and painfully walk to my rental car.

The next day as I drive to meet Riggs, the owner of one of the security firms, I can't get my mind off Samantha. I make a hasty decision and pull into a parking lot. Before I know it, I'm dialing the restaurant from last night to place an order for delivery. Knowing her home is in shambles from the construction, I don't want her going hungry again. Besides, her beautiful smile keeps playing on a constant loop in my mind. Maybe she'll think of me and smile again.

With that task complete, I continue driving. As I arrive, I'm not surprised to see an unobtrusive brick building that looks more like a warehouse. It's in an industrial area. If I were an untrained observer, it appears like every other building around. What my trained eyes show me is that Riggs owns this entire area. There are likely dozens of cameras on my approach and I would be willing to bet the clarity of those images could even describe the freckle on my inner wrist. I saunter up but before I reach the door, it swings open.

A man about my age and build dressed in black cargo pants and a matching t-shirt approaches me with an outstretched hand. "You must be Harper." His grip is firm and no-nonsense like, though his facial expression is a little hard to read. But like most of these situations, I'm sure he's sizing me up as much as I am him. "I'm Boone, Riggs sent me to meet you. He's on a conference call and will be with us shortly."

I nod, following him through the door. We enter a small reception area. There is a desk with a computer and phone set up. Most would just assume a small business was running behind these doors. Boone continues to walk and motions for me to follow. We turn right, down a hallway. It quickly becomes quite evident, this isn't a normal office suite. Placing his palm on a scanner, he waits for a door to open. After going down another hallway with no other points of entry, we reach another door. This one is steel and from the looks of it, thick. Boone scans his retina, then I hear the whoosh of locks.

We enter the next area and it's as if we've entered a tech geek's wet dream. There are monitors everywhere. Along one wall are all sorts of electronic devices. Some I've seen and used before while on routine missions, while others I have no idea what their intended uses are. A couple of men sit at monitors using code and completely locked into their task at hand. Along another wall are cabinets from floor to ceiling. I keep my well-trained mask in place to not give any of my thoughts away as we move toward another room at the back of this one.

We enter a conference room with a large table and about twenty plush rolling chairs around it. There's obviously long meetings held here if they go to such measures to have comfortable chairs brought in. I guess that's a perk of moving to the private sector. Boone gestures for me to sit as he says, "I'll let Riggs know you're here. Have a seat and I'll be back in a few. Can I get you anything to drink?"

"I'm good. Thanks," I reply, taking the seat closest to me.

With that, Boone exits, and I'm left in this enormous room by myself. Upon further scrutiny, this must be their tactics and operations room. The walls itself are stark white and as I turn around, I see a huge flat-screen monitor on the wall behind me as well as multiple smaller screens along each side of the middle one. There's also another door at the other end.

I'm not left with much time to myself before Boone and Riggs join me. My military training and manners have me standing to greet them. I shake Riggs' hand as he greets me. "Good to see you've made it."

"Glad to be here. It's been a while since we last met up." His team had helped with one of our missions about six months ago. After experiencing first hand my flight abilities out of more than extreme conditions, he'd told me to come talk with him when my contract with the Air Force was up. At the time, I brushed him off, but now as that date could be a real possibility, I'd be a fool not to keep my options open.

"Let's cut to the chase." Riggs lets out a breath as he folds his over six-foot broad body into a chair. "I've done my homework and know we'd be a good fit for one another. I've seen your records and they stand for themselves. I've also witnessed firsthand what a badass you can be in any cockpit. Are you here to tell me you're finally going to take me up on my offer and join my team?"

His bluntness catches me a bit off guard. I thought this would be an interview, not a formality. Riggs has always been known for his matter-of-factness. I shake my head and chuckle. "I'm seriously considering it. I have four more months on my contract with the Air Force, but I feel too young to completely retire. It doesn't hurt that your home base is close to my family here in Portland either."

His eyebrows raise as his head tilts knowingly in my direction. "Family is important. If you work for us, that's where you'll be when we're not out on a job. Don't get me wrong, sometimes there is little time between getting the call and wheels. They can also last a few weeks at a time. Usually, we're home within a few days. Trust me when I say, compared to what you're doing, the compensation's worth it."

He knows exactly what I'm looking for. This is by far the oddest of interviews I've ever been on. Can I even call it an interview? It seems more like he's interviewing for me now.

I place my hand on my chin, letting my fingers rub against it as I contemplate his offer. It'd be nice to get a place of my own and not be gone for months at a time. I could spend more time with my parents and get to know my nieces and nephews. Perhaps someday I'd even settle down and have a family of my own now that I'm not moving every couple of years and distance won't be an issue. An image of Samantha's beautiful face flashes before my eyes and I shake the thought away before it takes any merit. *Christ, I just met the woman yesterday. She has no business being in my thoughts today. Besides, she has a family and a life of her own. What in the world would she want with an Airman who is always away on a mission?* But... if I could stay in one place long enough... ENOUGH! *Get back to your interview, dumbass.* I feel the pull of a slight smile spreading across my face for letting my mind wander and being so stupid. Hopefully, Riggs and Boone will take it as I really like the possibility of being at home.

"What would the terms consist of?" I ask, knowing I'd be a good fit for this operation. I've already met and worked with many of the men and a few women working for Riggs. I also know I'd be an asset to his flight crew with my skill set. I think it's time to get the logistics taken care of, so I can make an informed decision for my future.

A smug smile forms on Riggs' face. His dark eyes crinkle in the corners, the only sign showing his age. I know he's near forty, like me. Riggs hands me a small packet of papers. "I took the honor of drawing this up, in case you came to your senses."

Once again, I'm taken back by his bluntness. I begin looking through the papers. It's essentially my contract. It discusses my salary, compensation, benefits, and even an additional retirement package. When I look at the numbers, my eyes widen slightly. There's even a huge signing bonus. Taking a few moments to let everything sink in, I realize there's some perks working in the private sector, especially for a job I'm currently already doing. This opportunity could be hard to pass up.

Trying to contain my eagerness, I place the papers back on

the table and coolly ask, "When would I have to let you know?"

Riggs and Boone both smirk at each other before glancing back at me. Just as I think Riggs is about to comment, Boone states, "You take your time. Enjoy your leave and let us know in the next couple of weeks. We know you can't start until you are done with the Air Force, so we're in no hurry to know the answer."

Riggs adds, "If you'd like, we're having a barbeque at my place on Saturday. You can stop by, visit with the rest of us, and get a real feel for the men and women you'd be working with. Feel free to bring a friend. The families will all be there. My wife would have my ass if I didn't tell you about it."

I laugh. I can't help it. The man before me is as gruff as they come but the moment he mentions his wife, he's a walking contradiction. There's a lightness to his features I can only hope to experience for myself one day. Knowing I shouldn't pass up the opportunity to get to know the team I'd be working with, I reply, "Sure. Just give me the time and address and I'll be there." Besides, after what he's shown me, it's highly unlikely I won't be taking him up on his offer. I want to meet with another buddy of mine before making my final decision.

After my meeting with Riggs and Boone, I drive toward my parents' house. But before I go too far, to make the phone call that's been weighing on my mind, I pull into a nearby parking lot and find my buddy Carson in my contacts and hit dial. We served together for many years and when I told him about my meeting with Riggs, he told me to call afterward. His deep voice greets me, "Hey, Harps! What's up?" I can hear music in the background and he sounds slightly out of breath.

"Not much, just finished meeting with Riggs." I shake my head, realizing the entire process was merely a formality, rather than an interview.

"Awesome. So... are you going to finally play with the big boys?" Carson teases. He's been working with Riggs for the past five years. I know if I join their team, I'll be with good people. I met Carson shortly after I enlisted in the Air Force and we've been friends ever since.

"I'm thinking about it," I nonchalantly say, to evade giving a direct answer. "I still need to talk with the CO at the Air National Guard before making any major decisions."

A low chuckle comes across the line before Carson says, "I hear ya. So, how'd you like Riggs and Boone?"

I try to figure out how to put my experience into words. Before I can say anything, Carson interrupts, "So did they act as if it were a done deal?"

"Um... yeah, actually they did," I reply. "I'd thought it would be more like an interview of sorts, but it was almost as if everything were just a formality. It's definitely the strangest job interview I've experienced."

"Ha... that's how they roll. You've already worked with us. They know you'll click with our team." He takes a deep breath and lets it out heavily. "Besides, they know if they make you a lucrative enough offer, you'll have no other choice but to sign with us. I know you love what you do, or you wouldn't do it. Why not do the same thing, making a shit-ton of money while you're at it? The best part is you'll be able to work with yours truly and see my handsome mug every day," Carson teases. "Fuck, you know you love me, Harps."

I shake my head and can't hold back my laughter. "Yep, that might just be a reason NOT to sign," I joke. "I know you snore like a boar in heat and all sorts of other crazy-ass shit about you." I continue to smile as some of my favorite memories with Carson flash into my mind. The thought of some alone has me in stitches again.

"You know you love me, Harps, even if you won't admit it!" Carson taunts as if he doesn't know I'd lay down my life for him or any member of my team. It's just the way we are. "So, what are your plans for the rest of the weekend?" Carson asks, changing the subject.

Once again, Samantha's beautiful face fills my mind. But I quickly divert my thoughts to answer his question. "Well, I will probably just hang with my parents and see my family. Riggs invited me to a barbeque at his place on Saturday, so I will make an appearance there as well."

"Good to hear. If you want to come out Saturday, a couple of us are going to head out to McMenamins'. You're welcome to join us. My buddy Todd's girlfriend always brings a few friends along. The more the merrier."

"I'll keep that in mind," I say noncommittally, but then amend my thoughts once another flash of Samantha's sexy smile and wicked sass fill my mind. "But I wouldn't count on it. I'm pretty sure I'll be busy."

Why the hell would I want to spend a night with a stranger? I may not be into long-term commitments, but I don't juggle women either. I'm sure as hell not stupid enough to walk away or blow any chance I have with Samantha. I have no idea what's gotten into me, but there are some things I just don't do. I haven't been able to banish her from my memories, and with any luck, she'll still be up to going out again tonight and make some more.

"Suit yourself." Carson chuckles then adds, "Listen... I gotta run. I'll see you Saturday. Oh, and for what it's worth. I think it'd be an honor to work with you again. I hope you make the best decision, for you."

"Don't worry, Cars, I will." I add before ending the call.

I glance at my watch. It's now a little after three in the afternoon. I contemplate where to go next, but those rich mahogany eyes keep calling to me and a decision is quickly made. *It is the afternoon.* Since I didn't think to get her number like the dumbass I am, I guess it's only fair I show up to see her, like I promised. I point my car in the direction of the sexy woman I can't seem to get off my mind and wonder what the hell she's doing to me.

6

SAMANTHA

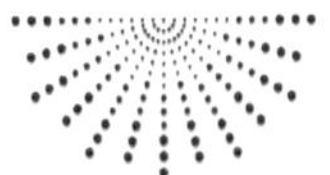

ALL MORNING, MY MIND KEEPS REPLAYING MY TIME WITH ENZO, as if it's on a loop. I find myself lost in thought as I touch my lips, recalling his taste. I can't remember when I'd ever been kissed so senseless. He managed to unhinge me in just mere moments with that sexy wicked mouth of his. *Fuck, that man can kiss.* I thought I'd burst into flames on the front porch and the neighbors would have to call the fire department. I might be incinerated if I were to experience more than just his delicious mouth.

I've tried over and over again to read the manuscript I'd started yesterday, but my mind keeps wandering back to Enzo. The construction crew is busy at work, so I do manage to get some work done. Thankfully, I'd read most of it yesterday and don't have as much to do today.

Around noon, I'm pleasantly surprised when I answer my door and find take-out from last night's Thai restaurant being delivered. There's no note, but I know it must be from him.

Who else would send me chicken and broccoli with peanut sauce? It makes me a bit giddy to know he's thinking of me. I wish I could call and thank him, but since neither of us thought to exchange numbers, I'm left with wondering if he'll show up today like he said. I'll admit, I've had my doubts. I keep trying to pass everything off this morning as if last night didn't matter, but now that I sit on my back porch eating my favorite Thai food, I know without a doubt he will be showing up today. *Though I wish I knew when.*

Around three-thirty, while the construction crew is still hard at work, I hear the doorbell ring. Not knowing who it is, I quickly rush to answer it. Pulling open the door, I'm greeted by the devilishly handsome man who's taken over my thoughts throughout the day. His short, dark-blond hair is messy on top and his gorgeous green eyes glint as if he holds all the secrets in the world. A slow smile spreads across his face, revealing that delicious dimple on his left cheek, instantly making my knees go weak. His dark blue t-shirt stretches heavenly across his broad defined chest. I'm at a loss for words as I take in my spectacular view.

"Um, is this a bad time?" Enzo asks, shaking me from my thoughts.

I shake my head to clear my suddenly lust-filled thoughts away. "No, not at all. Please come in."

With all the noise coming from the kitchen. I motion for him to follow me through the house to the back patio. I've created my own private oasis in our backyard, as I love to be outside any chance I can when the weather is decent. It's covered, so I can even be out here in the winter months or enjoy the rain, as only true Oregonians can do, while curling up with a great book. Lounge chairs and patio furniture are set out so I can entertain in our big backyard as well. When we finally reach my intended destination, I turn to face Enzo. "I... uh... didn't know when to expect you," I admit sheepishly. "I wanted to call and thank you for the fantastic lunch, but we forgot to exchange numbers last night."

"I'm glad you liked it." He reaches for my hand and I realize the zing of electricity from last night wasn't in my imagination. It's still there and back in full force. "I didn't want you going hungry again today. Mind if we sit?" Enzo's green eyes gesture to the double chair next to us.

"Sure," I say, guiding us to the oversized chair. From this spot, we're guaranteed not to be overseen by any of the crew working on my house, unless they come out to join us for some reason.

Before we reach our destination, he tucks one strand of hair behind my ear with one hand, while he continues to hold mine with his other. He lightly brushes a kiss on my cheek as he asks, "How was your day, beautiful?"

"Fine. They're making a lot of progress on the house. I managed to get some work done earlier." *Well, at least I tried to work... when I wasn't thinking about you!*

He pulls me down next to him on the chair as he states, "It was a grave oversight for not getting your number." He digs out his phone from his pocket. "Please, let's rectify this now, so it won't happen again. What's your number?" A sly smile pulls at his lips, making me catch my breath.

When his eyebrows raise at my hesitation, I quickly regain my thoughts and rattle off my number. Seconds later, I receive a text notification. Grinning, I smirk at Enzo. "I take it that's from you." I leave my phone unchecked, laying on the table next to us. I don't need to see his number since he's right in front of me. Shaking my head at his thoroughness, I ask, "So what did you do today?"

As Enzo tells me about his day, I can't help but be entranced in his deep timbre and sexy tone. If he were a narrator for one of the books I promote, I could listen to him read the phone book all day long and still be completely satisfied. The man just exudes sex and confidence, and I find myself more entranced with each thing he says. He tells me about having breakfast with his parents and catching up with his sister and her kids earlier this morning. Her children sure know how to keep everyone on their toes. Enzo's enthusiastic expression while explaining how he had to chase a half-naked toddler out the front door has me nearly doubling over. He ends by telling me about the most interesting interview I've ever heard of. I'll admit I'm a little shocked at Riggs' approach, but overall it sounds like an opportunity worth considering.

Enzo surprises me by changing the subject when he asks, "I know this is short notice, but do you have plans for tonight?" He eyes me hopefully, awaiting my answer.

"Well..." I say sadly, "I've been waiting around to see if a guy I went to dinner with last night is going to show up. You see, he forgot to ask for my number. I wasn't sure if or when he would get here," I tease mercifully. "What do you have in mind, maybe you'll have a better offer?"

Enzo lets out a deep belly laugh at my sass. "Well, if you think it's a better offer, I was going to see if you wanted to grab a bite again tonight. We could go to a restaurant I enjoy each time I'm home... but if you're waiting for that fool, I understand. Only a complete tool would walk away from a beautiful woman like you and not at least score her digits."

"Hmmm." I pretend to think it over for a bit. "Decisions, decisions!" In a sing-song voice, I add, "He was kinda cute and a fairly decent kisser." I put my hand on my chin, pretending to contemplate a decision.

Enzo grabs me around the waist, pulling me closer before growling, "Cute and decent?!?! *Those* are definitely two words I've never been described as..."

Suddenly, I'm pulled closer. I feel his warm breath on my lips. My body begs to close the gap. To taste what I haven't been able to get out of my mind all day. But my inner sass continues to shine, as I innocently say, "Would you prefer handsome and fair? I think I might need another reminder. It's been a while. I may not have judged you accurately." *Who is this woman that has taken over me? I have NEVER been this bold or flirty in my life. What is this man doing to me?*

Without even a second of hesitation, Enzo's hand engulfs my cheek and pulls my lips toward his. The lightning bolt which struck between us last night seems to have set off an inferno. His tongue slides across the seam of my lips, parting them, just as he had done last night. The fierceness of his kiss and complete consumption of my mouth makes my body hum like nothing I've experienced. I can't seem to control my actions because before I know it, one hand grips his short hair while the other cups his chiseled face. I find myself pulling him closer to me, if that's even possible. One of his hands slides to my waist and rests on my hip above my jeans while the other remains at the base of my neck, guiding my efforts to reciprocate this passionate kiss. Hours... days... an eternity could have passed, and I wouldn't have been any the wiser to anything that wasn't Enzo. When he breaks the kiss, *all too soon,* I'm surprised to find I have nearly crawled into his lap and I'm panting as if I just sprinted a marathon.

"Holy shit, woman, what have you done to me?" Enzo growls as he looks into my eyes, his hands firmly keeping me in place.

A furious blush spreads across my features as I realize what I've just done. I try to avert my eyes, but he won't have it. He pins me with his glorious green stare, *which are now several shades darker* and whispers, "Do you still think I'm cute and decent?" This sends a shiver across my entire body as it fights its carnal reaction to this man.

As if his touch and kisses were a truth serum, I blurt out, still regaining my breath, "No... definitely sexy and all-consuming."

7

ENZO

Holy fuck, what's this woman doing to me? She has me panting like a randy teenager, fogging up the back windows of his parents' car. I have no idea what just happened between us. It took everything, and I mean EVERYTHING in my power to put a stop to it. I'd heard a saw turn on from the crew working inside, which brought reality crashing back. She's somehow millimeters away from finding out just how much of an impact she has on me, too. I shift her a fraction of an inch away from my raging hard-on but hold her in place because I have no desire to let her go. The sheepish smile spreading across her face is one I'd kill for to experience over and over again.

"Do you still think I'm cute and decent?" I growl in a whisper to keep the crew from hearing me.

When she responds with, "No... definitely sexy and all-consuming." I nearly lose it. I couldn't keep my mouth off hers if she was the last drop of rain in an impending drought. I crash my lips onto hers once again to experience that delicious taste of sugar. This time I'm mindful of a potential audience because I don't share. Period. And if this continues any further, we're at risk of being exposed in more ways than one.

When I feel as if I might internally combust or *have an experience I haven't had since I was a teenager,* I force myself to put on the brakes. It's harder than fuck to say no to this irresistible woman nearly climbing in my lap, but somehow, I manage.

"Hey, sugar," I say as I steal one more taste from her delicious lips. "We'd better slow things down a bit, or we might just put on a show," I tease and kiss her softly once more, lightening my touch.

She suddenly pulls back, shaking her head as if she just became aware of our potential audience. "Oh my goodness... I... I... I've never done anything like this." She starts to pull away from me, but I can't let her go entirely.

I place her next to me, continuing to hold her hand. Her cheeks are pink and mortification settles on her features. Fuck, she has no right to feel this way, so I assure her, "You've got nothing to be embarrassed about, Samantha. You've done nothing wrong." I glance down at the evidence in my lap and smirk. "In fact, I have firsthand knowledge of just how right you feel."

She glances down at my now severely tight jeans and slightly gasps. She covers her face with her only free hand and mumbles almost to herself, "That's what I get for going years without so much as kissing a man... ugh... how embarrassing. I nearly mount him in front of his father's work crew..." she says something else, but I can't quite catch it all.

I'm stuck on the amount of time she said... Years?!?!?! What the ever-loving fuck is this incredibly sexy woman going years without so much as kissing a man for? I must clarify this, because obviously, I've heard her wrong. "Um... did you just say years? Without so much as a kiss?"

"Yes," she squeaks and squeezes her eyes shut. "This is so embarrassing. Just forget I ever said anything." She tries to brush the thought away by waving her hand in the air.

No Way. There's no way I can let this go. She can't really be serious? Before I give it much consideration, my previous thoughts come crashing out of my mouth, "What the ever-loving fuck is an incredibly sexy woman, such as yourself, going years without kissing someone for?" This catches her attention. She immediately opens her eyes to stare at me.

"You think I'm sexy?" she whispers as she shakes her head in disbelief.

"Umm... you have no idea, sweetheart," I say but she's still looking at me with denial. I'm a man and must prove myself, so I grab her hand. I place it on the bulge in my jeans, giving her direct proof of just how sexy I think she is. She gasps a little but doesn't move her hand as it clasps around my now even larger erection. "Is that proof enough?" I raise an eyebrow at her as my dick decides to give her his own salute. This causes her to blush and immediately pull her hand away.

"Why?" I say quietly. "Why is it that you haven't been kissed in years?" I'm still dumbfounded by this revelation.

She pulls in her lower lip and chews on it with her perfectly sculpted teeth as she tilts her head to the side, as if she's weighing a decision. Then I pin her rich mahogany eyes and she seems to give in. She lets out a deep breath, pulls another quick breath in, then quickly rambles,

"Because...my husband cheated on me three years ago... and I haven't kissed another man since." she says all in one blur of a sentence.

"Excuse me?" I ask in both disbelief as well as for a confirmation of what I think I heard.

Much slower this time, she closes her eyes and whispers, "Because... my husband cheated on me three years ago... and I haven't kissed another man since."

Fuck... what an asshole. She has no right to feel ashamed of anything she has done tonight. I squeeze her hand, waiting for her to look at me. After a few moments, her eyes finally meet mine. "Samantha," I say to make sure I have her attention. "Samantha sweetheart, you have absolutely nothing... and I mean NOTHING to be ashamed or embarrassed about. I completely reciprocate your feelings and I'm just as into kissing you, trust me. If it weren't for the fact there are people just on the other side of that door," I point to the French doors we came through, "there would've been nothing except you stopping me from taking just what I wanted. But you should know, I don't share."

Samantha's beautiful eyes widen at my boldness, but they darken a few shades as well. "But, it's just so embarrassing. Sure, I've dated a few times since my divorce, but I've never just kissed anyone the way I attacked you just now." She peers at the ground as she finishes that comment. "What is it about you?" she whispers aloud in wonder.

Once again, I'm caught in confusion and need clarification. "You mean to tell me that you've dated other guys, but haven't been kissed since your divorce?"

She shakes her head no and I can't help but ask, "Why?"

"There wasn't any chemistry. It didn't feel right to kiss someone just for the sake of kissing them." She peers at me through narrowed eyes as if I should understand, yet a glint of sass from before shines through her expression.

"Woman, that's definitely their loss. I'm honored to have you devour me," I tease. "In fact, I'm so honored, feel free to kiss me anytime." I pull her to me, kissing her senseless one more time before releasing her. I'm not sure how long it lasted. All I know is I didn't want it to end. "You're a FUCKIN' AMAZING KISSER and I only hope you'll devour me like that as often as you can!" I wink at her before giving her a peck on the nose. "Please, baby, practice on me all you want!"

"I'm sure it'll be a hardship." Samantha's beautiful eyes shine with mirth. "I suppose. If you insist." She boldly leans in, brushing her lips against mine. When she pulls back, she shows no sense of embarrassment. I'm relieved.

"So, dinner? Are you interested?" I ask, trying to regain control of my body. *Maybe if we talk about something else, I'll be able to move before too long.*

"Yeah. Sounds good." Samantha straightens her clothes and brushes down her hair. As my eyes rake over her, she appears as if she's been thoroughly kissed. Her beautiful lips are slightly swollen, her cheeks pink, and her eyes are slightly dilated. *This is definitely a look I want to see on her again.*

I glance at my watch and realize it's too early for dinner. But the thought of taking her to one of my favorite places comes to mind, so I say, "Why don't you go and freshen up. Grab your things and tell the crew to lock up when they leave. I'm going to make a call and then we'll head out." She eyes me suspiciously but doesn't say anything. *She's good with surprises. That's good to know.*

"Just wear what you have on," I tack on as an afterthought. There's no need for her to change from that scrumptious loose tank and sexy-fitting jeans. Besides, it's still warm for September and the weather is perfect for what I have planned.

As soon as she's through the door, I stand to adjust myself. *God, that woman has an effect on me.* I call and let my parents know something's come up this evening, so they shouldn't expect me. I also pull up a few websites to help me make my decision for what to do later tonight. *I can't honestly think of when I've gone to this much effort for a date.* Usually, I keep things casual and low key. But Samantha is special. I still can't believe a woman as sensual as she is hasn't kissed anyone else in years. I shake my head in disbelief. How on earth does someone go that long??? Geesh, I consider a dry spell a couple of months... but years? All that untapped energy. I can't believe I'm the lucky bastard she wants to let it out with.

8

SAMANTHA

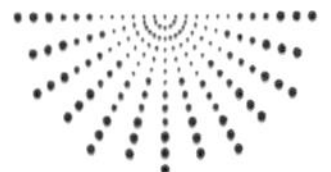

I RUSH INSIDE FEELING A LITTLE DAZED FROM MY BRAZEN MOVE on the patio. *What in the world was I thinking? I wasn't.* It felt so amazing to be caught up in the moment, I hardly knew what to do with myself. *God, the way he made me feel!* First thing's first. Go upstairs and freshen up. Then talk with the crew to let them know they will need to lock up when they leave.

I nearly sprint up the stairs as soon as I'm out of view from anyone. I rush into my bathroom to find a woman I hardly recognize staring back at me in the mirror. My face is flushed, my lips are swollen, and my hair looks as if I have been thoroughly fucked. This isn't that bad of a look on me. *God, how long has it been?*

Suddenly, another thought fills my mind, leaving me a bit apprehensive as I stare at my reflection. Crap. Enzo is only home on leave. This isn't permanent. Am I sure I want to do this? My hormones must get the best of me because they're

55

screaming *"Hell Yes,"* as my mind weighs the decision. Why do I have to be so logical all the time?

After a few moments of hesitation, I look at myself in the mirror and say, "Stop it! You deserve every moment with that man downstairs. He's gorgeous and makes you feel sexy, why not have fun and enjoy it? What's the worst that can happen?" Decision made.

I take another moment to calm myself. I glance at my clock then do my best to tame my wavy, yet tousled hair. Luckily, it only takes a few minutes to get it under control. I opt to leave it down around my shoulders. I quickly brush my teeth and throw on some lip gloss. I rush to my closet to reach for my light-blue leather jacket to bring, should it get cold later. I have no idea what Enzo has planned. But it should keep me warm enough. *He did say, not to change.* I shrug at myself in the mirror one last time before peering down at my sandals in my full-length mirror by the closet. *This will just have to do.*

It isn't even ten minutes before I'm back out on the patio, excited to see Enzo once again. Just seeing him has my body fully humming like before, even though he's standing feet away from me. When I walk outside, he glances up from his phone, an enormous smile slowly spreads across his devilishly handsome face. Of course, that dimple on his left cheek chooses this moment to pop out. I feel myself go weak at the knees. *Jesus, Samantha, get it together. You've been on a date before. Yes, but it's been an incredibly long time*, I quietly remind myself.

"Samantha," he growls in a deep timbre that has my heart picking up its pace. "You. Look. Amazing." He stands and closes the distance between us with little effort. He reaches out, grasping my hip to pull me in closer. He shakes his head slightly before whispering, "What you do to me..." the words trail off as he brushes his lips quickly across mine.

The grinding shrill of a saw is heard from inside and he steps back slightly, still keeping his hand resting on my hip. "Are you ready to go?" Enzo asks in a lighter tone.

I can't help the laughter that escapes my mouth as I take in the scene. I had suddenly forgotten what was on the other side of the doors. "Sure. Let's go."

Not wanting to be stopped by the crew for any reason, I allow Enzo to take my hand in his as I direct him to the gate on the side of the house. When we reach the driveway, he tugs me in the direction of his SUV. Effortlessly, he opens the passenger door and waits for me to get settled before closing it. I sit back and relax into the soft leather seats as I watch him privately take the few quick strides to make it around the front of his vehicle. This man sure is a sight to see. His green eyes twinkle with awareness as he catches me blatantly pursuing him from head to toe. *Busted... again! Gaaahhh! He must think I'm a nut job.* I need to get a hold of myself... or become stealthier.

By the time he enters the car, I have control of myself. I place my purse on the floor of the SUV and fold my jacket over it. He gives me another panty-melting smile, sexy dimple included, before he quickly buckles, adjusts the mirrors, and backs out of my driveway.

Enzo drives out of my neighborhood and approaches the freeway. He glances in my direction with one hand on the wheel, the other resting on the center console comfortably. His dark-blue shirt stretches across his chest to perfection. For a moment, I'm at a loss of what to do or say, but I do my best not to show my thoughts, *because that would get me into trouble.*

His chiseled jaw flexes as he smiles in my direction. I'm forced to stop my ogling and respond when he says, "I hope you don't mind. I haven't been home in a while and I absolutely love the Gorge in the fall. I thought we'd take a trip out there and have dinner."

"Sounds good. It's beautiful this time of year." I try to tear my eyes off him and look out the window. *If I don't stop staring... this will get awkward.* I pretend to take in the scenery around me instead as I gather my wits.

"So, last night you told me about your kids and work. I want to know more about you. What do you like to do, for you?" His deep voice fills the car and has my entire body humming once again.

Without even thinking, I burst out laughing. "Ummm... that's my life. I try to do a few things for me like run a few mornings a week. I hang out with a few close friends occasionally when our schedules allow it. Sometimes, we meet for drinks or get pedicures together, if I don't have the kids. My best friend Lexi and I see each other at work. Right after my divorce, she was my rock. But she has a life of her own, too." I shake my head when I realize my life isn't all that interesting. "What about you? What do you do when you're not flying?"

"I manage to keep myself out of trouble." He chuckles softly to himself. "Honestly, my life has been the Air Force for a long time. I spend a lot of my time working off base, which doesn't give me much time to be at home, wherever that happens to be. I love to hang out with my buddies because our off time is spent preparing for the next time we're back in the air. We're tight. We work hard and play even harder." A deep laugh escapes before he adds, "Well, I guess we have to be, our lives depend on each other." He suddenly goes quiet and his eyes appear distant, so I let that conversation go.

After a moment of comfortable silence, Enzo glances in my direction and an enthusiastic expression spreads across his features. "So, have you been to Multnomah Falls lately?" he asks as we leave the hustle and bustle of the city behind us. "I haven't been in years. Do you mind if we stop by?"

"Not at all." The fall leaves will be a spectacular sight to see with the waterfall in the background. I try to remember the last time I visited the state park along the Columbia River. Hmmmm... I've been so busy with work and the kids. I don't even want to think about the last time I went for a drive without a specific place and time to arrive. I miss feeling this relaxed. I stretch and let my muscles fall further into the seat. I take a deep breath and realize I could get used to this. I peek at Enzo, trying not to be too obvious about my intentions. *I could get used to this view, too.*

Enzo smiles at some unknown thought and I find myself blurting out, "What are you thinking about over there?"

He shakes his head to clear his thought but gives me a sideways glance with a lopsided smile. "I was just thinking about one of the last times I was out this way. My brother Zane bet me I couldn't beat him to the top of the trail. So of course, we had to race. Even as adults, we're still competitive. Zane thought I might be getting soft in my old age." He chuckles aloud as he shakes his head once more. "I still managed to smoke him." His voice now mischievous.

I look down at the sandals I'm wearing. "Uh, I might not be

wearing the right shoes to race to the top." I give him a questioning look and he immediately brings my mind to ease.

"Oh, I'm not planning on hiking to the top, or a race, Short-Stuff." There is a wicked gleam in his eye as he continues, "Just maybe getting out and looking around a little."

Short-Stuff? "I'm five-foot-seven. Since when is that considered short?" I'm never referred to as being vertically challenged. "Not all of us are six-foot-four gargantuan beasts," I tease in return. "Besides, if I had my running shoes, you just might be on."

He clears his throat, suddenly looking slightly humbled. "Um, actually I'm six-foot-six, not that it matters. But relax. I'm not here to race you, sweetheart. I just want to relax and enjoy the view."

He grins once again, and his smile has me losing my thoughts completely. *Wait! Six-foot-six?!?!? He's almost a foot taller than I am. No wonder I feel like a bit of a dwarf around him.* But still, I'm by no means considered tiny or short for that matter. I shake my head, trying to regain my thoughts.

"I thought we could kill some time there for a while before dinner at one of my favorite places. You couldn't believe how much you miss the Pacific Northwest when you're gone. Sure, Germany is beautiful, but it isn't home. Not that I spend much time there anyway."

From his comment, I can tell he must be out on missions a lot. "You seem to travel more than you're home."

He shrugs his shoulder. "I go where I'm needed. I've been flying a lot throughout Europe and the Middle East, occasionally to Africa and South America. If there's a hostile area, I've been there. But it's not like I get to be a tourist. I get us in and get out as safe as possible. My team depends on me. Most of my view is from the cockpit, not on the ground."

"Wow. That has to be stressful." I try to picture myself in his shoes. I honestly can't.

"It's not that way all the time. Sometimes it's a lot of fun. The team I work with is tight. We're like our own family, so it isn't a hardship," he reassures me.

I can't help but wonder. "Will you miss it if you retire?"

He gives it serious thought before answering, "Not really. If I work in the private sector, I'll be working with great people, too."

He takes the exit on the left of the freeway and we suddenly enter the parking lot for Multnomah Falls. It's between the east and west bound lanes on Highway 84, which always feels weird to enter. Enzo pulls into a place close to the pathway, to cross under the freeway. This beautiful September afternoon has brought on a few visitors to the state park, but not as many as there would be in the summer or on the weekend. Before I can even get out, he's at my door, opening it for me. He reaches for my hand with a god-like smile, making me tingle in places I've thought were broken. His strong grip on me sends that ever-present electricity zinging through me when I'm near him. I reach for my purse but opt to leave my jacket. It's still quite warm so it won't be necessary.

He keeps his hand linked with mine as we walk toward the tunnel. I can't help but feel my heartbeat quicken as he rubs my thumb with his. It's as if we've been holding hands naturally for years, rather than just knowing each other a couple of days. As we walk, I notice a tattoo peeking out from his dark-blue sleeve between us. I can't quite make it out, but

I'm now more than curious as to what it might be. Thankfully, I have some social grace and realize it might be awkward if I point it out, so I do my best to ignore it. But with each flex and movement of his arm, I'm more and more intrigued. At least when we get through the tunnel, I'm distracted from my ogling by the beautiful view of the tree-filled hill ahead of us.

"Magnificent, isn't it?" Enzo's husky voice breaks the silence and my reverie.

The colors are so vibrant, a gasp escapes as I nod my head at its beauty. I take in the rich reds, burnt oranges, yellows, and greens variegated throughout the magnificent hillside. The waterfall sporadically reveals itself as we walk along the path no bigger than two people side by side. Off to the right, a stream swiftly moves past us along the way. Finally, I see the bridge to get us to the visitors center and the falls itself.

As we follow the trail, the viewing area for photo ops of the falls quickly appears. It's a beautiful place to stop and admire the view. Enzo leads me to the handrail at the center of the platform. Since there are only a few people hanging around off to the side of the center, I don't hesitate to follow him. He pulls out his phone and uses the full force of that sexy dimple as he grins. "I want to take a picture of this gorgeous view." I immediately attempt to step out of the way, so I don't obstruct the view. He looks at me knowingly, pinning me to my place. "Um, you're part of the view, Samantha." He shakes his head as if I should have figured that part out, then motions to the spot he originally had me stand.

I return to the railing and raise my eyebrows. "Only if I get to take some of you, too." I reach for my phone in the pocket of my jeans.

Enzo laughs loudly. "If you insist. Though I won't look as beautiful as you." He rolls his eyes, and with a teasing tone, boldly states, "Get over there and pose, woman, before I put you there myself."

After a few shots of me, I dig out my phone and insist we trade places. I manage a few pictures of him before my arm is tugged, forcing me closer to Enzo. He places his closest arm around my shoulder, holding his phone so he can snap a selfie of us. He pulls me so close, I must place my hand on his chest to keep my balance. Glancing up at him, I realize I'm a goner. His hypnotic green eyes capture my attention and I can't help but get lost in them. He grasps me tighter and I gasp at the sudden closeness, as I involuntarily react to his movement. I stretch up on my toes, making our faces closer for the photo, while not taking my eyes off his. He briefly closes the gap with a peck on my lips as he holds out one arm with his phone. I barely register the phone is still taking pictures. Suddenly, a man next to us clears his throat.

"Um, would you like me to take a photo of the two of you?" he asks, trying to be helpful. Eyes darting between the two of us, he's about sixty years old, with kind eyes and graying temples. His wife is behind him, waiting to see if we want his help.

"Sure thing." Enzo chuckles as we focus our attention on him. He backs up and snaps a few pictures as we both beam at the camera.

He hands Enzo back his phone as he gestures to it. "Did they turn out?"

Enzo sweeps through the photos quickly. "Yes, sir. Thank you so much." He reaches out to shake the man's hand. Then

Enzo motions for the woman behind him to join us. "Can we return the favor?"

She steps forward without hesitation. "That would be lovely. I absolutely love the falls in autumn." Enzo takes the woman's camera, snapping quite a few shots. He tries to get as much of the background in them as possible. When he's finished, the couple thanks him.

"No problem. You have a great evening," Enzo tells them, as they turn and walk down the path toward the visitors center.

9

ENZO

As I hand the camera back to the couple, I thank them once again before they leave.

"Come on, Samantha." I grab her hand to walk up the path to the next bridge. "Let's go take a picture from there," I say, pointing at the bridge high above us. I'm not really one to want my picture taken, but she's breathtaking, with the sun shining on her and the fall leaves behind us. Her sexy sass and wicked smile make me want to completely devour her, but since we're in public, I'll just enjoy her company. We walk hand in hand further up the path as I do my best to adjust my pace to hers. She's by no means short, but with being a foot taller, it's something I'm conscious of. We should reach the bridge in a matter of a few minutes, but when I see a turn in the path completely obstructed by the eyes of others around us, I pull her to a stop.

Unable to wait any longer, I growl as I tug her closer to me. "What you do to me," comes out as a growl and my lips are on

65

her within a fraction of a second. I crush my mouth onto hers. My tongue darts out and parts the seam of her luscious lips. Her mouth is heaven. Ever since we were in her backyard, I've been wanting to get another taste of her deliciousness. Keeping an awareness of our surroundings, not willing to let things get out of control, I keep our kiss brief. Well, as brief as I can before I force myself to pull away. I graze her lips once more before standing to my full height, trying to casually adjust myself as I brush a light strand of hair back behind one of her ears.

Samantha's eyes darken as they regain their focus, which is gratifying. I know the effect she has on me, but it's nice to know she might feel the same. I shake my head, trying to regain my thought, but the look on her face brings a huge smile across my face as my heart thunders. What is it about this woman that I can't get enough of? I've *never* had such an instant pull, not even Vanessa and I was about to marry her. This is how it should have been. Dodged a bullet there!

WHAT. THE. FUCK? *Why am I thinking about marriage?* I just met this woman for CHRIST'S SAKE! She has kids, a family, and a life I barely know anything about. I'm more the type of being "Mr. Right Now," not "Mr. Right," and certainly not "Mr. Forever." But I need to know more about her and figure out this connection we share.

I hear a group of people coming up the path. Before they get to us, I pull myself out of my own head. "So, are you ready to keep walking?" I gesture in the direction of the bridge. She pulls away to continue our walk, but I just can't seem to let her go. I grab a hold of her hand once more, absentmindedly stroking her thumb with mine. I've never really been a touchy-feely guy. But Samantha is like a magnetic force set on high, and I can't fight the pull.

Conversation flows easily as we walk along the path. I tell her about the time my parents took us here when I was a teenager. "One time, my mom nearly had to bribe us to get one decent picture from this bridge." I point at the spot we stood, fondly remembering the experience. "None of us wanted to even be here, let alone stand together for a picture. My brother stood off to the side, barely in the picture, refusing to smile. My sister glared at me because I had done something to annoy her and I was doing my best to just take the ridiculous photo and get it over with. It was the early 90s, so there was big hair, flannel shirts, and hiking boots on every one of us. The total grunge look, now that I think about it. Ma was ticked." I laugh again at the memory. "I don't remember what she said but the look on my dad's face made us all comply with her wishes, immediately. It was a horrid photo, but in the end, we'd made her happy. She still has it hanging in the family room." I shudder at the thought, but the sound of Samantha's laughter has me willing to tell her more embarrassing stories if I continue to get a reaction like that.

Of course, she, too, has stories about trying to get her three kids together for one photo. I burst out laughing as she explains one of her favorites. Frankie's nearly running out of the screen, Declan's pouting, and Maddie smiling like a trooper. When she mentions it's framed in her home office, I'm dying to see it. It must be hysterical, but from the sense of contentment on her face as she recalls the memory, I know she cherishes it.

When we make it to the bridge overlooking the waterfall,

Samantha and I take in the beautiful view of the Gorge itself. As far as the eye can see, the magnificent Columbia River is lined with trees of varying shades of autumn colors with steep reddish-brown cliffs of weathered basalt far off in the distance. Once again, I can't control my need to capture the beauty before me. As if on autopilot, I find myself pulling out my camera to capture this moment with her. The more I've gotten to know Samantha, I find she's so modest and completely unaware of the exquisiteness within her. At the same time, she's bold and confident in some ways, sassy the next, and I love that I never know what she's going to say or do. I'm doing my best to keep my distance, but as I get to know more about her, I find myself losing the battle. My intrinsic need pulls her in for another kiss, but I force myself not to get carried away. We *are* in public. Throughout our entire time at Multnomah Falls, I find myself touching her in some way as if I can't let her go. *What kind of spell has she put on me?*

Later, as we drive further up the Gorge, I hold her hand casually across the console. Our conversation easily flows from one subject to another. I'm about to ask her another question when her phone rings. Samantha quickly pulls it out of her pocket, checks the caller ID, and mouths, *Sorry,* to me as she answers, "Hey, Maddie. What's up?"

From her side of the conversation, I can tell her daughter's just checking in. The sense of pride Samantha shows for her daughter is unbelievable. I admire the fact she stops whatever she's doing to give her full attention to Maddie. They talk about an upcoming dance and at one point, Samantha promises to go shopping for a dress later this week. Once that's settled, they chat about Maddie's plans for the weekend.

After a few minutes, Samantha's voice changes when she talks to her youngest daughter, Frankie. Frankie's obviously excited about something because I can hear her enthusiasm burst through the phone. Though, I have no clue her reason for such excitement because Samantha can barely get a word in edgewise. But as she listens, the smile which spreads across Samantha's face is infectious.

Eventually, her voice becomes more businesslike, causing me to glance her way to make sure she's okay. From her side of the conversation, I hear. "Hello? ...I'm not really sure. The place was still torn apart when I left... No... They won't be working on the weekend, so it looks like it might be early next week... Are you sure that's okay with you? I can still pick them up from school to drive them to practice. Yes... I think that'll be best. Okay. See you Monday afternoon. No, I'll get them something to eat along the way. Thanks, Devin. I'll talk to you later."

When she hangs up the phone, she turns to me with an apologetic tone in her voice. "Sorry. That was my girls and their father. We needed to make arrangements for next week, so everyone's on the same page." Samantha's face fills with an expression I can't read before she groans, "Ugg, I miss them like crazy, but with my house under construction, it's what makes sense. They love homemade breakfasts and cold lunches, so it's easier this way. Besides, Devin's always been a fantastic father so the kids will enjoy spending the time with him." She lets out a heavy sigh. "He'll keep them until Monday when he drops them off at school and picks up Declan from practice like usual." She lets out a deep breath before adding,

"They usually return Sunday evenings," as an explanation for the change.

"Do they stay with him often?" I ask, not knowing what else she might be thinking as she stares out the window.

"Usually it's just Wednesday nights and every other weekend, unless either of us goes out of town on business. We try to co-parent as much as we can. He helps with the daily drop-offs and pick-ups. The kids' schedules are so crazy, it's impossible to manage alone. It's not easy, but Devin and I try to get along for our kids' sake." Samantha takes a deep breath and seems to steady herself before adding, "Believe it or not, Devin actually only lives about five minutes away, so our kids can ride the bus to either house depending on where they need to go." She tucks her hair behind her ear and looks out the window as I continue to drive.

I can't imagine getting along so well with an ex. From what she told me earlier, she was the one cheated on. Samantha must make a tremendous amount of effort to make this happen. I don't think I could do that. The woman next to me must be a saint. I glance over at her in awe once again. Samantha has so many facets to her, it's a miracle she's still single. Devin was an idiot to let her go. She's smart, sexy as hell, and an amazing mother. Everything I learn about her just keeps drawing me in further. What the hell could've been so wrong for him to look elsewhere?

Trying to keep my voice indifferent, I say, "It's obvious you're a great mom who loves her kids. Not a lot of people would put forth the effort you do. Your kids will appreciate it."

She looks taken back by my compliment. She shrugs before letting out a deep breath. "Some days are easier than others, but I wouldn't have it any other way. We both chose to have the kids. Just because one of us chose a path that didn't involve the other doesn't mean our kids should be the ones to suffer. Maddie, Declan, and Frankie are the best things to ever happen to me. I can't imagine my life without them. Sometimes, I wonder what life would have been like if I hadn't gotten married in college, but then I wouldn't have them in my life." She smiles at her realization.

As I glance over in her direction, I can tell she means what she says with conviction. The love that flows from her eyes is unmistakable. Her positive attitude and an outlook on life, in general, amaze me. Most women would be evil and vindictive toward their cheating exes, but not Samantha. She handles it with grace and dignity. Just one of many traits I'm quickly coming to admire about her. "I can't wait to meet them," comes out of my mouth before I give it any thought. *Wait? Did I just say I wanted to meet her kids? That could be a cluster fuck...* but when I think more about it, my nerves calm. They're a part of her and from what I can tell, she's amazing.

We pull off our intended exit in Hood River. I take the necessary turns to make our way to the part of town overlooking the waterfront. I manage to snag a place to park along a side street. I get out of the car to help Samantha with her door. It's a bit windier here in the evening, so I suggest she take her jacket. I grab a hoodie from my "go bag" in the back of the SUV. I never am far without it, even when I'm not on duty.

The magnetic force sizzling between us makes it so I cannot keep my hands off her. I guide her down the sidewalk with my arm around her lower back. Instead of resting my hand in the middle of her back, I find it comfortable to rest it on her outside hip. This settles her closer to me. I take a huge breath, inhaling the delicious scent of her hair. It's a mixture of honey, mint, and something that's entirely Samantha. It's intoxicating, making me wish I hadn't driven so far to take her out for dinner. Being in public has its disadvantages.

We walk down the sidewalk, peering into shops along the way to the restaurant. She stops at one storefront to admire the dress on the mannequin. It's a sleeveless, green lace dress. The top seems to wrap around itself, while the bottom flows out like an A-line. I only know that type of dress because I had a sister growing up. *Not that I have a clue about much else.* I just remember my mom and her endlessly talking about how flattering the shape was.

"Why don't you try it on?" I suggest when I see the longing in her eyes. As she turns to face me, she seems a little confused by my suggestion.

"No, it's okay. I'm just window shopping." She glances at me sheepishly as if she doesn't know what else to say.

"It isn't a problem to stop in. That would look gorgeous on you," I suggest. *What the hell has come over me?* I'm never one to purposely choose to shop. In fact, everything I own can be grouped into two categories, military issued or bought on a brief trip to a department store. I'm not one to browse, or even indulge in fashion sense. It's for function only that I even bother. But for some reason, when I saw her eyes light up, I picture her in that dress. Now I want to see if the real thing does my fantasy justice.

"Are you sure? It seems weird to shop on a first date. I don't want to bore you." She chews on her lower lip and I can't help but want to free it with my teeth.

"I never say anything I don't mean," I huskily growl at her, fantasizing about those luscious lips. "We're here. If you want to try it on, go for it." *I certainly wouldn't mind seeing your sexy curves in that dress.*

She bites that lip some more and I nearly lose it. "Okay…" she whispers. "If you insist."

We walk into the small shop and a saleswoman quickly helps Samantha get a dress in her size. I browse a little while she's trying it on, but stay near the dressing room, hoping to get a view of her. My prayers are answered a few minutes later when she steps out of the dressing room.

Damn! Her curves fill out that dress perfectly. As she walks toward me, my mouth suddenly goes as dry as the Arabian Desert. I must pick my jaw up off the floor and smack my head against a wall to form any coherent thought. She smiles shyly and gives a quick spin. The skirt portion of her dress nearly does a Marilyn Monroe impression, but nothing indecent. The only indecent thing about it is my thoughts and how I wish I could get her out of this spectacular dress. Or just going back into that dressing room would do, too.

"What do you think?" she asks, wanting an honest opinion.

I clear my throat, trying to gain the capacity to speak. When I finally find my voice, I growl, "It belongs on you."

Her face blazes with the perfect color as if she's never received a compliment before. "Thanks," she whispers.

It takes everything in my power not to devour her on the spot. Eventually, I regain control of myself and say, "Go change, I'll have the saleswoman ring it up."

Samantha looks at me questioningly before she turns to head back to the dressing room. While she's in there, the saleswoman asks if there is anything else we need. I ask her to point me to the area for accessories. The saleswoman assists me in finding some handmade jewelry, which is made locally. I pick out a necklace and a pair of earrings to match. I have her ring them up and place them in the bag. To speed things along, I also ask her to ring up the dress as well. When Samantha arrives, she hands the dress to the saleswoman but has no idea about the accessories I bought her. A flash of irritation crosses her face when she finds I just purchased this dress for her. She starts to put up a fight.

"Get over it, beautiful. My plan is to take you out tomorrow night to reap the reward of seeing you in that exquisite dress." I raise an eyebrow, challenging her to question me. I can't help but chuckle when her mouth opens like she's about to rip me a new one, quickly changes her mind, then attempts again.

Finally, her spit-fire self comes through. "What makes you think I'm going out with you tomorrow night?"

"I have my ways of convincing you," I tease as I pull her in for a side hug and kiss the top of her head. I reach for the bag and lead her out the door. "Besides, who says I'm letting you go tonight?" I let her ponder over that as we walk out the door to the restaurant.

SAMANTHA

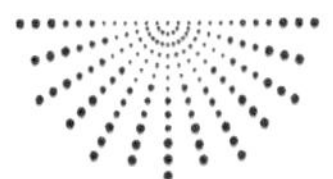

He bought me a dress. *He bought me a dress? Why on earth would he do that?* I'm perfectly capable of buying my own dress.

His words keep cycling on a loop through my head. *"I have my ways of convincing you. Besides who says I'm letting you go tonight?"*

What the hell does he mean by that?

I know I'm completely attracted to the man, but to go all alpha-male, is it really necessary? Yeah, sure, my panties just burst into flames, but to be so brazen and bold? Heaven help me if he follows through with his threat. I can't remember the last time I even had sex, let alone thinking about having it. *Before I met him, that is.* Yep. And there he goes, bringing that delicious dimple into the mix and… BAM! I might as well not be wearing any underwear, for all the good they're doing me. My jeans will have a wet spot in them if he keeps this up. Oh, who am I kidding? If we weren't on a public street, I'd be climbing him like a tree. Holy hell, this man is pure sex on a stick.

As I glance at him, I notice his five o'clock shadow makes him look even more scrumptious. He has the perfect amount of scruff for running my fingers along his strong jawline. He slings an arm over my shoulder while carrying my bag in the other hand. His masculine scent sends my body into overdrive. I do my best to keep my emotions under control as we walk together along the sidewalk. But my mind is reeling. I can't imagine where he's going to take me so I can wear my new dress tomorrow night. *Slow down, Sam. You haven't even gotten through tonight, you need to get through dinner first. Yes. That's it, focus on dinner and just take it one step at a time.*

As we arrive at the restaurant, I pull myself out of my head, focusing on the fact I need to concentrate on the here and now. Not of the possibilities to come. *Oh, but those possibilities...*

There wasn't a wait, so once we're seated we spend a few minutes to peruse the menu. I can barely concentrate on the words in front of me, as Enzo has yet to release my hand from across the table. The electricity zinging between us makes me feel like a fixated teenager, staring at her first crush. I'm grateful for the interruption when a perky waitress arrives. She explains the special tonight and I'm easily sold. It's steak with grilled asparagus and a side dish unique to the restaurant.

When the waitress leaves, I do my best not to ogle Enzo. I force myself to think of something to say to keep from staring at him like a fool. Focusing only on his gorgeous green eyes, I find myself asking the first thing that pops into my mind aloud, "Tell me, if there was a book made about your life, what would the title be?"

Enzo seems a little taken back by my question, but soon appears to be giving it some thought. Eventually, a slow smile spreads across his face and I brace myself for the full force of his scrumptious dimple. Slightly shaking his head, he lightly laughs. "I have no freaking clue." He lets out a deep sigh, leans back in his seat, and gazes up at the ceiling as if he's still pondering my question. His jaw juts out and his lips purse. His hand that isn't holding mine reaches up to scratch at his chiseled jaw. Finally, after a long moment of thought, he chuckles once loudly and sucks in a deep breath. "Maybe... Man on a Mission?" His eyebrows rise along with his shoulders, awaiting my response.

There are so many ways I can take this. Yeah, he's a pilot in the Air Force, and then his comment from the boutique comes to mind. My face immediately feels as if it will burst into flames from the last realization. Thankfully, I don't have to respond because we're interrupted by the arrival of our food.

After we have both taken a bite, Enzo clears his throat. "So, what about you? What would the title of your life be?"

He catches me mid-bite, so thankfully I have time to think about it while I clear my mouth. Phrases like Derailed and Matronly Mom pop into my mind. But then I consider Enzo's glorious greens which stare back at me, filled with such intensity, my mind heads in a different direction. Now the phrases Bound and Determined, Rejuvenated, Revitalized, Hot and Horny come to mind and I smile. *There's no way I'm telling him that last one.*

I shake my head to rid my thoughts from going into the

gutter. "I don't know, nothing I'm thinking of really describes it."

"Well..." His deep, husky voice rumbles. "Why can't you make it up as you go? Nothing says you must let one thing define you. The more I get to know you, the more facets I'm enamored with." He takes his hand to brush a strand of hair back from my face. As he places it behind my ear, a shiver runs through my spine. He blows me away when he continues with, "I think resilience is key to your success. You're a single mom of what sounds like three amazing children. You're career oriented and you overcome obstacles that get in your way. You are strong, fierce, and from what I can tell, loyal. Not one title would justify your life. At least, as I've come to know it."

Holy Crap. I just met this man, and he already knows me better than Devin ever did. I stare at him a little dumbfounded at my revelation. "I—Ummm... I don't know what to say," I whisper as I bring my hand to cover my chest. I feel my eyes prick with tears, but I blink them away as fast as I can. "No one's ever said that about me before."

"Was I wrong?" Enzo's deep voice questions. "I—Uhh... hope I didn't offend you. I consider myself to be a great judge of character. It's a necessity in my line of work. That's just... well, I tell it like I see it." He clears his throat and holds my gaze as he awaits my response.

The look in his eyes slays me. The thought he could have offended me is crazy. That was the nicest, sweetest compliment I could've ever received. "No. Thank you." I stare into the great depths of his eyes much longer than I should and they smolder. I finally add, "I appreciate the compliment."

He eyes me dubiously before he lowly growls, "You'd better

fuckin' believe it. You're unlike any person I've ever met."
Seeming to be taken back by his own words, his eyebrows
suddenly rise to meet his forehead. He appears to recover,
then smiles with the full force of his dimple at me.

All I can do is stare at him in return. That's it. I'm in
complete shock and unable to mentally process anything else
at this moment.

The waitress returns and interrupts my gawking. "Can I get
you two anything else?" She briefly smiles at me and then
turns her attention to Enzo. His eyes remain on me while he
shakes his head no.

"No, thank you," Enzo mumbles.

Thank God, for the interruption. *What in the world has
come over me?* I've received compliments before. It's not like
I live my life completely devoid of them or anything. I rack
my brain to think of something else to say to get the
intensity of our connection to turn down a few notches.
What do people talk about when they're first dating?
Sports! He's a man... and it's a subject we have yet to talk
about.

When the waitress saunters away, I ask, "So... do you
follow any sports teams?" *Gaahh... could that sound anymore
forced?!?!*

Enzo finishes the food he'd just placed in his mouth before
smiling back at me. "I'm known to watch a game now and
then. I like to watch the usual, football, hockey, and soccer if I
get the chance. Though it's been a long time since I've seen
any in person. What about you?"

"Well, I love to watch football. I'm an avid fan of the
Seahawks. I try to go to a game each season, but mostly I just

yell from my couch." I laugh at my revelation. "I'm a huge fan of Russell Wilson."

Enzo gives me a mischievous smile. "They're my favorite team, too. I'd love to catch a game while I'm home on leave." He takes a bite of his steak and chews it before adding, "They've had a good run lately. I hope this season continues the way it's started."

"Do you watch the games in Germany? Or do you just keep up on STATs?" I ask, thinking it must be hard with the time difference and all the traveling he does.

"Well, I don't always see them live. But I enjoy it all the same. Sometimes, I just keep track of the score."

"They play Monday this week," I casually mention. "You're welcome to come over and watch the game with me. I'll have to leave at some point to pick up Declan from soccer, but you're welcome to hang out. I must warn you, though. I might be known as being part of the twelve that makes noise," I tease, then realize what I've just said.

Shit, Sam… that's a sure-fire way to scare him off. Meeting your kids after just three days? Talk about baptism by fire! I can't believe I just asked him that! I immediately close my eyes, not wanting to see his response.

"Can I bring pizza and beer?"

My eyes go wide, and I feel my mouth take the form of an O. I stare at him blankly, not knowing if I've really heard him right. *He wants to meet my kids? WOW! Okay. This will be a first, but I can handle it, and they will, too. Who am I kidding? I have no idea how they will react, but I deserve to have a life.*

"Is everything okay, Samantha?" Enzo's deep timbre pulls me out of my panicked state.

I briefly shake my head, regaining my thoughts. "Yes." I inhale deeply and let it out slowly. *I might as well be honest. Here goes nothing.*

"Just to give you a warning, my kids have never met anyone I have dated," I quietly state. When I look up, I find a bit of surprise on Enzo's features. I immediately backpedal. "Don't get me wrong. It's not like I've dated a lot of men, or hardly any for that matter, but this is new for me."

"I can't say I've ever met anyone's kids before either." Enzo's eyes hold my gaze in place as he adds, "But I'm looking forward to it. After all, it's just football and pizza. It's not like we're getting married or anything. Your kids are a part of you, so they can't be too scary. They're past the biting stage, right?"

I laugh at the sudden seriousness I'd brought to our situation and realize he's right. It's just football and pizza. Enzo puts me at ease without even knowing it. For that I'm grateful. "I'm pretty sure they are. They might fight or bicker, but you should be pretty safe," I tease. "Frankie grew out of that stage a couple of years ago."

The rest of our meal goes by effortlessly. By the time we finish, I've learned more about his nieces and nephews, and the various stages they had gone through. I almost spit my drink laughing when he tells me about the time his nephew gave himself a hickey with the vacuum cleaner in the middle of his forehead. It's evident from the way he talks about his family, Enzo's an amazing brother and uncle. As we leave the restaurant, Enzo takes my hand in his and we walk hand in hand to the car.

ENZO

ALL THROUGHOUT DINNER, I CAN'T TAKE MY EYES OFF Samantha. Not only is she stunningly gorgeous, but she doesn't seem to comprehend the hold she has on me. She is fun, witty, and keeps me on my toes. I never know what she is about to say. When she goes deep into thought or is unsure of how to say something, she tends to pull her lower lip in and nibble on it until she could come up with something else to say. It takes all my effort not to reach over and tug that luscious lip out from the capture of her perfectly sculpted teeth, *though I'd rather do it with my own teeth. Fuck! This woman could be my kryptonite.*

As we walk to the car, I find myself completely drawn to her. I hold her hand in mine, with her purchases in my other. A cool breeze has picked up this evening, so Samantha is now wearing the light jacket she brought. I assist her in putting it on and once we're outside, I'm assaulted with her scent and force myself to keep from taking her immediately.

"Do you want to go down to the waterfront?" Samantha asks as we reach the car.

It's easier to drive to it, so I suggest, "Yeah, why don't we get in and drive down?"

Within a few minutes, we're down by the river. There are a few other people out enjoying the remains of this beautiful fall evening. On a hot summer day, countless people are down here. Most will be windsurfing. Now there are only a few die-hards in wetsuits enjoying the evening breeze. The shore is fairly empty, but I guide her further away, wanting to be alone with her.

Our conversation flows with ease as we stroll along the river's edge. We talk about how delicious dinner was. Never having it far from my mind, I mention how I can't wait to see her again in the dress I bought her. Just thinking of how she looked coming out of that dressing room makes me want to devour her. It doesn't help when color fills her face as I reveal my thoughts. The desire flowing through me makes me want to surprise her like that again soon. I shake my head at the preposterous thought. *This is so unlike me. When have I ever invested this much into someone in such short of time? Never.*

When we get further down the shore, we stop to take in the view. As Samantha admires the beauty of the Columbia River and the Gorge around it nearing sunset, I enjoy my view of her. Her mahogany hair blows lightly in the wind as it's pushed back from her face. The fading sun brings out lighter streaks of color throughout and illuminates her beautiful face. She lifts her head and takes a deep breath, seeming to relax. After all too short of time, she catches me watching her. Her smile nearly takes my breath away.

"It's so beautiful here," she whispers.

"Yeah, it sure is. Can't get much better than this," I huskily growl. Without any thought, I find myself stepping forward to embrace her. My arms fold around her waist as I nuzzle into her neck. It's like she was made for me. Her body fits perfectly with mine. No other woman has made me feel so unhinged. I've never met anyone more addictive. I'm drawn to her like a moth to a flame. I pull Samantha to me so her back is against my chest. Taking a deep breath of her heavenly scent, I kiss her neck lightly, just at the crease of her shoulder. I feel a slight shiver pass through her body, so I must be having some effect on her, too.

Before I know it, she turns around. Her arms drape around my neck. Having everything else around me fade into the background, I pull her to me and close the gap with my lips, needing another taste of her. One hand glides to the back of her neck beneath her hair while the other remains at her lower back. Her hooded eyes may be the death of me. The spark that ignites as soon as our lips touch could incinerate me on the spot and I could care less. Without another thought, I deepen the kiss with pressure from my hand at her neck. I'm rewarded for my efforts as I seem to have set off a magic switch inside her. She nearly climbs me and I'm thankful for my years of working out and quick agility. Effortlessly, I put my hand under her ass to pull her up to match my full height, so we are not thrown off balance. Her glorious legs naturally wrap around my waist and I remind myself not to get carried away. The small moan that escapes her mouth as her hands run through the back of my hair, nearly has me finding the first available flat surface to take her on. But I manage to keep my control. *Barely*.

To keep my composure, I reluctantly break off the kiss. Instead, I pepper kisses down her neck, continuing to hold her close. Her legs squeeze me tighter as if she's trying to find some release as well. I kiss her once more, though it's not as consuming, and slowly lower her back to the ground.

"Wow," she whispers as she looks into my eyes. "How do I always seem to lose all control when I'm around you?" The look on her face tells me there's no shame in her words, just wonder and awe. A sense of warmth spreads over me.

A slow grin spreads across her face when I clear my throat and say, "Trust me. You're not alone."

Knowing movement is the best course of action to keep from letting things burn out of control, I take her hand and walk back toward the parking lot. "Let's get back to the car before I get too carried away." By now, the sun has nearly set, and dusk is settling in. We can still clearly see where we're walking, but it won't be long before it's dark.

It doesn't take long until we're back in the car. Before I can drive the distance back to Portland, I kiss her one more time. Her hands wrap around my face and it takes everything... and I mean *everything* in my power not to take her right here. Eventually, I pull away from her and start the car, although my body curses at me and I regret this decision.

There is a sexual charge that could fuel the car if we could harness it, as we drive back to Portland. It doesn't take me long to reach over and take her hand in mine once again. I need to touch her, caress her, just be close to her. *Who the hell is this woman? I don't remember being so touchy-feely before.*

In fact, I'm usually the one to keep things at a distance. I wouldn't say I'm being clingy. I'm just quickly becoming addicted to her. It's like I can't help myself. *What the hell, man?*

So far, we've kept our conversation light, but suddenly Samantha catches me off guard when she asks, "How exactly are you still single?"

"Um... what do you mean by that?" I give her a confused glance to see what she's thinking.

She sighs. "Never mind." Then shakes her head. "I didn't mean for that to be said out loud." From the lights on the dashboard, I see her face turn chagrin. Then she mumbles, "Gaahh... what is it about you? It's like I have no control over my thoughts or actions."

I laugh aloud. "Samantha. You've got no idea the effect you have on me. It took all my effort not to take you in this car once we got back to it from the river."

"No way!" She shakes her head in disbelief.

"You have no idea," I grumble and adjust my jeans. "You're magnificent. I could feast on you for days."

She's quiet for a few moments. I fear I've offended her. "Everything okay?" I ask, needing reassurance since I can't quite read her expression in the dark.

Her voice turns sultry as she replies, "Yes. I'm fine. You've just got me thinking..." she trails off.

"About..." I prompt, needing to know what's on her mind. God, I hope I haven't offended her.

"What it would be like..." Her voice is barely audible.

She's killing me. Literally. I might even wreck the car because all my blood supply is traveling south while I'm supposed to be driving the car west. After another long moment, I ask, "What, what would be like?"

Thankfully, I see her peek over at me. Then I see her brazen smile as she straightens her back to face me directly. "Like… what being with you would be like. It's been so long… until I met you, I thought I'd never feel this way again. You have me nearly attacking you… AGAIN… in public no less." She shakes her head. "The funny part is I would have been totally on board with your train of thought… and I have NEVER done anything like that in my life!"

"What do you mean?" *I NEED to hear it. I NEED to know so I can be completely sure. I want nothing more than to pull this car over and have my way with her.*

"I've never had sex anywhere remotely public." She makes a weird noise with her throat, somewhere between a laugh and a snort before she adds, "I haven't done much outside my bedroom in so long I can't remember." Then she full out laughs. "And I can't even remember when the last time would have been. For all I know, my lady bits have shriveled up and died."

"Fuck, beautiful, you're killing me," I growl. When I see an exit ahead, I don't even think before I pull off, leading us to who knows where. I'm barely aware of the fact that it's a side road leading to the middle of nowhere. I don't even care. My only goal is to get to a place where I can park this damn car and not be bothered by anyone.

I know there must be a god when I see a turn-out that's half hidden by trees on one side. I quickly slam the car into park. Before I know it, I have unbuckled my seat belt and am reaching for her. She must read my mind because without hesitation, she's grabbing at me across the seat as well. Our mouths fuse together and we kiss passionately for endless moments. The electricity zinging between us is indescribable. It's like I can't get enough, no matter how hard I kiss her or caress her. I part her lips and delve into the depths of her. Samantha has me nearly losing control within moments.

I must get closer. I tear at her jacket and have it removed within seconds. I slide my hands up her smooth skin as I bring her loose tank over her head. Her body ignites when I unclasp her bra as I continue to kiss her. She sheds it quickly and I growl when I finally reach her magnificent breast with my hand. I tweak and pull her dark nipple with my thumb against my forefinger as I knead her flesh with the rest of my hand. Her nipple pebbles magnificently as if it were made for me. Wanting to give equal attention, I switch sides and assault the other one with the same intensity. Within moments, she lets out a sound I don't think I will ever forget.

"Fuck, Samantha. I need more of you," I moan as I let go with one hand and recline my seat before pulling her over the console to be on top of me. I scoot up the seat to give her more room in front of the steering wheel. Gone is the shy girl from before, replaced by a woman who knows her needs. She eagerly straddles me as a low growl escapes and grips tightly onto my shoulders.

Loving this new angle, I pull one ample breast into my mouth as I tease the other with my hand. Her skin is delicious. The scent that makes her uniquely her has me completely entranced. I lick and suck each delicious bud in my mouth to get more of those addicting sounds to come out of hers.

When she moves along my hardened length, digging my

zipper into my full erection, I reach for the button of her jeans to open them. "Oh, Enzo," comes out on a harsh breath as she seeks a release I know she needs. I take a moment and reposition us so that I can get my hand between us while enjoying her nipples the entire time with my mouth.

When my hand finally reaches her slick, wet center, I'm rewarded with her fisting my hair and guiding my mouth back to her delicious breast. Loud moans escape each of us as I nip, pull, and tug, making her addictive nipple taut and fully extended. My tongue slides across its peak as my long fingers find what they have been searching for. I curve my finger and give it a 'come hither' motion into her front wall and the gorgeous woman before me nearly screams.

"What are you doing to me?" she moans breathlessly, so I continue my efforts in full force.

"Oh, Enzo... there... right there." Her head falls back, giving me easier access to her heavy, erect breasts. I press my thumb across her clit, massaging it for mere seconds before she detonates.

"There you go, beautiful," I growl. "That's it. Give me all you've got," I whisper into her ear as I nip on her lower lobe. "I wanna watch this all night long."

Now any woman coming apart is a beautiful sight to see, but when Samantha comes apart, it's more than I can even comprehend. I nearly embarrass myself and come right along with her in my jeans, but I manage to hold on. *Holy Shit! I have no idea how much longer I can hold back. I haven't felt like this since I was seventeen.*

As she comes down from her glorious high, she kisses and sucks on my neck. Soon, she buries her face in my shoulder and I hold her tightly in place. Though she seems unaware, her ass rests squarely on my straining erection. I do my best to ignore it and pray it doesn't try to start a conversation with her on its own. Right now, this is about her and nothing else matters. After a few moments of stillness, I break the silence with a rough whisper, "You okay, beautiful?"

A soft sigh escapes before she answers, drawing out the word, "Perfect."

I push her back slightly, cupping her chin to have her look me in the eyes. "Are you sure?"

The utter sincerity almost slays me. "Just blissed out at the moment..." Her smile is infectious. "Give me a minute. I'm sure I'll manage to move soon." She rests her head back on my shoulder as her body remains slightly limp. "Sorry to squish you..."

I readjust her so she sits on my lap, rather than on her knees, by swinging her legs across the console. "Take your time, Samantha. I'm not going anywhere." I rub her bare back in slow circles and take another deep breath of her delicious scent, feeling mostly content. *Well, except for the fact that my erection has yet to stop making his presence known. Maybe if I think about car crashes, pre-flight checks, anything except for this beautiful woman before me, he will disappear or at least give me some reprieve.*

After a few minutes of listening to nothing but our breathing returning to normal, what she said before this all began hits me and I let out a low laugh. "I guess your lady bits haven't shriveled up and died. They felt pretty fucking amazing to me." *And he's back.*

Samantha buries her head in my shoulder. "Gaahh... Enzo.

Why can't I have a filter around you?!?! I swear it's like I can't contain anything. Are you sure you haven't slipped me some truth serum or something?" She laughs, trying to make a joke of it.

"I wouldn't have it any other way, Samantha," I say with all honesty. "Please don't ever hold back."

I notice a light in the far distance and reach for her shirt. Pointing in the direction of the oncoming car, I suggest, "We'd better get you dressed." She immediately scoots over the console and puts on her shirt, sans bra. Before I can say anything, she stuffs her bra into her purse. She buckles up, acting as if nothing has happened, before she innocently asks, "Ready?"

I can't take it. I pull her face to meet mine and kiss her thoroughly once again. I completely devour her mouth and I can't help it when my hand snakes under her shirt to cup her ample breast. The moan she lets out is satisfying and I can't help but grin. "Samantha, you're incredible," I whisper as I kiss across her lips. The interior of my car suddenly becomes illuminated with the passing of the vehicle I noticed earlier. I pull back, placing my hand on her thigh, and put the car in gear. It's going to be a long ride to Portland. My body is on fire and I want to be inside this woman before the night is through. Samantha gives me a knowing look and places her hand over mine, showing me she feels it, too.

SAMANTHA

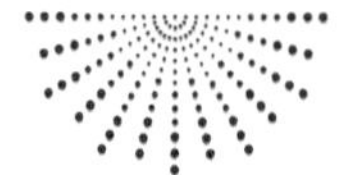

THE RIDE BACK HOME IS QUIET. I'M LOST IN MY HEAD AS ENZO drives with his hand on my leg. My body is still tingling from earlier. As I sat on Enzo's lap, I couldn't help but feel his length under me. I'm dying to know more about that part of him up close and personal.

I haven't had an orgasm like the one he gave me, ever. It's been so long since I've even had another person involved. Thank goodness, for my battery-operated boyfriend, or I'd be certain parts of me had withered up and died. Oh! My! Freaking! God! I can't believe I told him that. I seriously about died when he mentioned it. I was sure I'd only said that in my mind.

As we enter the city, Enzo breaks the silence, "What are you thinking about over there, beautiful? Your face keeps going from serious, to happy, to mortified, to something I can't entirely read. You're killing me over here." He squeezes my thigh he's been holding on to since we left.

Not really sure what to say, I go with the truth. "Just taking it all in."

"And you're sure you're okay?" he asks hesitantly. "That we're okay?" he rephrases. "...you're not upset with me, or anything?" I'm slightly shocked at the uncertainty I hear in his voice. Since I've met him, he's oozed confidence and his vulnerability is my undoing.

"No," I implore him. "I'm perfectly fine. I was just thinking about how I couldn't wait to get you home where we won't be interrupted by anyone... and there goes my lack of a filter. What is it about you that seems to have me misplacing it?" I tease, trying to shake off my mortification.

Enzo's deep baritone voice hypnotizes me when he says, "Oh, Samantha, we're just getting started. I have plenty I want to do to you, too."

My jaw drops, and my cheeks burst into flames as I think about what he might have in mind. Thankfully, we're only a few blocks from my house, so I won't have to wait long.

The moment he puts the car in park, he's out of the car, bounding to my door to get me. He reaches for my hand and we're at my front door within seconds. Thankfully, I have my keys ready, so we don't have to wait long to get inside.

The moment we shut and lock the front door, Enzo's mouth is on mine. I drop my purse and keys on the table next to the door before throwing my arms around his neck. Effortlessly, he hoists me up so that my legs snake around his waist and I'm propped up against the door. Every nerve ending is on fire. I want him more than I've ever wanted anyone. Each touch, each caress, and each kiss send electric pulses across my entire body. I. Want. More. I need more. I pull at his shirt because I'm dying to explore that sexy body beneath his clothes. Thankfully, he gets the hint and removes it over his head with only one hand.

"Only if yours goes, too," he huskily growls into my ear.

I gasp as I take in a deep breath. Enzo is sexy with clothes on, but shirtless... I may expire on the spot. Holy Hell! The man has thick, broad shoulders, with a few tattoos scattered over his chest and upper arms. I recognize the Air Force symbol on the upper part of one arm. I also see some that I would love to know the meanings of, but not now. Now, I'm going to lick each. And. Every. Muscle, across his delicious abs. I was convinced people only obtained sculpted bodies like this through Photoshop. He has a V traveling down his lower abs. You know, the kind that makes smart women drool and do and say stupid things.

"You can't be real," I moan as he reaches for me again. I could care less that being up against my door isn't comfortable. All I care about is the fact Enzo grasps my shirt and pulls it over my head in one swift move that I can't even begin to comprehend.

"You'd better fucking believe I'm real," he growls. Instantly, his mouth is back on mine and I'm devouring all that is him.

Finally, we're skin to skin. Chest to chest. The contact feels absolutely amazing. His lightly covered chest hair assaults my hardening nipples and I can't help but let out a soft groan. *I want this man. No! I need this man.*

"Bedroom," I moan as I break our kiss.

"Next time," he growls as he sets me down and unbuttons my pants. I try to help him by kicking out of my shoes as he pulls the length of my jeans down. He manages to grab my underwear in one tug, and now I'm standing in my living room in all my naked glory. I have no time to get embarrassed or think about anything other than him. He reaches into his wallet and picks something out before he drops it on the table beside us. When I realize it is a condom, I reach for his jeans. He brushes my hands aside as he unclasps them himself. With his boxer briefs in tow, they drop to the floor and he steps out of them. He kicks them aside and I'm in awe of the glorious man before me.

He's utter perfection. He catches me as I lick my lips. I'm about two seconds from dropping to my knees to get a taste of him when he takes a step toward me. He kisses me fiercely as he guides my hand to him. When I wrap my hand around his length, he moans. After only a few tugs, he pushes my hand away and says, "Condom." He hands it to me and I roll it on him. He tugs it down further than I had, in a practiced motion, then he grabs my hands and places them above my head against the door. He devours my lips, kisses my neck, and uses his other hand to pull my body close to him. I feel his entire body against me and I almost explode with my eagerness. He dips a hand down to spread me open, taking my own juices to drag them up and rub along my clit.

"Oh! My! Fucking God!" I almost scream as I feel my body work itself up. I have never had multiples but with this man, I could only hope.

He slips a finger into me for a few strokes. Then he adds more, stretching me wide. Just when I think I'm about to go over the edge, he stops, and I groan my frustration.

"Not yet, beautiful. I want it to be with me." With one quick motion, I feel him lifting me at the waist and placing me on his thick length. My legs naturally close around his waist and my back leans against the door behind us.

"Samantha," he growls as he slowly pulls out and reenters me, giving me time to adjust between each thrust. "God! You feel amazing!"

After I've completely adjusted, I urge him to pick up the pace. "Faster..." I moan my needs as I grasp his body tighter with my legs and clench down with my inner muscles. He grasps my hips with both hands. So hard and controlling, I know I will see bruises in the morning. *But. I. Don't care!* He pistons in and out of me and I lose myself completely. Being with Enzo is complete and utter bliss. He reads me like a book and has a secret code to get me to detonate in record-breaking time.

As the tingles form at the base of my spine, I let him know. "I'm close. So close, Enzo," I draw out his name as he ratchets up his pace even further. Suddenly, I feel one of his hands loosen his grasp on my hip and slide under my ass. His fingers slide along my backside and suddenly, I feel pressure in a place I've never felt before. He doesn't enter but massages it, putting pressure on me. It's an unbelievable sensation and once I get past the unique feeling, I find myself barreling over the edge into the most explosive orgasm of my life.

I hold on for dear life as Enzo continues until he reaches his release only moments behind me, with a long thrust and a loud groan. His release only spurs me on and I feel for the first time in my life what it's like to experience true multiple orgasms. *And I thought the last one was the best! Holy fucking hell! This man is a god! I have only read about this in books, never actually experienced it. What else have I been missing out on?*

For a long while, he holds me in place against the door. He rests his forehead against mine and stares into my eyes. When our breathing returns to normal, a lopsided smile appears on his face. Even after the out of this world experience I have just had, when his dimple appears, my insides clench, causing us both to groan.

"Samantha," he whispers. "I don't know what you think you've been missing out on, but I guarantee I'm willing to help you find it."

I can't help but roll my eyes. "Once again, I can't believe I said that out loud. But I've never experienced anything like this in my life." I might as well own this.

"Me neither, beautiful. Me neither," Enzo mumbles as he kisses my lips softly again. After a few minutes, he says, "Um... I need to take care of this." He points down at our joined bodies. I can feel him hardening again and I grin in surprise.

"Already? Holy shit! You're a god," I mumble.

"No... just Enzo." He grins impishly, but his face morphs into seriousness. "I'm sorry, Sam, I need to change the condom." He squeezes me tightly as he embraces my body once more. Then he lifts me off him and I feel a sudden loss.

"The bathroom's right there." I point to the door down the hallway.

"I'll be right out," he says as he takes off the condom to tie it.

While he's in there, I quickly gather our clothes, placing them in a pile. I'm about done when he reenters the hallway. "You didn't have to do that." He gestures to the pile of clothes in my hands.

I shrug. What can I say? Old habits die hard.

When I finally get a look at him in all his beauty, I almost have to pick my jaw up off the floor. He's utter perfection. His body is ready for me again and just the thought of it makes my mouth water. "Upstairs?" I gesture.

"Show me the way, Samantha," he growls as he picks me up and throws me over his shoulder.

"I can walk, Enzo!" I pound on his back, until I get a glimpse of his glorious ass flexing as he climbs the stairs and all the fight in me dissolves. I can't help myself when I reach down and slap his ass.

"Hey, now!" Enzo warns.

"Oops, Sorry!" I laugh. Who the hell am I? I haven't ever smacked anyone in my entire life. "I couldn't help it." As I glance at his ass once again, I find myself reaching to cup his scrumptious cheek in my hand. "I've never been a butt girl before." I chuckle loudly at my realization.

"Oh, Samantha. What am I going to do with you?" Enzo chuckles as we enter my room and he sets me in the middle of my bed.

As I stretch and open my eyes, I find my body is stiff and sore in places I'd forgotten existed. Flashbacks from the night before cause a blush to creep over my body. I can't help but sigh as I remember each lick, touch, or moment of intense pleasure Enzo gave me last night. Just the thought of the things we did makes me want him all over again. *But there is no way I can go again.* I'm going to be lucky if I can walk. I feel an arm snake around my waist which pulls me back against his hard length. *Hello, Hardness. Good morning to you, too.*

"Good Morning, beautiful," Enzo's deep sleepy voice whispers in my ear.

"Morning," I hoarsely whisper. I roll over and I'm met with the greenest eyes I've ever seen. His now reddish-blond scruff is sexily displayed across his jawline. His dimple makes an appearance and I forget any coherent thought I was about to say.

His hand glides from my hip up to cup my face. "Sleep well?"

"Yes," I whisper, nodding my head.

"What do you have planned today? Wanna get some breakfast?"

"That would be great. I'd offer to cook... but that's not an option," I tease as my hand reaches for his chest.

"What are your plans for later today?" Enzo's deliciously sexy morning voice asks.

I need to think for a moment. He's all too consuming. I'd love nothing more than to stay right here all day. I can't even imagine the last time I've had a night as spectacular as this. But reality must rear its ugly head.

Before I can get my train of thought clear in my head, Enzo's mouth is on my bottom lip. His teeth pull my lip free from the confinement of my teeth as he growls, "I've been waiting all night to do that."

Confused, I pull away and look at him. *Not that I mind his teeth on me but what in the world is he talking about?"* I raise an eyebrow at him, awaiting an answer to my unasked question.

He huskily whispers, "You pull in your lip when you're in

deep thought. I've been wanting to release it with my teeth since last night."

I purposely roll my lip into my teeth and pretend to contemplate something. But I'm not very successful because before I know it, he has my lip captured with his teeth once again. But this time, he parts my mouth and quickly devours me with a kiss. He rolls me onto my back and straddles me in an instant. He kisses me as he makes his way down my body. Before he has a chance to explore me too far with his hands, I break the kiss and moan. As much as I want everything this man has to offer, I can't have him again. *I may never walk again properly as it is.* I groan in utter dissatisfaction, "Ugh... Enzo, I want nothing more than to continue this train of thought... but I do want to be able to walk again. Last night was more than I've had in the last five years combined." I give him an impish grin before adding, "Please take mercy."

A satisfied expression crosses his features. He bends down and kisses his way up my body. When he gets to my ear, he pulls lightly on my lower lobe with his teeth. Then he whispers sexily in my ear, "I'm sorry you're hurting, beautiful. I'll make it up to you." He slowly extracts himself from me. I cry out, not wanting him to leave. "Do you have a tub in that bathroom of yours?" he asks, standing at the edge of my bed completely naked, distracting me from his question.

I stare. I can't help it. I feel my mouth part and jaw drop. The next thing I know, I see him smirk and cover himself. *Wait! Don't move. Let me enjoy the view.*

"Samantha," he chastises. "You can enjoy the view all you want, but let's get you into the tub first."

I quickly close my mouth and squeeze my eyes shut. I cover my face with one hand as I pull the sheet up with the other, hoping I can disappear into the bed.

Before I know it, the sheet is ripped back from me. Strong hands approach me from the side and snake under my back and knees. The air swooshes around me and I smell the heavenly scent of Enzo before my body collides with his chest. I peek one eye open to see what he's doing, and he lets out a deep belly laugh, shaking my entire body. "No reason to be embarrassed," he rumbles. "Let's get you into a warm bath."

He sets me on the floor and reaches for the faucet. As soon as I hear the water, I realize I have other business to attend to. *I have had three kids after all.* "Um... Enzo. Do you mind giving me a moment?" I look up, not wanting to ruin the moment, but I also don't want to do a potty-dance, like a three-year-old. "You can come back in a moment." I glance at the toilet longingly before looking at him for his response.

His wide smile slays me with his dimple. "No problem. Take all the time you need." Without another word, he leaves the bathroom, shutting the door. *God Bless This Man.*

It takes us a lot longer to get ready than I would on my own. It doesn't help that Enzo joins me in the bathtub. Once he gets me all relaxed, he somehow manages to rile me up. Then, of course I must devour every part of him. *And I mean every part.* He tastes just as delicious as I imagine he would. I have no freaking clue as to when I last felt so bold or sensual. Even with nearly twenty years of marriage, I've never experienced anything like this. I know he'll be leaving soon and this will end in disaster. But for once, I'm going to enjoy this moment, as if I may never get it again. *Hell, I don't recall ever having it before. This man is one of a kind, a temptation like no other and I have no idea how long this will last.*

13

ENZO

As we sit down at a local diner for breakfast, I can't help but feel relieved when Samantha orders a full meal. Not that I make a habit of getting breakfast with many women, but I absolutely hate it when they order only yogurt or fruit. That's like ordering only a salad for dinner. I want a woman who eats, not pretends she's a rabbit. How in the hell will they survive in life on only tidbits of food? I maintain an active lifestyle. I must eat to sustain my energy. Who wants someone who just stares at me while I eat during a meal, as they move the food around their plate, but never really eat it?

After chewing a bite of my buttermilk pancakes, I ask, "So what are your plans for the rest of the day?" I wasn't going to invite anyone to that barbeque this afternoon, but I don't really want my time to end with Samantha.

"Ummm…" She pulls that fucking lip into her mouth as she thinks. "I have Declan's soccer game at three and that's about it, why?"

Well, the barbeque is out. Maybe I'll be able to pull a plan out of my ass and get to see her in that sexy dress again. I still can't believe I bought her that dress. It's not like I care about the money. It's more about the fact I have never, in my life, done that for anyone. I don't think I've even taken my sister shopping. Though if she needed one, I would gladly buy her a dress. *Who the hell buys a woman he just met a dress, anyway?!?!* I do, apparently.

"What do you say to going out later this evening?" I suggest as I fork some hash browns into my mouth, trying to be nonchalant.

"I might be up for that," she coyly states as she cocks her head to the side, showing me that sass I enjoy so much.

"I'll make sure the occasion will suit your new dress." I place my hand on my chin, acting as if I'm contemplating world peace. I really need to move boots, if I'm going to find anywhere decent to take her this evening. Maybe one of my buddies who owns an upscale restaurant will help me out. Shit. I didn't bring home any dress clothes. I guess shopping will also be on my list of things to do today.

Samantha's eyes light up with delight and a slight blush spreads over her. I can't help but be in complete awe of the woman before me. If this is all it takes to cause that look, it seems I will be investing in multiple new shirts today. "Would you be available by six?"

"Yes, I should be home before five," she states, then continues to eat a piece of bacon that she had been holding. "It won't take me too long to get ready."

By the time I drop Samantha off, it's almost noon. I know I won't have much time, so I google to find what I'm looking for and head straight there. It's a big and tall store, specializing in suits with an on-site tailor. I know they will have what I need, and I can get in and out without much fuss. Besides, if they need to make any alterations, I can always come back to pick it up later this afternoon.

Thankfully, there is a salesman who is quickly able to measure me and help me find an entire suit that fits within about thirty minutes. Their tailor is available and tells me it should be ready to pick up within a few hours. I even managed to pick up a few shirts in different colors and a new pair of shoes that looked sharp but are still comfortable. My usual wardrobe is entirely function over fashion, old habits die hard. But knowing how Samantha will look in her new dress tonight, I need to step up my fashion game for our date.

I don't even hesitate as I swipe my card at the cashier. I'm pleased by the little amount of time I had to spend shopping. Besides, what do I really spend my money on? What's the use in having it if I never get the chance to spend it? I may not wear this suit often, possibly never again, but at least I'll have it if it's needed. Not only that, Samantha deserves a nice night out.

I glance at my watch and realize I still have plenty of time to pick something up for the barbeque on the way to Riggs' home. I should still make it there on time, too. For someone who avoids shopping like the plague, at least I'm efficient.

As I sit at a red light on my way to the barbeque, I pull up a buddy of mine from my list of contacts, who owns a prestigious nightclub in Portland. I did him a solid a few years back while we were on a mission. I'm hoping he can do one for me in return. I know there's always a waiting list for people to get a table at his restaurant, but maybe he'll give me a break and fit us in tonight. If not, I'm sure I can find something else. My main mission is seeing Samantha in the gorgeous green dress. The best part might also be the fact I will get to see her out of it, too.

Fuck! Now I'm thinking about Samantha's sexy curves and everything else about her.

Thankfully, before I'm too far out of control, I'm interrupted by Rowan's gruff voice. "Holy fuck! Has the world come to an end? Is this really Harps?" Before I can say anything, he laughs as he continues, "To what do I owe the pleasure?"

I can't help but grin as I greet him, "Hey, Ro! What's up, man?"

"Not much, just about to head to work."

"About that…" I start, but then realize I'm not sure how much I should divulge.

"Yes?" he drawls out and I can hear his sarcasm drip through the phone.

I might as well just get to the point. "Look, man, is there any way I could score a table at your place tonight? I know it's incredibly short notice…"

Before I can say more, he interrupts with, "I could probably work it out… for how many?" By the end, I can hear the humor in his voice.

"Just two," I say nonchalantly.

"Hmmm… I see."

"You see what?" I ask, not getting what he's hinting about.

"Well, since you willingly ask for favors, I take it there must be someone special," he induces, as if I've been holding out on precious intel.

I can't spend years working with someone and not know his tells. Sleeping in less than desirable conditions for days on end will do that. I can play this two ways. I can feed him a line of BS, or I can be straight with him. Not being one to put up with much shit, I keep it simple. "Yeah. I have. I want to take her to a nice place like yours. Do you think you can make it happen?"

"Only if I get to meet her," he hedges. "Your game is usually at the local dive bar, so I'm interested in who you've met. Especially since I know you haven't been stateside for a while."

"Hey now," I defend myself. "I don't usually go to dive bars."

Rowan lets out a belly laugh. "Relax. I know. I was saying that to get your goat!" He takes a deep breath. "Seriously, if you want a table, it's yours. I'll put your name on the list with the hostess. Text me when you're on your way and I'll make sure a table is ready for you."

"Thanks, man. I appreciate it."

We spend a few more minutes catching up before disconnecting. He tells me how business is doing, and I tell him about my leave, as well as the decision that lays ahead of me. He doesn't ask about Samantha, but I'm sure he's waiting on that for tonight. Knowing Rowan, it will just be a matter of time.

We disconnect just as I get to Riggs' house. The driveway is long and filled with vehicles. Most are some form of 4x4 or

SUV. Upon further inspection, they're also nondescript, but high end all the same. I find a place to park, ensuring I won't get blocked in. There's no way I'm going to be late to pick up my suit or Samantha. Approaching the house, I hear most of the noise coming from around back and the side fence is open, so I head in that direction.

Carson is the first to greet me, "Harps! Glad you made it."

He lifts the hand he's holding a beer within greeting, as he breaks from the small crowd he was talking with to meet me in person. When he gets closer, he shakes my hand with one arm, pulling me closer to pat me on the back with the arm he's holding his beer with. "Nice to see you, Cars!"

"Same here, Harps! Same here." Carson steps away and points in the direction of the food tables. "Are you hungry? There's plenty of food over there."

Motioning to the bag I'm carrying. "Thanks. I'll just add this to it."

He follows me to the table. "So how have you been, Harps?" In a lower tone, he asks, "Make any decisions?"

"Not yet. I like the thought of being near Portland though." Once again, a flash of Samantha's beautiful face comes to mind. "I'm meeting with the CO at the Air National Guard later this week."

"Are you sure you want to switch over?" Carson asks, giving me a knowing look. He and I both know I wouldn't be doing what I am currently, and it'll affect my years of service, but I'd be guaranteed to be stationed here in Portland. More than likely, I'm going to take Riggs up on his offer, but I'm not making any decisions yet.

Carson introduces me to many of the people I'd be

working with. Each welcome me eagerly and have nothing but good things to say about working on Riggs' team. I'm pleased to discover I know most of them already. I know I'd be a good fit. I just don't know if I'm officially ready to retire from the Air Force altogether.

Riggs and his wife, Stella who also happens to work for him, make quite an impression on me. He's exactly like I expect, what you see is what you get. But he has a soft side for his firecracker of a wife. It's evident as the day is long that he loves her above all else. She may be petite, but I've no doubt that woman can pack a punch. She's quick as a whip, and if you're ever on her bad side, I'm sure her tongue lashing would be impressive. She's in no way a bitch. The woman has a heart of gold, but I can tell she knows her shit and won't be afraid to put you in your place. She's such a spitfire. It's pure entertainment watching her keep Riggs on his toes. That itself is a sight to behold. I thought the man was unflappable. Stella is true to her stereotype of being a redhead. But from what I gather from the guys around here, it's best to never mention that fact to her face. Together, they're quite the dynamic duo. Both badasses of their own right, but each bending just slightly to fit each other perfectly. It would be an honor to work with them.

I keep an eye on my watch as I enjoy the gathering of what could become my closest friends. These are good people. Even if I don't take the job with Riggs, I'm sure they'll be people I see often. I feel right at home as I relax and enjoy my afternoon.

As I walk into Ma's kitchen that afternoon after picking up my suit, I'm greeted with her warm hug. There's never a loss of affection growing up in our house. Ma may be a petite woman, *well, almost anyone is compared to me,* but she knew how to keep us in line.

"So, what've you been up to, love?" she says as she kisses me on the cheek I've lowered toward her. I take a seat on the barstool next to the counter she's working at. The kitchen smells delicious.

"I'm just stopping by to check in before I head back out this evening."

Eyeing the garment bag I've hung on the back of the stool next to me, she gives me a knowing grin. "And I suppose that," she says, gesturing to the bag, "has something to do with the fact I won't see you until tomorrow, either?"

I'm thirty-seven years old. I've lived on my own for the better part of the last twenty years. Traveled all over the world. I'm in the Air Force for crying out loud, but she can make me feel sixteen all over again.

Never being one to lie, I say, "More than likely."

The knowing twinkle in her eye pierces my heart. Ma is the best mom one could ever ask for. "So, you've found someone special." She doesn't ask. It's said like a fact. Which I guess she's right. The woman has always had her Spidey senses from the time I could walk.

I hesitate for a moment, trying to figure out what to say. Samantha is special, there's no doubt about it. But I've just met the woman a few days ago. From the glimmer of hope in Ma's eye, I don't want to squash it if it doesn't work out, so I go with the truth. "It's still very new."

"Lorenzo Dean Harper, you can pull your BS with your buddies. But I know you, remember? So, spill it. Who is she?" And there it is, the BS radar that could have grown men groveling on their knees. I could be held prisoner by hostiles and they couldn't get the truth from me, but one raised eyebrow from Ma... *SHIT, I knew better.*

I cough and run a hand through my hair, taking a moment to look any direction but at her. Never being one to cower, I finally come to my senses and nod. "Yeah. There is someone, Ma. I just met her, so don't get your hopes up. I wasn't lying when I said it's new."

"But she has you buying a suit..." There it is. That cocked eyebrow reaching further away from her hazel eye. The woman should have been an insurgent interrogator. There would be no world secrets with her seeking the truth. She missed her calling in life.

I can't help the lopsided grin that takes over my face. I shake my head as memories of Samantha come flooding back to me. I try to keep as nonchalant as I can, but that would almost be as effective as raking leaves in a hurricane, around my mom. I stick with simple. With her, less is always more.

"Apparently..." I shrug dismissively.

"Correct me if I'm wrong, but the last time you actually bought a suit to go out with a woman was in high school, right?" She taps her finger on her chin as if she's trying to remember for herself when the last time was.

Hell, I don't even remember. She might be right.

"Ma, it's not like I've never bought a suit since then," I say in my defense. "It's not that big of a deal."

But of course, it is. I usually just wear my dress uniform for special occasions. Not that I purposely choose to wear that often either. Only when I'm forced to or strongly encouraged is my usual rule of thumb.

Ma interrupts my thoughts, "Enzo, I really can't remember you wearing anything but your dress uniform other than at your sister and brother's weddings," she states, not making accusations, just recalling memories.

A slight chuckle escapes. "You're right, Ma, me neither. But I had to class it up a little to go with her dress." Damn, what a dress it is, too.

And then I see my mistake. Simple as can be… but epic at the same time. I just opened another can of worms that my mom won't let rest until I give her the entire scoop. Yep! There it is… the eyebrow. She doesn't even need to talk. It's like she has subliminal powers to make me tell all. Dammit to hell.

Before I know it, I tell her all about my date with Samantha last night. Well, the very G-rated version. She can draw her own conclusions as to where I've been all night. She may have powers for being "all knowing," but there are some things I just don't share with my mother, not that I'd share them with anyone else, for that matter.

Ma doesn't seem to get overly excited or really say much for that matter. She just listens as I tell her about taking Samantha up the Gorge to have dinner. She chuckles when I tell her about finding a dress. I do get another brow raised when I mention that I paid for the dress, but luckily, she doesn't press me about it. She knows as well as I do that this entire situation is very uncharacteristic of me. Since Vanessa, the type of girls I've dated in the past usually didn't hold my attention past the first date, if you can even call some that. I'm sure Ma's given up hope of me ever settling down, figuring that ship had long since sailed.

Eventually, I excuse myself to get ready for my date with Samantha. The word "date" sounds weird to think about. *But what else would you call it?* Usually, I just casually hang out or meet up at a restaurant. Not since high school have I gone to this much trouble. But the thought of Samantha's gorgeous smile reminds me there is nothing I wouldn't do to see it again.

By the time I return downstairs, Pops is still not home and Ma's waiting in the family room reading a book. I didn't exactly divulge the fact Samantha is dad's client. I'll cross that bridge when I get there. He being gone makes it easier to keep that bit of information to myself for a while. *This is still very new.*

As soon as I walk in the room, Ma lets out a slight gasp. "My, don't you look handsome!" A knowing smile spreads across her face as she stands up to inspect me further, making me feel as if I'm back in high school going to prom.

"Thanks, Ma," I say as I bend down to kiss her goodbye. "I'll see you later."

Traffic is light, and I get to Samantha's house with plenty of time to spare. I glance at my watch and see it's five thirty. It's a habit, being early is considered on time, being on time is considered late in my book. Years of being in the Air Force will do that to you. I even stopped by a flower shop on my way here to pick up a bouquet of dahlias for her since she mentioned they're her favorite. It doesn't hurt that they're in full bloom this time of year. I knock on the door to her house, but there's no answer. Her car's in the driveway, so I know she's here. Maybe she's in the shower. I take a seat on the bench next to her door and send her a text, letting her know I'm here.

14

SAMANTHA

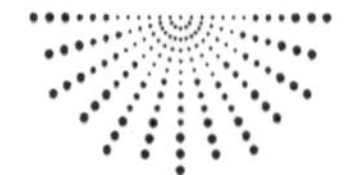

FROM THE TIME ENZO DROPPED ME OFF, I'VE BEEN RUNNING NON-stop. As much as I've wanted to bask in the delicious memories of last night, I force myself to stay busy. I throw in some laundry and shower again. This time, I take extra care with the razor and blow-dry my hair so it'll be easy to style when I return from Declan's game. I also flat iron it, knowing I won't have much time later. Not wanting to look too done up, I keep things casual for the game. Before leaving, I switch over a load of laundry to the dryer and pack some extra snacks for Frankie and Maddie during the game.

I rush to the field, armed with my snacks and chair to watch the game. I make it there before Devin and the kids, so I choose a spot on the sideline to take a moment and relax. To pass the time, I pull out my e-reader to keep my thoughts occupied. *But that, of course, is an Epic FAIL!* Enzo's been on my mind since the moment he left and I'm more than eager to see him again this evening. Eventually, I'm able to get into the

114

manuscript I'm reviewing for a chapter or two before I'm nearly knocked over by Frankie and her infamous hugs.

She sneak attacks me from behind, as she screams into my ear, "Mama, I've missed you! Is the kitchen done yet?"

"Not yet, Sweet Pea," I say as I pull her around to sit on my lap for another squeeze. "I've missed you, too." We sit like this as she tells me about her morning with Devin and her siblings.

Just as she's in the middle of some story about eating the biggest pancakes ever, Devin, Aubrey, and Maddie come to sit down beside us. I give them a nod in greeting, as I do my best to keep up with Frankie's explanation of her cooking breakfast.

I notice Maddie deliberately sits next to me while Devin and Aubrey set up their chairs on the other side of her. Declan is with his team warming up for the game. Maddie seems distracted by someone she's texting, but overall, she looks content. *Just another day at the soccer fields for us.*

Frankie's still talking a mile a minute, but suddenly I hear, "...so then Aubrey said I could have the next one. Mom, it was almost bigger than my plate..."

Wait. What? Aubrey was there for breakfast? I try not to let my reaction show. *I guess things are more serious with her than I expected. I'm not sure how I feel about this. When did Devin start having sleepovers?* But then my mind goes to my evening last night. Memories of Enzo and his delicious body replay on a loop. Suddenly, I'm not the least bit worried about Devin because my mind is filled with all thoughts of Enzo.

After a few more glorious memories flashing through my mind, I take a good look at my kids. They each really look okay. *Well, no different than normal.* They seem to be fine with what's going on between Aubrey and their dad, so I guess I could be, too. *Besides, it's not like I want him back. That ship has sailed, caught on fire, and sunk.* I think for the first time ever, I'm really not jealous of Devin and his relationship. *Huh, that's an interesting thought.*

When Frankie finishes telling how syrup got everywhere, and Devin made her take a shower, I take a moment to check in further with Maddie. "Hey, Mads, how are you?"

She looks up from her phone and smiles. Genuinely smiles. "I'm good, Mom."

I can't help but tease her, "So... what's got you into such a good mood?" I gesture at the phone in her hand.

A slight blush crosses her face. *There must be a boy involved. She never blushes like this.* "Well, you know I'm going to the dance this Friday..."

"Yes. I remember you telling me about it." I wait for her to go on. I've found it's usually best to wait for her to divulge information. I get a lot further with her if she thinks it's her idea to share.

"Well, at first, I was just going with a bunch of friends. But then Soren Silva, you know the junior I told you about. The one that plays lacrosse... well, he asked me to be his date instead."

A date. My daughter wants to go on a date. Okay. I knew this time would come, but it's still hard to let her grow up. She's still my baby. We told her she could go to dances, but dates? Well, I knew it would happen eventually... just hoped it'd be later.

I try to be as nonchalant as I can when I respond, not to give my thoughts away. "So, what did you tell him?"

She sheepishly looks at me, then glances at Devin. "Um, I told him I'd have to ask my parents. I'm talking to you first, because well, you know how Dad can be. If you don't think it's a good idea, there's no reason in even telling him." She starts to speed-talk by this point. "So, what do you say, Mom, can I go? Can I tell him yes?" By now, she's nearly bouncing in her seat.

"How exactly would you be getting there?" I ask, trying to stall for time. I need more information before I can say yes. I know I started dating at her age, but it feels different being on this side of the scenario.

She suddenly looks even more nervous than before. "Um, he's had his license for about a year. He makes the honor roll every term and he's never been in an accident. I know, I asked. I even asked his brother to check." She still has a pleading look on her face.

"That's nice, honey. But I'd at least have to meet him before I make a decision."

"Mooommmm! That's so not fair," she protests, but Devin cuts her off.

"What's not fair?" He raises an eyebrow in question to me.

I, in turn, look pointedly at Maddie. I won't lose her trust by spilling the beans to her dad. She can tell him if she really wants to go on this date, though I'm sure he won't make it easy on her.

I can't help but be proud of her when I see her turn toward him, sit up taller, and say, "I was asked to go to the dance on Friday, by Soren Silva. I'm asking Mom if I can go."

Hmmm... this boy must be someone worthy if she's telling Devin so openly about it.

Devin's eyes go a little wider, but that's the only sign he

shows of being unprepared for our conversation. "And… what did your mom say?" He glances in my direction.

Maddie lets out a little sigh. "She said she has to meet him first."

Knowing Devin, I can tell he's holding back a smile as he keeps the solemn look on his face. "Well, that's not unreasonable, Mads. I would like to meet him, too."

"Daddy…" She puts her hands over her face as if she's suddenly embarrassed. *I don't blame her really.* Devin's been putting the fear of God in her ever since she looked like she might notice boys. She knows he'll do something to completely embarrass her, or at least he's been threatening to do so, for as long as I can remember. She also knows I won't let him get away with too much, *but a parent has rights.*

Attempting to put her out of her misery, I state, "How about we invite him out to dinner one day earlier in the week? Then we can meet him and not have it be a big deal when he picks you up for the dance."

"Mom, since his practice usually gets done around mine, do you think we could make it less formal and just let me introduce you when you pick me up?" She gives me a pleading look.

I look to Devin since we're trying to co-parent the best we can. He gives me a slight nod. "Sure thing, sweetheart. Why don't you have him plan to meet us Tuesday evening after practice? Then I'll take you dress shopping if all goes well."

She hops out of her chair to give me a hug. "Thanks, Mom, you're the best."

Not letting her get away with anything, Devin states boldly,

"I still reserve my right to meet him, too. *Before* your date. I'll be there when he picks you up."

I must hold in the chuckle that wants to escape. *Dad's will be dads!*

"I'll be there, too!" Frankie chirps in, not wanting to be left out, making us all laugh.

Thankfully, for Maddie's sake, Declan's game is about to start, so our attention is soon diverted from her to the game. The team they're playing is a tough one. The score has stayed at zero for both sides for quite some time. Finally, Declan assists in the first goal, and the crowd goes wild! Sure enough, at one point in the game, he does that new maneuver where he flips as he throws the ball in, giving me a near heart attack. *But at least it looks cool, right? Don't worry, poor mom's over here having palpitations.*

After the game, I wait to congratulate Declan on his win. As his team huddles afterward for a talk with their coach, the sidelines pack up the gear they brought to make room for the next game. I stay near Devin, Aubrey, and the girls. Aubrey and I make small talk while we wait. It still feels a little forced, but it's a lot easier than last time. I guess the shock factor is over. Devin does his best to remain respectful to each of us and breaks in to contribute to our conversation.

Within a few minutes, Declan runs over. He high-fives or fist bumps his sisters, Aubrey, and his dad before reaching me. I'm lucky, I get a hug. "Great game, Dec! I'm so proud of you," I say as I squeeze him tighter.

"Thanks, Mom!" His smile stretches clear across his face and his arms remain wrapped around me for a while longer.

Then he looks up mischievously. "So, did you catch that new maneuver I learned?"

I tickle him on his side as I say, "Yeah, thanks for the near heart attack, Dec. I've always wanted to go to an early grave! If I get gray hair, it's because of you, squirt!"

Declan laughs and tries to pull away, but I'm still quicker. I continue to dig my fingers into his side, tickling him where I know he's weakest. Right under the armpits. *Yep! A mother knows best.*

"Enough... Enough," he pants, still trying to squirm away.

I give him mercy by letting go. "Way to go out there, champ. You're pretty impressive!" I wink to let him know just how proud of him I am. His grin in return is priceless.

We spend the next few minutes talking about his game. I make sure the girls know I'll be picking them up after school on Monday since Devin usually picks Declan up for his practice. I still can't believe Maddie's going on her first date. With our spectator gear in tow, we head to the parking lot. Each of the kids gives me one last hug before they get into Devin's car with Aubrey. It's never easy to say goodbye, but with my plans for this evening never being far from my mind, I'm eager to get home all the same.

By the time I get home, it's nearly five o'clock. I know it won't take me too long to get ready, but I still want to look my best for Enzo. *When was the last time I've had the opportunity to put this much effort into a date?* Knowing how the night will end, I opt for taking another quick shower, taking care to pull my hair up, so it won't get wet. That was the point of using my flat iron earlier.

Before getting dressed, I take the time to apply my makeup

and put the final touches on my hair. By the time I'm ready to exit my bathroom, I check my phone to see the time. Crap, he's here already. I send Enzo a quick text to give him the combination that unlocks our door, telling him to wait inside for me.

I rush out to my room to retrieve the dress out of the bag. I'd forgotten to hang it up last night. Thankfully, the material isn't the kind that wrinkles easily. I can't help but feel flushed when I recall how preoccupied I'd been when we arrived. *Though, I wouldn't have stopped to hang the dress up for a million bucks.*

I take the bag to my bed and pull out the dress, ready to inspect for tags needing to be removed. As the dress is freed from the bag, a small wrapped cluster of tissue falls to my bed. Curiosity has me forgetting the tags for a moment to see what this could be. As I grasp the tissue to pick it up, I feel there's something in it. It's lightweight but has a square shape, like a cardboard tag of some sort.

As I take care to unwrap it, I'm shocked to find a matching necklace and earrings to my dress. I know I didn't pick these out. This is all Enzo. My heart melts a little. These are just what I would've picked out to go with it. The man has good taste. *This must be too good to be real, right? What man picks out accessories? How in the hell has he stayed single for so long?!?!*

Suddenly, I'm in a hurry to see Enzo. I quickly put on the dress and earrings, *after removing the tags, of course.* I grab a pair of my favorite black heels as I clutch the necklace in my hand. *I think I'll ask for his assistance in putting this on, so I can get to him quicker.*

As I quickly descend the stairs, I notice Enzo is pacing at

the bottom. There's a bouquet of dahlias on the sideboard that wasn't there before. I can't see him entirely, just his backside. But when he turns as I approach, I'm completely awestruck.

OMG! Enzo is pure perfection in his stunningly gorgeous black suit and light-green shirt, sans tie. It's cut to precision. It lays perfectly across his broad shoulders, forming the perfect inverted triangle. His muscular form is sexier than I've ever seen. Even the models I use for covers have nothing on him. If I wasn't eager to find out what he has planned for me this evening, I'd say to hell with it and drag him upstairs.

"Hey, beautiful," his sexy voice calls to me. "You look exquisite. My memories of you in that dress didn't do you justice."

I quickly close the distance between us and meet him at the bottom of the stairs, as I reply, "You're not so bad yourself, handsome."

He grins shyly, and that delicious dimple makes an appearance, making his sexy smile reach his potent green eyes. *Yep, this is the perfect combination to make a grown woman go weak in the knees and lose all train of thought. God, what Enzo does to me is unbelievable.*

Remembering I still have the necklace in my hand, I hold it up and ask, "Can you help with this?" I force myself to turn away from him, lifting my hair off my back to keep it out of the way.

Before I know it, I'm enveloped with the scent that's entirely Enzo. His strong, muscular arms, hidden behind that magnificent suit come around, placing the necklace near my collarbone before clasping it in the back. As soon as he's done, he embraces me with those welcoming arms while snuggling into my neck. His breath on my skin makes me tingle in all the right places. He kisses me once at the base of my neck, then places his hands on my hips to turn me to face him.

"Hi," I whisper, as I'm still caught in his trance.

"Hi yourself, beautiful. Are you ready?" He matches in a whisper.

"Just let me get my coat and purse, and we'll be on our way."

Reluctantly, he lets me go and I walk to the hallway to get my burgundy knee-length trench coat and my purse. It's still warm, *or at least I feel warm,* so I opt to just carry it. When I turn around, I see Enzo's outstretched hand waiting for mine. I eagerly take his as we walk out the door. I can't wait to see what he has planned for this evening. With the way he looks in that suit, it could be a food cart downtown and I'd be completely satisfied just to be in his presence.

As we drive over the Fremont bridge, I take in the cityscape and all that is Portland. Dusk is nearing on this magnificent, clear, fall evening. The twinkling of lights from below never fail to entrance me. As we take an exit, Enzo drives us further into downtown. Before I know it, we're in a parking garage and he's leading me out onto one of the busy streets.

Figuring we're about to go to one of the street-level restaurants, I readily follow his lead. I'm a little surprised when we enter a lobby to one of the many high-rise buildings lining the streets. I eye him skeptically when we enter the elevator and he presses the thirty-sixth floor. A group of people who are dressed up like us also enter the elevator, so I don't get the chance to ask Enzo what he's up to. He pulls my back flush against his body, as we make room for the crowd. The ride to the top is silent between us since other couples are having conversations around us. My body instantly hums by the nearness of Enzo, though I do my best to ignore it. *We are in public.*

When we reach our floor, I'm surprised to see we've arrived at a waiting area. There's beautiful art hanging on the walls around us, along with a sculpted silver sign hanging above a hostess stand that reads "Allure." The script is done beautifully, leaving me very intrigued as to where Enzo has taken me. We wait our turn to get to the hostess. From what I can tell, there's going to be a substantial wait. But when Enzo gives his name, we're immediately ushered right back to an incredibly dressed table overlooking the Willamette River and the twinkling city of Portland. A gasp involuntarily escapes as I take in this incredible view. I almost forget I'm supposed to be finding my seat. I'm too busy staring out the window at the miraculous view.

Enzo pulls me out of my trance when he steps around me to pull out a chair. He places his hand on the small of my back as he ushers me to my seat. He assists me in scooting back into the table before taking a seat across from me. By the time he sits, I realize my jaw is hanging open as I stare at him in disbelief. The waitress says something, and he replies, but I have no idea what it entails. I'm too lost in thought. Finally, he gets my full attention with a raised eyebrow when he asks, "Problem, Samantha?"

Re-gathering my wits, I blurt out the first thing I can catch from the swirling thoughts in my mind, in a whisper, "Come here often? Isn't there a month-long waiting list for this place?"

Enzo's only response is to grin sheepishly.

I wait for an answer, but my mind reels out of control. *He must have already made reservations here when he knew he was coming home. Just whom did he plan on taking here?*

Before my thoughts get too out of control, he shakes his head. "No, this is my first time actually."

I give him a look that clearly says I'm not buying it. "And…"

He clears his throat, looking around nervously. "I… might know the owner."

Tension I didn't realize I had been holding on to suddenly releases. "Oh."

Well, there goes that theory. What the fuck had I been thinking? And where did that sudden pang of jealousy come from? I seriously had no right to jump to that conclusion. He's given me zero indication there's been anyone else. I guess old habits die hard. He shouldn't have to pay for Devin's sins. *Thank God, I'd managed to keep my filter in place for once.*

When I don't say more, he adds, "Ro and I go way back… I called in a favor."

Before I can say anything, a man in a suit approaches our table. He looks much too classy to merely be a waiter, but he commands my attention just the same when he blatantly states, "Ma'am, what on earth are you doing with this tool?"

"Excuse me?" I blanch, then glance at Enzo who now has his head in his hand, shaking it slightly, looking very embarrassed.

The man stands straighter and clears his throat and with a straight face says, "I said, what are you doing here with this tool? You are the most beautiful woman in this room, and you came here *with him*?" He points at Enzo, who is now rolling back his shoulders as if he's itching for a fight while keeping his hand over his eyes blocking his full reaction from me.

I push back my chair to stand as I quietly hiss, not to draw too much attention, "What business is it of yours whom I come with? The man you just insulted I might add, could kick your ass in a New York minute." I point my finger at his chest and step closer. "He's served our country for the past twenty years, and he's *anything* but a tool!" By the time I finish my rant, I turn my head toward Enzo to find he of all things is nearly rolling out of his chair with silent laughter.

"You're right," the bastard before me states. "She's special." His icy façade melts and he roars with laughter.

Between gasps of air, Enzo coughs out, "I... told you... she was." Enzo stands and is suddenly hugging the man before us. "It's good to see you, Ro!" Then he lowers his voice and says, "I can't believe you just pulled that shit. I thought this was a high-class establishment." Enzo pats him on the back then looks at me, holding out his hand. "Samantha, I'd like you to meet Rowan Evans. We served together before he got out and decided it was time to change in his boots for fancy loafers. Rowan, this is Samantha O'Reilly."

Rowan doesn't give me a chance to say anything before he pulls me into a hug and whispers, "Keep this one on his toes. He deserves it." I can't help but laugh and feel more at ease.

"I'll keep that in mind," I reply as he releases me and gestures for me to return to my seat.

"Seriously, it's good to meet you," Rowan says apologetically as he grabs a chair from a nearby table to join us. "I was just messing around with Harps. That man can prank like the best of them. It's good to finally get one over on him. I didn't mean for the joke to be on you, too. Sorry."

I glance at Enzo and the gleam in his eye is infectious. I can't help but let my guard down and enjoy the moment. Man, I was really riled up. I don't know what came over me. It's not like Enzo couldn't defend himself. *He's six-foot-six for crying out loud.* But that was a good prank... he got me good. I decide to let Rowan off the hook. "It's all good."

"So where did you kids meet?" Rowan finally asks.

"We're not here to play twenty questions, Ro. Thanks again for getting us a table tonight. I appreciate it."

"Yes, thank you," I add.

"Any time. I had to meet the woman who turned this sorry bastard's head enough to get him to call in favors." He shakes his head in disbelief. "And after you handled that stunt I just pulled, I know you're worth it."

I can't help but blush. I really was about to cause a scene. I don't get to say anything before Enzo reaches for my hand across the table. "She totally is, man. She totally is."

Rowan stands and places the chair back at the table next to us. "Well, I put your name on the list upstairs at the club as well. Feel free after you leave here to go up and use a table in the VIP section. Dance the night away and enjoy!"

Enzo once again stands and reaches his hand out to Rowan. "Thanks again, man. I really appreciate it." He dubiously looks at me and states, "You might just get me out on the dance floor yet, Ro. We'll see..."

After Rowan excuses himself to go check on something on the other side of the restaurant, our waitress soon comes over to tell us the daily special as well as hand us our menus. We're quiet for a few minutes while we look over the selection. Everything looks amazing and I can't help but grin as I take in the entire ambiance of the restaurant. Enzo really did well in choosing this place. It's spectacular.

After the waitress comes back to take our orders, Enzo breaks the silence with, "You handled him like a champ, Sam. I can't believe he tried to pull that on you." We both laugh at the memory, but Enzo grips my hand in his before continuing, "You really are an amazing woman. Thanks again for coming out with me."

"Enzo, I still can't believe you pulled this off with so little notice. Though I must warn you, I haven't danced outside my house in years. I might not be the best of partners, but I'd love to check the club out if you're willing. I don't think I've been to a club since college." I bite my lower lip as I try to recall the last time I've danced, other than at a wedding.

"Then we'll check it out." Enzo shrugs as he squeezes my hand. "I might have been known to throw down a move or two back in the day."

"Bring it on, Enzo. Bring it on," I tease.

After we finish our dinner and even have dessert, we end up going to the club upstairs. As we enter the wide hallway from the elevator, I realize the club is decorated as well as the restaurant below us. Art hangs as well on the rich blue walls that lead to a room at the other end. Music you can dance to greets us, the bass pulsing like a heartbeat. As we make our way into a large room, I take in the space around me. The bar stretches across one entire wall, with several stations set up for multiple bartenders. It has modern gray-stone masonry as the entire wall behind it. There are tiered shelves behind the fogged-glass bar that has blue backlighting. Those shelves must be filled with every type of alcohol imaginable. The countertop of the bar itself is reflective and every color imaginable reflects from it. There's an obvious VIP section, with plush seating and tables, up the stairs with an incredible view of the enormous dance floor. Patrons are strewn all throughout, and everyone seems to be enjoying themselves. A deejay is set up in one corner and a stage in the other, filled with musicians.

Enzo guides me to what must be the VIP section. He gives his name to the gorgeous woman in her twenties standing at the podium before the section and she escorts us to a large lounge chair with a table in front of it. Before she leaves, she takes our drink orders as well. I order a lemon drop and Enzo orders a beer of some type. He slides down next to me and places his arm around my back as we wait for our drinks. For a few moments, we take in the atmosphere around us.

Finally, Enzo breaks the silence, "Well... what do you think?"

"This place is incredible. I thought I'd feel old and out of place, but I don't. People of all ages are out enjoying their evening." It's a relief to know this. I thought a club would mean it was for barely twenty-one year olds at a rave or something. I guess since this place is more upscale, everyone of all ages comes here to enjoy the evening.

Enzo chuckles in my ear. "Samantha, you're not old." His

voice suddenly gets deeper. "In fact, you're the sexiest woman in this room. I can't wait to get you on that dance floor."

Just the thought of being in Enzo's arms has me shivering with anticipation. "Me neither," I softly speak into his ear. I finally give into the pull that's been between us all night and kiss him on the cheek. "Thanks again for this incredible evening."

"It's my pleasure, beautiful." Enzo grazes a quick peck on my lips before the waitress interrupts us with our drink orders.

I sit back to enjoy my lemon drop. It's the perfect concoction for this evening. As I relax, I can't help but head bop a little as I sing along under my breath to a song I recognize. After a few moments, I realize I have Enzo's full attention. I immediately stop and take a large drink, almost getting a brain freeze, to keep myself from singing further.

"Don't stop on my account." Enzo sweeps a strand of hair behind my ear, so he can fully see my face. "I was rather enjoying the view."

Embarrassed, I shake my head. "Sorry. Got lost up in the moment. This is one of Maddie's favorite songs, so I know it well."

He takes a long pull on his beer. "It's a great song. Wanna go out there?" He gestures to the dance floor below us.

"Sure, why not." I shrug.

By the time we get down to the floor, one of my absolute favorite songs makes an appearance. The melodic start to Ed Sheeran's *Shape of You* begins. I pull Enzo out into the middle of the floor and dance like no one's watching. I can't help it. I feel the need to move when I hear this song. After a few bars, Enzo grabs my waist with one hand and pulls my body to his.

He clasps his other hand with mine, and we move around the dance floor. *The man can dance.* He guides me effortlessly and even puts in a few spins at the appropriate moments. When the song gets to the chorus about the smell of bedsheets, memories of last night flood my thoughts. Enzo's now hooded eyes don't help with my suddenly lust-filled mind.

Enzo had left his jacket at our table with mine. His shirt sleeves have been rolled, so his muscular forearms keep flexing right along with the music. His shirt is open at the collar and I can't help but want to undo a few more buttons and feel his magnificent chest without the barrier of clothing. *But we're in a club, not my bedroom.* After dancing with him like this, I don't think I'll ever be able to hear this song and not think of the sexy man before me. I shake my head to keep my thoughts from lingering so I can simply enjoy the rest of the song. By the time the song ends, we're so in tune with one another. Maroon 5's song *Sugar* starts immediately afterward, and we can't help but dance to the beat, moving with the music. In fact, we stay on the dance floor for countless songs, just enjoying each other on the dance floor.

I soon find Enzo is pure magic and I simply cannot get enough. I laugh when I realize I haven't let loose like this in years. It's primal and our connection continues to grow throughout the night. Enzo is sexy as hell and the more I'm around him, the more I want him in every way possible. When I finally can't dance anymore, we head back to the table to reorder drinks. Though it's not long before we're out on the dance floor getting caught up with one another once again.

15

ENZO

From the moment I picked Samantha up, I've been dying to get my hands on her. It's not like I'm a randy teenager, but I haven't felt this way since my early twenties. She looks amazing in that dress. I wasn't kidding when I said my memory hadn't done it justice. By the time we get out onto the dance floor and she begins to dance, I nearly lose it. When she lets loose, she's the most beautiful woman in the world. She owns her moves and I can't help but want to sway right along with her. As I guide her around on the dance floor, I notice Rowan off to the side of the room. He gives me a knowing look that says, *'I never thought I'd see the day.'* I know, I haven't been out on the dance floor willingly in years. I quickly dismiss him and focus my entire attention on the sexy woman before me.

By the time we head back to her house, it's two o'clock in the morning. Neither of us drank much throughout the evening, as we spent most of our time out on the dance floor. I'm still cautious as I drive because others might not have made the same choice.

After dancing, the sexual tension between us is even thicker than last night, if that's possible. I can't wait to get Samantha home and refresh my memory of what she looks like out of that glorious green dress. The woman moves in heels as if they're just an extension of her. I might just have to insist she keep those on for a bit, but as beautiful as that dress is, it's gotta go!

Once again, clothes are flying as soon as we enter her house. Our bodies passionately entangle the moment the door is shut. I'd like to say we make it to the bed because I'm a gentleman, but it's just too far away. Being a man to use the resources around him, I find the stairs to be quite an effective tool. In a not so suave move, I hurriedly try to kick off my shoes and pants after grabbing a strip of condoms from my wallet. I end up falling to the stairs in a sitting position. Samantha takes this as an invitation and climbs me like a tree. I haven't even gotten my shirt undone.

Seeking to resolve the problem with my shirt, Samantha straddles me and slowly unbuttons it. Her soft, warm hands ignite a fire deep within me. She kisses my chest and each muscle as she makes her way down my abdomen. I'm going to burst into flames if she keeps at it. I can barely contain myself. I must fist the stairs to keep from directing her. When she gets past my navel, she stops and takes a good look at my straining erection that's begging to greet her personally. Not wanting her to feel obligated to go any further, I reach out with one hand and grab the side of her face to get her to look at me.

"Come here," I encourage.

"I'm a little busy." She smirks, letting that sass I'm quickly becoming to love shine through.

"Well... don't let me interrupt. I'll be right here when you're ready," I tease.

Without any warning, she cups my balls with one hand and gently massages them. With her other hand, she strokes at my base. All the while, just looking at my cock as it turns a darker shade of red. When a bit of precum makes an appearance, she surprises me by licking it free. Then she uses her tongue by rolling it around my tip, making swipes down my shaft and causing me to utterly lose my mind.

"Fuuuccckkk," I growl.

I'm trying with all my might to let her keep control of this situation, but I can't not touch her. I reach out to place my hand at the base of her neck, my fingers entwine in her hair, and I can't help but guide her head as her spectacular mouth slides up and down my cock. Between the massaging, stroking, and sucking, she creates the perfect rhythm that's unlike any I have ever experienced. My toes curl as the tingling at the base of my spine makes its presence. I don't know how much longer I can hold on, so I try to encourage her to stop.

"Come here, beautiful," I groan, needing a release.

She looks me directly in the eye as she continues without missing a beat and shakes her head no.

"Are you sure?" I pant. "I'd rather come with you." *HOLY HELL, I'm going to lose it!* She keeps her eyes on me, but she somehow manages to increase her effort at the same time. *OH. MY. FUCKING. GOD!!!!*

"Right there, beautiful... just like that!"

I can't help it when my grip goes stronger on her hair. My

entire body is so taut, it could rip apart. When the tingling sensation at the base of my spine explodes throughout my entire body, I'm sure I let loose a string of expletives. She continues to keep up her efforts until I'm so sensitive I don't think I can handle any more. *Is that even possible?*

"Jesus, Samantha," I huff out. "That was unbelievable." She pulls off with a pop from my still semi-erect cock.

I pull her up to me and before she can say anything, I kiss her as if she's my last breath of air. Sure, I can taste myself on her, but like I give a shit. She tastes of the perfect mixture of the two of us. I pull her body further up mine, so I can stroke her core. Like expected, she's drenched. I slip a finger inside her and drag the wetness to her clit. I massage her clit with my thumb while I use my fingers to bring her more pleasure. Like in the car, I find that perfect spot and the sound she makes is all I need to know I'm on the right track.

After a few more moments, I realize I can't take it anymore. I need to taste her, too. I scoot down one step as I lift her body higher. I don't give her much time to think as I hoist her up even further. Her arms fall out in front of her and brace themselves on the steps above me. She protests when she realizes what I'm about to do, but the moment my tongue strokes between her outer lips, she suddenly relaxes. When my tongue and dexterous fingers find the perfect rhythm, she nearly screams. I use my middle finger to make the 'come hither' motion, pressing against that magical spot and her body trembles from the inside out. I swipe my tongue across her clit before clamping down on it with suction and she explodes beautifully on my hand.

When she comes down from her sated bliss, I lower her to

my lap. She presses her ass right into my straining erection, but I ignore it for now. Her hands wrap around my neck as her face falls against my chest. This is the most content feeling in the world. Slowly our breathing returns to normal and she traces the tattoos on my chest.

"What does this mean?" she whispers as she traces my Pararescue tattoo. It's an angel holding a globe.

"That's my Pararescue tattoo. Everyone got some version of it when we became part of the team. Traditionally, it also has the words 'that others may live,' but I know the words, no need to repeat them." I shrug as if it's no big deal.

"Wow," she whispers as she kisses it softly. It's on my right pectoral. I have a few other tattoos but she doesn't ask for more information. She kisses me on the lips once again, but before things get too carried away she suggests, "Wanna take this upstairs?"

"Sure thing, beautiful," I say as I help her stand. I look around the entryway and see our clothes are once again scattered. I can't help but chuckle as I see the evidence of our passion around us. "We sure do like this entryway, don't we?"

"It seems that way." She shakes her head and laughs as she gathers her things. "Let's go upstairs."

Who am I to disagree. "I'll follow you, beautiful." *Anywhere. What the fuck? Where did that come from?* As soon as I catch sight of the beautiful sway of her ass, my thoughts are soon distracted. I quickly pick up my things and run up the stairs after her.

The next morning, Samantha is sprawled out across my chest. Her hair covers one of my shoulders and her face looks toward me. I can't help but draw circles on her back with the hand that's under her, as well as study her unique features. From this angle, I can see she has a slight dusting of freckles across her nose, as well as the way her eyes flutter from time to time while she's asleep. The sheet rests just barely over her hips and mine, leaving her on display for viewing. Never having been one to sleep in, no matter the time I get to sleep, I take this moment to fully enjoy all that is Samantha.

Her bedroom is entirely her. Off to one side, she has a reading area. There's a window seat with cushions, a soft, gray leather loveseat and an oversized dark-gray chair that has a cozy tan blanket on the back of it. That must be where she likes to sit the most. I can almost picture her with her legs pulled under her as she curls up with a book. There's a walk-in closet leading into a full bathroom on the other side. I know from personal experience she has a large tub, as well as a walk-in shower and double sinks. Across from the bed we're lying in is a large black dresser with pictures of her family displayed on top. The bed itself is a large black platform. It rests against the wall I'm leaning against. The headboard is built into the wall. It's well-padded and covered in black soft leather.

I glance at the clock on the table next to me and it reads nine o'clock. I don't recall the last time I've been in bed this late, but then again, I think we were up until dawn. I try my best to just relax and let her sleep. Listening to the soft cadence of her breathing puts me deep into thought. I mull over my delicious memories of the past few days.

Has it only been four days since I've met her? I can't believe I'm here in her bed again. *Fuck, I usually try to make a habit of being gone before morning, not trying to find ways to be back again.* I've made a habit of keeping women at bay since Vanessa. There's no point in settling down if I won't be around long enough to see where it might go. I've always been upfront about that. It's always been casual or time constricted. When my next mission called, I always beat feet to be back with the Air Force.

But not with Samantha. With her, I've been completely enamored. And besides, who knows if I'm really going to be Air Force much longer? *That offer with Riggs is nothing to be taken lightly.* If I do take that job, I'd be guaranteed to be based here in Portland. Sure, I'd still have to travel and there'd be distance between us at times, but those will be for a few weeks, not months at a time. Samantha doesn't seem to be the type who would move on without telling me first. From what I can tell, she knows first-hand what cheating can do to a person. She waited three years just to kiss another man. Who knows how long she's waited to do more. *Ugg... I can't think about her and other men. Not going there.*

Something about Samantha completely draws me to her. I don't even have words to describe it. She's smart, funny, and caring. She's sexy as sin and completely in tune with my needs and desires. I can't recall a time I've ever been more satisfied. But it's more than just sex. With her, I want to go out of my way to make her smile. *She has me willing to put on a monkey-suit and dance.* When was the last time I've felt this way? *Never.* I think my mom may have been onto something, as well as Rowan. But there is still so much unknown.

From what I've gathered, Samantha is smart, independent,

and is what I'm sure a wonderful mother. *Fuck, she has kids.* Yes, I'm a great uncle, but I have no idea how to navigate around being in a relationship with a woman with kids. This is uncharted territory for me. I'm totally out of my depth here. Maybe I'm not what she needs in her life right now. Maybe this is going too fast and I should slow things down.

Fuck. That. Shit, Dumbass! Just the thought alone of attempting to end things has my gut churning inside. There's no way I'm ready for my time with Samantha to end. I'll just have to take her lead and see where this goes. I'm set to meet her kids tomorrow evening. It could be a disaster and she might dump me on my ass. There's also that little bit about figuring out how to tell my dad that I'm suddenly very interested in one of his clients.

Four Days. I've only known her four days. It's not like I'm going to be proposing or anything. *I just want to date the woman. That's all. Jesus, I need to get a grip on my emotions.*

I look down at her beautiful face and see Samantha's beautiful mahogany eyes studying me. Before I can say anything, she asks, "What are you thinking about over there? World peace?"

What the hell do I even say? There's no way I'm ready to repeat even a fraction of the thoughts bulldozing through my brain. I go with the truth. "Just about you, beautiful. Just about you." I bend down and kiss her on the forehead as I brush her hair out of her face.

"What time is it?" she asks as she stretches her body and yawns.

"Almost ten o'clock."

She snuggles back to my side, laying her head on my chest

and her arm across my waist. "I don't remember the last time I slept in this late. But snuggling with you is something I could get used to."

Her stomach rumbles and I suggest, "What do you say to breakfast? Wanna get dressed quickly and come back to take showers later? Just put on something casual and I'll run down to my car and get something out of my bag."

She grins mischievously. "You brought a bag, knowing you'd be staying?"

I shrug. "Not really. I always have my "go-bag" with me. You saw it when we went up the Gorge. It just has everything I need, so I won't ever be without."

"That's very prepared of you," she teases as she tries to tickle my side.

"Hey now. If you start that, we'll never get breakfast. I'm starving, woman!" I roll her onto her back and tickle her until she's convulsing with laughter. Her naked body has me wanting to have her for breakfast instead, but when her stomach rumbles for a second time, I stand next to the bed and pull her in for a quick kiss. I keep it brief before turning her toward the bathroom.

"Go! Get dressed and I'll get my things." As she walks away with a sway, I'm dying to follow. I smack her on the ass and chuckle. "Don't tempt me, beautiful!"

She walks to the bathroom while I search for my pants and shirt from last night. We brought them upstairs, but they're combined in a pile of his/hers discarded clothes. I quickly put my pants, shirt, and shoes sans socks and head out to my vehicle for my things. I don't bother to look at myself in a mirror because I can already see that my clothes are rumpled, needing to be washed. I haven't done a walk of shame in years. Though with Samantha, if it doesn't tarnish her reputation, I'd gladly do it every day.

When I get to my car, I decide to just bring the entire bag inside, so I'm not going through it in the driveway. *I really need to do some laundry if I keep using this as my source of luggage.* When I'm back inside, I use the downstairs bathroom to get ready. I know if I go upstairs, we'll never leave her bedroom.

By the time I'm dressed, I realize Samantha has yet to come downstairs. Not wanting it to get in the way, I take my bag to my SUV. Then I go into the living room to wait for her. I have no intention of rushing her; she can take all the time she needs. I can hear Samantha moving around upstairs, but so far, no sight of her.

Suddenly, I hear the front door bang open. I look up in surprise to find Samantha's youngest, Frankie, running through the door. She's at a sprint, heading for the stairs when she stops dead in her tracks as she notices me. She doesn't say anything, just stares, doe eyed. *Well, this is awkward.*

I might as well break the ice. "Hi, you must be Frankie."

She nods but doesn't respond. Shit. Now what am I supposed to do?

I try again. "I'm Enzo. I'm a friend of your mom."

Before she can respond, two things happen at once. An unknown man approaches the wide-open door as Samantha hollers from upstairs. "I'll be down in a second. Just switching over some laundry before we go."

The man in the doorway has yet to see me and scolds Frankie. "Frankie, I told you to wait for me. I don't like it when you ride your bike so far ahead of me."

The man in front of me is about six-feet tall. He resembles the pictures of Declan, but an older version. He has dark-brown hair and appears to have kept himself in shape. He notices Frankie staring and turns his attention to me. *Well, this is one way to meet her family.* His look of pure shock is almost amusing, if it hadn't been for the fact his daughter just walked into a room with a stranger in it.

Before either of us say anything, Frankie turns to him as if it isn't a big deal. "Dad. This is Enzo. He's one of Mom's friends." She looks back to me before continuing. "I'm Frankie. This is my dad, Devin." Wow, what manners for an eight-year-old… and she saved me from having to introduce myself.

I step toward Devin with an outstretched hand. "Nice to meet you, Devin."

Truth being told, Devin still looks out of sorts. It takes him a moment, but eventually, his manners kick in. "You, too. Enzo?" he asks my name, questioning.

"Yes, Enzo Harper," I clarify.

Devin acts as if he's trying to solve world peace, he's concentrating so hard. Then he whispers my name again before almost shouting, "Oh, I remember now. You're the contractor Sam has hired for the remodel. I'm surprised to see you here on a Sunday. Sam said you weren't working this weekend."

"I'm his son actually." I want to add that I'm not working. But I'm not sure how Samantha wants this to play out with her children.

"Well, it's nice to meet you." Devin seems a little more at ease.

Frankie tugs on her dad's arm. "Daddy, I'm going to get the ballet slipper I forgot. I'll be right back."

"Okay, Frankie. I'll be right here."

Well, at least he doesn't just make himself entirely at home in Samantha's house, though just waiting in the doorway is awkward. What the fuck am I supposed to say to him? Finally, after a few more moments of uncomfortable silence, I gesture to the couch. "Would you like to have a seat?"

He sits down and there is still silence.

Finally, he breaks it. "So, how much longer do you think the remodel will take?"

I laugh. "I have no idea."

He gives me a face that looks as if he's saying, 'what the fuck?'

Just then, I hear Samantha call as she runs down the stairs, "I'm starving, are you ready to g...?" She freezes when she sees Devin sitting across from me on the couch. She looks back and forth from him to me. She suddenly shakes her head as if to clear her thoughts and asks, "Devin, what are you doing here?"

"Frankie lost one of her ballet slippers. She's upstairs looking for it now."

"Oh..." Samantha still appears as if she's unsure what to say.

Devin stands and calls upstairs, "Frankie, did you find it yet?"

"It's under my bed. As soon as I get it out, I'll be right down," Frankie hollers from what I presume is her room.

"How in the world did she lose it under her bed?" Samantha grumbles. "She just wore those shoes a few days ago."

Devin laughs. "Will she be able to find her way out is the better question?"

"Who knows? That is her go-to place for cleaning her room. At least she knew where it was." Samantha then looks at me. "I'm sorry, Enzo. Have you been introduced to Devin?"

"Yes, we've met," I reply.

"So... he says he has no idea how long the remodel will take..." Devin eyes me suspiciously as if I'm not qualified to be doing the job.

Samantha's beautiful laugh fills the room. "Well, that's probably because it's his father doing the work, not him. Enzo is in the Air Force. He doesn't work for his father." She shakes her head at Devin's misconception.

Devin is back to looking more confused than ever. "Oh," is all he says for a moment. "Where are you stationed?"

"Ramstein Air Base in Germany," I reply automatically.

Devin puts his hand over his chin and scratches it before adding, "So, how long are you on leave for?"

"For the next month and a half," once again comes automatically. I'm used to that question, but not sure why it would be a concern to him. But then I eye the beautiful woman standing next to me and I'm pretty sure I can guess.

"I see..." Devin states.

Before anyone can say another word, Frankie comes barreling into the room. She rushes up to her mother and squeezes her tight. "Hi, Mama," is muffled, but can be made out.

"Hey, sweet pea," Samantha replies with a smile on her face. "Did you find your slipper?"

"Yep, it was stuck between the wall and my bed. I had to

crawl under to get it." Frankie holds the slipper up proudly for all to see, making us all laugh.

"Well, we'd better go, Frankie. Everyone is waiting for us," Devin states as he turns her toward the door.

"Okay, Daddy, race you!" Frankie shouts as she rushes out the door.

I stick out my hand. "It was nice to meet you, Devin."

"You, too," he replies. Then he looks to Samantha before turning back to me. He appears as if he's about to say something about me being here but changes his mind. He clears his throat then states, "Sorry for the interruption." He walks toward the door. "I'd better run, or she'll beat me home."

"Goodbye," Samantha says as she follows him to the door.

He leaves without another word, but Samantha just stares at the door in silence.

I come up behind her and snake my arms around her waist. "Everything okay, beautiful?"

As if I have shaken her out of a trance, her body has a slight tremor. "Yeah, it is." Then she looks around at the entryway and suddenly giggles. "We'd better start using the deadbolt if we're going to continue using the entryway like we have."

I turn her so she's facing me. "If you say so..." I lean in for a kiss and then pull away. "Are you ready to eat?"

"Sure. Let's go."

16

SAMANTHA

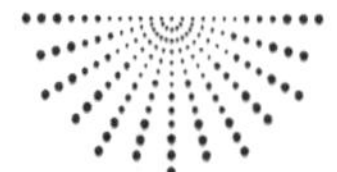

DEVIN BEING AT MY HOUSE TOTALLY SHOCKED THE SHIT OUT OF me. I tried to pull it off like it wasn't a big deal, but I'm not sure how well I managed that, or if my shock even went unnoticed. *What the hell had he and Enzo been talking about?* That look on Devin's face when he realized Enzo wasn't the contractor was almost hysterical. It seems it finally has dawned on him that I've met someone else. This is a first since I've never gone on more than one date with anyone. And I certainly haven't brought anyone home, but he can suck it. He doesn't deserve to know the details of my private life. He made the choice long ago not to be privy to that information. I've silently watched him move on. God, it feels so good to be on the other side in this situation. Meeting Aubrey was difficult for me, and she hasn't even been the first person Devin's brought around the kids. I can only imagine what is running through Devin's mind.

"What are you laughing about over there, beautiful?" Enzo asks, breaking me out of my trance on the way to the restaurant.

I shake my head, not really wanting to divulge my thoughts, but I do ask the question I'm dying to know the answer to. "So, what did you and Devin talk about?"

"After Frankie came bursting through the door, he came in and seemed a bit surprised to see me in your living room," Enzo states matter-of-factly.

"Wait, they didn't even knock?"

"Nope, the door burst open, scaring the shit out of me, I might add. But before I could react, Frankie came barreling in. She was on a mission. As soon as she saw me, she froze on the spot. Wouldn't even say a word to me when I introduced myself."

"Okay..."

Enzo lets out a chuckle. "Then, when her dad came in, she introduced me like we're long lost friends. Your kid's a riot. I've never seen anything like it. She ran in and out like a hurricane. Does the girl ever slow down?"

"That's Frankie for you. She's a force of nature. You will never have to guess with her; she has no filter. Her heart is bigger than the ocean and she's as silly as they come." I can't help but chuckle. I love that girl more than life itself.

"I'm looking forward to seeing that," Enzo says as he turns into the parking lot.

Does this mean he plans on sticking around? Samantha, I chide myself, *focus on the situation at hand. Let that be tomorrow's worry when he actually meets my kids again.*

"Did Devin actually say anything to you?" I press again.

"Not really. He seemed interested as to why I would be there. He mistook me for my dad, and I didn't really correct him until you came in."

"Oh..." *So, I didn't miss that much.*

"There's nothing else to tell you, Samantha. No need to stay in your head about it." Enzo pulls into a spot and reaches for the back of my neck to pull me toward him. He lightly kisses me on the forehead. "You can always ask me anything."

I sigh. "I know." Not wanting to miss out on an opportunity, I reach up and kiss him on the lips before saying, "Thanks."

Just as we're finishing breakfast, Enzo's phone must vibrate from his pocket because he suddenly pulls it out and looks at the screen. He apologetically looks at me. "Sorry, gotta take this."

"Hey, Ma," he greets warmly. He listens for a while before looking at me hesitantly and saying, "I'm not really sure... Yes... I know." He lets out a huge sigh. "Yeah, Ma. You're right. Sure. I'll see you soon." Before he hangs up I hear, "I love you, too, Ma," in closing.

Enzo looks as if he's contemplating something, but I'm not sure if I should press the issue or not. I decide to just finish my coffee instead. It has cooled but at least it keeps me from having to be nosy.

"So..." Enzo seems more resolved in whatever he was in deep thought about. "What are your plans for the rest of the day?"

I try to remember if there is anything I must do this afternoon. "I might do some laundry, but other than that, it's wide open." I eye him closely to try to get a read on his thoughts. But there's nothing giving them away. "What do you have in mind?" I tease, trying to get a reaction from him. I have no idea what he has in mind, but I certainly wouldn't mind spending more time with him.

"Well…" He clears his throat and it miraculously becomes even sexier as he sits across from me at the table where we're eating. "I'd love nothing more than to spend the day with you." He clears his throat before he continues. "Actually, Ma just told me she's expecting me for dinner." He raises his shoulders and a slight grin makes his dimple pop. *Holy shit. It does it every time to me, my inner muscles clench in anticipation. What is it about this man?*

He pulls me from my thoughts when he continues, "She's invited my brother and sister's families over, too. Kind of a homecoming celebration of sorts." Enzo shrugs humbly and shakes his head as if he doesn't think it's worth the fanfare. "And…" he hesitates.

For the first time since I've met him, Enzo almost seems a bit shy. *What in the world has him behaving this way?* I manage not to say my thoughts aloud as I nibble on my lower lip to keep myself from blurting them out. I just raise an eyebrow and wait as patiently as I can for him to continue. *Though patient is the least I'm feeling about now.*

I'm about to give into my temptation by asking him to continue when he suddenly pulls a hand through his hair and states, "She wants you to come, too." He looks apologetically and then as if he's bracing himself for my reaction.

What. The. What?!?! She wants me to come, too? How does she even know about me?

"She does?" I manage to say, as my thoughts hurdle at top speed through my head and I can barely catch one to keep a hold of.

Enzo looks a little chagrin. "Um... I might have mentioned you to her last night when I went home to change." He tries to brush it off like it's no big deal.

"Okay... what exactly did you tell her?" Mortification fills my mind. *His mother must think I'm a two-bit hussy since he's been staying over, and I haven't even known him a week.* I can't help when I shudder at the thought.

"Relax, Samantha. Breathe. Your mind is like a freight train that's lost its brakes on a steep incline." He laughs lightly before adding, "I can see your wheels turning ninety miles a minute barreling out of control."

I take in a deep breath and try to stop from letting my thoughts get out of control. He's right. I'm doing that. *How is it that he knows me so well already?*

He puts my mind at ease when he explains how his mom saw him come home with his new suit. She knew it was for someone special because he may have mentioned the part about getting me a dress, which sent her into detective mode. We both laugh when he gets to the part about his mom giving him a hard time about not having bought a suit since high school and the fact she missed her calling as an international interrogator. By the time he's done, I don't feel as mortified and am looking forward to meeting the amazing woman who raised him.

"Well, I guess I could go," I tease, then I'm hit with another thought. "What about your dad? Does he know about us?"

"Not that I know of. I guess we'll just be honest and tell everyone how we met that first afternoon when I went back to get my car."

"Are you sure you want me to meet your family? It's only been a few days," I try to explain my hesitation, but he gives me a stern look, cutting me off.

"Samantha." Enzo's deep voice sends shivers up my spine. "I have no idea where this," he points between the two of us, "is going, but what I do know is that I want to spend as much time with you as possible." *I feel the same way, but isn't it a little fast?*

"And… you're not just… horny?" I try to tease again, and he adamantly shakes his head with complete confidence. The emotion shining through his glorious green eyes pierces through me. I've never seen anyone with more conviction.

"You and I both know there's something else here or we wouldn't even be sitting at this table together. I don't know about you, but I've never felt this way about anyone. Ever." His declaration continues to slay me. The wall I've been holding up for so long cracks.

I nod my head in agreement. *It's true. I never even felt this way with Devin, and I was married to the man. I don't remember having feelings for anyone so quickly like this.*

Before I can say anything, he continues, "I don't know where this will lead us. Hell, I don't even know where I will be living in four months, but I do know that while I'm on leave, I plan to spend as much time with you as possible to figure it out."

I can't do anything but stare at the beautiful man before me, laying all his thoughts out there. I'm in pure shock. No one's ever been that blunt with me before. I don't even know what to say. If I wasn't tongue tied, that is.

Thankfully, he continues as he runs a hand through that glorious thick, blond hair. "Fuck, I don't know what will happen. Your kids might hate me, or I might annoy you to death and you'll kick me to the curb." His dimple-wielding smile hits me again. "But I do know that I want to see where this goes." He stops and stares at me, trying to get a read on my thoughts. "So... what do you say? Are you willing to see where this goes?"

He hit everything in one fell swoop I could have used to argue against him. He mentioned the newness of our relationship and my kids. But, our connection is incredible. Maybe it's the lust-filled haze he keeps me in, maybe it's just the fact that it's all new and exciting, but there's something about Enzo that makes me want to see where this goes. So, I say the only thing that seems right, given our situation.

"Sure," comes out in a whisper.

"Come again?" He lowers his head to truly study my face. His glimmering green eyes look hopeful as they bore into my soul, taking my breath away. I nod my response again.

He cocks his head to the side, squinting his eyes toward me, willing me to say more.

Finally, after what feels like an eternity, I find my voice. "I'm willing to see where this goes, if you are."

Relief spreads across his features and he lets out a breath he had been holding. He reaches for his wallet, places some bills on the table, then he stands, holding his hand out to me. I take it as I stand, but he surprises me by pulling me in closer to him. He wraps his arms around me in an enormous hug, so I wrap my arms around his waist and melt into him.

When he releases me, he simply states, "Okay then. Are you ready to get out of here?"

17
ENZO

WHAT THE EVER-LOVING FUCK WAS I THINKING? AFTER ONLY A few days... days?!?! I just laid everything out on the line for Samantha. And she said yes? She feels our connection, too? A part of me is freaking the fuck out, while another part is riding cloud nine. I must get her out of the restaurant, I must get her alone to show her just how much she means to me. When I reach for her hand, and she willingly takes mine, everything just clicks into place. It feels so right.

Hell, I have no idea if we'll make it work. She has a family she must consider, too. It's not just about us. Am I even ready for something like this? Holy Shit. Family. Can I even be a stepdad? Do I even want to be? Wait! *I'm thinking about marriage?!?!?* I take a long, hard look at the beautiful woman before me and I reach for her hand. The moment her hand contacts mine, I realize for the first time since Vanessa, I'm willing to see where it might lead with someone, even if it means taking on an entire family in the process.

Not wanting to be apart from her any longer, I pull her into me for a hug and brush a kiss on the top of her head. "Okay then. Are you ready to get out of here?" I take her hand and lead her out of the restaurant.

I'd like to say I spent the rest of the afternoon wooing Samantha and romancing her, but I just couldn't think about anything except being with her again. I drove directly to her house. I remembered to lock the deadbolt before I rushed her upstairs, lavishing her body the only way I know how.

About an hour before my mother was expecting us, Samantha sexily unwove herself from my body and insisted on taking a shower, alone I might add, to get ready for dinner. I reluctantly used the guest shower down the hall to get ready. I guarantee that we would never have left the house again had I stepped into that bathroom with her. She's so damn addictive.

We manage to arrive at my parents' house about twenty minutes before my mom said dinner would be ready. Samantha's quiet on the way over and I'm a little lost in my own head, too. I pull a hand over my freshly shaven jaw and scratch it absentmindedly, trying to remember the last time I brought someone home to my parents' house. Hell, I don't have a clue. High school? Vanessa? *Holy shit. I haven't brought home anyone since Vanessa, and that ended shortly after I enlisted.* Hmmm... this should be interesting to see how my family reacts.

"Contemplating world peace over there?" Samantha teases, breaking me from my trance.

I shake my head and a smile forms on my face. "Nope. Nothing that serious. Just taking everything in, that's all."

She cocks her head to the side to get a better read on me. "Everything still okay? You're not having second thoughts about bringing me here, are you? I could totally Uber it home or something if you'd rather I not come."

She looks as if her comment was serious. I'm not having any of that. "Samantha, if I didn't want you here, I never would've asked." I reach for her hand to bring it to my mouth for a kiss. "Get those crazy-ass thoughts out of your head, beautiful. You've nothing to be nervous about. Besides, I'd never let you Uber it home." I glare at her to show my seriousness. Then I add, "You already know Pops, and Ma already likes you. I can't promise you anything else from the rest of my family. They could go rogue at any moment, but overall keep in mind they're good people."

She takes in a deep breath before letting it out slowly. "Okay, I know," quietly escapes her mouth. "I just haven't met anyone's family since college. I guess I'm getting a little nervous." She shrugs as if it should make sense.

"Well, if it makes you feel any better, I haven't brought anyone to meet them in about that long either." I give her a side glance, pulling my mouth into a smile. "I'm not feeding you to wolves, Samantha," I attempt to tease.

Pulling into the driveway, I kill the engine. I keep a hold of her hand for a moment to make sure I have her attention. "We can leave at any time, I promise. If you don't feel comfortable, just say the word and we're out of here. I'd like to spend time with my family and let them get to know you. Time is precious, and I don't want to miss an opportunity to be with you either." I lean in and kiss her firmly on the lips. I must remind myself to not get carried away because the driveway's full of vehicles and I don't want anyone getting a free show. Knowing my family, I'd get the razzing of a lifetime if they witnessed anything as well. Thankfully, I feel her relax in my embrace. In all too short of time, I pull away to give her a reassuring smile. She audibly sighs, then gathers things from around her to go inside.

It turns out Samantha had nothing to worry about. As soon as we're inside, Ma greets her with open arms and Pops acts as if this is just a normal occurrence. I did see a slight eyebrow raise discreetly in my direction as to ask, *"So this is who you are spending your time with*?" But nothing is said aloud. I'm sure at some point he will ask me about it… but knowing Pops, it won't be in front of anyone.

Ma offers to take Samantha into the kitchen where the girls are visiting while they get dinner ready. The guys are outside with my nieces and nephews for the moment. Pops casually mentions that he'd like to show me something in the living room. I silently ask Samantha if she's comfortable going alone with my mother, but she just flashes a confident smile that nearly takes my breath away. When she's out of sight, my dad clears his throat, reclaiming my attention.

"So…" He keeps his face stoic, but I can see the gleam in his eye that tells me he finds this amusing.

"So…" I counter, not wanting to give too much away.

"It sure is nice to see Samantha O'Reilly again. I'm a bit surprised though. I didn't realize you knew her."

"It's still pretty new, Pops."

"I see…" he draws out, waiting for more.

Never being one to keep secrets, I launch into the story about how I met her outside her house after he dropped me off. Pops has a slight grin on his face the entire time I reveal everything to him. He bursts out laughing when I mention the fact my stomach rumbled just as she said she was going to dinner.

"No shit? You couldn't have timed that better if you tried, son." He leads me over to the couch in the living room. We can now hear kids somewhere in the house and adult conversations from the kitchen, both male and female.

"I know, right." I shake my head at the memory of my embarrassment.

"So, Ma says that Samantha has you taking her to a place fancy enough you needed to buy a suit," he presses on, giving away the fact he already knows everything, but just wants to hear it from the horse's mouth.

"The dress she bought was amazing and I didn't want to look like a dumbass next to her." The memories of her in that dress flood my mind, as well as the night we spent afterward. Holy hell, the woman is hot! She's smart, sexy, and does things to me that I have never experienced before. I admit, I've had my share of women, so that's saying something. Samantha O'Reilly sure is special.

I shake my head to clear my thoughts and get back to my conversation at hand. "Besides, I took her to Allure, you know, the restaurant and club my buddy Rowan opened a few years back. I couldn't go in looking like I just stepped off the airplane. I didn't bring anything home other than casual clothes."

"No. You couldn't," my dad agrees. "I'm more interested in

the fact you've seemed to deem her worthy of bringing her around here." He gestures to our family in the other room.

"She's special, Dad. I'll give you that." I shrug. What else can I say?

"What about her kids? Have you given much thought about them?" He raises a good point and thankfully, I already know my answer because I told Samantha about my thoughts on her children earlier.

"Samantha is the type of person you don't let slip through your fingers, Pops." I'm a little shocked at my own wording. It's true, but at the same time, I'm not used to thinking that way about anyone. Ever.

"We're taking it slow…" When I think about these past few days with her, I amend my thought. "Well, one day at a time. I plan to meet her kids tomorrow. I'm going over to watch the Seahawks play tomorrow night. Who knows? They could hate me. She could get bored of me… and hundreds of things could happen, all making her want to kick me to the curb." I shake my head, hoping it doesn't go in that direction because that would suck.

"Kids are tricky, son, but I think you'll know how to handle it." He pats me on the shoulder. "If it's meant to be, it'll all have a way of working out." He stops for a second, looking as though he's thinking about something before he continues, "Does this mean you'll be taking a job around here then?"

"Ha… believe it or not, Samantha has little to do with my decision." My dad nods like he thinks I'm full of shit. Before he can say anything, I add, "I think I'm ready to be in one place, rather than moving every couple of years. I'm pretty sure I'm going to retire one way or another. I still have a meeting later this week with the CO for the Air National Guard. But, I'm ready to have a permanent home, regardless of which direction I go. It doesn't hurt that Riggs offered me a lucrative position with his team either. I still have a lot to consider, though."

"Whatever you decide, Ma and I will support you. I know she'll be relieved to hear you're at least strongly considering returning to Portland, that's for sure." There's suddenly laughter from the kitchen that draws our attention.

Pops beats me to my thoughts. "What do you say we go in there and find out what the ruckus is all about?"

By the time we enter the kitchen, the roaring laughter has me more than curious. I don't even get a foot into the room when a screaming, naked toddler comes barreling past me, trying to escape. Her hands are full of Cheerios and her body is doing the best she can to stay upright as her feet move faster than her torso. The grin on her face is pure bliss.

"Zoey!" my sister-in-law Ann hollers. "You get back here! I need to finish putting on your diaper and changing your clothes!"

Doing my best to help with the situation, I bend down and scoop her up into my arms, keeping her from her great escape. Quickly, I bring her up to blow a raspberry onto her belly, making her squeal in delight. "I think you're missing your booty cover, Zo! Let's get you covered up before you go traipsing across Granny's carpet."

"You do it, Zo!" she screams at me in her cute as can be toddler voice. "Not Mama!" She's still giggling as she says this. "Git my belly 'gain!"

Of course, I oblige. I give her another raspberry and reach

for the diaper Ann's holding. I quickly get it in place. *Yep, I'm a great uncle. I do know how to change a diaper, and I know the severity of needing to put them on quickly and accurately.*

I'm kneeling on the floor, just having fastened the diaper securely, when the rest of my nieces and nephews come over to get in on the action of picking on me. Before I know it, they all dog-pile on me. I tickle them and do the best I can to keep the upper hand. They're like slippery fish and bursting with laughter. I love moments like this. *Of course, this is why I'm their favorite uncle.*

Soon, I hear Ma say, "I think that's enough. Who's ready to eat?" One by one, they all dismantle the pile we have created. Brandon, Riley, and Nick all rush to the dinner table, while Zoey and Isabel continue to climb all over me like little monkeys. Thankfully, their parents rush in and pick them up, so all I need to do is get myself upright and head to the table.

Samantha's beautiful smile nearly knocks me back on my ass. Her amusement over what she just witnessed is evident. She walks over to me to lend me a hand. Still laughing, she asks, "Want help?"

I reach out to take it, but not really using it to get the momentum to stand. The spark that shoots through me is completely electrifying. Without even caring about the present audience, once I get myself to fully standing, I find myself reaching under her hair at the base of her neck to pull her closer to me. It's as if I *need* to get my lips on hers, the pull is so strong. I give her a heated kiss, entirely caught up in the moment, but my obnoxious family quickly reminds me of their presence.

Several noises erupt at once. Everything from, "Ewww," to loud whistles to, "Get a room."

I pull back and see Samantha completely blush from head to toe. *Shit. I didn't mean to embarrass her.* "You okay, beautiful?" I ask, tipping her chin to make her eyes meet mine.

She looks around the room and shrugs as if that should explain everything and she pulls on her lower lip with her teeth.

I look at my family who all, except for the kids who yelled 'Ewww,' look at us with a mixture of awe and hope. My brother and sister's mouths are both opened so wide they could catch flies in them. Obviously, my behavior shocks them. But I don't give a shit. All I care about is the woman before me.

"Sorry if I embarrassed you, Samantha," I whisper, though I'm sure everyone can hear me. "But there's nothing to worry about. I've seen each of them," I look pointedly at my brother and sister and their significant others before adding, "kiss one another as well as my parents and it's not a big deal." I kiss her once more to prove a point. "I just can't help myself; you're irresistible." I shrug as if that should answer the unasked questions running through her mind.

When I pull back this time, she has a smile on her face, but not from embarrassment. "Oookkkaaay." She sucks in a deep breath to steady herself.

"Get used to it," I whisper as I take her hand in mine, leading her to the dining room table.

Dinner itself goes off without a hitch. My brother and sister attempt to bring up stories to embarrass me from my past, but I have no problem with it. I've dished out my share over the years. Payback is a bitch, but I honestly haven't done that much to be too worried about. My most embarrassing moments are secretly kept just that, a secret.

By the time dinner is complete, Samantha is well at ease with my family. My sister Erin, Mom, and Zane's wife, Ann, are all avid readers, so they have a lot to talk about. Samantha seems in her element when she talks books and authors. The passion in her eyes ignites a flame that will never burn out. I can see she loves her job and takes great pride in representing authors who are worthy of being promoted. When Erin mentions she has written a little since becoming a stay-at-home mom, I'm even a little shocked. I had no idea she was interested in publishing a book. She and Samantha set up a lunch date to discuss this idea further because Erin wants to know what the next steps are for getting her book out there.

When dinner is over, Pops shoos all the girls out of the kitchen so us guys can clean up. It's a tradition in our house. My parents raised us to be an equal opportunity family. If someone cooks, the other cleans. Ma didn't want us boys going off and not knowing how to fend for ourselves, so it's proven to work out well for all involved over the years.

I set into clearing the plates from the table and prepare myself for the razzing I'm about to receive. My guess is that it'll be less than thirty seconds after the women and children leave that either Zane or my brother-in-law Nate will say something. I count in my head as soon as the room is just us guys.

They make it to eighteen seconds before Zane casually asks, "So, how is it you're back in town less than a week and you have a woman as hot as Samantha here for dinner?"

Before I can respond, Nate adds, "Since when did you ever bring someone to Sunday dinner?"

I pointedly look at Zane. "Dude, you're married. You shouldn't be calling Samantha hot." *She sure as fuck is, but that shouldn't be his concern.*

"Reality check, Enzo," Zane mocks. "I'm married… but not blind or dead. Samantha's hot by anyone's definition. Even Ann whispered that to me earlier."

I can't help but nod in agreement. I'd be lying if I didn't acknowledge that fact. But then I turn to Nate. "Ma asked her to come for dinner."

"Didn't you just get into town a couple of days ago?" Zane asks.

"Yep." I glance at Dad and he just smiles as he loads the dishes into the dishwasher. *The bastard. He knew this would happen.* It was inevitable the guys would give me a hard time. Might as well get this over with. I've certainly dished out my share of shit to them.

"So, how'd you meet her?" Nate asks with sincerity, no longer teasing me.

I chuckle at the thought. "Well, I actually went to surprise Pops and I happened to meet her. He's remodeling her kitchen. Pops and I went out for lunch and he showed me around his job sites. When I got back to my car, I ran into Samantha and we went out to dinner."

"You remember the rule Pops had about not messing with clients, right?" Zane chides.

I glance at Pops whose smile just gets wider by the minute. *Shit. I knew the rule. I'd never even thought of breaking it before. But fuck the rule. I'm a grown man and I'm not about to fuck up Pops' business. This is different. Besides, we're all adults.*

Pops interrupts before I can continue. "I only had that rule in place when you boys were randy teenagers. I had to keep you away from the daughters of clients or the Mrs. Robinsons of the world. Enzo's a grown-ass man. If he wants to date Samantha, I have no problem with it." Pops shrugs nonchalantly and I can't help but want to hug him. This will surely get Zane and Nate off my back.

"She's special," I sincerely state.

"No shit, Sherlock." Zane chuckles. "You haven't brought anyone home in nearly twenty years. We knew you aren't batting for the other side, too many rumors from your youth to dispute that, but I never thought I'd see the day you'd bring home someone like her. Are your manwhoring ways finally over?"

Offended, I bodily state, "I was never a manwhore. I just didn't see the point in settling down when I would never be in one place for long."

"So, does this mean you're going to be sticking around? Finally getting out of the Air Force?" Nate asks, sounding a little shocked. I look over to Pops, and I can tell he has kept my business mine.

"I'm thinking about it. I have a few weeks to decide whether I'm going to re-up or do something entirely different. That's part of the reason I'm home on leave. I'm here to make some decisions about my future." I tell them about my meeting with Riggs as well as the one coming up with the CO at the Air National Guard as we finish up with the kitchen before meeting up with everyone else in the family room.

18

SAMANTHA

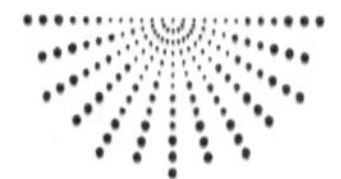

BY THE TIME ENZO COMES OUT OF THE KITCHEN, I FEEL completely at ease with his family. I love the way they joke and tease one another. I can't believe the way he kissed me in front of them. I'm not one for much PDA, but when a man like Enzo kisses me like that, who gives a fuck about my surroundings?

Sara, Anna, and Erin are all people I could become friends with easily. Their children are adorable. Of course, we have a lot in common: kids, books, and Enzo. *Though that last one is the one subject I do my best to avoid talking about. I don't want to give them any reason to think less of me since I've known Enzo for such a short time.* Thankfully, no one does or says anything to make me feel as if I don't belong here.

I can feel Enzo enter the room before I see him. My back is to the entrance, but the prickling up my spine is the sensation I experience whenever he's near. He comes to sit next to me on the couch, instinctively grabbing my hand to hold once he

166

arrives. He kept his hand on my leg all throughout dinner. Like now, my nerve endings are spasming out of control. It's as if each nerve is a live wire, waiting to explode. It's taking all my energy not to climb him like a tree and have my way with him.

Eventually, we say our goodbyes. I promise Erin we will get together for lunch soon. She texts me her number so I can call and schedule something once I have my calendar in front of me. Enzo's parents each give me a hug and we make our way out the door, heading back to my place for the evening.

The next day, I awake in Enzo's arms. His delicious scent envelops me, and I swear, if I died right now, I'd go happy. As I recall each delicious thing he did to me, for me, and with me last night, I realize I can still feel the tremors of the after effects throughout my body.

I had to set my dreaded alarm today because I have the contractors coming, as well as meetings in the office I can't get away from. Fortunately, I still have some time before my alarm, so I decide to be a wake-up call of my own for Enzo. Let's just say he's more than satisfied with being awakened earlier than the alarm this morning. *That man is pure heaven!*

I make it to work on time, even with his help in the shower this morning. He left my house when I did, even though I insisted he could stay for as long as he liked. He didn't really tell me what his plans were for the day, but I know I will be seeing him tonight for pizza and the football game.

I can't stop thinking about him throughout the day as

scenes from last night play on a loop through my mind. It's hard not to picture him as the hero of every story I read throughout the morning, either. He's absolutely mind consuming.

By the time one o'clock comes around, I find Lexi standing at my door. I apparently have been staring out into space because she actually knocks, which never happens, and her greeting is almost yelled, "Earth to Samantha! Come in, Samantha!"

I, of course, quickly snap out of my lust-filled stupor and jump out of my chair to greet her with a hug. She has been out of town for the last few weeks and I have been working from home as much as I could, so we haven't seen each other in a while. "It's so good to see you. How was your trip?" I ask as I pull away from our hug.

"Great. I had the best time in New England. The fall leaves were something to write home about." She looks around at my desk and then peers back at me. "So, what do you say to lunch? I skipped breakfast this morning for that meeting with Morgan. I'm starving."

Jay Morgan is our client who is about to launch a new mystery series. Fortunately, when we discovered him, most of his stories already had been written, so all we had to do was help him brand, edit, and get his series published. Then we will roll each book out strategically to get the optimal readership. Lexi is our go-to gal for that part of the process; she thrives on marketing.

Not even thirty minutes later, Lexi and I are sitting at our favorite Mexican restaurant. Our orders are in and Lexi is telling me all about the trip across New England. She'd always wanted to go in the fall to see the leaves change and she finally made it happen this year. Lexi and her husband Tim took a kid-free vacation since her high-school aged kids stayed with their grandparents to attend school. She even managed to tie it into meeting with a client in Vermont to keep from getting behind while on her travels.

I'm excited to hear all about her trip, but thoughts of Enzo keep flashing through my mind and I'm a bit distracted. I have no idea how Lexi is going to react, or even what I'm going to reveal for that matter. I have never been with anyone like Enzo. Nothing has ever been this fast or as intense... and the things he makes me feel. *Damn, that man is sex on a stick.* I inwardly groan as I feel my well-used muscles clench, just thinking about him.

Suddenly, Lexi stops talking and my attention is back to being on her, due to the silence. She stares at me for a moment. Her head turning to the side while her bright blue eyes scrutinize me. "All right. Spill it. What's going on with you?"

I've never kept secrets from her, but with everything being so new, I'm just not sure what I should say. I manage to get an, "Uh..." out before her face suddenly lights up like the Fourth of July.

She blurts out, "Oh, this has to be good. I haven't seen you this spacey since you were in college and starting to date Devin." Lexi pauses for a moment to look me over closer. "OH! MY GOD! You've met someone!" She nearly screeches at the end. Then, as if there is a God in Heaven, she lowers her voice before she continues, "You have that *'just been thoroughly fucked'* look about you." Sudden shock comes with her realization, but then I see curiosity wins out. "So… who is he, Sam?"

Yep. This is my best friend. The knower of all things Samantha O'Reilly. The keeper of my confidences. There's no stopping her once she catches hold of the possibility of a secret. When she sniffs something juicy out, she sticks to it like a dog to a bone. I might as well just come clean. There's no point in stalling. She'll find out anyway.

"His name is Enzo Harper," I quietly state as I pull my lip into my teeth to figure out what to say next.

Since this is Lexi I'm dealing with, there's not much chance of being able to think for long. "Annddd…" she prompts.

I can tell she's trying to keep her enthusiasm under control… but this is Lexi. She knows everything I have been through over the years. She's dying to know what has me acting this way. I hold on to her gaze as she penetrates me with a dubious smile. I finally concede and break the silence. "It's still pretty new…" Still trying not to give much away. *I wouldn't be her best friend if I didn't make her work for it a little.*

"But you've slept with him." It's not a question, but an assessment.

I want to hold out on the details, but this is my best friend. I can't keep secrets from her. Besides, if I'm being honest, I've been dying to dish out the details, so I can wrap my head around things. I burst out laughing at her attempt to pump me for more information.

I shake my head to clear my thoughts before giving in. "Lex, there's just something about him. I don't know what to say. Ever since I met him, I can't get him off my mind." I shrug as if that should make all the sense in the world.

"How long have you been seeing him?" Lexi eagerly asks as her eyes fill with more excitement.

She knows me. She knows I don't date anyone and let things get serious. I'm sure she thinks I've been holding out on her. I can't wait to see her reaction to this. I casually state, "Thursday."

Yep, there it is, her eyes go wide, her mouth forms a perfect 'O.' Lexi never disappoints. "Come again?" She finally asks, a little weary.

"Thursday," I repeat.

"Samantha, *today*... is *Moonndaay*," she slowly exaggerates.

I smile and nod in agreement. "Yep."

"And you've already slept with him? Who the hell is this man with the magic mojo who got you out of the funk you've been in for years, *in just four days?*"

"Two days," I quietly correct her, but I quickly continue with other facts before she can respond. "He's the son of my contractor. He came to surprise his dad one day and later that evening, I ran into him. I ended up asking him to dinner Thursday and we've seen each other every day since."

"Wait... You, Samantha O'Reilly, the woman who rarely dates. Even if she does, never does anything but give a polite kiss at the end of the night, are saying that YOU asked a man out?"

I tell her about how we met on Thursday and went to Thai food together. Being my best friend, I give her all the details she will require to be satisfied. When I get to how Thursday night ended, she suddenly interrupts again, "Wait. You said only two days. As in, you slept with this man on Friday at some point?"

"I'm getting there. Be patient." I proceed to tell her about my lunch delivery and going up the Gorge for dinner. She seems really impressed with him when I tell her how he bought me a dress. She prods me for more information and nearly falls out of her chair with laughter when I tell her about the car after dinner.

"No WAY," she gasps. "You did *not* almost have sex in a car!"

I feel my cheeks heat and I own it. "You think *that's* hot, wait until I tell you about when we got home."

She's fanning herself by the time I finish explaining the rest of my evening. "Holy hell, Sam, that's HOT!"

I nod in agreement. What else can I say? Enzo has done things to me I've never experienced with any man.

"So, where did he take you to wear that sexy dress?" Lexi asks as she takes a drink of her margarita. She insisted we each order one after I began to tell her about what she's now deeming as my 'sexcapade.'

"Allure," I say nonchalantly, once again waiting for her reaction. She knows it's an exclusive restaurant and club. Now that I've been there myself, I recall her telling me about it once.

Her jaw drops, and before she can say anything I add, "He's friends with the owner." I tell her about my amazing experience there, too. Lexi is nearly crying when I finish telling her about the stunt Rowan played on me. Her laughter is infectious. I can't help but join her. Eventually, after our laughter dies down, I give her the sordid details of the rest of our evening and yesterday morning.

"I may never look at your entryway the same," she teases when I finish explaining my adventures of the evening.

"Neither will I," I gasp, before laughter makes its appearance again. "The man does unbelievable things to me. I'm telling you, Lex, he's sexy as hell and can read me like he was given his own personal instruction manual."

"So. What did you do yesterday?" Lexi asks as she eats a tortilla chip. "Well, after our unusual encounter with Devin and Frankie, we went to breakfast then eventually went to his parents' house for dinner."

"WTF?" Lexi nearly yells with a look of complete shock covering her face. "You've already met his family? Moving a little fast, aren't you?"

I can't help but feel a little shy and guilty when I say, "Well, I've kind of been monopolizing his time. I don't really blame them for wanting to see him."

"Sam," Lexi says sternly. "You've been with him for four days. How is that monopolizing his time? PLEASE tell me he doesn't have mommy issues or anything?"

"He's on leave. He actually just arrived on Thursday," I say as if it's not anything important.

She hedges with, "On leave from where?"

"Germany. He's a pilot for PJs... pararescue men in the Air Force."

"Only you would find a man who you connect to so well and he lives halfway around the world." She shakes her head teasingly. "Sam, what are we going to do with you? Is this more like a rebound thing?"

I shake my head. "I don't think so. I've been over Devin for some time. Enzo is something else." I try to put my feelings for him into words, but too many thoughts go through my head at once to really grasp a definition of it all.

"But he lives in Germany. As in Europe. How will this work?" I can tell she's just looking out for me at this point.

"I have no idea, but I'm willing to see where it goes. Who knows what'll happen? Besides, there's a good chance he's retiring from the Air Force and moving to Portland when his tour is over."

"When will that be?" She looks sad.

"Um... he has less than six months to go and he's on a nearly two-month leave, I think." I try to figure it out in my head, but I realize I don't really have the specifics.

Lexi lets out a deep breath as if she finally found the information she's been waiting on. "Okay. Now it makes sense why you want to try it one day at a time..."

"For the past few days, it's been amazing to be wrapped up in our own personal bubble. But now that I'm away from him, I'm having other thoughts about him, too."

Lexi suddenly appears weary as she slowly asks. "Like what?"

"Well, for starters, what about my kids?" I start out slow with my reservations, but the more that comes to mind, the more rapidly I fire the questions to Lexi, never giving her the time to respond. "What on Earth am I going to tell them tonight? Do I not tell them much and let them jump to their own conclusions? Do I tell them that I'm dating him? Ugh... I've never been in this situation. What if they don't like him? I think he's wonderful. I've seen him with kids. Believe it or not, he's even sexier while playing with them, but if my children hate him, there's no way it'll work." I gasp when another thought hits me. "Lex, what about when he goes to Germany? Will he get bored with me and find someone else? What if..."

"Stop," Lexi firmly states. "Sam, you're going crazy with questions. You've only known the man for four days. You don't need to have all the answers right now. It's not like he's asking you to elope tomorrow or anything. Chill out. Relax." She places her hand on mine across the table and I feel myself relax and mentally thank her for pulling me off the edge of a cliff.

I take in a deep breath and calm myself further. "You're right. I need to calm down. I'm just so gun shy since finding out about Devin's infidelity issues. I completely trusted him, and it was a blow to find out about his affairs. I've never brought anyone around the kids and I'm just nervous."

"Oh, hon, you're going to be just fine. Anyone who can break through your barriers in such a short time must be worthy of meeting your kids," Lexi reassures me in only the way my best friend can.

"Thanks, Lex." I shrug and shake off the negative thoughts. "I don't know what I'd do without you."

"That's what I'm here for, Babe. Just keeping it real. I love you and can't wait to meet this devilishly handsome man that's got you so tied up in knots. He must be special, or you wouldn't have given him the time of day."

After Lexi and I have our almost two-hour lunch break, I decide to call it quits for the day so I can pick up the kids. I drop by the grocery store to pick up some snacks for the girls after school. I can't wait for my kitchen to be finished so that I can just cook a regular meal again. Just as I am leaving the grocery store, I receive a text from Enzo and I can't help but smile.

Enzo: Hey beautiful, how's your day going? I haven't been able to stop thinking of you. I'm looking forward to seeing you this evening.

Holy Crap. What a way to start a conversation. The man sure doesn't mince words. Just the thought of seeing him again soon has me tingling all over. But what do I say in response? After a few minutes of thought, I finally tap out

Me: Me, too. I had a good day. How was yours?

Gaahhh... so lame. But it's already out there, what can I do?

Enzo: Great. Met with CO. Tell you more later.

Before I can respond, another text comes through.

Enzo: What kind of pizza do your kids like?

I'm curious as to how his meeting went, but I decide to wait for later, so I just answer the second question.

Me: Pepperoni or Canadian Bacon and Pineapple.
Enzo: What's your favorite?

Me: I usually just eat what they do, but I like garlic chicken or meat lovers as well. But whatever you like is fine.

Enzo: Any preference on drinks?

Me: You can just pick up what you like. I should have the drinks for the kids covered with what we have at home.

Enzo: What time do you want me there?

I want to say *now.* But instead I type:

Me: The game starts at 5:30. I should be home by 4:30, so any time you'd like.

Enzo: Gotta run. See you then.

I spend the rest of the afternoon in a lust-filled haze as I drive around taking the kids to their activities. My mind doesn't wander far from Enzo, but I manage to pick up Declan and Maddie from each of their schools on time. As I rush to feed Dec a snack so he can be at practice by four, I casually tell my kids we'll be watching the Seahawks game with a friend this evening. Neither of them gives much of a response, but then again, we're rushing from one place to the next and it's not like I haven't had people over for the game before. Just never a man I've been dating.

In the process of picking up and dropping off, I get a text from Maddie saying her friend Nicole will be dropping her off at home after practice. I'm relieved to have one less thing to do this afternoon. It takes a village to raise children and I'm thankful for all the help I can get. Usually, Devin picks up Declan at six from his practice, so I'll just meet him back at the house.

Before I know it, it's just Frankie and me driving home in the car. She's telling me all about her day and I contribute to the conversation the best I can. By the time we make it to our driveway, I've learned all about her friend's new haircut, what her dad made her for lunch, as well as a funny story her teacher told her about why it's important to learn how to read with punctuation. The amount of enthusiasm Frankie has for learning astounds me.

When we pull into the driveway, I notice Enzo waiting on the front porch. There's a bag of groceries next to him on the bench out front and he's looking at his phone. When he realizes we've arrived, he nearly takes my breath away with his greeting smile.

"Mama, isn't that Enzo?" Frankie asks.

"Yeah, honey, it is. He's here to watch the game with us," I remind her as I park the car.

Enzo greets me at my car door, by opening it. "Hey, beautiful, how was your day?" His husky voice sends shivers up my spine.

While Frankie's still in the car, he brushes a light kiss on my cheek, making me wish we could do more than that.

"Great. I had lunch with Lexi and I don't have to go back out to pick up Declan or Maddie tonight. They're both getting a ride home, so we can just watch the game."

"Fantastic. I ordered some pizza. It should be here around the time of kickoff." He closes my door and turns to greet Frankie, as she's finally managed to gather her things and climb out of my SUV. "Hello, Frankie."

"Hello." Frankie looks from me to Enzo, then back to me.

I remind her of our conversation in the car, "Hey, sweet

pea, why don't you go inside and get your homework started, so we can watch the game in a little bit?" I gesture for her to move along and not doddle.

"Okay. I'll do my math. Then we can check it and read together," Frankie says without any fuss, thankfully. Sometimes she likes to procrastinate or play a while first.

As Frankie runs inside and closes the door, Enzo and I slowly make our way to the house. Enzo reaches for my hand to hold on the way to the front porch. Before we can get into view of any of the windows, he stops and pulls me in for a kiss.

"Damn, you taste good. I've been waiting for that all day." He keeps the kiss short, but it still has a lasting effect.

I reach up on my toes to kiss him once more before forcing myself to pull away. "Good to see you, too, handsome."

He lets out a slight groan and pulls away completely. He does lean back in to gruffly whisper, "I have no idea how I'm going to behave around you this evening. You've spoiled me this weekend. How do I refrain from touching you whenever I damn well please?"

"I feel the same way," I sigh. Then I look at the house. "We'd better get in there before she gets distracted and forgets to do her homework."

We walk to the porch in silence next to one another. He reaches down to pick up a grocery sack and we go inside. Just as we enter the door, I hear Frankie yell from the living room, "Mama, can you help me with this math?"

Since we don't have a working kitchen, I just tell Enzo to go put whatever needs to be put in the refrigerator in the spare one we keep in the garage. The rest can just be brought back into the living room since it's the only place we still have usable furniture and a TV. I point to the doorway off the kitchen so he knows where to go. He takes care of what's in his bag.

I settle down on the couch to help Frankie with her math. It's only a few minutes before Enzo returns and asks Frankie, "So, what are you working on?"

"Ugh," she sighs loudly. "I just have to do some multiplication and division." She points to the page she's working on.

"Want some help?" he asks, melting my heart just a little more. "I'm pretty good at math." He gives her a genuine smile and waits for her response a bit apprehensively. I don't think Frankie notices this though.

Frankie looks from me to him. She usually digs her heels in with me, so I'm so relieved when she eagerly accepts his help. "Sure, I guess so." *I can't believe she acts as if this is just an everyday occurrence.*

He sits on the couch and she scoots closer to him to show her work that's spread out all over the coffee table. She sounds so official and excited when she explains her homework to him. He has her read the directions at the top of the page to him then he asks her what she's supposed to be doing.

I sit back on the couch for a few minutes to watch. I'm quickly impressed with the fact Enzo has a natural way with her that makes her feel like math is fun, not a chore. He even teaches her a few tricks for how to do nines on her fingers as well as some basic chants to help her remember her facts like, "eight and eight, ate some more, eight times eight is sixty-four." She giggles and soon her homework is done. *I wish he would be here every night to make homework this easy.* Not that she's too difficult, but she seems to connect with him and didn't argue about the right way of doing it like she does with me. Sometimes, parents know nothing when it comes to schoolwork, according to the kids. I should know, I've been told many times. I guess it's just a rite of passage.

By the time they're finished, she is even eager to read her book she brought home. This never happens. I usually break it up and read before bedtime, so it doesn't become a fight. I'm shocked when she asks Enzo to read her *Magic Fairy* book with her. When she suggests, "How about... I read a page and you read the next, Enzo?" The look on his face is priceless. She crawls right up on the couch next to him, so they can both read the book together. He gestures to me for assurance and my ovaries nearly explode. The man is magic. *Apparently, I don't need to worry about Frankie liking Enzo. They seem to get along just fine. One down, two to go.*

She finishes her reading just as the game starts and the pizza arrives. Before I can even answer the door, Enzo is up and off the couch, paying for the pizza he had delivered. When he comes back from the door, he has at least three pizzas in front of him and a few smaller boxes on top. *Who the heck does he plan on feeding?* They all seem to be large pizzas. From the delicious aroma that fills the room, I can tell there must be a dessert pizza in the mix as well. When I count just how many things Enzo ordered, I see there are five boxes.

"Are you expecting company?" I exaggerate as I look around the room to see if there's more than just the three of us in the room.

Enzo looks as if he's a kid caught with his hand in the

cookie jar. He's so damn adorable when he clears his throat. "Well, I didn't know exactly how much everyone would eat, so I just ordered one of each."

I can't help but laugh. "Um… the kids and I usually just eat one pizza, and sometimes there are even leftovers from that. This has to be over a hundred dollars' worth of pizza here."

"Well, since Maddie and Declan are just getting done with practice, I thought they might be really hungry. I know I always was when I played sports as a kid. Besides, I can usually eat at least half a pizza on my own." Enzo shrugs as if it's not a big deal.

"That's because you're six-foot-six and work out regularly. If I eat more than a couple slices, I'm definitely going to have to go running in the morning."

"What time can I join you?" he suggests eagerly. "I haven't run since I've been home. Although I have been able to burn some calories in *other* ways." He waggles his eyebrows suggestively and I burst out laughing.

"Yeah… right…" I look over at Frankie who is completely oblivious to his suggestions. I can't help myself when I add seriously, "I usually run around six a.m. before I have to get the kids up for school."

"I'll be here," he whispers. Then, looking at Frankie, he changes his tone from deep and sexy to cool and kind as he addresses her, "I hope you're hungry. What kind of pizza do you want?"

Frankie eagerly helps us set up the pizza boxes on the coffee table. We put them in stacks on top of another, planning to pull from just the ones we need. Enzo pulls out some paper plates and a roll of paper towels from the bag he sat beside the couch. *The man thought of everything.* He tells Frankie there are containers of chocolate milk and juice staying cold in the garage fridge. Enzo and I burst into laughter as she pops off the couch and runs toward the garage to get a drink. I'm guessing she comes back with chocolate milk since it's her favorite.

Enzo doesn't waste any time while she's gone. He moves closer to me and plants a scorching kiss on my lips. Like usual, it doesn't take much from him to have my body become a sudden inferno. *Fuck, I wish we were alone. I want him to know my kids but being around him and having to control myself is torture.*

As if he reads my mind, he pulls away and whispers in my ear, "I know. I feel it, too."

The sounds of Frankie's feet making a fast track back to the living room has us pulling further apart. She has a container of chocolate milk in her hand and an enormous smile on her face. "Thanks, Enzo! Are you ready to watch the Hawks crush the Packers?"

Enzo's deep laughter fills the room. "Sure thing, Kid." To my surprise, she chooses to squeeze herself between Enzo and the other side of the couch. *I guess I no longer rate.*

"Um… Franks, do you think you should give him some room?" I eye the tiny space between the end of the couch and Enzo.

"Well, if you scoot over, we'll all have plenty of space," she states matter-of-factly, then shouts at the TV, "Way to go, Wilson!" as Russell Wilson, the quarterback for the Seahawks, just threw a long pass into the end zone for a touchdown. Frankie then cheers, and our conversation is forgotten, at least by her.

I look to Enzo and he just beams. Then he whispers in my ear, "Yeah, Sam, just move over so we can watch the game." He high-fives Frankie and we're glued to the TV until the next commercial break. Then he moves closer to me, so his entire leg presses against mine. Though the action might be innocent, the thoughts that swirl in my head about the sexy man next to me are anything but.

19

ENZO

Samantha wasn't lying when she said she and her family are huge fans of the Seahawks. Both she and Frankie continue to yell at the screen, as if they're at CenturyLink Field. I don't think I've ever seen two girls so into football before. They cheer for their team as if they're playing in the Super Bowl right now. I can't help but find Samantha sexy as hell as she hoots and hollers at the television. I find myself cheering right along with them, enjoying every moment. In fact, I don't think I've ever had so much fun watching a football game before.

Within a half hour or so, two teenage girls come through the front door. From the pictures I have seen, as well as the resemblance to Samantha, I can tell which one is Maddie immediately. The girls are in deep conversation as they enter, but as soon as they see us here in the living room, they stop dead in their tracks.

"Uh, hi," Maddie says as she stares at her mother, Frankie, and me on the couch.

"Hey, Mads," Frankie greets.

Samantha follows with, "Hey, Maddie. Hi, Nicole. How was practice?"

"Good." Maddie still seems to be locked in place as she eyes me up and down.

Samantha takes notice and introduces us. "Maddie, this is Enzo Harper. Enzo, this is my daughter and her friend Nicole."

I stand to shake both of their hands, telling them it's nice to meet them. Then I gesture to the stacks of pizza still left on the table. "Care to join us for pizza?" I almost laugh when Maddie's eyes go as big as saucers when she takes in the number of boxes. *I guess I did go a little overboard. So sue me.*

"Are you expecting more people, Mom?" She looks to her mom for clarification.

Samantha shakes her head. "Nope. Just you and Declan. Thank goodness, Nicole is here. Maybe we won't have to eat pizza for a week." Before Maddie says anything else, the sassy woman next to me pins me with her beautiful mahogany eyes. "Apparently, Enzo thought we eat like savage beasts. He bought out the place." Her beautiful laughter fills the room as she motions to all the food.

"In my defense, I didn't want anyone going hungry." I hold my hands up as if to surrender.

"That won't be a problem, Mr. Harper. You bought enough pizza here for an entire army," Nicole adds with a grin as she eyes all the choices before us.

Okay. So... I went a lot overboard. I just remember my friends and I always being hungry. Wait. Mr. Harper? Since when have I become my old man? "Um, you can just call me Enzo or Harper. No need for the mister."

Maddie and Nicole look at me quizzically. They glance at Samantha, as if they're unsure of what to do. Before either of them can say anything, I cut them off and clarify, "Mr. Harper is my dad. Last I checked, he's not here. Enzo or Harper is what I respond to if you want my attention. My buddies usually shorten it to Harps. I'm used to all three since that's what I'm usually referred to. Twenty years in the Air Force will do that to you, I guess." I shrug as if this should explain everything. No need to go to such formalities.

Just then Samantha yells, "Go! Go! Go!" at the TV, as if it will personally usher Wilson into the end zone for another touchdown. *God, I love her enthusiasm.* Now we're all glued to the TV to see if he can score or not.

Nicole and Maddie sit on the other couch in the living room and watch the game. All of us are completely enthralled with the action on the screen. Hoots and hollers can be heard sporadically as we sit on the edge of our seats. The Hawks have stopped the Packers on the one-yard line and there's less than a minute until half-time. Rodgers, the Packers' quarterback, receives the snap and throws it to one of his wide receivers for a touchdown, but it's picked off by Sherman. Everyone goes wild. The screams that can be heard throughout the room are insane, considering they're coming from a mom and three kids.

When it finally quiets down, we notice Declan has entered the house with his dad at his side. Declan seems to be in awe of the celebration that has taken over the room. He greets us, "What's going on?"

Maddie jumps up from the couch excitedly. "You missed it, Dec! Griffin got another pick and stopped the Packers from scoring!" He looks at the TV, which is now in a replay of the scene.

"Sounds like a good game," Devin states. He appears to be interested in the game, but I can't help but notice the brief look of surprise that crosses his face when he notices me here. He doesn't say anything, but I can tell he's not expecting to see me.

I decide not to make this any more awkward for him than necessary. "It's a great game. You're welcome to stay and watch. It's just about half-time and I've ordered plenty of pizza." I point out the piles of boxes on the coffee table.

"Nah, I think I'll head out so I can watch the rest of the game at home. Thanks for the offer," he sincerely states before turning to head to the door. Before he can leave, Samantha stops him.

"Hey, Devin, do you think you could keep Dec tomorrow after practice until I can pick him up from you? I'm taking Maddie shopping after her practice, so I won't be home until later."

"Shouldn't be a problem. Do you want me to pick up Miss Muffet from school, so you can just go with Mads? Tomorrow is when you're going to get the dirty deets on that boy Maddie is going to the dance with, right?"

"Dad," Maddie huffs out in complaint. "That right there is why you aren't meeting him first! You're horrible."

"Only doing my job, Mads. Only doing my job," Devin reminds her with a grin spread wide across his face.

I can't help but smile at their interaction. *God knows what I would do if I had a daughter who wanted to date. Heaven help me there.* I think if it wasn't for the fact Devin cheated on Samantha, I could see myself liking this guy. *But then again, his loss is my gain. If the fucker didn't screw things up with Sam, I wouldn't be here.*

"Who says I'm not going to give Soren the third degree?" Samantha perks up trying to get in on the ribbing.

"Mom. Not you, too. You're the sane one. The nice one. The one that doesn't make threats or embarrass me," Maddie reminds her sweetly.

Samantha looks very serious at me and says, "You know how to hide a body, right?" Then she looks back to Maddie and adds with a straight face, "I'm sure I could get some help if I needed."

All that can be heard from Maddie is a sudden intake of air.

Without missing a beat, I casually state, "I'm sure I could figure something out."

"This is insane," Maddie huffs. "Come on, Nicole. Let's go upstairs. It's only a dance; it's not like I'm going to marry the guy or anything. You guys need to give it a rest." She and Nicole each take another piece of pizza on a plate and head upstairs while the rest of us try to contain our laughter.

"She's ticked," Samantha says under her breath as Declan comes into the room and helps himself to pizza.

Frankie exclaims, "There's chocolate milk in the fridge out in the garage, Dec!"

"Awesome!" Declan puts his pizza down and heads to the garage.

"Well... I'll leave you to it," Devin states awkwardly. "Let me know if you need anything, Sam." Devin looks up the stairs and shakes his head in disbelief. "I still can't believe she's going on her first date this week. Time sure does fly."

"Yes, it does," Samantha agrees. "Don't be too hard on them when you come to meet him on Friday."

He grins dubiously. "I have rights as a father, Sam."

"Would you rather she sneak around?" Sam points out, raising an eyebrow. Devin slumps in defeat. "No... no, I wouldn't. I guess I'll talk to you tomorrow." With that, he shakes his head and walks out the door.

Sam and I both sit back on the couch. Frankie takes it upon herself to sit on the other side of me again. The girl hasn't left my side since I've been here. Well, except to get her chocolate milk. Which is a hit in this household. I'll have to remember that for future use. I'm just about relaxed on the couch when I look over and realize Declan is eyeing me suspiciously. Shit. I forgot to introduce myself. He's giving me a *'what the fuck are you doing here with my mother look.'* I immediately stand to rectify the situation.

I hold out my hand to him. "Hey, you must be Declan. I'm Enzo."

He shakes my hand firmly and looks me in the eye. "Nice to meet you." He then looks toward his mom.

"Sorry, honey, I forgot to introduce you. He's already met everyone else and with the drama stunt your sister just played, I got distracted." Samantha then asks, "How was practice?"

"It was good. What's the score on the game?" He motions to the TV.

"21-7, Hawks," I interject.

Declan cocks his head to the side and looks me over with care. I notice him glance at his mother, then back to me. I want to ask him what's on his mind, but I'm not sure how to handle this. This is uncharted territory and I'm making it up as I go.

I finally break the scrutiny with, "So what position do you play?"

Declan smiles and tells me about his position as forward. He can play all positions, but from what I gather, this is where he shines. With the help of strategic prodding on my behalf, we have a real conversation that seems to easily flow. I glance from time to time at Samantha, and she just smiles in a way that could take a grown man to his knees. The pride she has for her children is evident.

When halftime is over, we all go back to watching the game. Samantha remains at my side as we laugh at commercials, joke with each other, and cheer for our team. Her touch is addictive, so I keep one leg along hers most of the evening. I know I can't have more now, but I like being close to her. The more I get to know Samantha, the more I find myself completely drawn to her.

When the game's over, Samantha tells Declan and Frankie that it's time to get ready for bed. Nicole had left awhile ago and Maddie is still upstairs, having yet to resurface. Declan heads upstairs without an argument to take a shower and finish his homework. Frankie hangs around for a while longer. She doesn't seem to be ready for bed. She laughs and jokes around with me as easy as my nieces and nephews do. Finally, about twenty minutes later, Samantha pulls out the mom voice.

"Frankie, it's already past your bedtime. Tell Enzo goodnight and head upstairs. I'll be up in a few minutes to tuck you in."

For the first time all night, I hear a whine come from her, "But, Mom... I don't wanna go to bed."

"Sorry, Charlie, it's bedtime for you." Samantha comes over to her, cocks her head to the side, and places her hands on her hips. If she wasn't trying to be stern, I would burst out laughing. I give her a look asking if I should leave, and she shakes her head no. *Okay then. What should I do to help the situation?*

Frankie looks to me as if I can rescue her. "Can Enzo tuck me in and read another story with me?" She looks at me with pleading eyes and I can't help it when a small laugh escapes. She's fucking adorable. The eight-year-old extortionist. That should be her new name. Frankie's way too cute for her own good.

I look to Samantha for direction. She looks... a little shocked, if I'm correct in my assessment. Finally, she shrugs. "If Enzo is okay with it." I nod in approval. "But you," she looks to Frankie, "need to get upstairs, change into jammies, and brush your teeth. Enzo won't come up until that's done. And he will only read one chapter. Got it?"

Frankie looks as if she could jump up and down and scream with excitement. But instead, she shoots me a look and asks, "Will you really read me a story before bed?"

"Sure thing, kiddo. But do what your ma tells you first. Then I'll be upstairs," I reassure her.

"But you don't know where my room is." Frankie protests.

Samantha sighs. "Frankie. I'll show him. Now, scoot up the stairs, so he can come and read."

Frankie turns and runs up the stairs. It's finally just Samantha and myself. She comes to me and I pull her body close to mine in an all-enveloping hug. After a moment, I place my hand under her chin and turn her face to look at me. "You are amazing, beautiful." I lean down and kiss her gently on the lips.

I seem to have ignited the flame between us because she takes our kiss to a whole new level within moments. I do my damnedest to keep aware of our surroundings because there's no way in hell I want to have her kids walk in on us at this moment. Yes, I feel my arousal course through my body. Yes, I'm sure she wants it just as bad as I do. But I can't. Get. Carried. Away. It takes everything in me to pull away from the gorgeous woman before me. I hold her close for a moment more before letting her go. Well, almost. I'm still holding her hand.

She starts to walk toward the stairs, but I stop her. "Um... give me a sec," I whisper.

She looks at me questioningly and I can't help but show her what I mean when I adjust myself. *Jesus, what is it about being around her that makes my jeans shrink?* "There's no way I can go upstairs and face your kids in my condition."

The challenging grin conspiring on her face is the only warning I get before she walks over to me and feels for herself, just how much my condition is affecting me. "Samantha," I groan. "You're not helping."

She whispers, "Payback's a bitch. My panties have been drenched since before the game started." She leans up on her tiptoes and kisses me lightly. Then she turns and walks up the stairs. The sway of her ass has me wanting to follow her for an entirely different reason.

Suddenly, Frankie yells, "Enzo, are you coming?"

I wish. I grumble to myself. Samantha stops at the top of the stairs and almost falls back down them with silent laughter. She turns to me, shaking her head. "They always do have impeccable timing."

"Good to know," I try to grumble, but laughter wins out.

Samantha walks me to Frankie's door and tells me she's going to check in with the others after she discovers I'm going to be fine on my own with Frankie. As an uncle, I've told a lot of bedtime stories. I pull out all the punches and do special voices for the characters. Frankie insists on me sitting on her bed next to her, so she can see the words on the pages, too. She's wearing fuzzy pajamas with feet in them. The kind that looks way too warm to wear, but she digs them. She's lying on top of the soft purple quilt on her bed. As I look around her room, I see her walls are a light purple as well. That must be her favorite color.

"So, what are we reading tonight, kiddo?" I ask as I sit beside her, keeping my shoes hanging off the side of her bed.

"*The Twits.* I just got it from the library. Mama said I can only read one chapter with you, but they're really short. Can we just read for a while?"

I realize she's right. The first chapter is only a paragraph or two. It's about noticing beards. Now that I've read it, I can't help but think about how many beards I notice when I'm out and about. The next chapter has Frankie squirming when she realizes how disgusting Mr. Twit is. I can't help but laugh. I've never read this story before, but it's very entertaining. The part about how dirty beards can be makes me never want to have one again, not that I've ever worn one. Damn, that man is disgusting. Keeping morsels of food for later, never showers, and his being an all-around Twit makes me want to vomit. I flip the front cover to see when this was published. Wow. I wish I'd read this as a kid. I totally would've loved it.

After about fifteen minutes or so, I tell Frankie it's time for bed. To my surprise, she doesn't argue. Instead, she says, "Thanks, Enzo. I had fun tonight. Will you be back again soon?" She yawns heavily, and I take that as my cue to stand from the bed. She pulls her covers up closer to her chin.

The look she gives me floods my heart with emotion. There's complete trust and comfort. *I could get used to doing this every night.* I shake my head to clear my thoughts. I ruffle her hair and clear my throat to hide how she's affected me. "I sure hope so, Kiddo. Night."

"Night, Enzo," she calls to me as I walk to the door to turn off the light.

"Do you leave it open or closed?" I point to the door.

"Closed. I have a nightlight." She rolls over to face the wall as I close the door.

I don't get much further in the hallway when I see Samantha leaving Declan's room. She shuts the door and motions for the stairs. I make my way over and walk down. I can feel Samantha behind me. But I don't say anything until I'm in the living room.

"How is everything?" I point upstairs. "Was Maddie upset? She never came back down earlier."

"She's fine. She just had a lot of homework and was talking

with Soren on the phone after Nicole left." Samantha shrugs. "She's just about done and is about to go to sleep."

"What about Declan?" I walk over to the pizza boxes and consolidate as many of them as possible.

Samantha helps me. We manage to get it all into two boxes. The kids devoured the dessert pizza earlier. "He just had me turn out his light. He will be sawing logs soon. He wears himself out at practice."

She gathers the full boxes as I gather the empties. "Let's take these to the garage," she suggests.

As soon as we rid ourselves of the boxes, I stalk over to Samantha, who's next to the fridge. "Thanks for inviting me over tonight. It's great getting to know your family." I pull her close to me. One hand is reaching for the nape of her neck while the other snakes around the small of her back.

"I should be thanking you..." She looks as if she's about to say something else, but suddenly seems distracted.

Samantha pulls in a deep breath as she locks her eyes with mine. "I've missed you," comes out before I can think about what I'm saying. I pull her even closer than before.

"Me, too." She willingly closes the gap between us.

Having lost all my restraint from earlier, I slowly consume her with a kiss. The contact alone has me nearly losing all my control. It doesn't help that she's reaching under my black t-shirt and scraping her fingernails against my abs. I take a step to the side, bringing her with me so that her body can be hidden behind the fridge, should anyone walk in on us.

I press her body up against the wall and one of her legs encircles my hip. I grab her ass to hoist her into the air, pinning her against the wall and my chest. This reminds me of the first night at her front door.

"Enzo, I can't wait any longer," Samantha practically pants. She pulls me back, devouring my mouth.

Thank fuck, she's wearing a skirt. I've wanted to reach under it all night and have my way with her. I inch it higher, running my hands up her inner thigh. When I get to the delicate fabric of her panties, I find them completely soaked. She hadn't been kidding earlier... had I only known. I would've found a way to help her out. I push them to the side and tease her. The quiet noises she makes let me know that I'm right on track. With little effort, I slide one finger inside, then quickly add another. I work her up until I know she's close to teetering over the edge by mimicking the motions of my mouth with my hand. The minute I change the position of my fingers to reach that perfect spot inside her, she detonates around me. I feel her inner muscles clamp down as spasm after spasm spread through her.

Each sensational tremor makes me want her even more. I pull my hand out from under her skirt to steady her as I reach for my wallet. And that's when I realize. FUCK!!! Fuckity, Fuck, Fuck! I knew I'd run out of condoms and I was in such a hurry to get over here, I'd forgotten one very important item on the list. Then I think it is for the best. I shouldn't be having sex with her while her kids are here. What the ever-loving fuck had I been thinking?

Samantha can tell there is something wrong and opens her mouth to ask, "Wha..." She slides down my body to put her feet on the floor.

"Nothing to worry about, beautiful. Let's see how quick we

can make another orgasm rip through you." Making my entire focus be on her, I do my best to forget about my own needs for now. I drop to my knees and pull her legs over my shoulders. I hold her against the wall with one hand resting against her hip while I push up her skirt with my other to get to what I need desperately. *Shit, this underwear must go.* My hands find a seam and all that can be heard is the quick rip of fabric. Samantha gasps at my bold move. Within mere seconds, my mouth reaches the promised land of all that is Samantha. I make good on my promise of bringing her to another crippling orgasm quickly. I lick up every drop of her arousal as she comes down from her high.

As I set her feet on the floor, her legs almost buckle beneath her. I pull her down onto my lap and cradle her as both of our breaths return to normal. Having her in my arms is more than enough. I wish I could take her to bed and have her wake in my arms as I have for the past three mornings, but with her kids at home, that isn't an option.

Wait! When the fuck did I start wanting sleepovers all the time?
Since you met this amazing woman, dumbass.

As if reading my mind, Samantha sexily whispers, "I wish you could stay. I've gotten used to waking up with you."

"Me, too, beautiful. Me, too. But I'd better get going or I'm never going to be able to leave." I absolutely hate that I said that aloud. But it must be done. "I need to go home and take a very cold shower. I have very little self-control left. I know that kids can walk in at any time, as I've heard many embarrassing stories from my siblings about their own kids interrupting times like this." There's no way I'm going to compromise Samantha in any way, shape, or form. As much as I try to test my limits on a regular basis, I know I only have so much self-control.

Samantha sighs deeply with as much regret on her face as I feel. "I know."

"I'll be over here at six-thirty to go running with you tomorrow." There's no way I'm going to miss out on any time I can have with her.

We get up and I help her adjust her clothing. I notice she grabs her shredded panties off the floor and fists them in her hand. She kisses me gently one last time before I pull away. *If we keep this up, we'll be sleeping in the garage tonight.*

With all the resolve I can muster, I motion to the garage door. "I think I'll just head out this way. I don't want to risk the chance of your kids seeing me still here. I wouldn't want them to get the wrong impression."

Samantha shrugs and gives me a nod of understanding. "I appreciate that."

With one last goodbye kiss, I whisper, "Goodnight, Samantha. I'll see you in the morning."

She walks me to the door and kisses me one last time before saying, "Goodnight, Enzo. Thanks for coming over."

With that, I leave. *Fuck! Being honorable sucks. My dick wholeheartedly agrees with that sentiment as well.*

20

SAMANTHA

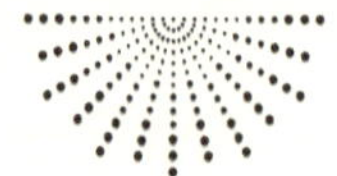

MY DREADED ALARM GOES OFF AT FIVE FORTY-FIVE A.M. THE only thing that gets me out of my all-too-comfortable bed is knowing I'll be seeing Enzo shortly. That sexy man made it so I could hardly walk up the stairs last night, as my legs feel like Jell-O. As soon as my head hit the pillow, I barely had time to contemplate what he'd done to me in the garage because I was sound asleep. Now that I think about it, I realize I hadn't returned the favor to him. He had made me blissfully climax twice and I didn't even offer to reciprocate. I know he didn't want to get caught, and neither did I, for that matter. I can't help but think I was a bit of a shitty girlfriend.

Girlfriend? Since when did I think of myself as that? Well, what else would I be? We agreed to see where our relationship would go, didn't we? Doesn't that make me his girlfriend?

I glance at the clock again and realize I have been daydreaming about Enzo for longer than I thought. I rush to the bathroom to brush my teeth and run a brush through my hair. It doesn't take long before it's in a high ponytail. I come back to my room and dress in a pair of running pants, tank, and a long-sleeved shirt with holes for my thumbs. I know it's still going to be dark outside, and there's no way I'm going to be cold. The shirt and pants have built-in reflectors in them, so I can be seen. I also grab my visor that has a built-in headlamp and flashing light on the back of it. *Always better to be safe than sorry.*

I rush down the stairs to put on my running shoes that I usually leave in the hall closet. Then I leave a note for the kids, should they get up before I get back. I'm about to grab a glass of water when I hear a quiet knock on the door.

It is just after six, so I know it must be Enzo. I'm learning to expect him to arrive earlier than he always says he will. *I might want to remember this for the future.* I feel like a schoolgirl with her first crush. My stomach has a thousand butterflies swarming inside as I walk to the door.

Without a word, Enzo pulls me in for a mind-shattering kiss. When he pulls back, he has a smile on his face that would sell millions of copies of romance novels based on that alone, if he worked in the book industry. *Damn! He would make bank in the modeling world.*

"No, beautiful. No one would buy a single copy if I was on the cover. You, on the other hand, might sell out within minutes."

Did I say my thoughts aloud? Again? Shaking my head, feeling slightly embarrassed by the comment I hadn't intended to say to him, I say, "There I go without my filter again."

"Thanks for the compliment though. That was one I've

never heard before," Enzo teases. "Are you ready to go?" he asks as he gives my body a full assessment.

I take a moment to ogle him as well. He's in a black t-shirt that looks as if his muscled body is trying to escape. The hard planes of his chest are on display, thanks to the taut fabric. His black running shorts perfectly display his thick, muscular thighs. Upon further inspection, I realize he, too, has reflective strips throughout his clothing to be seen better.

"Wanna stretch in here or outside?" he asks as he glances upstairs to see if anyone else is up.

"Let's go outside."

We head out and begin stretching in my driveway. Before long, I put my visor on and we jog down my driveway and into my neighborhood. We run at a conversational pace. It dawns on me I never asked him about his meeting with the Air National Guard. *I'm a shitty girlfriend.*

"So how did your meeting with the CO go?" I ask as we round the corner on my block.

"Not bad. They don't have any jobs in the area I was hoping for and it would screw with my retirement. So, I won't be going in that direction." He shrugs.

Wanting further clarification, I ask, "What does that mean?"

"I'm leaning pretty heavily on taking Riggs up on his offer." It's still dark, so I can't see his facial expression clearly.

"Oh," I reply. We jog a few more paces in silence and I consider what his comment could mean. When I realize I don't have a clue, I decide to ask him. "Would it be much different from what you're already doing?"

"Not really. I would get to relocate and have a permanent

home though. I'd still go out on missions, sometimes without much notice. My job would be to get his people in and out of locations safely. I might have to do other things to help the team, but transportation would be my focus."

"Is it safe?" I ask, suddenly working my lip between my teeth.

"That's what I'd be there for. To get everyone in and out safely. I'd be behind the scenes unless it was necessary for me to be out in the field. It would be a team situation with a lot more money and eyes on the game than what I'm used to." Enzo is quiet for a few strides. Then he continues, "You know, Samantha, I don't take risks that aren't necessary. I keep my head in the game and I do what's best for everyone involved. Is this job risk-free? Hell no. But I can promise you this. I'll do my damnedest to get back to you as often as possible."

Did he just make a declaration to me? Did I really just hear that?

"What do you mean?" I ask, wondering where he's going with this line of thought.

Enzo suddenly stops under a lamp post so I can clearly see the expression on his face. He sets his hands on his hips and says, "I want to move to Portland and really see where this thing goes between us. Before meeting you, I'd decided I didn't want to stay in the Air Force. I want a permanent home and not have to move every couple of years, but I'm not ready to give up flying entirely. I want to spend more time with my family. And... while I'm being honest, now that I've met you, I want to spend more time with you, too."

"I'd love that," is all I manage to say because my heart is fluttering out of my chest.

"Good to hear." He smiles smugly and his dimple pops. *I'm a frickin goner. This man's dimple gets me every time.*

Suddenly, I think of something that should've been my first thought. "What about my kids?" I whisper.

His eyebrows raise, and his smile turns into a smirk. "Uh... Sam... You're kind of a package deal. I know that. So, quit worrying."

A rush of relief I didn't know I was holding on to barrels through my body. He wants to be with me; he wants to see where it goes. "Okay."

"Okay? Is that all I get after baring my soul to you? Just, okay?" Enzo's lips quirk, so I know he's teasing, but there's a hint of seriousness that shines in his eyes.

I'm a little overwhelmed by his declaration, but relieved at the same time. *Who knew those few simple words would be such a big deal? My kids and I are a package deal for him.* Of course, I wouldn't have it any other way. Even though everything is still new, and I'm in completely uncharted territory, I look at the man before me and am stunned by the complete sincerity in his glorious green eyes. There's also a slight sense of vulnerability to him as well, so I clarify my thoughts, "Okay. I want to see where this goes, too. Besides, it'll be a whole lot easier to find out what happens if you're closer to me each day."

He steps closer to wrap his arms around me, pulling me into an enormous hug. He smells so incredible, even after working out. Soon, Enzo pulls us apart enough to kiss me, showing the emotion of his unspoken words. But when he's done, he says, "Those are just the words I needed to hear, beautiful."

I can't help the laughter that escapes when I look around and realize our surroundings. *Here we are in the middle of the street, declaring ourselves to one another and the sun hasn't even risen yet. What will happen by breakfast?* I try to make light of everything by taunting, "You ready to run, hotshot?" I adjust my visor and run down the street faster than our pace before, but he catches up to me with ease. We keep this pace for a while, making it difficult to have any conversation, but I'm in the zone, flying high not only on endorphins but on the words from Enzo as well.

After a couple of miles, we slow back down to a conversational pace. Enzo lifts the end of his shirt to wipe the sweat from his face. I can't stop myself from gawking at his washboard stomach. Without even processing the words, I blurt out, "How in the hell did you get those?" I point at his stomach in disbelief. *Yes, I've seen his body before, but now that I'm working out with this man, I know he must do more than just run each day to get abs that look photoshopped onto his body.*

At first, he obviously doesn't know what I'm talking about because he asks, "My shorts?"

I laugh, I can't help it. "No, hotshot. Those abs." I point at them again while we run a little further.

He shrugs his shoulders. "I was born with them?" he offers, trying not to make a big deal of it.

I give him a pointed look to let him know I'm not buying it.

"Samantha, I work out regularly."

"Ugh…" I moan. "Please don't tell me you're actually a gym junkie?" Not that that would be a big deal, but I would feel like I need to step up my workouts and I just don't have a lot of time.

He stops running completely and bends down to place his hands on his knees. His body shakes and when he looks up at me, I can see a full belly laugh ripping through him. "Shit, Sam, you should have seen the look on your face. I don't spend much time in a gym. I do lift a little, but usually, it's more CrossFit and resistance type training. I don't need to bulk up. I prefer to be able to scratch my own ass."

That last comment has me nearly doubling over in hysterics. What a picture to paint in my head. Geesh! *What a smartass. He's got good looks and a sense of humor.*

"You don't appear to be the type that lifts in front of a mirror to see his progress on a daily basis." I take a deep breath to steady myself.

"Sam, most of what I do to work out involves limited space and time. I just fit it in when I can." He once again shrugs as if it's not a big deal. "Do you have a problem with going to the gym?"

Oh. My. Goodness. I'm a complete dork. I stop dead in my tracks when I realize how ridiculous I just sounded. I shake my head. "No, Enzo. I don't have a problem with going to the gym. I was just teasing you." I look down at myself and shake my head, feeling a bit mortified. "I was just caught ogling you… and tried to give *you* a hard time for being the cause of it. You tried to pass off your hotness as not a big deal. But look at you! I could put you on the cover of almost any of the romance books I work with and you'd have an instant following." I raise my hand up and down as if to point out his hotness even more, but by the end, I can't help but close my eyes as I wait for his response.

He's shaking his head. Trying to contain a laugh as he says,

"The look on your face is priceless... you didn't offend me. You looked as if you're completely mortified and have absolutely no reason to be. I just wasn't expecting you to compliment my body after all that we've done together." Enzo reaches out to grab a hold of me and pulls me close to his body. He perfectly executes a huge bear hug, but I can still feel tremors from his silent laughter. "Your lack of filter is definitely one of the many things I enjoy about you."

I let out a big huff but hug him back. He feels amazing against me. I don't even care that I'm sweaty and likely stink. I take a deep breath. *The man even smells sexy. This is so not fair.*

"What's not fair?" *he asks. UGGG!!! My fucking filter.*

I look up to him sheepishly. "Even when you work out, you still smell sexy."

"You're delusional, Samantha." I feel his body rock with another tremor of silent laughter. "I reek just like everyone else. Just give me time. I promise."

"If you say so..." I take in another breath and all that I smell is Enzo. No reeking involved. I wish I could bottle what I smell. I'd make a fortune... but then again, I wouldn't be willing to share.

We finish our run and head back to the house. The kids are already up and dressed, but still getting ready for school. Enzo asks if we have time to go out for breakfast, and after looking at the clock, I tell him, "Only if we drive them to school." My two younger kids are ecstatic and rush to finish getting ready. Maddie is also eager to go because it sounds better than a cereal bar, so she retreats to her room to finish gathering all her things for school. Enzo asks if he can use one of the spare bathrooms upstairs after getting something he needs from his bag outside. I rush upstairs and take a quick spin in the shower. In record time, we're all back downstairs, ready to go within fifteen minutes. I decided to just towel dry my hair because there is no way I would have had time to dry it this morning. Enzo offers to drive and we all pile into his rental SUV. He takes us to his favorite diner not far from my house.

Conversations flow easily all throughout breakfast. The waitress overhears me telling the kids there won't be time to dilly-dally as we eat, or we'll be late for school, and without even asking, I hear her put a rush on our order. Thankfully, our food is out with plenty of time to eat leisurely. Maddie opens up and I can tell she's excited to go shopping this evening for the dance on Friday. Declan and Frankie chat Enzo's ear off and I can't help but smile at how eager he is to hear what they have to say.

We drop the kids off at their respective schools with plenty of time before the arrival bell rings. Enzo brings me back to my house and as we approach, we can tell his dad's crew is up and running for the morning. With any hope, things will be back to normal before too long. "Would you like to come in? I have to be at the office later for a meeting, but you're welcome to stay for a while."

He puts the car in park and peruses the driveway and trucks lining the street. "Um… Sure. I'd love to. I guess I could go see how Pops is doing." He points to a truck that must be his father's.

We head inside through the front door and the sounds are evident that progress is being made in my kitchen. No one sees us approach or hears us, due to the noise I'm sure. Lorenzo Harper has his back to us, and when the sound of a saw stops,

Enzo makes our presence known. "It's about time you got out of bed, Pops."

Lorenzo turns around with a huge grin on his face. "I was surprised to find you gone when I left this morning actually."

Enzo looks over to me. "Wanted to get a run in. Samantha works out before the kids go to school. Then," he points around the room to the beautiful kitchen for an explanation, "we took them to breakfast. We just got back now."

"Busy morning, 'Zo." He winks at me and says, "Nice to see you again, Samantha."

"Nice to see you, too," I reply. "You guys are making a lot of progress."

"We should be done taking out the floors by the end of the day. Your current tile is being stubborn in some places." He points to a spot where men are chipping as we speak. "Then with that wall removed…" He points to the wall in question where two other men are working on it since the floor around it has been removed. "We hope to be ready for floors tomorrow."

"Wow, you do quick work." I marvel at the amount of work that needs to be done beforehand.

"Need a hand?" Enzo asks.

Lorenzo looks around at his crew. "Naw. We've got it covered. I was just popping in to check on everything. I'll let you know if that changes. You just enjoy your time off." He gives me a wink and then walks over to help one of the guys from the crew hold a new piece of drywall they're replacing under my new bay window. From across the room. Lorenzo hollers, "I'm going to head out to another site in about thirty minutes if you want to join me."

"Sure, Pops, sounds like a plan." Enzo smiles then turns toward me. "Do you need to get ready?"

"Yeah, I'm going to head upstairs to finish getting ready for work." I motion for the stairs. "You're welcome to come visit with me while I do."

Enzo's eyes turn a darker shade of green and the look on his face is evident of his intent. "Sure, sounds good." The playful mirth dancing in his eyes and sexy smile give away his intentions.

As I sit at my desk later that afternoon, I can't help but contemplate the events of my morning. After Enzo and I went upstairs, we made good use of my bathroom counters. I had every intention of just getting dressed and ready for work. But knowing that we won't have much time alone together this week, we made good use of our time alone. Thank God, my bathroom is the furthest from the crew working downstairs.

As I leaned forward to put my makeup on in the mirror, he came up behind me and whispered in my ear how sexy he thought I was. One thing led to another, and the next thing I knew, I was pushed forward over my counter, the skirt of my dress was around my waist, and my panties were easily discarded. It was H-O-T! I watched Enzo's intense gaze through the mirror as he showed me just how sexy he thought I was. Our connection was so unbelievably strong, the house could've caught on fire from our combustible chemistry alone. When we were done, he helped me clean up, then he cleaned himself. *Always the gentleman.*

Once he was put back together, in all his usual perfection, he kissed me goodbye and went downstairs. I, on the other hand, stayed upstairs to make myself look presentable once again. It was a lot faster without his sexiness distracting me. But, I missed him all the same.

I made it to work and met with my client as I was supposed to. All went better than I expected, and we should see some amazing returns on our efforts. Now, I find myself staring out the window and daydreaming about the man who is starring center stage as my real-life fantasy. I know I should be working, but the manuscript I'm working on is another contemporary romance and when the scenes get sexy, my mind shuts off to all things, other than Enzo. *God help me.* I need to get my work done at some point.

When I realize I can't concentrate on the words in front of me. I pick up my phone and call Enzo's sister. I try to keep it as professional as possible, telling her my available time to meet with her early next week. She eagerly takes me up on my offer and we agree she will come into my office to meet one afternoon.

When I hang up, I notice a text came through from Enzo while I was talking.

Enzo: Hey, beautiful. How's your day going?
Me: I just got off the phone with your sister. I'm meeting with her next
week. How are you?
Enzo: I can't stop thinking about bending you over that counter this morning.

I can't help the blush that creeps over me. He must be a mind reader because our sexy scene has been playing through my mind on a loop all morning. *What the hell do I say to that?* I go with the truth.

Me: It was incredible. I won't deny that it has been on my mind, too.
Enzo: What are you doing now?
Me: I was just going to finish up with a manuscript, then grab something for
lunch.
Enzo: Want some company?
Me: I'd love some.
Enzo: I'll be there in 20.

I'm about to ask if he needs the address when another text comes through.

Enzo: Make that 5. I'm closer than I thought.

21

ENZO

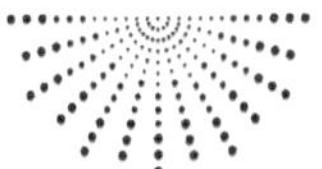

EARLIER THIS MORNING...

After I leave Samantha this morning, I head out with Pops to look at a few job sites. On our way to the first one, he asks me how things are going with Samantha. Of course, I tell him the truth. I've never felt this way about anyone else. We also talk about my job possibilities again. I tell him I'm heavily leaning toward the job with Riggs. He makes the situation crystal clear when he asks, "What's holding you back from making your decision?"

I really can't come up with anything. I think long and hard about it while Pops picks up an order from our local hardware store. It's just for a small tool, so I stay in the truck to ponder my thoughts. Every pro and con for each of my potential choices make it that much clearer that I want to be in Portland. I've wanted to retire from the Air Force, and I've wanted to go to the private sector, rather than stay in the military, so I have control of my future. If truth be told, Samantha did have an influence on my decision as well. The thought of leaving and going back to the single life after experiencing what I've had with her makes me shudder.

I've been dating for the better part of the last twenty years. I've never, and I mean *never*, come across a woman who has captured my interest the way she has. I know it's still new. I know she has a family and there will be a lot of obstacles in the way, but I have zero desire to walk away from her at this point. She may get annoyed with me and chuck me to the curb, but for now, I need to see where this goes.

By the time Pops comes back out to the truck, I've made my decision. Pops must see it in my eyes because the grin on his face becomes infectious. He lets out a deep chortle. "So, you've made your decision." *The man does know me well. But then again, that's my dad for you.*

"Yep, I'm going to take Riggs up on his offer," I state eagerly.

"I figured as much. I didn't see you staying in the Air Force much longer, after seeing you with Samantha this weekend and again this morning." He seems to think for a moment, but then another smile spreads across his face. "She sure is something."

"You can say that again, Pops. The more I get to know her, the more I fall for her. I can't honestly say I've ever felt this way about anyone, including Vanessa."

Pops lets out a low whistle. "That's saying something."

"You may as well make it official and let everyone else in on your decision, Son. Why don't I drop you back off at Samantha's? You must have some important phone calls to make. No need to keep anyone waiting any longer." *Damn. The man sure doesn't mince words.*

"Are you sure, Pops? I can hang out with you today if you'd like."

"Son, you do what you need to do. I'll be here. You can always hang out with your old man another day."

"Thanks, Pops." I give him a knowing look.

"Anytime."

When we get back to Samantha's house, I'm disappointed to have missed her before she left for work. But we both have things we need to do, so I'll have to catch up with her later. Not wanting to waste any time, I make my calls from Samantha's driveway.

First, I call my CO in Germany. It's still early evening there, so the timing is right. He had asked to know when I make my decision. I can tell he isn't surprised with my choice. Most people don't make it twenty years, let alone stay in longer these days. He seems happy for me and is looking forward to seeing me when I come back until I officially retire. Knowing the crew I work with, there will be a lot of ribbing coming my way, but it'll all be done in good fun. It does feel weird to know I only have less than four months to work with them now. They've been my life for so long, it will be strange to not have my team with me. The fact I have over a month left of leave makes this all seem even more surreal.

My next call is to the CO at Air National Guard. I don't owe him anything but my decision, so there's no hard feelings. He understands I've committed twenty years to being with the Air Force. Being thirty-eight allows for me to have a civilian retirement as well.

My next call is to Riggs. He wasn't expecting my decision so soon, but I can tell he's pleased. He's going to email me my contract to sign, as well as all the paperwork necessary to fill out as a new hire. I tell him I will get on it today and get it back to him within the next day or so. We talk about my potential start date and I tell him I will have to get back to him on that. I mention that I will need a couple of weeks for my move back from Germany as well. Overall, things seem to be falling into place, making it evident this is the best decision for me.

By the time I finish my calls, there's only one person I have left to tell. I look up her office on my phone and find the address. I realize I know exactly where it is, without even having to get directions. I shoot off a quick text to her.

When I arrive at her office and walk to the entrance, I can tell she has established herself and has done well for herself, as it looks upscale. As soon as I open the door, I see a receptionist to one side of the office suite. She looks to be about twenty-five, dressed professionally with straight strawberry-blond hair, pulled into a high ponytail. She locks eyes with me for a second, acknowledging my presence before taking a breath to greet me with, "Hello, how can I help you?"

"I'm Enzo Harper, here for Samantha O'Reilly."

She appears to be looking over a schedule but before she says anything, I hear another woman approach from the hall behind me. "You're Enzo Harper?" A mixture of shock and awe fill her voice.

I turn to find a woman in sky-high heels, black pencil skirt, and a blue top staring at me wide eyed through quirky red glasses. Her curly brown hair has a life of its own as it spirals in all directions. From the expression on her face, it's clear she's heard of me. And then it all clicks. "You must be Lexi."

"Correct." She beams. Without having a chance to react,

Lexi closes the distance and embraces me with a hug as she loudly states, "So nice to finally meet you. Samantha has told me wonderful things about you." *Okay, she's a hugger, who squeezes the life out of you,* leaving me slightly stunned. When she's about to let go, she whispers, "But if you hurt her, I will hunt you down."

I can't control the laughter that bubbles out of my mouth as she releases me. "That's perfectly fine with me, Lexi, since I don't plan on hurting her. Nice to meet you, too."

She gestures for me to follow her down a hallway, to where I assume Samantha is. I can't help the smile that spreads across my face when I spot Samantha about to walk through another door. "Hey, Samantha," slips out without a second thought.

Needing to be close to her, I close the gap between us and kiss her cheek as she whispers, "Hello."

She appears in a daze for a moment but when Lexi clears her throat, Samantha suddenly shakes her head and remembers where we are. "Oh, Lexi. Have you been introduced to Enzo?"

I turn my attention to Lexi who darts a mischievous grin at Samantha before turning her attention to me. "Yes, we met in the lobby." The woman knows more than she lets on. "What do you the two of you have planned for today?"

I run a hand through my hair as I answer, "I came to take Samantha to lunch."

Lexi beams in my direction. "Well, isn't that nice? Don't let me stop you."

"You're welcome to join us," I offer. It would be nice to get to know some of Samantha's friends.

She sighs as disappoint fills her face. "I'd love to, but I have a meeting across town in about an hour."

"Maybe next time," Samantha offers.

"Absolutely!" Lexi declares. "So, Enzo... are you enjoying your time on leave?"

I can't help but smile when I look at Samantha. "Yes. I've gotten to spend time with my family as well as get to know Samantha so far. As much as I don't want to go back to Germany, I can't wait until the next few months are over, so I can be back in Portland permanently."

Samantha's jaw drops, and I hear Lexi gasp. Neither of them says anything for a moment.

Lexi's the first to break the silence. "So, you've decided to retire, huh?" Obviously, she and Samantha talk, but I'm surprised she knows all the details.

"Yep. Twenty years is enough. I met with Riggs again this morning and they should email my new contract this afternoon." I'd planned to tell Samantha this bit of information during lunch, but I can't contain my excitement.

Finally, Samantha finds her voice, "That's amazing!" She throws herself in my arms and I hug her for all I'm worth. I'm so relieved this is her reaction.

When we pull apart, I explain, "After our run this morning, I had time to think about it more and it was an easy decision for me to make."

Lexi interrupts with a sly comment before I can continue. "You and Enzo went running this morning?" I can tell by the look on her face that she's jumped to the conclusion that I stayed the night.

Before she can get any more out, I set her straight. "Yes, I met her this morning at her house to run before taking her to breakfast."

At first, Lexi looks confused, but then she must remember Sam's kitchen is in shambles. "Oh, right. Her kitchen is a wreck."

"Yes," Samantha interjects. "And he even took the kids with us. The man seems to be a glutton for punishment."

I love her kids and I don't want her thinking otherwise. "Your kids are no punishment, Samantha. In fact, I think they're quite amazing."

"Thanks. I'm glad you think so," she responds with pride and my heart melts a little. I can't believe how much I enjoy her family. It's hard to believe I've fallen for all of them in such a short time.

"Well, I need to jet if I want to be on time." Lexi turns and surprises me with a hug. Lexi is a hugger apparently and her sheer strength takes me a bit off guard "I'll see you two later. Have fun this afternoon!" With that, she turns and walks to her office.

"So, you're really retiring?" Samantha asks when we're finally alone. Her eyes scrutinize me to gauge my reaction.

"Yep. I really am." I smile with delight at the thought of being able to spend more time with the beautiful woman beside me. "The timing's right, the offer was almost too good to pass up. Besides, I'm ready for a change."

"That's so amazing. I'm happy for you, Enzo." She leans in for a hug and I can't let her go without a kiss. I could kiss this woman for days on end and never tire of her. Of course, I remember we're at her place of business in the parking lot, so I don't let things get too carried away.

We decide on a little café a few miles away to have lunch. I've never been there before, but then again, I'm not picky. I eat anything. Samantha tells me about her day and I mention that at some point I'll need to log onto a computer and check my emails from Riggs. I usually use my phone for everything, but when reading fine-print documents, I'd rather do it on my laptop, which is at my parents' house.

"Why don't you just use the conference room at my office?" She casually suggests. "Lexi is out of the office for the rest of the afternoon. I don't have any client meetings, and no one will be using it."

"Are you sure? I don't want to bother you while you're working. I need to print everything out so I can sign them." I have no idea how much paperwork I'm going to receive. I'd rather read them on hard copy so I can make note of any changes I might want to suggest.

She sighs. "Enzo, I wouldn't have offered if I'd thought you'd bother me." She has a flicker of something I can't quite read spread across her face before she adds, "Besides, I don't have to be anywhere until I pick up Maddie from practice this evening. Maybe if we're really good and get our work done, we could skip out early." She waggles her eyebrows and I can't help but fall even more for her.

"A woman after my own heart," I say as a smile spreads across my face.

After lunch, we spend the next few hours back at her office. She shows me the conference room and sets me up in there while she retreats to her office. I'd be lying if the thought of following her to her office to have my way with her doesn't cross my mind once or a hundred times. But I manage to keep my focus. We both have a job to do. I am thirty-seven, for Christ sake. Get it together, man. Stop with the one-track mind already.

Once I'm buried deep in my contract, I curb my thoughts of Samantha to a certain degree. Riggs has everything laid out for me. I'm surprised by the benefits being offered. It's a larger pay grade and a lot more options as an employee. Don't get me wrong, I've enjoyed serving my time in the Air Force, but the private sector will absolutely have its advantages.

When I get to the section about benefactors, I involuntarily think of Samantha, which is ridiculous. We've only known each other a week. But if I have any say in it, we will know each other a lot more when I'm stateside. Instead, I put my usual response, my parents. Should anything happen, I can always change it later.

By the time I have read and filled out the last form, I realize I have been working for over two hours on this. I had to leave my official start date blank, but since I've already discussed this with Riggs, it shouldn't be a problem. I get up and stretch. I'm used to sitting in a cockpit for hours on end but staring at a stack of papers is different. I gather my things and place them in the envelope Samantha left for me. To make sure I don't leave them behind, I take them out to my car.

When I return, I realize that Brenda, their receptionist, is about to leave. She asks if I can tell Samantha she has to leave for her class this evening. Of course, I have no problem doing this. I notice that she locks the door upon her exit. She quickly explains this is their standard protocol so that customers won't enter after hours when it's just Samantha or Lexi in the building. I thank her and say goodbye.

I walk to Samantha's office and lean on the doorjamb. She doesn't notice me. I take a moment to just admire her. She has that delicious lip tucked under her teeth and is completely engaged in reading the stack of papers before her. A pencil plays in her hand and her hair is now in a messy topknot. This is her in her element, and she couldn't be sexier if she tried. I'm not sure how much longer I just stare at her, but eventually, I must move or make a noise, which draws her attention to my presence.

She finally looks up and pierces me with the most beautiful smile before saying, "You gonna just stand over there, handsome?"

I cock an eyebrow, not sure I heard her correctly. Damn, I love her lack of filter when it comes to me. From what I can tell, she never has the problem with anyone else, so it's flattering that I get her unfiltered side. Sometimes it's downright hysterical, the thoughts that come out of her head. The woman has a way of keeping me on my toes.

After just a few moments of staring at one another, I ask, "And just what are you going to do with me over there?"

Yep, as I suspected. She didn't intend for me to hear that because a warm blush creeps up her face. But I love how she suddenly steels her spine and owns it. "Well, get over here and you'll find out." Her eyes dance playfully.

I walk into her office and shut the door behind me. I stalk slowly over to her as if I'm a hunter and she's my prey. "I might not let you go once I get you," I warn playfully.

The look on her face is a cross between pure pleasure and complete mischief. I can't wait to see what she comes up with next. I love that I'm finding this woman is more adventurous than I could ever imagine. *How in the world did I get so lucky finding a woman like her?*

The minute I get to her, she stands to greet me. Her arms drape around my neck and I pull her in for a passionate kiss now that we're behind closed doors. What starts out as a slow burn quickly ignites into fiery flames.

"Did Brenda leave?" she pants out.

"Yes," kiss, "right before," kiss, "I came in here," kiss. My breathing is quickly becoming just as erratic as hers as I kiss my way down her neck.

"Good," she says, the word coming out as a moan as I get to the place between her shoulders and neck that I have quickly learned is a trigger spot for her.

The next thing I know, she's reaching for the buckle on my belt and popping the fly of my jeans. "What are you doing, beautiful?" I growl into her ear as my zipper retracts at a slow pace.

"Makin' my fantasy a reality." She grabs for the hem of my shirt. *What kind of gentleman would I be if I didn't help her?* Within seconds, I'm shirtless and my hard length is being pulled out to greet one of her hands while the other pushes me back toward her chair.

"Um... Samantha?" I ask, wanting her intentions known.

Between planting kisses down my chest, she pants out, "Sit down."

"Of course," I comply. I'm usually the one to take charge, but when Samantha takes control, it drives me wild. She manages to pull my pants down further as I sit while she kisses down my torso. The sensation she's stirring through me makes going Mach 3 feel like just a walk in the park. The minute her lips connect with my cock, it's all I can do to keep my hips planted in the seat and not take control. *Fuck, this woman will be the death of me.*

When I realize I'm almost to the point of no return, I pull her off me with a loud pop from her mouth that can be heard throughout the room. *There is no way I'm going to be the one to come first.* The look of disappointment is almost priceless on Samantha's face. But I have other things in mind. I push the papers she's working on to the side, hike up her skirt like I did this morning, and shred her underwear. Taking them off would just be too much time.

I reach into my jeans for a condom and suit up before she even has a chance to contemplate what is happening. I kiss her deeply as I reach my hand between her legs and feel that she is already drenched and ready for me. I swipe my fingers from her center to her clit and spend a few moments making sure she is just as ready as I am.

"Now, Enzo," comes out on a hitchy breath. "Please."

Wanting to give her what she needs, I reply with, "Sure thing, beautiful."

Within seconds, I line the head of my cock to her entrance. She arches her hips just as I push toward her, making me slide my entire length with one thrust. *OH. MY. FUCKING. GOD! This feels incredible.*

"Again!" she nearly screams. Her reaction alone has me wanting to come on the spot. Obviously, she loves that move as much as I do, so I try to match it again and again. Pulling out to the tip, then sliding back to the hilt in one fell swoop. My pelvic bone bumps her clit each time I'm fully seated within her. She writhes beneath me and I can feel her clench tighter and tighter with every thrust. When she spasms around me, I can't help but let loose. I pump into her with all my might and give myself entirely to her until we both reach our climax.

Holy fucking hell! That might have just been the best damn orgasm of my entire life. I'm entirely wrecked. As I steady myself, I realize I have lost all feeling in my toes and outer limbs. My breath is harsh, as if I just ran a five-mile sprint. I fucking love the way her entire body is clinging to me for life. It's as if her legs are now permanently locked around my waist and I'm the only one who will help her survive.

All too soon for my liking, her legs loosen their grip on my waist. Her body relaxes as she releases her hold on my shoulders and I feel her breath steady. She finally opens her beautiful mahogany eyes, which remain sexily hooded as she seeks out mine. For a long while, we simply stare at one another before she whispers, "That. Was incredible, Enzo. Life-altering. Holy shit, I don't think it'll ever be better than that."

I can't hide the grin that forms on my face. Because let's face it, I did that to her. I put that entirely blissed-out look on her face. And what she said was the fucking truth. That *was* incredible. *But to say it could never be better than that?* I don't even think when I throw down the challenge. "Don't be so sure. I'd sure love to try to top that, beautiful. We're just gettin' started."

The look on her face shows she completely agrees. Then that sexy sassy woman I'm growing to love appears, having heard my challenge. "Enzo... if it gets better than that, you just might break me."

"I doubt it. But it'd be fun trying, beautiful. It'd be fucking fantastic to try to top that." I bend down and kiss her once more. My cock makes his presence known, and she clenches me tight with a huge grin forming on her face. "Damn, you're beautiful, Samantha," I growl.

Knowing I need to take care of the condom, I pull out. As I remove the condom, I notice I'm wetter than usual. Maybe it's just from her arousal? But it feels too slick to just be from her. I tense as I make the realization. "Fuck, beautiful, the condom broke."

I pull out all the way and reach for the tissues on her desk to help clean up the mess. "I swear on my mother's life, I'm clean. You have nothing to worry about. I have ALWAYS, and I mean always used a condom," I say, hoping she knows how sincere I'm being. "Shit, I've never had anything happen like this before."

Samantha shudders. At first, I'm afraid she's crying or something, but when I finally look her in the eye, I realize she's shaking with laughter. *What the fuck?*

She takes a deep breath and continues to laugh. "It's okay, Enzo. Really. I'm clean, too. There's no need to worry so much. I was tested after Devin let his indiscretions be known and I haven't been with anyone else since. I get tested at each of my yearly visits. You have nothing to worry about either."

I bend down to kiss her, feeling the relief she isn't upset over this. But then another thought hits. "What about getting pregnant?"

She kisses me once again before she responds with, "Why don't we clean up and get dressed, then we can talk about it more? You shouldn't have anything to worry about."

We take the next few minutes to clean ourselves up with

the tissue she has on her desk. We right our clothes and I can't help but cringe and apologize for her lack of underwear.

She laughs it off, saying, "That's an amazing first for me. So is going commando for the rest of the afternoon."

Thank God, her sexy skirt goes past her knees. It's hard enough to control my erection, just knowing she's bare under that dress. But I do the best I can to control that urge. I'm only a man.

By the time we're both back to being presentable, she takes my hand and leads me to the couch across from her desk on the opposite wall. We both sit, and she keeps my hand in hers. She looks a little nervous, so I bend down and kiss her once more on the lips.

"Go ahead, beautiful. Tell me what's on your mind."

"Well, you asked about getting pregnant…" she starts but appears as if she doesn't know what to say.

"Are you on birth control?" I ask, trying to make things easier for her.

She shakes her beautiful brown hair and her rich mahogany eyes bore deeply into mine. "No, I'm not." She holds up a hand to stop me from saying more. "Let me explain why I don't think you should be worried."

"Okay," I slowly state. *Where's she going with this?*

"Well, the thing is, Devin and I tried for years to get pregnant after Frankie. Right up until I found out he was cheating on me, in fact." She shakes her head as if she's trying to rid herself of a terrible thought. Then she resumes with, "The point I'm trying to make is if I tried for over five years to get pregnant, I likely would have, don't you think?"

"I guess," I reply. I think I'm more concerned about the fact that she tried for five years to have another child, than the possibility of getting her pregnant now. *How devastating that must have been for her.*

"You see, with each of my other children, the moment we tried to have a child, I was pregnant within the first month or so. If I were going to get pregnant again, I think it would've happened." She takes in a deep breath, and now she looks as if she has the weight of the world on her shoulders. She looks away from my eyes, not wanting to see my reaction.

"Samantha," I say but she doesn't look in my direction. I reach out to put my hand under her chin to guide her eyes back to me. "Samantha, beautiful. I'm not worried. I'm sorry if I overreacted just then, but in the twenty plus years of using condoms, I've never had one break. I just didn't want to let you down. Or upset you."

Her deep mahogany eyes shine as a smile forms across her face. "I'm not upset."

"Are we good?" I ask, hoping she will release the stress that she has been holding onto.

She finally exhales, and I can visibly see her relax. "Yeah, we're good." She glances across the room and scares me when she yells, "Oh, shit!"

"What?" I grasp her shoulders to get her to look at me. "What's wrong?"

"I have to pick up Maddie in less than thirty minutes!" She runs her hands through her tousled hair and pats it down frantically. Then she takes it out of her topknot and goes through the process of brushing out her hair with her hands to position it again into another messy bun-like thing. This time it doesn't look as if she's just been thoroughly ravished, but still sexy as hell. Relief washes over me that the time is the only real concern she has. I can deal with that. She looks stunning with her afterglow from the best sex we've ever experienced.

"What can I do to help you?" I ask, wanting to be of some use to her.

"You must think I'm the shittiest of girlfriends. Leaving you behind after that out of this world experience." She suddenly stops and stares at me, as if she didn't want me to hear that comment. Panic covers her features.

"What's wrong?" I ask, suddenly concerned that she's becoming upset.

I barely hear it when she whispers, "I said girlfriend." She closes her eyes as if she doesn't want to see my response.

This woman is fucking adorable. I can't help it. I laugh. "Samantha, beautiful. Look at me." I wait a few seconds for her to comply. "You *are* my girlfriend in every sense of the word." I kiss her lightly on the lips, making her facial expression turn into a smile. "I'll admit I haven't had one in years. But I'm pretty sure that's what you are... that's if you want to be?"

Her nod is emphatic. "Yes. I want to."

"Okay then. You'd better get out of here if you're going to get Maddie on time. I want my *girlfriend*," I emphasize the word to make my point clear, "to drive safe and call me later this evening." I kiss her once more on the lips, then turn her in the direction of the door and swat her on the ass. "Go. You're going to be late."

She chuckles as she gathers the things on her desk and slips them into an envelope. She finds her purse in her desk drawer and is ready to head out the door within minutes. We walk hand in hand out her office door to the reception area. Since the door is already locked, all she does is set the alarm and walk out the door. I walk her to her SUV and kiss her once more.

"I really wish I didn't have to go," she pleads. "But Maddie's waiting. I have to meet her date for Friday and take her dress shopping." She kisses me once more. Then she whispers, "Apparently, I'm doing all this without any underwear." She smirks at me, then shakes her head and gets into her car. I swear I hear her say, "There's a first time for everything," before I shut the door and wave her off.

I can't help it. I burst into laughter. A deep belly laugh rolls through me as I watch her drive out of the parking lot. *This woman may be the death of me, but, man, I'm going to enjoy the ride.*

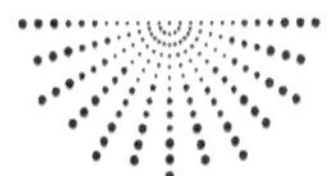

I CAN'T BELIEVE I'M GOING TO PICK UP MY DAUGHTER AND MEET her first date with no underwear. Really? Is this my life now? Not that I have a problem with it after the mind-blowing sex Enzo and I just had. How can I discreetly buy underwear without her knowing and slip them on?!?!?

When I think about how sexy it was when Enzo ripped them off me, I can't lie. I'd do it again in a New-York minute. He's every wild fantasy come true. Our chemistry is so combustible, I'm surprised I haven't burst into flames. It doesn't hurt that he's H-O-T either! Between his deep, gravelly voice, amazing good looks, and his huge heart, I don't think I could ever ask for more.

Though I'm glad we were alone at my office this afternoon, I don't think anyone could have stopped me from what I started with him, either. It was pure torture having to get my work done while he was just a wall away. I did eventually read through most of a manuscript before I noticed him standing at my door. Just thinking of the things we did in my office has me starting to clench all over again. That man is sexy, that's for sure.

I manage to maneuver my way down side streets to get to Maddie's school with time to spare. When I pull into the parking lot, I take out my phone to see if she's texted me. There's one notification, but it's not from her. Butterflies flip in my stomach just looking at the name that flashes on the screen.

Enzo: Hey, beautiful, your boyfriend is thinking about you.

A smile spreads across my face as I realize he's referring to me calling myself his girlfriend. Before I can respond, another text comes through from Enzo.

Enzo: Okay. That sounded much better in my head. I'm really not a loser. Please disregard that last text.
Me: I thought it was sweet.
Enzo: Aren't you driving?
Me: Just arrived at the school. Waiting for Maddie to get out of practice.
Enzo: So, my girlfriend is also a speed demon. Good to know.

The thought of him referring to me as his girlfriend sends butterflies to my heart. This man is more than I could ever ask for. But I can't let him get away with thinking I'm a speed demon.

Me: Just know good shortcuts. ;-)
Enzo: Good to know. Just arrived at my parents' a few minutes ago myself. I, too, may know a shortcut.

Another notification comes through but this time it's Maddie.

Maddie: I just got done with practice. Grabbing my things now. Want to meet me by the gym doors?
Me: See you in a few.

I return to my messages from Enzo. I love the way he makes me feel. I really wish I didn't have to wait until tomorrow to see him again. Since Devin usually takes the kids on Wednesdays, I'm looking forward to spending more time with Enzo then. *I just hope he doesn't have other plans.* I get out of the car and walk toward the gym as I type a new message to Enzo.

Me: Sorry, Maddie is ready for me. Do you have plans tomorrow evening?

Immediately, he responds, and I let out a breath I didn't know I was holding.

Enzo: Only if they involve you, beautiful.
Me: Sounds good. Gotta run. Meeting Mads. TTYL
Enzo: Call me when you make it home.
Me: Will do. <3

I love the fact he wants to know if I've made it home safely. It warms the corners of my heart to know he cares as much as he does. I can still feel occasional tremors passing through my body. I'm so looking forward to tomorrow night. I can only imagine what'll happen once we have an entire evening to ourselves again.

By the time I make it to the gym, Maddie is waiting on the steps with a boy who looks as if he could perform with a boyband. His curly brown hair is short on the back and sides, while longer on the top. It covers his face on one side. He's wearing athletic gear, in the sense; he has on fitted cuffed black sweats and a black hoodie over a white t-shirt. He's holding a large athletic bag with what must be his lacrosse gear. He's looking at Maddie with respect and admiration as she explains something to him. *Point one for him.*

When I reach the top of the steps near the door, Maddie greets me. "Hey, Mom. This is Soren." She points to Soren, then back to me. "This is my mom."

Soren looks me in the eye and holds out his hand. Impressed with this boy's manners, I shake it as he says, "Nice to meet you, Mrs. O'Reilly. Maddie's told me a lot about you." *Okay, the kid knows how to show respect. Another point in his favor.*

"Likewise," I reply. "So, what are your plans for Friday evening?" I ask, trying to remember all the things my parents asked my dates when I was Maddie's age. *Damn. Life really does bring things full circle. I've turned into my dreaded parents.*

Soren explains how he has had his license for over a year. If I'm okay with it, he'll pick Maddie up and they'll go to a local Italian restaurant. Then he'll take her to the dance and bring her straight home when it's over. He even makes a point to tell me he has an early lacrosse match the next day, so he won't be able to stay out too late. I must hand it to him. He seems like a decent kid.

"I'll even come over early enough for you to take pictures since this is a semi-formal dance. *Whatever that means.*" He smiles at his assessment.

"That sounds wonderful." I can't help but agree with his plan. "I will give you a heads up. Maddie's dad will be there to meet you as well when you pick her up since he couldn't be here this evening."

"Mom..." Maddie scolds, but Soren interrupts her.

"That won't be a problem, Mrs. O'Reilly. I have an older sister. I know how important it was for my parents to meet her dates as well." At first, I think he's pulling one over on me, but upon further inspection, I realize he seems genuine.

"So, what are you doing now?" Maddie asks Soren.

"Uh..." He looks from me to her before he answers. "I was actually going to head to the mall to pick out a new shirt for Friday." He seems a little nervous to admit he isn't prepared.

Maddie looks at me as if she's asking if she can invite him to come along. I nod in agreement. It will give me a chance to get to know him better. Though there will be fewer chances for me to slip away and purchase some underwear... *Geesh... the things I do for my kids.*

"We're heading to the mall now. Do you want to ride with us?" I offer.

"Are you sure?" he asks. "I don't want to impose. What about my car? It's parked here."

He looks to Maddie and me for confirmation.

"I can always drop you back here to get it, or you can drive yourself and meet us at the mall," I offer.

I see the hopeful look in Maddie's eyes, knowing she wants him to ride with us. Soren picks up on it, too. He suddenly says, "I guess I'll ride with you."

The ride to the mall is interesting to say the least. We all walk up to my car and Soren automatically goes to the back seat. Upon seeing that, Maddie walks around to the other side. *I guess I'm playing the role of chauffeur.*

As I drive, I learn a few more things about Soren. He's worked at a local restaurant as a busboy since he was fifteen, and now he's a waiter. He bought his own car and is hoping to get a scholarship to college with lacrosse. He's already talking with some coaches from universities across the country.

Since both Maddie and Soren just got out of practice, I offer to buy them both dinner in the food court. They both eagerly accept, and we head there first. We all decide to get Thai food and grab a spot to eat next to the restaurant. Our conversation flows, and I can tell Maddie really likes Soren, if the permanent smile stretched across her face is any indication. I'm impressed with him so far. He seems like a nice kid with a good head on his shoulders. He also has manners, which in this day and age is something to cherish.

When we finish eating, we make our way through the mall looking in every dress section. Maddie tries on a few, but she just keeps moving right along. She's a lot like me. She knows what she's looking for and seems to be on a mission.

Soren, bless his heart, is a champ. He doesn't look bored and takes interest in what choices Maddie makes. He even chats with me while we wait for her to come out to model some of her choices.

I soon learn he's a character, too. While we're waiting for Maddie to try on another dress, he picks up the ugliest dress I've ever seen. It's burnt orange with white polka-dots. It has huge ruffles on the arms, but the body of the dress itself looks as if it should be fitted. It's as if the 70s were on a bad acid trip and mated with the late 80s. It's a total retro-fail. He holds it up across his body and somehow manages a straight face when he asks, "Do you think this would look good on me? Maybe they have it in my size."

I lose it. I double over in laughter, tears are streaming down my face. Especially after he breaks his composure and does the same. Maddie comes out of the dressing room with a look of pure horror on her face when she sees what he's holding, and both Soren and I lose it again. Soren is a riot to shop with, I'll give him that.

Finally, after it feels as if we've scoured through every department store, leaving no dress unturned, Maddie finds the one she wants. It's stunning on her. The winner of our endless dress search is a royal blue short evening dress that has beaded lace over a sheer illusion bodice. It has a modest neckline, which her dad will approve of. There is plenty of coverage in all the right places, making it appropriate for her age as well. It has a gemstone band that breaks the dress apart, like a belt at her natural waist, and the skirt of the dress is multi-layered tulle and reaches the top of her knees. Maddie takes in our expressions and a smile spreads across her face. She does a little spin and the dress flares.

Soren speaks before I can, "Wow, Maddie. I think this is

the dress. You look beautiful!" The blush that creeps up her face and the knowing look in her eyes tells me she's flattered by his compliment.

"Yeah, honey. You look spectacular. This is the dress," I tell her.

I'm not sure I like the fact Soren is looking at my daughter the way Enzo looked at me last week in my new dress, but I can't fault him. This is *the* dress. It looks as if it were made for her and fits her perfectly. It's dressy but still fun and appropriate for her age.

"Why don't you change and we can check out the shoe department, then we will look for shirts with Soren." She nods and returns to the dressing room.

"Okay, Mom, but I'm getting flats. You can't pay me enough to wear the deathtraps you love to walk around in." Maddie snickers as her back disappears into the dressing room entirely, so I can't reply. I can't help but laugh. If she has her way, I'm sure she'll be wearing a pair of Chuck Taylors.

Soren has looked at shirts in each of the stores we've shopped, but I have my suspicions he's been waiting for her to pick out the color of her dress first. He mentioned at dinner he has a black suit, but just wanted a new shirt and tie for the dance. Maddie could have done a lot worse than Soren Silva as her first date. Just with my interactions with him tonight, I know she'll have a great time and I have little to worry about.

When we get to the shoe department, I shit you not, there is a pair of royal blue Chuck Taylors out front on display. Maddie's inner tomboy is still in there because her eyes dance with absolute joy as she screeches, "OH MY GOD! These would be perfect!" She looks to Soren and asks, "You wouldn't mind if I wore these, would you?"

Soren's smile is wide on his face. "Only if I get to have a pair, too. We can wear matching shoes for our photos. It'll be savage!"

Savage? What the fuck does that mean? I look to Maddie as she beams. "It will be total badass!" *Okay, I learn something new every day.*

A salesman comes over and gets them fitted for their matching shoes. *Who knew wearing matching shoes to a dance would be a popular thing to do?* But with the excitement and chatter that continues about how amazing this will be, it must be a thing to do.

Unlike Maddie, Soren doesn't take long picking out a shirt and tie. The department store we're currently in has a great men's section. He finds the perfect blue shirt that matches the color of Maddie's dress within moments, then tries it on to make sure it fits. Then he selects a silver and blue tie to match the shirt. Soon, with two pairs of Chuck Taylors in tow, we all make our way to the register and walk back to where my car is parked.

After dropping Soren off back at the school, Maddie and I head over to Devin's to pick up Dec and Frankie. It's later than I realize because when we pull into Devin's driveway, I glance at the clock and see that it's after eight thirty p.m. already. Maddie and I both go to the door to get them, but she rushes ahead of me and just lets herself in the door after telling me she needs to use the bathroom. I, on the other hand, wait at the doorway until Devin greets me and invites me in.

"Woah, Mads, what's the rush?" he hollers at her back as she climbs the stairs two at a time.

"Sorry, gotta pee, Dad!" she shouts in return.

We're both left shaking our heads. "Poor girl, she probably held it the entire time we were shopping," I suggest as an explanation.

"So, did you find a dress?"

I nod my head. "Yes. It's perfect. You'll even approve."

Devin sighs in relief. "That's good. So how was meeting this Soren guy? What did you think of him?"

"He's a pretty good kid. He seems like a hard worker with a good head on his shoulders," I honestly state. "Don't give him too hard of a time when you come over on Friday. He ended up going to the mall with us and I'm really impressed by him."

"I'm not making any promises." Devin laughs. "He's still a guy wanting to date my daughter."

"*Our* daughter... and I think you may actually like him," I counter.

"Hey, Sam?" Devin rubs a hand behind his neck, appearing as if he's going to give me disappointing news.

"Yes?" I prompt.

"Frankie went upstairs to read and fell asleep about a half hour ago. I didn't know how long you'd be and she was cranky this evening. Do you want to wake her or let her stay here? Dec's almost out, too."

Just then, Maddie comes back downstairs. "Where is everyone?" She looks around for her siblings.

"In bed, kiddo," Devin explains, then to me he adds, "I don't care either way, Sam. Maddie can stay, too. I can make breakfast and get them off to school."

I look to Maddie to see what she says. "That's great, Dad. I'll just grab my bag from the car so I can do my homework. Also, can I wash my practice gear tonight?"

"I guess that's settled," I say. "No sense in waking them. Do you still want to take them tomorrow night, too?"

"It isn't a problem. Besides, with your kitchen remodel, this will be easier for you. If you don't mind, they can stay until Friday with me. I'm going to leave for Seattle after I meet Maddie's date on Friday evening, and I like having the extra time with them."

"Okay." *This will certainly have its advantages for me and Enzo, too.* "Do you mind if I go kiss them goodnight, then I'll be on my way?" I know it won't be a problem, but I don't want to traipse through his house without asking first.

"Sure thing. You know the way." He gestures up the stairs to their bedrooms.

After going upstairs and kissing a sleeping Frankie goodnight, I knock lightly on Declan's room. He's awake and about ready for bed. I ask him about his day and tell him what his dad and I decided. He seems fine with it as well. I hug him once more before telling him I'll see him Friday after school, then I leave his room to say goodnight to Maddie downstairs.

As soon as I get out to my car, it dawns on me I'm going to be alone both tonight and tomorrow night. A tingling sensation spreads through my body, and I know just who to contact. I pull up his number and quickly type out a message.

Me: So... my kids are staying at their dad's for the next three nights. What will I do alone in that big house all to myself?!?!?! Hmmm...

Not even a minute goes by and I see an incoming message.

Enzo: Up for some company?
Me: I thought you'd never ask. I'm on my way home now.
Enzo: Be there in 30.
Me: I'm still not wearing any underwear.
Enzo: Make that 20.

ENZO

Waking up with Samantha in my arms is something I would love to get used to. The past three mornings have absolutely been the highlight of my week. Not only do I get to have my wicked way with her, but I'm getting to know her on a much deeper level. I can't imagine how I've missed out on this experience all this time. But no one else is the beautiful woman beside me, Samantha O'Reilly. She has everything to do with the way I'm feeling right now.

Spending our evenings together, sleeping in her bed, and waking up beside her has all been incredible. Samantha's even managed to make it to work on time each day, despite the fact I may be keeping her up late, as well as making it more difficult for her to get ready to go in the mornings. She's just so irresistible I can't help it, and she can't seem to keep her hands off me either.

We went to my parents' house for dinner again last night,

so I'm still spending time with my family while on leave, too. That was my original intent when I came to Portland. While Samantha's busy at work during the day, I make the most of my days by seeing other family members. Today, I'm going hiking with my brother Zane.

Zane is my younger brother, who recently turned thirty-five. He's an architect here in Portland and has done quite well for himself. He and his wife Ann live in a suburb, not too far from my parents. We used to be really close and I'm really looking forward to spending the day with him. When he called and said he had the day off, we immediately made plans to go hiking at Mount Tabor, an extinct volcano right in the middle of Portland. Our favorite trail is the Blue Trail Loop, which is by far the most challenging trail. The best part is the view from the top as you pass by the water reservoirs, which used to be Portland's main water supply, but now they're for aesthetic purposes only.

Wanting to spend as much time with Samantha as I could before her meeting this morning, I dropped her off after having breakfast at another local diner.

It's just before ten o'clock when I knock on Zane's door. I'm not surprised to find he's already in his workout gear. He greets me with a brotherly hug. There's plenty of back-slapping before we quickly release. "Good to see you, Zo," he says as he pulls away.

"You, too, Zane." I see him grab a bag by the door and head to the driveway.

"In a hurry?" I ask, wondering why we're leaving right away.

"Only to kick your ass, old man," he taunts.

I scoff at him. "I'd like to see you try. You spend your time these days behind a desk." *Yep. I went there. It's my duty to give him a hard time. It's what we do.*

Our thirty-minute car ride is filled with light conversation. He fills me in on how his kids are doing. He and Ann must stay busy raising three kids under the age of six. He tells me how thankful he is now that his oldest, Riley, is in first grade and no longer requires all-day childcare. Brandon, his four-year-old will be in pre-school full time this year and Zoey, his two-year-old, is still in daycare. I just about shit my pants when he tells me how much daycare is for a toddler. Holy crap. No wonder he's excited his kids will be in school.

The premise of the word "hike" is loose when it comes to my brother and me. I know we'll be running at top speeds up the trail in no time. We each get out of the car and stretch. He carries a light backpack that allows him to run and still carry water. Zane tells me the has water for me, should I need it.

Like I presumed, we have no time to talk during our run up the trail. At first, we jog next to one another, but when we get near other people, we're forced to run single file. Of course, Zane takes this opportunity to sprint ahead. I let him go, but keep close on his tail while we pass others to our right. When there is room for us to run side by side, I kick up my pace and pass him at the last minute before we take a sharp corner. I maneuver my way to the top with ease, with him lagging the entire way. *I may be almost thirty-eight, but I still take him every time.*

When we make it to the summit, I can't help but tease, "Who's the old man now?"

"Ha! You've still got it in you." He takes a moment to

unscrew a water bottle and take a long swig. "Glad to see you haven't gone soft yet, big brother."

Chugging my own bottle, I shrug my response as if to say, *'I've still got it.'* We find a bench to sit on and take in the view. Neither one of us says much while our heart rates return to normal.

Zane breaks the silence with, "So, you and Samantha..."

The smile that spreads across my face is involuntary. "Yep. Me and Samantha." Not sure where he's going with this line of thought.

"So, you're pretty serious?" Zane openly asks.

I nod my response. "Yeah, we are."

"She the reason you're retiring?" He takes another drink of water as he waits for my response.

"Not really. I've been wanting out for a while. I love the adventure, but I want to have a permanent address. When Riggs offered me the job, I just felt the timing was right. She's a huge benefit to choosing to stay in Portland, I'll give you that."

"She has kids, right? Have you met them?" He places his elbows on his knees and leans forward, keeping his water bottle in one hand.

"Yeah, I've met them. I went over for the Seahawks game on Monday. You should've seen their enthusiasm for the game. It was unreal. Samantha and the girls were screaming their heads off at the TV as if they were in the stadium itself. It was a riot to watch. Declan came in a while later and watched the end of the game. I think we hit it off okay. But it was Frankie who stole my heart that evening." I continue to tell him about how she insisted I read her a story and tuck her into bed.

Zane lets out a low whistle. "I never thought I'd see the day you'd be serious about anyone." He seems to think for a while, then adds, "Has there been anyone serious since Vanessa?"

I shake my head. "No one worth mentioning."

"So now that you're moving back to Portland, what are your plans? Are you going to get a place of your own, stay with Ma and Pops, or what?"

I take a deep breath, mulling over what he just said. I haven't even thought about any of this. I know I still have time, but it's something I should be thinking about sooner than later. I decide to just be honest when I answer Zane's question. "I have no idea, Zane. All of this is pretty new."

"Do you see yourself settling down with Samantha?" Zane raises an eyebrow waiting for my response.

Do I see myself settling down? Yes. No. I don't know. I'm going back to Germany in just over a month. The thought of even going away for the remaining months of my contract has me on edge. After the last three mornings, I know that's how I'd prefer the rest of my mornings to go. "Fuck, man, I don't even want to go back to Germany to finish my contract. I just want to get it over with, so I can come back and see where this goes."

"You don't know where it's going?" Zane asks a little shocked.

I might as well lay it all out for him. This is new for me, both in opening up about relationships as well as how I feel toward Samantha. "I know I absolutely adore her. She's smart, funny, adventurous, and always keeps me on my toes. I enjoy being with her." Zane gives me a look that insinuates I'm all about the sex. "Fuck, man, everything about her is incredible. But she means more to me than just inside the bedroom. I find I like being with her out and about, running errands, and just having lazy moments, too. Isn't it too soon to be feeling this way? I just met her a little over a week ago."

"When it's the right person, you know. It's as simple as that. I honestly knew within the first month or so that Ann would be the one."

"Didn't you date for a couple of years before you got married?"

"Yes, but that's only because we were still in college. We each wanted to start our careers before getting married. It's different for you though. You're at a different stage in life. And let's face it, you're not getting any younger." He holds up a hand and stops me from interrupting. "Hear me out. What I'm trying to say is perhaps you've already been with as many '*wrong*' women as you needed to be with to prove she's the right one for you. Sure, you need to juggle what's right with her kids and all, but I think you'll find a way to make it work. If it's meant to be, you'll make it happen. Why don't you just enjoy her company until you go back to Germany? If it's still going strong, you can decide from there."

"All I know is that I think about her all the time. Thoughts of her consume me when I'm not around her, and the thought of leaving makes me cringe. I don't even think I felt this way about Vanessa and we dated for years."

"That's the difference between your first love and your forever love," Zane points out.

"Forever love?" *What the fuck is he mentioning love for?*

Zane gives me a knowing look, then I think a flash of pity? *Why would he pity me?* "Enzo, if you're not already in love with this woman, you're at least halfway there."

I just stare at him dumbfounded. *Love. Hmmm... is it love that I'm feeling?*

"Dude, even I could see the way you were looking at her this week at dinner and Ann tells me I'm obtuse when it comes to noticing details. You act as if she has hung the stars and moon. You might not have noticed, but you even seemed to intrinsically know where she was, no matter if you're in the same room with her or not."

He must see an even more confused look on my face because he continues, "Okay. Answer me this. What's your first instinct when you think of her moving on without you, should you decide long distance isn't for you while you're in Germany?"

"I'd want to throat-punch any fucker who even thinks of touching her," comes out of my mouth before I have a chance to censor my thoughts. *Since when did I get so possessive?* I've always dated casually, and it's never bothered me before when someone was ready to move on. *Holy fuck. Maybe I'm already in love with her?*

Zane gives me a knowing look as if he knows I'm not telling him everything on my mind. "So... what aren't you telling me?" he finally says after I remain silent for a while longer.

I let out a deep breath and quietly say, "I think I'm already in love with her."

"No shit, Sherlock," Zane teases, but then his tone is serious. "So, what's holding you back?"

I shake my head. "Shit, I don't even know where to begin." Zane lets me mull it over in silence while he takes another long pull from his water bottle and enjoys the view before us.

When I think I finally get my head wrapped around the thousand stampeding thoughts charging through my mind, I break the silence once again by putting words to my swirling thoughts. "How have I fallen for her in such a short time? What the fuck is going to happen when I return to Germany? Will we survive it? Will I get another fuckin' 'Dear John' letter? What about her kids? How do I navigate a relationship with them? How do I…"

"Enzo, Stop," Zane encourages. "You're freaking out over things that don't have to be decided today. In fact, I think time will be your best friend in this situation. You can't rush things because you know you're going to have time apart. I think that's the best way to go about it with her kids as well. Let them get to know you while you get to know them. They already have a dad; you need to find your own relationship with them. Talk with Samantha. Tell her how you're feeling, then she won't be left in the dark either."

The mention of Samantha brings a smile on my face. *Fuck, I'm so lost to her. Just mentioning her name has my stomach doing Mach 3 maneuvers and I'm standing firmly on the ground. If I feel this strongly for her after just a week, how the hell am I going to get through the rest of my time in Germany?* "What about when…" I can't even bring myself to say anything about a 'Dear John' letter.

"Enzo, you're in a different place than you were with Vanessa," he states matter-of-factly. It's both a blessing and a curse at times that Zane knows me so well. *Today it's a blessing.* "Zo, you're not twenty-two anymore. It's not like you're going to be deployed for a year at a time or anything. You're only talking a few months tops. If Samantha's the woman I think she is, I don't think you'll have to worry about her straying."

I nod my head in agreement. After her ex cheated on her, it took her three years to even kiss another man. "You're right, man, she'd never cheat." I fill Zane in on the details pertaining to her and Devin's breakup, though I keep the intimate details to myself. *There are just some things I don't tell about my personal life. No matter who I'm talking to.* I give him the bare facts about Devin's cheating was so devastating to Samantha, and Zane comes to the same conclusion as me. *Samantha isn't a cheater.*

"Have her come to Germany for your birthday. Then you can break up the time being apart. It will also give you a chance to get to know her better when she doesn't have the responsibilities of having her kids," Zane suggests.

"That's a promising idea. I should look into flights to see if I can get her to come the week of my birthday. I actually still have a bit of leave I need to use or lose, so I can request some time off then, too." *How does he make this seem so simple?*

By getting my thoughts out with Zane, I feel much better about the situation. I've never been one to hash out my relationship troubles, but it feels good to put things into perspective. Besides, it also gets me thinking about a surprise I can give Samantha before I leave, should things continue to go in the direction they're heading.

Eventually, Zane and I make our way back down the trail to my car. We go out to lunch together after returning to his house to clean up first. He invites me to spend the rest of the afternoon hanging out at his place once we've picked up his kids early from daycare, so I can spend time with them, too. I shoot off a few texts to Samantha when I think I can get away with it and not be harassed too much for being distracted.

Me: How is your day going, beautiful?
Samantha: Good. I'm about to head out to pick up Frankie from school.

Before I can respond to her text, another one arrives.

Samantha: Would you be up to keeping me company while I wait up for
Maddie to come home from her date?
Me: I'd be honored. What time would you like me to come over?
Samantha: How about 7? No need to overwhelm the poor boy with two men to meet when he picks her up.

I wouldn't want to step on Devin's toes. I may not like the guy, but he's Maddie's father so I can't begrudge him for wanting to meet her date. I have no idea how I'd feel about a daughter of mine going on a first date. I also don't want to press my luck with Maddie.

Me: I'll be there at 7.
Samantha: I can't wait to see you. - XO
Me: Me, too. See you then.

To my surprise, an attachment comes through and the next thing I see is her beautiful face radiating through the screen. There's also a message attached to it.

Samantha: Here's something to make the time go by.

I wish it was seven o'clock already. This is sure to be a long afternoon. I decide to do something totally uncharacteristic of me. I reach my arm out and take a selfie. The smile she's put there is evident. I attach a message of my gratitude and send it to her.

24
SAMANTHA

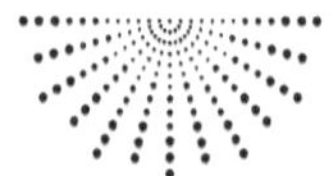

I RUSH HOME AFTER PICKING UP MADDIE FROM PRACTICE. Thankfully, they got out a little early today since the dance is tonight. I have Frankie with me and Devin is picking up Declan. I thought ahead and ordered take-out. Maddie seems a little nervous about going on her date; she is talking a mile a minute.

"Hey, Mom?" she asks from the passenger seat of my SUV.

"Yes?" I reply, knowing she's about to ask me for something.

"Do you think you could help me with my hair?"

"What do you have in mind?" Though I'm honored she's asked, I hope she doesn't want anything too intricate. I may not be able to pull it off.

"I was thinking about leaving the back of my hair down, but French-braiding a section across the front, like a crown and tucking it behind my hair on the other side. You know, like you used to do for me?" The last part comes out as a question. As if I wouldn't remember how to do that. Frankie asks for that style all the time.

"Sure, no problem," I tell her.

"I'm thinking I could leave the back down and curl it." She pulls her bottom lip under her top teeth before adding, "Do you think you can help me so it'll go faster?"

"Of course. You'll look beautiful."

"Thanks." She's quiet for a moment, then blurts out, "Mom, should I offer to pay for dinner?"

"I've picked up some cash you can have just in case, but I'm pretty sure Soren will pay for dinner. He's the one who asked you out, right?" I ask, wondering why she's suddenly bringing this up.

"Yes, he asked me. But what should I order?"

"Maddie, just be yourself, relax, and have fun. The restaurant he's taking you to is affordable. Pick something from the menu that you'll enjoy and have a wonderful time."

"My friends say to pick a salad, but do I have to?" She seems so worried, I feel for her. I remember being just as nervous on my first date.

I place an arm on her leg and pat it reassuringly. "Mads, no man, who is worth anything, will want to be with someone who only eats lettuce. Most guys truly just want to get to know the real you, not a version of who you *think* they would like. Anyone who doesn't like you for who you are is a fool."

"Are you just saying that because you're my mom?"

"No, I'm sure anyone would give that advice."

Frankie, who I thought was engrossed in the book she was reading, pipes in, "Ask Dad or Enzo what they think. They're guys. They've gone out with girls before. They'd know what Soren is thinking."

Catching both Maddie and me off guard by her profound response, we just gape at each other for a moment while at a red light. I know Devin would be Frankie's first choice to ask, but I'm surprised to hear Enzo's name added to this conversation.

Frankie takes in our expression and asks, "What? It's not like I can't hear everything you're saying? We *are* in the same car." The way she states it so matter-of-factly makes me laugh. *When did she become so grown up? She's supposed to be my baby.*

Maddie shakes her head at me. "Ut... Uh. No way am I asking Dad." Then she practically makes my jaw drop when she whispers, "Do you think you could ask Enzo, without it coming from me? He's taken you out on dates, right?"

I laugh. I can't help it. "Yes, we've gone on some dates. I'm sure I could call and ask him if you'd like." *Great, now I feel like I'm the teenager calling to get advice from a guy without telling him the reason why. What am I, fifteen? Nope. But I have a fourteen-year-old daughter who's looking as if she'd give her first born to have the answer. The things I do for my children.*

At the next light, I pull up Enzo's number on my phone. I'm connected through my car's speakers via Bluetooth, so I press send and whisper to myself, "Here goes nothing."

Enzo answers before the second ring. "Hey, beautiful, how's your day?" I can't help the blush that crosses my features. *This man has quite the effect on me.*

"Hey, Enzo, you're on speaker. I have a question for you and need your advice," I state calmly, not wanting to give Maddie away.

"Okkaaayy," he draws out, evident that he's wondering where I'm going with this.

"Hi, Enzo!" Frankie shouts out before I can reply.

"Hi, Frankie," he says back to her. "How was school today?"

"It was good," she replies.

I smile at their kind exchange before continuing, "Actually, there might be more than one question," I hedge when I realize how I'm about to word it.

"Shoot," his husky voice booms through the car.

"Okay, my first question to you is if you're going on a date, what do you think of a girl just ordering a salad?"

He chuckles, then replies, "I'd hate it!" His voice crackles through the speaker. "Unless it's a part of the meal as an appetizer, I find it annoying to go out with people who only order that. Who wants to sit and have someone watch you eat a full meal when they stopped at the appetizer?" He laughs a little at the end to show how ridiculous the thought is. "Besides, who can live off rabbit food alone? Unless it's filled with protein, that salad isn't going to fulfill its purpose of feeding you. Most women who only eat that are hungry and crabby later because they haven't eaten. No offense," he adds on the last part as almost an afterthought.

"Okay, thanks for the honesty. I have one more question for you. What kinds of things should a girl order while they're out on a date?"

"Um, whatever they're in the mood for?" I can hear the questions running through his mind, evident in his voice.

"I was thinking the same thing," I add. But then I want to answer Maddie's unasked question. "I was also thinking maybe not the most expensive thing on the menu, unless your date orders that, but not the cheapest thing either, right?"

"Sam, I would want my date to eat what she's hungry for. I don't want her to try to please me based on what she orders. I wouldn't have taken them to the restaurant if I couldn't afford it. As men, we research these things, if we're making the effort of taking someone out to dinner. Does that answer your question?"

I look to Maddie and she nods her head. The relief on her face is evident. "Yes, it does. Thank you, Enzo. I'd better get going. I'll see you later."

"Bye, Enzo," Frankie calls from the back of the car.

"Bye, sweetheart. You, too, beautiful. I'll be there at seven," Enzo's sexy voice draws out before disconnecting the call.

When I'm sure the call has ended, I ask Maddie, "So do you see that you should just be yourself and not worry so much? Honey, if Soren doesn't like you for who you are, he's not worth dating."

"Okay, Mom, I know. Thanks for doing that. Enzo seemed like he knew what he was talking about."

I don't even want to think about Enzo dating, but he did give good advice. "I'm sure he does, Honey."

Maddie's quiet for a while. Then she whispers, "Mom, what if he wants to kiss me?"

And... my heart falls out of my chest. Okay. I'm the mom. We've talked about this before, but now it could become a reality. I try to keep my features as calm as possible, though I'm feeling anything but calm. As much as I'm excited for her to experience this, she's still my baby.

I take a deep breath and blow it out slowly, not trying to

draw attention to myself before I attempt to casually say, "Sweetie, you just have to do what feels comfortable to you. If you want to kiss him at some point throughout the evening, that's up to you. Just remember, it's your decision and your body. Make good choices for yourself. Don't feel pressured to do anything you don't want to do. If he wants more than you're willing to give, he's not worth it."

"Thanks, Mom." She lets out a giggle before whispering, "I wonder what kissing him will be like?"

I decide her question is rhetorical, and not answer it. *Oh, God, this is so much harder than I ever thought.* Is this what my parents felt like? At least she feels comfortable enough to talk to me about it. I must be doing something right.

Devin and Declan arrive at the house a little before six. Declan runs up the stairs to put his things in his room while Devin joins Maddie, Frankie, and me in the living room. Soren told Maddie he would be here by six-fifteen, so we're all anxiously awaiting his arrival.

Maddie looks stunning tonight. With my help, it took hardly any time at all to get her hair done. I love the hint of the tomboy left inside her with the Chuck Taylors. The look on Devin's face is priceless. He doesn't say anything, but when he walked in and saw her standing there, he froze, eyes wide as he took in a deep breath to steady himself. Maddie had her back to him at first, so she didn't see. But when she turned around, she ran to hug him. Before she reached him, he slowly said, "Wow, Mads, you look beautiful."

"Thanks, Dad," she says as they hug tightly. She stands back and takes a spin to show him her entire look. Watching Devin's eye scrutinize everything is almost hysterical. As his eyes roam down her body to her toes, he seems to relax a little when he notices her shoes. He doesn't get a chance to say anything because the doorbell rings.

"I'll get it," Declan calls, heading down the stairs, almost to the door.

"Hey, man." Declan gives a fist bump to Soren as he steps through the door. "Mads is in the living room." He gestures for Soren to come in and join us.

Soren steps into the room. He looks handsome in his black suit. It looks as if it were made personally for him. The blue shirt and matching silver and blue tie he bought while shopping with us make his outfit. The matching blue Chuck Taylors are a unique feature, but when he comes to stand next to Maddie, they look like the perfect couple. In his hand is a wrist corsage with a white rose surrounded by blue carnations. The ribbon that's intricately placed around the flowers matches her dress perfectly.

"Wow, Maddie. You look great." Soren just stops and stares for a moment with a huge grin on his face, as if he has lost all train of thought. "Is this for me?" She points to the clear plastic box he's carrying.

"Yes, would you like me to help you put it on?" Soren asks as he opens the package. Within moments, he has it on her wrist and her face lights up from the kind gesture.

"I have a boutonniere for you as well." She turns toward me, looking for where it is.

"I'll get it," Frankie announces as she jets out of the living room to the garage where we kept it in the fridge.

Within seconds, Frankie bolts back into the room and hands it to Soren. "Here. This is for you." She shoves it at his chest and chuckles can be heard around the room as we take in the surprised look on his face.

"Be careful not to squish it," I warn as Maddie takes the boutonniere out of the box for him.

Soren is a saint as he patiently waits for Maddie to pin it on. She can't get it to sit straight on the black lapel of his jacket. Not wanting blood to be drawn, I volunteer to help her.

While I'm doing this, Devin continues his inquisition with Soren. He asks where they're going, who will be with them, what time they will be home. I can hear Maddie huff a few times, but overall, she's getting off easy considering this is her first date. When the basics are out of the way, he asks Soren which sports he plays and other 'get to know you' questions. Soren takes it all in stride and I can feel him relax as the questions continue.

When I'm done, Maddie walks over and stands next to Soren. She grabs her silver wristlet purse. It's tiny, but it holds her phone, lip gloss, and money. She looks at him and asks, "Do you mind taking pictures?"

"Not at all," Soren replies then looks to Devin and me. "Where would you like us?"

Maddie pulls out her phone and hands it to me. Soren hands his phone to Devin as he asks, "Would you mind taking a few pictures of us? My mom wants me to send her some."

"We should have invited them over," I state, feeling like a schmuck for being so thoughtless.

"It's okay," Soren states. "They're going out to dinner tonight with some friends."

We spend the next twenty minutes or so taking photos. I think Soren wins Devin over a little when he offers to take pictures of Maddie and her dad. Maddie asks to take a photo of her and me together, then Soren graciously steps into the photo as well. Frankie is eager to get her turn next to the happy couple while we force Declan into a couple photos. At least he manages a smile.

Enzo arrives just as we're finishing up. I thought it might be awkward, but oddly enough it isn't too bad. After the initial shock on Devin's face, he manages to school his features and is cordial. Frankie greets him with a hug, taking Enzo by surprise. Since we're trying to finish up the group poses, Enzo offers to take one of all of us, which is gracious of him.

The next thing I know, Maddie is off on her date. Devin says goodbye, reminding me he will be out of town until next Wednesday, so I'll have to get Declan to his practices. *Thank goodness for other team parents who are willing to help.* I tell him I'll manage and he's out the door. The delivery for our food arrives just as Devin leaves. *Whew! What a whirlwind.*

"Who's ready to eat?" I ask as Declan and Frankie settle in around the coffee table and eat the Chinese take-out I had ordered earlier. I didn't know what to order for Enzo, so I ordered a few extra of my favorites to make sure there is enough food for all of us.

Enzo comes up beside me and leans in to whisper in my ear, "Hey, beautiful, you doin' okay?" He plants a kiss on my cheek before pulling away, leaving a wake of tingles sprawling across my body.

I sigh. "Yeah, I'm fine. It's just a little surreal having her go out on her first date."

He raises his shoulders in a shrug. "I can only imagine. It all seemed to be going well when I got here. Did I miss anything?"

"Only Dad giving Soren the third degree," Declan chortles. "That poor guy must have been asked a hundred questions before he was able to leave."

"Watch it, buddy," I tease. "You'll be going on dates before you know it and you'll be the one in the hot seat."

"If that's what I'll have to go through, I think I'll pass," Declan says with a mouth full of fried rice.

"You might change your mind someday," Enzo adds to the conversation. "I know I used to feel the same as you, but I soon changed my tune. Besides…" Enzo sits down on the couch next to me as he dishes himself up some food. "When it's the right girl, you won't have any troubles answering those questions." Enzo winks at me and I sigh.

Then I turn to look at Declan. I can't help but laugh at the look he has on his face. It's a cross between being forced to eat a lemon and complete astonishment. "Yeah, Dec, you'll feel differently in a few years. Trust me."

"Whatever you say, Mom." He shakes his head and focuses his entire attention on his heaping plate of food.

While we eat, we each talk about our day. Declan seems interested in the hike Enzo took earlier with his brother. They even talk for some time about other places they would like to hike locally. It pleases me to no end to see them getting along. Frankie, being Frankie, tries to contribute and invites herself to join them. When Enzo asks if we would all like to go hiking this weekend, both kids light up like the Fourth of July. They beg me to go Sunday morning since Declan has soccer tomorrow. Of course, I say yes. *Like I'm going to turn down more time with Enzo anytime soon.*

As we finish with dinner, I ask Frankie if she has any homework. Knowing I'd rather her spend tonight working on it than Sunday, I encourage her to get it. She reluctantly admits she has some math and of course, reading. Enzo offers to help her, and she immediately changes her tune. I ask Declan if he has any work to do. To my surprise, Declan goes upstairs and grabs his bag and returns to do it in the living room with us. *Who are these people and what did they do with my children?* Maybe it has to do with the fact Enzo is here. Who knows, but I'm not going to complain.

It's almost eight when all homework for the weekend is complete. Frankie still has reading to do, but I know we will get that done over the weekend. She never lets me send her to bed without a story first, so I have no worries about it not getting done. All we have is a soccer game at nine tomorrow, and now apparently, hiking this weekend. *I'm so looking forward to a low-key weekend. Especially, if it involves Enzo.*

I'm learning many new things about Enzo tonight as well. I haven't missed his subtle closeness. From the casual brushing of his fingers across my skin, his patting my leg to make a point, or the way he brushes my loose hair from my face. All are signs he's thinking of me as much as I'm thinking about him.

My heart melts the way Frankie insists that Enzo sit between her and me on the couch when we settle in to watch a show before bed. Meanwhile, Declan stretches out on the other couch next to us. Enzo lifts his arm, resting it behind me, and I can't help it when I lean in a little closer and sniff the amazing scent that's all him. He puts his arm around me, then looks into my eyes to ask the silent question of, '*Are you okay with this?*' I don't say anything, but I lean in and put my head against his chest.

Declan has control of the remote. He's chosen something on the Disney Channel. It appears to be the kids of supervillains coming to live with the families of the heroes in fairy tales. All the major characters from the movies I've watched growing up now have kids and they're going to school together. It's a cute concept and I find myself being sucked into the plot. We're all sucked in because the next thing I know, the ending credits are rolling. Declan is almost asleep, and Frankie has conked out against Enzo's side.

"So, what did you think?" I ask Enzo as I stretch and ready myself to stand.

"It was surprisingly good. I don't think I've watched a Disney movie in its entirety for years."

"Mom, I'm going to head up to bed." Declan walks over and gives me a kiss goodnight. He may be getting older, but these are one of the few things I still cherish. "Night, Enzo."

He turns to walk out of the living room but stops. "Hey, Enzo?"

"Yeah, buddy?" Enzo responds.

"If you're not doing anything tomorrow morning, I'd love it if you came to my game."

Enzo turns to me with a brief look of awe crossing his features, but he quickly tamps it down. "Let me know the time and I'll be there."

"It's at nine. We'll leave here around eight." Declan looks to me. "You don't mind if he rides with us, do you?"

"Not at all, Dec. See you in the morning. Love you." I snuggle Enzo further after Declan leaves the room.

"What shall we do about her?" Enzo points to Frankie, who is now deadweight against his arm.

A light laugh escapes my lips. "I'll carry her upstairs." I get up to move, but Enzo stops me.

"No, I've got her. I just didn't know if you wanted to wake her," he says as he extracts himself from her. Within seconds, he has her scooped up in his arms and is carrying her up the stairs. Now that she's eight, it's a lot harder for me to carry her. He makes it look as if she's an infant.

"She sleeps like the dead. I'm afraid if we wake her, she might be up for hours," I tease as I follow him up the stairs. Once we reach her room, I pull back her blankets and he lays her down on the bed. I tuck her in and kiss her goodnight.

Once we leave Frankie's room, we walk down to Declan's. I notice the light is still on and the door is open. I knock lightly, and he tells us to come in.

"Hey, Dec, are you about ready for bed?" I ask him.

"Yeah. I'm just getting my gear ready for my game. Are we going to breakfast tomorrow? Or are we having cereal here?" he asks, knowing I had bought disposable dishes and silverware just for that reason.

"It depends on when you get up. If all else fails, I can get you a breakfast sandwich on the road to the game," I state as he zips up his bag of gear for tomorrow. "Want me to turn off the light?"

"Thanks, Mom. Love you."

"Love you, too," I say as I turn off the light and shut the door.

Enzo and I walk downstairs together. Once we're in the living room, he says, "Thanks for having me over. I had fun tonight."

I don't respond with words. I show him just how much tonight meant to me by kissing him for all I'm worth. The moment my lips touch his, the chemistry between us ignites fast and fiery. I can't control myself. *God, I've been waiting for this all night. I thought my kids would never go to bed. Being so close but so far away all evening has taken its toll on me.* I fist his hair in my hands and pull him closer to me. Instinctively, as he tightens his grip on my back, I wrap my legs around his waist and he walks toward the couch.

He lays me down on the couch and climbs up my body. "We can't do much, Samantha," he whispers, "But, God, how I want you."

"Me, too," comes out in a moan as I pull him closer to me so I can make contact with those delicious lips of his.

I'm not sure how long we kiss. Could be minutes or hours, but it isn't long enough. I have been craving Enzo since he walked in the door this evening. It took everything in my power to keep my desire for him to a minimum amount of PDA in front of my children. I'm a mom, but, God, when this man is around me, I want to be the randy teenager without a care in the world.

Suddenly, we're interrupted by my phone ringing. Enzo reluctantly pulls himself off me, but nuzzles me close, kissing my neck and collar line of my V-neck shirt. When I reach for my phone on the second ring, I realize it's Maddie. Panic replaces desire in an instant. Enzo pulls back when he sees me go rigid. "It's Maddie," I announce before answering the phone. Enzo is suddenly ramrod-straight on high alert. "Maddie? Are you okay?" I ask when I answer.

Through the phone, I hear, "Yeah, Mom, I'm okay. But there's been a bit of a problem."

I look at the time on my phone and the dance should have gotten over only a few minutes ago. "What kind of problem?" I ask hesitantly.

"Well, Soren and I were on our way home since the dance just ended. We got about halfway there and he got a flat tire."

"Are you guys safe?" I notice Enzo gather his jacket and pace the room.

"Yeah, we're pulled off into a parking lot. Soren's tried to change the tire, but his jack is missing. He's called for roadside assistance, but they told him it would be about three hours before anyone could get to us."

"I'll come and get you," I state. "Just tell me where you are."

I start to gather my things when Enzo interrupts my thoughts and our conversation, "Samantha?"

"Just a second, Maddie," I tell her to wait while I hear what he has to say.

"She has a flat tire?" he asks for clarification.

"Yeah, I'm going to get them. They don't have a jack and the roadside assistance will be a couple of hours."

Enzo looks at me pointedly. "I have no doubt you can get them home safely, but what about the kids asleep upstairs? I'd be more than happy to go. Besides, I have a jack in my rental and I can change the tire quicker than waiting for someone else."

"Are you sure? You don't have to," I hedge, not wanting him to feel obligated.

He gives me a '*Did you really just ask that*' look and I immediately see my answer.

To Maddie, I say, "Hey, honey, Enzo is here and he's going to get you."

"That's great, Mom. Soren's worried he won't make it home by his curfew and he can't get a hold of his parents. He also has an early game he needs to sleep for."

"Tell her to text me the address," Enzo states. "I'll be there as soon as I can."

I relay the message and Maddie and I get off the phone. A moment later, a text chimes on my phone. I immediately forward the address to Enzo.

"Thank you, Enzo. I appreciate it," I sigh and pull him in for a quick hug. *He really is a modern-day hero.*

"Not a hero, beautiful. Just someone who knows how to use a jack." He smiles, making that damn dimple pop and me at a loss for words.

2 5

ENZO

The ride to pick up Maddie is quick. I easily spot the black Jeep Soren had in the driveway at Samantha's house. The boy has a sweet ride, but I'll bet changing that tire is going to be a bitch. One of my buddies has one and it's one sick SOB to change. Oh, well. It can't be worse than a Humvee in hostile territory.

When I arrive, Soren and Maddie are safely locked inside the Jeep. I can see which tire is flat from across the parking lot. I angle my SUV so that my lights will assist in changing the tire. I put my vehicle in park and head to the back to get the jack out of the cargo space. By the time I approach the Jeep, Soren is out of the driver's side and Maddie hops out, too.

Soren shakes my hand as he greets me, "Thanks, man. I appreciate the help." He points to the back of his car. "I can't believe I didn't make sure there was a jack in here. I just assumed when I bought my Jeep a few months back, that it

270

had one with the spare. I guess I know what I will be buying tomorrow."

"Not a problem. I'm just glad I could help." Soren walks back to the driver's side and takes off his jacket. He comes around to the back passenger side to where the jack is and is about to crawl under to place the jack I brought.

As much as I'd like to let him show he can take care of things, I feel guilty for letting him get his suit potentially ruined. "Hey, Soren, wait up," I say as I step around to block him off.

He looks at me hesitantly. "What?"

"I'm sure you're perfectly capable of changing your own tire, but you've got a suit on. I don't want you to ruin it."

He looks a little hesitant. I can't say I blame him. Most men wouldn't sit back and let someone else do the dirty work for them. Then he looks down at his shirt and the wet pavement from the rain earlier this evening. "Are you sure?"

"Yeah. My mom would've killed me if I came home with my suit all muddy. You can assist me when you can but stay off the ground."

I look to Maddie, who is slightly shivering now that she's standing outside. Doesn't she have a coat? "Maddie, would you like to wait in my vehicle while we do this? I can start it for you so you can stay warm."

"Or you can wear my jacket if you'd like," Soren states as he opens the door to the passenger side and leans across to get it. *The guy's smooth, I'll give him that.*

"I'll take the jacket, thanks. I'll need to know how to change a tire when I get my license, so if you don't mind, I'll watch." *Strong and independent.* She sure is Samantha's daughter.

Before I place the jack, I loosen all the lug nuts. Then, I hand Soren the wrench to loosen the lug nuts on his spare tire, which is attached to the back of his Jeep. The tire is covered, so it shouldn't be too dirty once he gets that off. Within minutes, the spare is off the back of the Jeep. I have the jack securely placed, and the vehicle is lifted high enough to pull off the flattened tire. As I inspect it further, I see a piece of metal that is the culprit. I point it out to Soren so he can show the repair shop. "It looks like you ran over something."

"Yeah, it does." Soren runs his fingers over the two-inch piece impaled in the tire.

I switch tires with his spare. Thank God, it's full-sized because if he just had a donut, I would worry about him making it home. I'll still follow him, just to make sure there are no more problems. But at least I won't worry as much.

Soon, I finish and the tire is changed. I make a point of explaining each step as I complete it since Maddie's genuinely interested in learning how to do it on her own. When I finish, I notice Maddie is sheepishly rocking back and forth on her toes. Knowing this is her first date, I'm sure this isn't how she wanted it to end.

"Thanks again, sir, for your help. I'm going to call the car service and cancel it." Soren pulls out his phone and frustration fills his face. "Crap. It's later than I thought. I really do need to get home. I have to be at school by seven to get to our game on time." He then looks to Maddie with the utmost sincerity. "I've never skipped out on bringing my date home, but do you mind riding with him?" He gestures to me. "I'd rather you not ride in my Jeep until I can inspect the rest of the tires in the daylight. Can I make it up to you another time?" he asks hopefully.

"Of course, Soren," Maddie states, but continues to rock back and forth nervously as if she's unsure of what to do next. *And that's my cue to give them some privacy.*

"Why don't I wait for you in the car, Maddie. I'm going to move it so I'm parked legally. Take your time saying goodbye." I shake hands with Soren and state, "It was nice meeting you."

"You, too, sir. Thanks again for the help."

"No problem. Anytime," I state before walking to my vehicle.

Okay, so I *try* to give them some privacy. I really do. I move my SUV so that I'm no longer putting a spotlight on them with my headlights. I'm not facing them, but I can't help but see them both standing there awkwardly for a moment from my rearview mirror. I'll try to look away if anything should happen, but I want to make sure Maddie's all right. I know she's not my kid, but right now I feel responsible for her. I don't want that boy to take advantage of her. I didn't get any vibes that he would, but he's still a guy, not to be trusted with a young impressionable girl.

They seem to be talking about something important. The way she's looking at him shows me she's hanging on his every word. She nods her head yes. He says something, then she nods again with a huge smile on her face. The boy must finally feel like it's time to make a move. He places one hand on her hip and she takes a step closer to him. He brings the other to the nape of her neck and she steadies herself by placing her hands on his chest. He leans in and kisses her.

This is when I truly do look away. I'm not into voyeurism. I pull up my phone and text Samantha, letting her know I have changed the tire and will be following him home first to make sure he arrives safely. She thanks me again and I tell her it really isn't a problem. I'm happy to do this for her and Maddie.

I glance back at my mirror, thinking they might be done. They seem to have stopped for a moment but start once again. I've gotta hand it to him, Soren must have balls the size of Texas if he's giving her a kiss like that in front of me. I'm not her dad but being a good half foot taller than him, plus fifty pounds heavier, I'm not one to be messed with. I notice he tries to pull away and she kisses him once more. I can't blame the guy. If a woman kissed me like that, I wouldn't be wanting to stop any time soon either.

Finally, when I've looked in every direction I can but at them, I hear him holler, "Thanks again for a great night. Sorry, it had to end this way."

Maddie is almost at my door when she states, "No problem. You'll make it up to me." She laughs and slides into the seat next to me.

Maddie turns to me, cheeks flushed, eyes glimmering with emotion. "Thanks again for coming to help us. It's really nice of you."

"No problem at all. I'll be here any time you need me," I say as I pull out behind Soren and follow him home.

For the entire ride to Soren's house, Maddie appears lost in thought. She has a grin that says she's just been thoroughly kissed and her eyes are slightly glazed over. I can also tell what she's thinking by the fact she keeps running her fingers over her swollen lips. She seems to come out of this haze she's in when she waves to Soren before we pull away, but the rest of the way to Samantha's, she falls back into this trance.

When we're only a few blocks away, I decide I should ask, "Are you okay, Maddie?"

Her grin becomes wider, if that's even possible. "I've never been better."

"Just making sure," I add, not knowing what else to say.

She's quiet for some time, and then I hear her whisper, "So, this is what it feels like to have been kissed."

"Only when you're with the right person," comes out before I can even think to censor my thoughts.

"Are you going to tell my mom?" She looks a little hesitant.

"Not my story to tell, Maddie," I say honestly.

"You sure you won't tell her?"

"Did he hurt you? Or put you in harm's way? Did he take advantage of you?" I ask, trying to make a point.

"Not at all. It felt wonderful," she says dreamily.

"Well, then it's your business to tell your mom."

We pull into the driveway and get out of the car. I wait for her to walk around to the front of the vehicle so I can follow her in, but Maddie surprises me with a hug. "Thanks so much, Enzo. I appreciate your help tonight."

"You're welcome, Maddie."

We go inside and Samantha greets us. Maddie gushes about everything that happened, and we get a count-by-count replay of her evening. When she gets to the end, she can't hold it in any longer. "Guess what, Mom?" Samantha doesn't even get a chance to respond when she states, "He kissed me. Like, *really* kissed me, and it was wonderful." She lets out a big yawn. "I'm beat. I'm going to go to bed."

"Goodnight, honey. I'll see you in the morning." Samantha gives Maddie a huge hug, then kisses her on the forehead. "I love you."

"Love you, too, Mom," Maddie says.

Then she turns to me. "Thanks again, Enzo." She takes a few steps up the stairs then turns around. "Enzo?"

"Yes?" I ask, wondering what she's going to say.

"It's really late. Are you going to be able to drive safely?" The sincerity in her face pierces my heart.

"I'll be fine," I offer reassurance.

"We do have a guest room. I'm sure Mom would be fine if you use it." She turns and says nothing more.

Did she really just say that?!?!? I'd like nothing more than to stay over since our time is so limited, but we have been doing our best to stay respectful for the kids' sake. Hell, I don't even know what to say to that.

"She's right, you know. It's late. You said you'd be here in less than six hours. You might as well stay the night," Samantha says as she traces the collar of my button-down shirt and undoes the first button.

"Are you sure, Samantha? I don't want to give your kids the wrong impression of us."

"Maddie will set Declan and Frankie straight. Besides, the guest room is right next to mine. If they see you go in there and come out in the morning, it won't be a problem."

"Samantha," I growl. "Are you going to take advantage of me this evening?" I say with a hint of teasing among the seriousness of my gravelly voice.

"Only in the best way," she whispers to me as she places a

quick kiss on my lips. "Come on, let me show you where you will be sleeping."

Last night was amazing. Fuck, I honestly don't think it could get any better. When I think of every lick, suck, and kiss, I want to live it all over again. Jesus, I'm getting hard just thinking about it.

I'm at a friggin' soccer game. These aren't appropriate thoughts to have on the sidelines. But the beautiful woman standing beside me evokes something in me I can't get out of my head.

I wouldn't say we got much sleep last night, but what a night we had. She showed me to my room and had her wicked and glorious way with me. I can't even count the number of orgasms we shared. Trying to be quiet brought things to an entirely new level of intimacy. We eventually wore ourselves out and fell asleep. I had to wake her this morning at five to go back to her own bed since I didn't know when her kids start moving around the house. After the sensual wake-up call I gave her just before five, she stumbled back to her own room and got ready for the day. If the smile on her face every time she looks my way is any indication, I would say she's just as satisfied with our sleepover as I am.

By the time we get everyone up and ready, we're running late due to our extracurricular activities this morning. We rush through a drive-thru to order breakfast burritos at one of the kids' favorite 24-hour Mexican restaurants. Being a part of

Samantha and her family's routine this morning makes me realize I've been missing out on a lot. *God, how I loved waking up and being able to have my way with Samantha this morning. I'll gladly take the chaos of her family if it means getting to experience this.*

A whistle pulls me from my real-life fantasy into the present. FUUUCCKKK! I need to get a grip and get my mind off Samantha. Trying to get my head in the game, I watch Declan as he sprints down the field and takes control of the ball at the last moment before it goes out of bounds. He makes a swift bank to the left and shoots for the goal. The sound of everyone sucking in air as they hold their breath is audible around the sideline. The ball sails high into the air, misses the goalie's fingers by a fraction of an inch, and sinks into the goal in the top right corner of the net. The crowd suddenly goes wild. *Damn, that boy is good.*

The action on the field helps keep my focus on the game. Being a forward, Declan has several more attempts at scoring, but ends up with just two of the four scored this game. His team is ecstatic when they pull off a win. If I thought Samantha and her girls were avid Seahawks fans, that's nothing compared to their enthusiasm watching Declan play. Their pride shines throughout the entire game.

After the game, we all head back to Samantha's house. We pick up sandwiches on the way home for when we're hungry for lunch. Declan surprises me by asking if I'd like to go to a park and play frisbee golf when his sisters each beg Samantha to take them to the mall. The look on Samantha's face shows me she wasn't expecting this either, but I gladly accept. The next thing I know, I'm changed into workout gear and driving to the park.

Declan and I seem to be getting along well. We have a lot in common with us both being athletic and competitive. He's asked me about my time in the Air Force and seems genuinely impressed with the fact I'm a pilot. I tell him if it's okay with his mom, I'll take him out flying sometime. I don't have a plane of my own, but I know enough people that I can make that happen. Working with Riggs will certainly have some benefits, too.

Declan and I arrive at the park and start on the course with ease. Since it's late fall, not too many people are out and about this morning. We go through the course, laughing and joking the entire time, especially if a throw goes awry. Somehow, I manage to get one way off target. A huge gust of wind picks up just as I release, taking my disc about thirty-five yards off my course, nearly hitting a flock of geese roaming the grass. They scatter like crazy, making sounds of their displeasure known. Declan and I burst into laughter at the sight. *That didn't go as planned.*

It takes us a few holes to settle down, but then I notice Declan is unusually quiet suddenly. I figure I can let this go two ways, wait it out or ask him directly what's on his mind. Not being one to shy away, I decide to break the silence with, "What's on your mind, Declan?"

He stops and stares at me for a moment. I notice him straighten his spine like his mother does when she's about to confront something head on. This tells me something serious is on his mind, but it still shocks me when he blatantly asks, "So, what are your intentions with my mom?"

Nope. Didn't see that coming. "Well, I like her very much and we're dating." With eyes much older than a boy his age, he just stares at me as if that isn't a good enough answer.

"What do you want to know?" I ask, looking him directly in the eye. With the look he's returning, I feel like a teenager asking to date a man's daughter. But in a sense, this is like that. If he doesn't think I'm worthy, it will be a no-go with Samantha.

"You're still in the Air Force."

"Yes?" It comes out like a question because I'm not sure where he's heading with his statement.

"You're stationed in Germany. You go back soon, don't you?" He makes his questions sound like he's prompting me to say more. But for the life of me, I'm not following his line of thought.

"Yes," I say again. Still not sure what else he wants me to say.

He shakes his head in disgust. Then he strikes me through the heart. "So, are you just going to dump my mom when you leave?"

What. The. Fuck? I shake my head adamantly and quickly dispel his line of thought. "Not a chance!" *So, this is where he was going with this. Shit. I guess we haven't told him I'm retiring, have we?*

Now Declan seems confused. "What do you mean?"

I let out a low chuckle. "I guess you haven't been told," I say more to myself than him. "Yes, I'm going back. But only until the end of my service contract in February. Then I'm coming back to Portland to work for a private security firm. I'll be doing the same thing as I was in the Air Force, but in the private sector."

A huge relief washes over him. "Really?"

"Yeah, really."

"So, you're not just a fling for her?" Declan puts his hands in his pockets and rocks back and forth from his heels to his toes, no longer making eye contact.

Holy Shit! This is what he's thinking?!?!

"No!" I shout, then I get a little calmer with my explanation. "Your mom is special, Declan. She's the first woman in a very long time, if not ever, to make me feel the way I do. She's smart, funny, and beautiful. She's certainly not a fling and I'm not going to break up with her. I respect her a lot and I hope to continue to be with her when I'm stateside again."

"Are you going to marry her?" *If I thought I was shocked by his last question, I'm flabbergasted by this. Apparently, I'm unprepared for this conversation.*

Without a thought, I state, "It's a little early to know right now, but I'd be honored if it goes that way. You and your sisters are amazing, and I really care about your mom." *Holy shit. I just admitted to Samantha's son, I'd like to marry her. Did this just happen? Who knew this is what I was in store for when I said I'd play frisbee golf?*

"Okay." He turns toward the next target. "You ready for me to whip you at this?"

And just like that, we're back to frisbee golf. I would love to understand the inner workings of a ten-year-old mind. The kid keeps me on my toes, that's for sure.

The next morning, I arrive at Samantha's house a little after eight o'clock. When Samantha greets me at the door, I'm still stunned this gorgeous woman wants to spend time with me. I had the most amazing day with her and her family yesterday and it was a test of my will to drive home last night. I stayed late enough to have Frankie insist I read her a bedtime story, but since the other two kids were still up and watching a movie downstairs, I decided to make a respectable departure time. Man, did it suck sleeping alone.

"Good morning, beautiful," I draw out as I pull back from a passionate kiss. "How was your night?"

"Lonely." She pretends to pout.

I can't help but laugh at her put-out expression. "I'd have rather been here," I whisper in her ear as I continue to keep her embraced in my arms. Finally, after a few more moments of taking in her delicious scent and feeling her body against mine, I reluctantly pull back. This isn't the time to let things get out of control. "You guys ready to go hiking?"

She cringes slightly, making me wonder if something's wrong.

"What?" I ask, hoping it's nothing serious.

"Um, we kind of slept in. I woke up with just enough time to sprint through a shower and pull on clothes. I haven't gotten around to waking them yet."

"You didn't need to get dressed on my account," I whisper in her ear and I can feel her shiver.

"Well, Mr. Punctual, I didn't want to come downstairs looking like Medusa and scare you to death."

"I've seen you in the morning, beautiful. It's quite a sight to be seen. Nothing Medusa-ish about it." We step through the doorway and shut it behind us.

"Why don't I go upstairs and wake the kids? Then we can get going." She turns to walk back up the stairs.

"Or... if you're not in a hurry, we can just hang out and go when they wake. I'm in no rush and I'm sure we can think of something to occupy our time together," I tease, loving the way the subtle blush creeps over her body.

"I don't think that will be a problem." Samantha smiles, taking my hand and leading me to the living room.

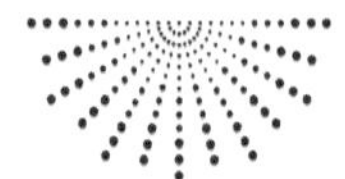

I LOVE MY KIDS. DON'T GET ME WRONG. BUT HAVING ENZO TO myself for an hour and a half is fantastic. We talk, we snuggle on the couch, and of course, enjoy some scorching kisses that send me upstairs to change my underwear before getting the kids ready for our hike.

Thank goodness, I had stocked up on snack foods. I was able to load a backpack for us to take hiking. We're heading up the Gorge on the Washington side to go to Beacon Rock. It's an easy hike with a beautiful view of the Gorge, Mt. Hood, and the Columbia River. We laugh and joke the entire way. Enzo drives my SUV because it has a DVD player in the back and Frankie is excited to watch a show.

When we arrive, we take our time getting to the top. We stop to take lots of selfies of us as a group along the way. *I can't help but feel like we're a family, although I don't want to get ahead of myself here.* At one point, someone offers to take our picture. After looking at it through my phone, I know this is one I will be framing. Enzo has his arm around me and the kids are standing in front of us. Everyone's genuinely smiling at something funny that Frankie just said. The kicker is that we all are looking at the camera at the same time, which is a miracle. Pictures like this never happen with multiple children.

As we reach the top, we get a call from Sara, Enzo's mother, inviting us to come for dinner this afternoon. When Enzo emphasizes the fact that my kids are with us, I hear her tell him 'the more the merrier.' I nod that it's okay, so we finish our hike and head over to his parents' house.

By the time we get there, his brother and sister's families have arrived, too. *Apparently, Sunday dinners are something they partake in each week. I should've figured this out by now. Silly me.* Thankfully, they welcome my kids and me with open arms. It doesn't take long before we're all sitting down to dinner. My kids are a lot older than Enzo's nieces and nephews, but everyone includes them the best they can.

Frankie and the rest of the grandkids that can eat on their own sit at a children's picnic table set up in a corner while Declan and Maddie join us at the table. As I look around the room, I realize it's filled with love, laughter, and lots of happiness. It gives me another glimpse of the life Enzo grew up in. Not that mine was much different, but we see each other less frequently now that everyone's older and has lives of their own.

"So... Pops, when do you think Samantha's remodel will be done?" Enzo's brother Zane asks after finishing a bite of food.

"Well," Lorenzo looks to me before turning to Zane, "I should be done with the cabinets, floor, and counters this week. All that we're waiting on is Samantha's appliances. Hopefully, they will arrive around the same time."

"When it's all done, I'll have you all over for dinner," I announce to the room. "It will be beautiful. I can't wait to show it off."

"We'll take you up on that," Sara says with a smile on her face. "Be warned though, this lot can get a little wild," she teases, making the room roar with laughter.

"I might even cook," Enzo adds. When jaws drop all around the table, including mine, I'm afraid, Enzo rebuts. "What? I can cook! You just wait. I'll prove it to you."

"I'll hold you to it," Sara teases.

The rest of the meal is filled with easy conversations and laughter. As we're about to leave, Sara reminds us that we're welcome to come next week as well. I mention that the kids will be with their dad, but I'll gladly be here. She also offers to have us over another night this week, with my kitchen in disarray, but once I tell her our weekly schedule with volleyball, soccer, and ballet, she understands completely why I must decline.

Later that night after Enzo leaves, my phone rings. He told me he would call when he got to his parents' place. Without looking, I automatically say, "Miss me already?"

"Uh... Hey, Sam. How's it going?" Devin's deep voice comes through the phone. Mortification creeps through me.

"Oh... Devin... hi," I reply, wondering why he's calling out of the blue. I haven't spoken with Devin on the phone in a while. His voice sounds so different compared to Enzo's. I remember a time when the voice on the other end of this phone meant everything me. *Boy, how times have changed.*

"Hey... ah... listen... I just found out I have to meet with a client in Denmark next week. They're going to pull their campaign if I don't go personally. Ugh... one of my employees really fucked things over and I need to smooth things out or it's going to be costly."

"Okay?" I draw out as a question. *What does this have to do with me?*

"Would you be willing to take the kids next weekend? I won't be back until Tuesday night..." He pauses like he's about to say more but doesn't.

"Sure. Just let me know when you get back into town and we can play Wednesday by ear." This is usually something we handle through texts. Why does he feel he needs to call me? He's so quiet, I wonder if he's still on the line. "Devin?"

"Yeah, Sam. I'm here... So..." he trails off again. He's usually quick and to the point. He sounds tired, but there's something else on his mind.

"So..." I prompt.

"So, the kids say things are getting serious with you and this Enzo guy."

Hmmm... Interesting. "Yep. I'd say they are." *Not that it's any business of yours.*

"But he's going back to Germany," he says as a statement, not a question.

"Yes, he's going back. He *is* in the Air Force and has obligations," comes out a bit snarky at the end.

"I know, but..." He trails off again.

Geesh, get to the point already. "But what?" comes out sharper than I intend. Before he can say anything, I remind him, "Devin, this really isn't any of your business. I've watched you move on and have said nothing. Not a word. Not a snarky remark. Nothing. What is it you have to say?"

"Aren't you afraid you're going to get hurt? Getting so close to him then having him leave. How is that good for you... or the kids? I'm okay with you making your choices, but I'm worried about the kids. They're getting pretty attached to him. Well, at least, Frankie is. He's all she talks about when she comes over."

I see, he's worried more about Frankie at this point. Okay. I get it. Taking a deep breath, I slowly release it before responding. "Once again, not that it's any of your business, but he's only going to be in Germany a few months. Then his plan is to return to Portland *permanently*." I stress the last word to make my point. Hopefully, he gets it.

"So, this is really serious." He seems more confident now.

"Yeah, I'd say it is," I sigh, and thoughts of Enzo flood my mind.

"Are you happy?" Devin asks, sounding sincere. *This is the Devin I remember.*

A smile forms on my face when I realize just how happy I am. "Yeah, Devin, I am. He totally caught me by surprise, but I don't expect him to go away anytime soon."

"Okay." He remains quiet for a moment before adding, "Samantha, I'm happy for you." Devin takes a deep breath and continues before I can say anything else. "Look, I know I've said it before, but I'm sorry for all the shit I've put you through. I never knew what it was like to be on the other side in this situation, until I saw him with you. I have to say it kind of sucks." He chuckles at the end. "But you seem happy and that's what matters here."

"I am," I almost whisper, still reeling from his revelation. But somehow, I find my voice again, "I know it's new, but he and I are going to see where this goes. I'm not going to do anything to jeopardize the kids. You'll just have to trust me, okay?"

"I do, Sam. You're a great mom. I just didn't know he was coming back. I don't want the kids, well, Frankie getting her mind set on him being around when there is a time limit, that's all." *Is he really saying this?*

"Well, I can't predict the future, but I don't see him leaving anytime soon, Devin. There's no need to worry."

"Okay, Sam. I'll leave you to your night."

As I hang up the phone, I can't help but do a little fist pump. I'm proud of myself for completely holding my own and not letting him interfere with my business. I finally told him my thoughts on his dating, too. Go me. I could care less what he thinks about Enzo and me, but I'm glad he cares enough about our kids to confront me about it. I know I'd want to do the same if I were in his shoes.

The phone rings again. This time I check the caller ID, and the smile that spreads across my face is infectious as I greet him. When I hear "Hey, beautiful," my heart melts even more.

It's been three weeks since dinner with Enzo's parents and my conversation with Devin. Enzo and I have somehow managed to see one another every day. When the kids are at Devin's, he stays the entire time with me. *Which is magnificent, by the way. I don't think I will ever tire of him.* When they're home with me, we still spend time together, but with much more focus on my family and, unfortunately, he goes home at night to his parents.

He's been a godsend to my family. Devin had to be out of town a couple of times and Enzo stepped in to help with carpool since I haven't figured out how to be in two places at once yet. Enzo tries to be at every soccer game or volleyball match that he's invited to. My kids seem to get along with him, which is a huge relief to me. I can't imagine how these past few weeks would have gone if they'd hated him.

Knowing he's leaving within the week, we're trying to squeeze as much time together as possible. Today, he told me to wear the green dress he bought me on our first date. He won't tell me where we're going, but he said to make sure I bring a coat since it's the middle of October and fall is in full swing. Living in the Pacific Northwest is unpredictable this time of year.

He showers in the guest bathroom while I put on the finishing touches to my outfit. We both know we would never leave my house if he was in here "helping" me get ready. *We've learned that lesson.* I'm thankful I'm my own boss because I've been late to work plenty of times in the past three weeks. The man is insatiable and turns me on like no other.

Once I'm ready, I meet Enzo downstairs in my beautifully remodeled kitchen. I can't be prouder of what Lorenzo Harper and his team did in here. We still haven't had the chance to have everyone over, due to crazy schedules, but Enzo assures them I will once he returns from Germany.

Enzo looks stunning in his suit. I'm breathless as I take him in. I honestly think he looks even better than the last time I saw him this dressed up. It might have something to do with the fact my feelings have exploded for him since then as well.

"God, you look beautiful," Enzo murmurs as he pulls me in for a kiss.

"So do you, handsome," I reply.

"Are you ready?" he asks with a gleam of excitement shining in his glorious green eyes. My stomach still flips and flops when I see that dimple pop.

He leads me to his rental SUV and we're on our way. I'm surprised when we don't go downtown, but to an industrial area. There's nothing but brick buildings around us, and I can't for the life of me think of where we might be going, especially dressed up the way we are. He's unusually quiet on our ride, making my senses heighten.

He pulls up to a high, chain-link fence with razor wire spiraling on the top and it opens without any indication of him doing something to move it. I quizzically look in his direction, but he just smirks a knowing look, telling me to be patient. *He should know by now I'm not a patient person. I'm a planner; I like to know what's happening. He's taking me out to Timbuktu, for all I know.*

"Not Timbuktu, Samantha. I'll keep you stateside for tonight." He chuckles at my remark. *Damn, my lack of filter around him.*

Once we drive around the building, I see a small plane with a private airfield behind it. I raise an eyebrow and ask, "Going somewhere?"

"Yep."

That's all I get. One word. He's grinning like the Cheshire cat, but nothing comes out of his mouth.

He parks his SUV and I notice a man standing outside the plane with a clipboard in his hand.

Enzo gets out and rounds to my door. He assists me in getting out and walks me over to the plane to where he holds out his hand to shake. "Good to see you, Boone. Thanks so much for helping me set this up."

"No problem, Harps. Glad to help." Harps. *Okay, so this has something to do with the military or with his new security team. At least I have some idea now. Sort of.*

"Boone, this is Samantha O'Reilly. Samantha, this is Nathan Boone. He works for Riggs." *Yep, I at least guessed part of this.*

I hold out my hand to shake. "Nice to meet you."

"Likewise," Boone says, smiling at me kindly before turning to Enzo. "Harps, I've pre-checked the plane myself. I have your flight logged and you're ready for takeoff. Need anything else?"

"Nope, that about covers it. Thanks again for all your help. I'll see you in a few months, if you're not here when we return."

With that, Boone leaves and Enzo walks me over to where a plane is waiting for us. I've flown on plenty of planes, but nothing small and private like this. "So, I guess we're flying the rest of the way?" I tease.

"Yep." There's that word again and that's all I get.

He assists me into the plane. Apparently, I'm sitting in the co-pilot seat. *God help us if Enzo needs any assistance.* There's a small cabin where I could have been comfortably seated, but all I get from Enzo is, "I want you to have the best view."

He goes through the process of checking the instruments

on the monstrosity of a board in front and around us. He puts on a headset and talks with someone in aeronautical gibberish I don't understand. But when the plane moves, I take it he's said the right things. We taxi down the runway, and soon, we're high in the sky above the beautiful city of Portland. I can't believe the view from the cockpit.

"Wow! This is incredible," I whisper as I take in all I see. I can see all the mountains in our vicinity: Mt. Hood, Adams, St. Helens, Rainier, and Jefferson. Sure, I've seen them from the small window of a plane, but this view is phenomenal. We turn south once we get to the elevation and I give a look to Enzo asking, "Where are we going?"

"Have patience, beautiful." He fiddles with a control then continues, "I have a weekend planned for us."

"What?" I exclaim, yet question at the same time. "What do you mean a weekend?" Suddenly, I'm beyond excited. I can't believe Enzo planned all of this.

"Well, since Devin has the kids, I packed us a bag of clothes. We'll be back tomorrow evening. Don't worry, I spoke with him about our plans and he knows you're out of town until tomorrow evening."

"So, Devin knows where I'm going, but I don't have a clue?" I pretend to pout.

"Relax, Samantha. You'll know soon enough. It's only a two-hour flight."

Where the hell will we be in two hours? I rack my brain and try to think of flights I've taken.

I must pull my lower lip between my teeth because Enzo suddenly growls, "Samantha, if you don't remove that lip, I can't promise what I'll do to you when we land."

As tempting as that sounds, I decide to play along. "Okay… Okay. Calm down, Rockstar. I was just thinking about where we could be in two hours."

The flight to wherever we're going seems to go by fast. Enzo and I talk about many things. Eventually, there is a lull in the conversation as I take in the forests below us. I can see the ocean in the distance and I can't for the life of me figure out where we're going.

Enzo breaks the silence with, "So what do you think of flying?"

"It's pretty impressive. I'll never forget this experience, that's for sure."

"What do you think of longer flights?" I look at him, wondering where he's going with this.

"They're okay. But nothing will top this. Thank you for planning this trip, to god only knows where you're taking me." I can't help but add that last bit on. I still haven't figured out where the heck our destination is, and it's driving me crazy.

"You're welcome," he says, glancing at me with a smile. "What do you think about hanging out with me for my birthday?"

"Isn't your birthday December sixth?" I ask, thinking about the fact he will be in Germany at that time. The thought alone makes me a little sad.

"Yeah, it is. But I have big plans for my birthday."

"What do you mean?" I'm confused, and my interest is piqued. He has plans, but he wants me to hang out with him? How will that be possible?

"I want you to visit me in Germany. I still have some

vacation time left, so I'll be off for a long weekend. I'd love to have you come visit me."

Me, go to Germany? Not only would I get to spend more time with Enzo, but I'd get to go on an incredible vacation. This is a huge step in seeing where things will go between us. But uninterrupted time with Enzo? Only a crazy person would turn that down. "I'll have to look into tickets," I say, thinking I might be able to afford them by using my air miles or something.

"Well, what would you say if I already bought the tickets?" He waggles an eyebrow in my direction.

"Are you serious?" I ask, my excitement filling the cockpit.

"Yep. I'd love for you to visit. I've gotten used to seeing you every day and it's going to be hell being apart from you. My birthday is right about the midpoint for my time left in the Air Force. If you come to Germany, we won't have to be apart from each other much longer than a month before and after."

"How long will I be there?" I ask excitedly, but also to know so I can make arrangements for the kids.

"About ten days. With it being a long flight, I want you to enjoy our time together and not be exhausted from travel."

Wow! Ten days without my kids? Sure, I'll miss the heck out of them, but ten days of uninterrupted time with Enzo sounds incredible. There's no way I can pass this up. "I'm sure I can arrange something for the kids. Devin goes out of town frequently, so we swap our time with the kids when necessary. My parents could even come into town if I need them."

"Lexi said she would help out with them as well," Enzo casually mentions.

"You've told Lexi?" *What else does this man have planned?*

"Yes. I wanted to make sure you could take the time off.

She helped me plan this weekend as well." He shrugs as if it's no big deal.

"I'm going to kill her," I mumble. She has some major explaining to do when I get home.

"Are you mad?" he asks with genuine concern.

I shake my head. "No, I'm just frustrated she's been keeping secrets and I'm the last to know. We don't usually keep secrets, but I can't wait to see Germany." I look at Enzo and smile. I feel so fortunate that he took the time to plan all of this for me.

"I can't wait to show you, beautiful. Besides, I don't think I can go months without seeing you. I can't come here in that time, so I figured you can travel."

We settle into an easy silence, but my mind is anything but quiet. It keeps racing back and forth between all the surprises he has in store for me. I can't believe he and Lexi pulled this off. I'm beyond ecstatic! Lexi and I talked about Enzo going away. She knew my worries about him going away for so long and forgetting about me. Not that he'd forget, but from my experience, distance makes dicks wander. Enzo's a man. He has a dick… I don't think he'd cheat on me, but we haven't been dating for very long. He could meet someone else.

"What's on your mind, Samantha? You're about to chew through that delicious lip of yours. Spill it."

Where do I begin? "Well…" I let out a sigh. I might as well lay it all out on the table for him. "I'm so excited to be going on this trip. I was kind of afraid you'd go back to Germany and forget about me."

"Are you serious, Samantha?" Enzo asks in a shocked tone. "I don't think I'll ever have you far from my mind. I love you, and it's going to be pure hell being away from you for any amount of time, let alone for a couple of months on the other side of the world."

I'm not sure he realizes what he just said, but all I can focus on is the fact he said he loves me. *He loves me!* "You love me?" I ask him, my heart about to jump out of my chest.

Enzo looks over at me, and sincerity is clear in his eyes. "Hell yes, I love you, Samantha. I have for some time now. I hate the fact I must go away from you. I've grown to love both you and your kids in the time I've been home." He stops and shakes his head with a light laugh escaping. "I honestly don't think I've loved anyone more." He reaches out and takes my hand, giving it a hard squeeze for reassurance. *It's amazing how just a single touch from him can center me.*

"I love you, too, Enzo. I was afraid you'd find someone else once you got back to Germany."

"Samantha Elizabeth O'Reilly. You get one thing straight in that beautiful mind of yours. I. Will. Not. Cheat. *Ever*! I've been on the other side of that act and I'd never put anyone through that pain."

"Okay," I say quietly. "I believe you."

"I don't think I've told you about Vanessa, my ex. Well, at least not to the full extent. We were high school sweethearts. We started dating at the end of our junior year and it lasted until I was in the Air Force. We were young and in love, or at least I thought we were. I'd known for a while my plan was to go into the Air Force. She told me she was completely on board with it. I went through BASIC and was stationed at McChord Air Force Base near Tacoma, WA. We got a place together and lived off base in a small apartment. Within a year or so, I was ready to propose, but I got deployed overseas. She was going to school and wanted to get her degree before we got married, so we decided to wait until I got back." Enzo stops for a moment and seems to gather his thoughts. I don't want to interrupt, so I wait in silence.

"About three months into my year-long deployment, I got an infamous 'Dear John' letter. To say I was devastated would be an understatement. She told me she didn't think she loved me because she'd met someone else. He was in one of her classes and he was there for her in ways I wasn't."

"Oh my God. That's awful," I whisper and place my hand on his lap to give him reassurance.

"Right then and there, I vowed as long as I'm in the Air Force, I'd never be serious with anyone. I'd never commit to anything long-term because I just wasn't cut out for it."

"What changed?" *I need to ask, but do I want to know the answer?*

"You," he simply states. "I walked into your home, fell into your heart, and don't ever want to let you go." My heart skips a beat at his sweet confession. "I'm older now. I know not everyone cheats. I'm sure you understand. You waited three years to kiss anyone after your husband cheated on you. I highly doubt you're the type of person to cheat either."

He's right. I'd never cheat on anyone. "You're right. I won't. What Devin did, shattered me. It wasn't even just once. He cheated on me multiple times before we finally called it quits. I'd never do that to anyone."

"I'm sorry you had to go through that, Samantha. He was a fool. But..." He leaves off, making me wonder what he's about to say.

"But what?"

"But if he hadn't done that to you, I wouldn't be with you now. So, things do have a way of working themselves out, don't they?" The smile on his face is wide and I can see the love he has for me pouring through.

"They sure do, Enzo. They sure do."

"I love you, Samantha." Enzo's deep voice sends shivers up my spine.

"I love you, too," I tell him with my entire being.

Suddenly, I'm distracted by the sight below me. I notice we're approaching a larger city in the distance. Before long, I see the Golden Gate Bridge. "We're in San Francisco?" I say gleefully.

"Yep. We're going to lunch by the Fisherman's Warf and spending the day sightseeing."

"Wow, you are a rock star. This is an incredible trip you've planned."

Enzo is suddenly busy radioing the tower to land properly. All I can do is look out the window in awe. I can't help to steal another glance at the sexy man who's completely in his element for the moment. As he radios back and forth and adjusts the gadgets in front of us to make a smooth landing, I'm even more in awe of him. I can't wait to show him my gratitude for everything.

From the small airfield, we take an Uber to the Fisherman's Wharf. We walk along shops and go to a fantastic seafood restaurant. Then we take a trolley car up and down the expansive hills of San Francisco. I've been to the airport before, but I've never explored the city. Being with Enzo just makes it that much better.

I should be tired when we reach the hotel. But I only have one thing on my mind when we step behind those doors. I want to show him my deep appreciation for everything he has done for me. He's carrying a small overnight bag with him, which I hope has a change of clothes for me. If not, I really don't want to wear anything for the remainder of our trip anyway.

I immediately strip out of my clothes the minute I hear the door click closed. I kick off my shoes, unzip my dress, and turn to face the gorgeous man beside me.

"In a hurry?" He laughs, his eyes roaming up and down my body.

I nod as the dress slips to my ankles and I step out of it. I'm only wearing a lacy green underwear and bra set I bought to match the magnificent dress Enzo bought me. Enzo's eyes darken to a deep green as they take in what I'm wearing. He's already removed his jacket and is unbuttoning his shirt, but I stop him. I want that glorious task. I close the distance between us, reaching my hands to his chest.

I slowly make my way down his shirt, placing a kiss under each button I open. I enjoy the flex of each muscle as his scent envelops me and slight moans escape his lips. When I finally reach the last button, I push the shirt off his broad shoulders, running my tongue along his collarbone as I trace my hands over his strong shoulders and sculpted arms. I can't help but stare at his chest, filled with the perfect combination of tattoos and muscle, making him the sexiest man I've ever seen. I don't think I'll ever get over how much he turns me on. My body is on fire as my need takes over.

He kicks out of his shoes as I reach for his belt, undoing it so I can get to the fly of his trousers. I can see his cock vying for my attention, but I ignore it for a moment as I slide his pants and underwear over his thick-muscled thighs to the floor in one motion. I quickly make work of his socks. I want to see this man in all his glory.

Finally, the only thing Enzo is wearing is the sexy smile, which makes his dimple pop. *God, I could stare at him all day.*

"I hope you do more than stare, beautiful." His sexy voice makes my panties want to spontaneously combust.

"Oh, I'm sure I'll think of something to do," I tease, my voice sounding gravelly. I lead him to an oversized chair next to us and force him to sit down.

Feeling sexier than ever, I slowly dance in front of Enzo. Though his thick, beautiful cock bobs for my attention, I focus on his green eyes, turning darker with need, as I do a strip tease, removing my bra. I sway to a rhythm in my head and soon my panties are on the floor as well. I dance for a while longer until Enzo shows he can't take it anymore and gives me a firm warning, "Samantha." His voice is barely controlled, and with his hands bunched into fists, resting on the arms of the chair, I can tell he's doing all he can to keep himself from reaching out to me. *I love that I have an effect on him.*

Careful not to touch anything else, I reach for his cock to take it in my hands. I slide one hand up his shaft while the other reaches for his balls. He widens his legs without any prompting and I kneel between them. I start to lick, stroke, and tug the perfect rhythm, using my hand and mouth in such a way that drives him wild. I hear his breath catch every now and again, letting me know this is what he needs.

When I can't take it anymore, I release the hand cupping

his balls and slide it into my own wetness. Within moments, I find my clit and work it roughly as I continue to enjoy the taste of Enzo.

"Samantha," he growls in a low warning, letting me know he's close. He tugs my arm to get me to stop. "I want to come with you."

Without a second thought, I stand and he guides me to straddle him. I know I'm drenched, so there's no need for any preparation. I place both my thighs on the outside of his and slide home to the base of his cock. He can't stay passive. Enzo takes control from the bottom and it's all I can do to hold on for dear life. His lips lock onto mine as he thrusts into me over and over again at a relentless pace. *God! I love this man. I love this feeling.* Feeling myself build higher and higher, I need to take Enzo with me. I put every amount of effort I have into showing him how I feel and taking the pleasure he gives me.

I scream, "I love you!" as one of the best orgasms of my life rips through me. I feel Enzo thrust into me a few more times and his body stiffens. He holds onto me as if I'm his last dying breath. Then he fills me with love from the inside out.

"I love you so much, Samantha. You're so beautiful," he says as he rests his forehead against mine.

Holy Hell! It's going to take a long time to recover.

Nothing can be heard except the panting of our breaths and the beating of our hearts as we both come back to Earth from that out-of-this-world experience. *How is it that each time keeps getting better?* I think as I relax into that perfect place between his shoulder blade and chest.

After a long while, Enzo breaks the silence. "It does get better each and every time, Samantha." His voice then turns playful as he pats me on the ass to move. "Are you ready to see what we can do to top that?"

I swear to God, with his words alone, he grows once again from inside me. He doesn't even remove himself as he lifts me to a standing position and carries me to the bed across the room. He gently lays me down on the bed, careful not to slip out and proceeds to show me just how much better round two can be.

2 7

ENZO

Saying goodbye to Samantha is one of the hardest things I've ever done. She takes me to the airport, but I won't let her walk me in since there's no point with security, so we say our goodbyes in the departure lanes at the Portland International Airport. My legs feel like lead as I walk away from her. My only saving grace is knowing our time apart will be short.

We spent the last of our time enjoying every moment with one another. Devin had the kids while we were in San Francisco, then Samantha took a few days off to spend more time with me. In the evenings, we enjoyed activities with her family. Life couldn't have been any better. Well, except for the fact I have three months left on my contract. It sucks being away from her.

As soon as I get back to Ramstein, I realize my vacation is over. I talk with Samantha whenever I can. But time differences and being on duty proves to have its challenges. I sleep near my phone so I can answer her calls. We video chat or talk every day, except when I'm required to go radio-silent for the mission I'm on.

I have literally flown all over the world for the past few weeks. I'm glad to say I safely made it in and out of various places in Sudan, Afghanistan, and Pakistan. There have been some touchy situations, but I know I had to make it out unscathed. The men and women who depend on me to be their wheels make it essential I return, not to mention I now have Samantha counting on me, too.

Thank the fucking Lord time flies when I'm busy. Knowing there's an end in sight to my misery has made it bearable. I miss Samantha like crazy. Each time I close my eyes, her rich mahogany eyes stare back at me. I can't wait until she arrives at the airport.

Knowing I can't spend another minute without her being mine, I managed one important shopping trip while I was off duty last week. I had to guess at her size, but I'm pretty sure I have it right. I just can't wait until she gets here. I never knew I could miss anyone so much.

These last two hours have been the worst. I have flowers waiting for her as I pace the lobby of the airport. The monitor keeps changing for when her flight should arrive. It appears as if they have a good tailwind, so they're making up time. I'm in civilian clothes, wearing dark jeans, t-shirt, and a thick sweater. In Germany, it's cold in the winter. I have a plan in place for tonight; I just hope she's up for it.

I paid for her to fly first class, with only one layover at JFK. I hope she was able to stretch out in a sleeper bed and rest the entire way here. It's still morning, so I'm hoping she got some sleep to help with jetlag.

When she finally approaches, I feel as if I'm dreaming. She looks even more beautiful than I remember. When she reaches me, I pull her in tight. Damn, I've missed her. I can't get enough of her. I kiss her thoroughly and completely. I don't care that we're in the middle of a crowded airport. I lift her off the floor and she squeals as I spin her around.

"God, I've missed you, beautiful," I whisper before setting her down.

"I've missed you, too," she whispers as I kiss her once more.

When I finally put her on her feet, I hand her the flowers I've been holding onto. Then, I take a good look at her. She's wearing a beautiful, dark-red, flowing top with black skinny jeans and short brown boots. She appears as if she just stepped off a runway, which brings an even bigger smile to my face because she has no idea about our plans this evening. She appears a little tired, but not dead on her feet. Her hair is flowing perfectly around her shoulders and the smile she has plastered on her face makes me feel as if I'm the luckiest guy in the world.

I take her carry-on bag and direct her to baggage claim. It doesn't take long before we're out of the airport and climbing into my silver Land Rover. She seems in awe that she's here. Her eyes take in the scenery as we drive down the highway, and the smile on her face is infectious.

"Are you hungry?" I ask, wanting to make sure she isn't starving after her long flight.

"I could eat," she says as she takes in the sites outside the Frankfurt Airport.

Knowing we'll have to go inside to dine, I take her to the place I think she'll love. It's located in a small town just outside of Frankfurt. As we pull into town, she lights up at all the beautiful Christmas decorations lining the streets. I find a place to park and we make our way to the restaurant. On our way inside, Samantha spots a shop with Christmas ornaments displayed in the window.

"Oh, can we go in there? I'd love to bring home an ornament to remember this trip."

"Let's go, beautiful." I take her hand and pull her close to me once we're on the sidewalk. Thankfully, she brought a warm jacket because it's freezing out here. I wrap my arms around her, so fucking relieved she's finally with me. When she pulls back, I reach for her face, and with a kiss, show her once again how much I've missed her.

All too soon, I remember we're in public and I need to curb my enthusiasm. Fuck, it sucks being honorable sometimes. I motion for the shop she wanted to look in. "Let's go see what's inside."

Christmas music with German voices being sung fills the shop. It smells like sugar cookies and pine trees and the blast of warm air that welcomes us is inviting. The small shop is lined with shelves. Samantha peruses them, and I follow along with her hand in mine. Even though I usually despise shopping, being with her is worth every moment of torture. Seeing her enthusiasm as she browses through the trinkets makes me feel things I've never felt before.

"Oh, Enzo! Look at this." Samantha holds up a hand carved Santa ornament. At the bottom, it has "St. Nicholas Day" and the year carved into it. "Do you realize that your birthday is on St. Nicholas Day?" she asks when she realizes in Germany, they celebrate that on the sixth of December.

"Yeah, I know." I hold out my hand, asking her for the Santa to inspect it further. "You should get this. It's beautiful."

"I think I will, but I want to look around some more." She turns to look at more decorations around her.

"Uh, Enzo?" She seems a little hesitant.

"Yeah?"

"What's up with the pickles? They seem to be everywhere." She holds one up, then looks around at the variety of choices she has before her.

"Ha! For St. Nicholas Day here in Germany, the parents decorate the tree. Then the first time the kids look at the tree, they search for the pickle. The first one to find the pickle gets an extra present under the tree," I explain.

"Well, we should get one of those, too. It'd be a fun tradition to start."

"Would you like to find *my* pickle?" *I'm a guy. I can't help it.* The burst of color that explodes across her face was so worth it. Samantha winks at me, then picks out her favorite before continuing to shop.

By the time we're finished with this shop, Samantha has quite a few new things to decorate her home with. God, I wish I could be there with her this year. It's going to suck spending the holidays alone again, especially now that I have someone I want to share them with. But I'll be home at the end of January for good.

When we finish shopping, we walk down a few doors to the restaurant. There is no wait, so Samantha and I are seated right away. Since this is a small town and the woman who greets us speaks only in German, I take the liberty of asking Samantha what she's in the mood for, then I order for both of us. *You can't live in a country and not pick up on at least the basics of the language.*

We fill our time talking about everything and nothing. She fills me in on each of the kids and I tell her what I can about my most recent missions. Granted, I can't say much, so I tell her about some of my buddies stationed here at Ramstein. She's eager to meet them. Though I'd rather keep her to myself, I realize I want to share that side of my life with her, too. I warn her that some of them are rough and rowdy, and she doesn't miss a beat by telling me those are the ones she should meet first.

There's about an hour drive to my apartment off base. To my surprise, as soon as Samantha gets settled in the car and the heater flows through the frigid space, she falls fast asleep. *She did just travel over fifteen hours to get here.* I just lay my hand on her thigh to keep a connection and make the trip with ease.

Samantha is as cute as can be when we arrive. She doesn't appear to be willingly waking up anytime soon. At one point, I reach for her hand to hold it, and it drops like a lead weight when I try to wake her. I've made plans for this evening, but I think I'll just postpone them until she can enjoy them more.

When I open her door to help her out, Samantha wakes, seeming embarrassed to have fallen asleep. "Shit! I fell asleep. Are we already here?" She looks around in a panic.

I try not to laugh as I reply, "Relax, beautiful. You didn't miss much. I'll take you sightseeing another time."

She eagerly gets out of the car, taking my hand as she says, "Now that I've rested, what do you want to do this afternoon?" I lead her to my one-bedroom flat. "Let's get you settled, then we can decide."

Now that I'm looking at my flat from an outsider's perspective, I realize there isn't much to it. "I hope you aren't expecting anything fancy." I look at Samantha, who seems to be taking my living space in. "It's basically a basement that has been converted into an apartment. There's a three-bedroom flat above me, which is also rented out. Three guys live in it. All are stationed at Ramstein, though not in my unit. We get along okay."

"I'm sure it will be fine, Enzo. Don't worry." She leans up on her toes and kisses me quickly once more.

"I've warned you that I'm not home much, right?" I feel like shit inviting her to this place now that she's here. "I just got this place so I could come and go as I please, have some privacy, and stay out of base housing. It's nice to get away from it all, if you know what I mean." We reach the door and she puts her hands on her hips.

"Enzo, I could care less what it looks like. I didn't come here to stay at the Ritz. I came here to see you."

"If you don't like it, I can get a hotel for the week you're here," I offer, knowing it only has the bare necessities.

"Don't be ridiculous. Does it have a clean bed and shower?"

"Yes," I sigh. "It's not a dump, just tight quarters. You're used to living in a big, beautiful home. I just don't want you to go without."

She shakes her head and laughter comes out. "As long as I have you, I'm fine."

With that, I open the door and let her walk in. I give her the five-second tour because that's all it takes. My kitchen lines one wall and a living room the other. There are two doors off the back of the living room wall. One goes to a bedroom that's at least big enough to fit a king-sized bed along with my dresser, the other goes to the bathroom.

I take her things into my bedroom and place them near the dresser on the floor. "If you'd like to hang anything up, feel free to. There's plenty of room in the closet."

"Thanks. Do you mind if I take a shower?" she asks innocently.

"Sure. You can grab your things and go through that door. It also opens to the living room, so if you don't want the neighbors to see, be sure to shut the other door," I tease.

She walks in and I hear the other door shut. Wanting to give her some space, I do everything I can to force myself back to the living room. After a few minutes, I hear Samantha call, "Enzo, can you help me with something?"

Not knowing what she should need, I rush through the bedroom and stop dead in my tracks. There she is, in all her naked glory, standing before me. One arm is held high against the bathroom doorjamb, the other is casually on her hips. Her body is on full display and the look on her face lets me know the help she needs.

Trying to play coy, I ask, "Need something?"

Her rich mahogany eyes grow darker. "Only you."

It takes me less than thirty seconds to rid myself of the clothes I'm wearing. There's no way I want to have our first time after a month of being apart to be in the moderately sized shower. I bend down and swoop her up without giving her a chance to comprehend my intentions. Within two strides, I'm laying her on the freshly washed bedding. Then I pause to stare at the beauty before me.

"Took you long enough," she teases. I'm not sure that she meant to say that aloud, but I can't help but chuckle.

"I was giving you some space, beautiful. I've wanted to attack you since you stepped into my arms from the plane. I was *trying* to be a gentleman."

"Have your wicked way with me, Enzo. I can't wait any longer." The invitation couldn't be clearer if it was tattooed on her forehead. I don't wait any longer and I don't disappoint. I spend the next several hours worshiping her body the only way I know how. We do make the time to refuel with dinner, but we eat it in bed and I continue to sing my praises to her throughout the night.

The next morning, I awake to a retching sound. It makes me bolt out of bed once I realize Samantha is no longer beside me. I find her naked body hovered over the toilet, praying to the porcelain God. "You okay?" Fuck. She isn't okay. She's puking. What a stupid thing to ask, so I try again. "Anything I can get you?"

"Go away, I don't want you to catch this," Samantha croaks.

"Not happening, beautiful." I may feel helpless, but I'm not going to be a complete douche and leave her when she is sick.

I walk over to her and pull back her hair. I rub her back as she seems to dry heave over the commode. I realize she's freezing, so I take a towel I set out for her to use and wrap it around her body.

"Thanks," she whispers weakly.

When she stops trying to heave, she slumps against the wall and the toilet. I realize this can't be comfortable, so I ask, "Do you think you're done puking for now?"

She nods, then rolls her head to lean it against the wall. I take this as my cue to help her move. Within moments, I have her lying back down in bed. I cover her up, then walk over to my drawer and get her a pair of boxers and a t-shirt. I'm not about to take the time to get into her suitcase. Besides, there's no reason she should ruin her clothes if she gets sick again. I slip on a pair of boxers for myself, then walk back over to the bed and pull back the covers to help dress her. At first, she protests, but then she realizes what I'm doing and eagerly accepts what I'm offering.

I walk to the kitchen and get my largest cooking pot. It isn't much, but it'll do if she needs it again. I place it on the floor next to the bed with a towel underneath. Then I attempt to crawl back into bed to hold her, but she protests.

"Enzo, I don't want to get you sick."

"Samantha, we've swapped enough DNA since last night. If I'm going to get sick, I'm already exposed," I try to tease, but then I take mercy on her. "Beautiful, I just want to hold you. Please let me do this. I feel helpless right now. Not to mention there's no way I'm going in the other room after spending the last six weeks apart."

She reluctantly agrees. The next thing I know she's snuggled into my chest, sound asleep. I hope she just ate something that didn't agree with her, or that this is just a twenty-four hour virus. I settle in and eventually fall asleep again with her by my side.

A few hours later, she wakes up. She gets up to go to the bathroom, but all she does is use the facilities. I hover around in case she gets sick, but want to give her privacy if she needs it. When she returns, I notice her hair has been brushed and she smells like mint, so she must have brushed her teeth.

"Are you feeling better?"

"So much better. I'm a little hungry. Do you have any toast?"

Thankful for something to do, I quickly get up to put some bread in the toaster. She joins me in the living room and sits on the couch. While the toast is cooking, I walk over to the closet by the door and get a blanket to place over her.

"I don't know what I did to deserve you," she whispers as I kiss her lightly on the forehead while tucking her in.

"I'm the lucky one," I whisper back, and I can tell she hadn't meant for me to hear. A beautiful blush brings color back to her cheeks.

"Damn filter," she mutters, and I can't help but laugh.

"I love you, Samantha, lack of filter and all."

She pretends to glare. "You're lucky I love you, too, Enzo."

"Damn right I am."

After fixing her toast, we lounge around for a few more hours. When it's one o'clock in the afternoon, Samantha groans. "Can we go do something? It feels like such a waste to come all this way just to sit in an apartment."

"Are you sure you're up for it?" I ask, remembering how much she heaved earlier this morning.

"Yes. I feel fine. Let's stay out of public areas, so I won't spread germs if I'm sick, but I really want to see the sights. We can drive around and see them from the car and come back to them after we know I'm better."

Of course, I honor her wish. Within the hour, we're loaded into my car and driving around. I take her to Ramstein Air Force Base and show her around. She says she's hungry again, so I run in and grab something for us to eat at a deli on base. Unfortunately, we don't even make it thirty minutes after she eats before she's begging me to pull over. She empties her stomach in some bushes and begs me to take her back to my place, claiming she has embarrassed me enough for one day. We spend the rest of the evening watching movies. She seems to do better after a few hours, so I feed her some chicken broth for dinner, not wanting to take any chances.

The next morning, I feel like I'm Bill Murray in the movie *'Groundhog Day.'* My life is stuck on repeat. Samantha's back to retching on the floor and once again, I'm feeling helpless. I help her take a shower, keeping things task oriented, then get her back into bed. I feel awful for her. She seems lethargic and I can hardly get her to eat anything for the remainder of the day because she can't keep it down. She has me worried.

Thankfully, the next day she's better. It happens to be my birthday, so *Happy Birthday to me!* She seems vibrant and full of energy. Back to her normal self, or at least not knocking on death's door at any moment. She begs me to get dressed up and get out of the house to celebrate my birthday. *Who am I to complain?*

I'm on cloud nine because today might finally be the day I get to follow through with my original plans. While Samantha is getting ready, I make sure I have everything I need to make my dreams come true. She nearly knocks me on my ass when she greets me in the living room in that stunning dress I bought her on our first date. She looks spectacular.

Even though it's only early morning, we decide to make the most of the day and start celebrating early since she claims we have a lot of lost time to make up for. To be honest, I could care less what we do today. I just want to be with her.

"So, are you ready to finally show me around?" she saucily asks.

"You keep that look on your face and we won't ever leave this place," I tease in return. God, it feels amazing to have Samantha back in the land of the living.

From my flat, within thirty minutes, we can drive to three different castles. I start with the closest. It's the Nanstein Castle. It was built in 1162 in Landstuhl, Rhineland-Palatinate. Thankfully, Samantha brought knee-high boots, so we're able to get out and tour the grounds of the castle. It has spectacular views that overlook the city. We learn that it was built after Holy Roman Emperor Frederick I demanded its construction as an additional defense for the Palatinate. Samantha and I take several pictures of the architecture, as well as the views from the castle walls. I sneak quite a few pictures of Samantha, too, because she's absolutely glowing with excitement.

Afterward, we stop at a local café. Samantha claims her stomach isn't completely back to normal yet, so she only wants a light pastry and coffee for breakfast.

After we eat, we go to another castle, in Thallichtenberg,

Germany. It's the biggest castle ruin in Germany, and it's a fantastic sight to see. Samantha is in awe of its vastness. It sits upon a large hill, overlooking the farmlands below.

Samantha can hardly control her enthusiasm for the history we're experiencing. I can't help but laugh when, "This is what fairytales are made of," comes out of her mouth. The brilliant woman before me is always referencing books.

"Does that make me your Prince Charming?" I tease.

Samantha doesn't respond, just kisses me soundly on the lips, making me wish we were back at my flat again.

***

Unfortunately, just as I'm about to take her to our final destination for the day where I have my big surprise planned, she begs me to pull over. Yep. She gets sick once again.

When I feel her head, it's clammy and I can't help but notice she has lost all color. Maybe we overdid it and I'm overreacting but throwing up for three days straight and not keeping anything down in all that time has me extremely worried. She just lies limp in the car as we head back home, which scares the shit out of me even more. When she moans and rubs her upper stomach, I nearly lose it.

Screw this. I'm not taking any chances. Instead of taking her back to my place, I make a rash decision. I drive straight to the on-base hospital. I know she's a civilian, but it's the closest hospital around. When Samantha figures out my plans, she throws a fit. "Enzo, I don't need to go to the hospital. I've just got the flu. There's no need to go to this much trouble."

But suddenly, she turns completely green and points to the

shoulder of the road. I barely have a chance to get off safely before she's opening the door and releasing the remaining contents of her stomach.

I give her a pointed look and ask, "Will you just humor me? Let's go make sure that's all this is. I can't idly sit back and watch you suffer like this, not knowing the cause."

"Okay," she reluctantly agrees and falls asleep within moments.

Fuck! Her lethargic state is scaring the shit out of me. I step on the gas and get her there as safely as possible.

When we enter the waiting room, I explain her situation. Samantha is offered a wheelchair because she can hardly stand on her own. Thank the fucking Lord, there isn't a long wait. Most people are home celebrating St. Nicholas Day and we've beaten the evening rush, according to one of the nurses.

The entire time, I can't help but hold Samantha's hand or have some part of me touching her. I feel so fucking helpless. She moans a little more and I nearly take out my frustrations on a nurse that finally comes to get us.

The nurse asks if I'm family and I say, "I'm her fiancé," before any questions can be asked. There's no fucking way I'm going to sit out in a waiting room because I'm not family. Besides, if I had had the chance to ask her, I would be telling the truth right now anyway.

The nurse records her vitals and asks her a series of questions. What feels like eons later, a doctor comes in and does a quick exam. Samantha's sore throughout her stomach, so the doctor orders a series of tests to be done. Blood is drawn, and a nurse asks Samantha if she can give urine. She smiles weakly and the nurse assists her to the bathroom. It takes everything in my power not to insist I be the one to go with her, but Samantha gives me a knowing look, putting me at ease. A little, anyway. Who the fuck am I kidding? I'm still a nervous wreck.

The doctor has been throwing words around like appendicitis, gallbladder, kidney infection, and about four other things they will test for. In a little while, they will be taking her for an ultrasound. Samantha has been the voice of reason through it all. Just the touch of her hand on my skin is enough to calm me to the point of being reasonable to be around.

While we're waiting for her tests to be done, I realize I can't take it anymore. I'm a fucking ball of nerves and I must let her know how much she means to me. "Samantha," I almost shout.

Surprised, she looks in my direction. "Yes?"

"I need you to know how much I love you," I start, but she interrupts me.

"I love you, too," she whispers, placing a hand on my forearm and I immediately calm once again.

I clear my throat and begin again, "Samantha, I need you to know how much I love you. I've never met anyone like you. You've become the most important person in my life."

Finally, I have her full attention, as her round eyes are entirely focused on mine. I kneel on one knee and I bring both her hands in mine as I lean against her hospital bed. I hesitate for a moment until I finally get a grip on my emotions and continue, "Samantha, no matter what those test results say, I'm going to be with you in sickness and in health. I want you to know that I will always have your best interests at heart. I'm sure there'll be times you're going to have to put me in my place because I can be a little thick headed…" I can't help but laugh when she chuckles at my comment. "…but know I will always do it out of love."

I take a deep breath to collect my thoughts once again.

"These past six weeks of being apart have made me a miserable bastard. I don't want to spend another day without you being mine." I take another deep breath as I keep to my mission, getting the words I desperately need to say out, "Samantha Elizabeth O'Reilly, would you do me the honor of being my wife? Will you marry me and make me the happiest man alive?"

My heart pounds in my chest with anticipation and of course, Samantha chooses this moment to stay silent. Her face is a mask, void of emotion, and her beautiful mouth remains firmly closed.

Christ, was this the wrong place to ask her? Should I have waited until she was well again or stuck with my original plan and been more romantic? Where the fuck is her lack of filter when I need it?

To be continued…

Ready for the conclusion of this story?

Download Resolution Today!

https://amandashelley.com/books-by-amanda-shelley-2/

ABOUT THE AUTHOR

Amanda Shelley loves falling into a book to experience new worlds. As an avid reader and writer, sharing worlds of her own creation is a passion that inspired her to become an author. She writes contemporary romance about characters who are strong and sexy with a twist of sass.

When not writing, Amanda enjoys time with her family, playing chauffeur, chef and being an enthusiastic fan for her children. Keeping up with them keeps her alert and grounded in reality. She enjoys long car rides, chai lattes and popping her SUV into four-wheel drive for adventures anywhere.

Amanda loves hearing from readers. Be sure sign up for her newsletter and follow her on social media. Join her reader's group Amanda's Army of Readers to talk about her books and stay up to date on her latest information.

www.amandashelley.com

Readers group: https://www.facebook.com/groups/Amandas ArmyofReaders/

Newsletter: https://geni.us/AmandaShelleyNL

Goodreads: https://www.goodreads.com/author/show/19713563. Amanda_Shelley

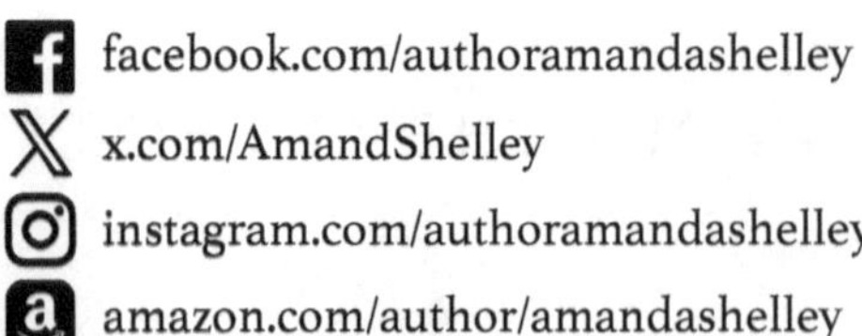

facebook.com/authoramandashelley
x.com/AmandShelley
instagram.com/authoramandashelley
amazon.com/author/amandashelley
bookbub.com/profile/amanda-shelley

ACKNOWLEDGMENTS

I have to say I truly appreciate those who have supported me along the way. Whether you read my books, have listened to me talk about my characters as if they're real people, or simply been a cheerleader, I wouldn't have been able to do this without you, so thank you.

To my four beautiful daughters, thank you for allowing that "one more minute," as I finished a scene, read over what I'd written, and for letting me follow my dream. I know it wasn't always easy but your continued support matters the most. I love you all.

To Kay, for being the first to read my work and encouraging me to continue. I will make a reader out of you yet!

To Cara, I'm beyond thankful that fate intervened, causing you to reach out to me. You haven't only become an amazing friend, but this writing experience wouldn't have been the same without you.

To my beta readers Jackie, Heather, Becky, and Zee, thank you for your invaluable feedback and for taking the time to read my words and being a part of the process to bring the world I created to life.

To Jennifer and Katie, I appreciate your willingness to read my book and help me find teasers and quotes to share the best of this book with others.

To Andy for always answering my random questions, for seeking out the answers if they were unknown, and for getting your buddies involved if needed. Your willingness to pick up the phone and not shake your head continues to amaze me.

To Aly Martinez, you aren't only an inspiration but you are a gift. I appreciate the time you took to work with me on my blurbs and to help fine tune them. After listening to you speak at the Indie Tea, I hope we one day meet again.

To Corrine Michaels, Meghan March, and Whitney Garcia, after speaking with you and listening to your advice at the Indie Tea, I was inspired more than ever to make my dream a reality. I want you all to know your words didn't go unheard. I appreciate the time and effort you put into to helping others along this journey.

Thank you Marquita Valentine for giving me my first ARC years ago and showing me a glimpse into the world of self-publishing. Little do you know just how much you have influenced me. I am still a huge fan and please know you hold a special place in my heart.

To Amy Queau at Q Design, thank you for your invaluable advice and amazing covers. Your cover designs rock and I can't tell how satisfied I am with them. You brought my vision to life and I will be forever grateful!

To Mickel Yantz, thank you for my kickass logos.

To SJS Editorial Services, thank you for working with me to make my story become what it is today. I look forward to working on many books with you in the future.

To Deaton Author Services for proofing my books and

catching my mistakes. I don't know what I would do without you.

To my reader's group Amanda's Army, thank you for being loyal and supportive. Your encouragement reaches far beyond what you'll ever know.

Last, but certainly not least, I want to thank all the bloggers, readers, and reviewers out there who have supported me along the way. Your word of mouth and enthusiasm is priceless. I can't wait to share more with you in the future.

plans, which potentially will bring them closer together or rip them apart.

Will Enzo and Samantha get the resolution they desire?

Making The Call

Dani

As a bestselling romance author, most assume my life's glamorous, filled with combustible chemistry, and most of all, romance. Ha! I can only wish. With a deadline looming, I've escaped to my family's cabin on Anderson Island to free myself from distractions. My plan's great, until a man, who could pass as a cover model on one of my books, comes to my rescue. Is there chemistry? Sure. Is he everything I'd look for in a guy? Absolutely. But will my career be at risk if I give into my desire?

Luke

For a player, women line up outside the locker room. For coaches, we're lucky to get in the game. As the youngest NFL coach in the league, I live, eat, breathe, and even sleep football. To gear up for this season, I return to my home on Anderson Island for a much-needed break. When Dani literally crashes into my life, my mind's suddenly on the sexy brunette with a sailors mouth, rather than my team's next play. She has me dusting off another playbook entirely, making me wonder, did I make the right call?

https://geni.us/AmandaShelleyBooks

The Boy Upstairs

I ran into Derek while trying to escape the neighbor from hell.

Instantly, we hit it off. Since he's only here for three months and the microbrewery leaves me little time for commitments, it's the perfect setup for a fling.

He's adventurous, challenges me, and he just gets me from the inside out.

With our expiration date quickly approaching, I'm left to wonder...
Will my heart ever be the same without the boy upstairs?

https://geni.us/AmandaShelleyBooks

He Saved My Boy

Davis is the first guy to catch my attention since... hell, I don't even know.

Instantly, he makes me think and feel things I've forgotten existed. It has been forever since I put my needs first, so I take the chance and let him light me up from the inside out.

Our night is the kind that will ruin me for all others.

But then I get the dreaded call.

I rush out without a second glance, knowing I'll likely never see him again.

My son will always come first—Always.

Imagine my surprise when Davis walks in, and I find he's the only one who can save my boy.

This cannot be happening—*I guess it's time to pull up my big girl panties and see what happens.*

https://geni.us/AmandaShelleyBooks

Zander: A Perfectly Independent Series Novella

Zander's known for being a player both on and off the court. When his name shows up as my next client, my heart stalls, and not in a good way. There's no way I'll survive the semester with him. I just don't have the patience.

However, when I need help, Zander makes a proposal I can't refuse. He'll be my fake date to my best friend's wedding so I don't have to face my ex and his new girlfriend alone.

The weekend goes off without a hitch as we effortlessly pretend to have the time of our lives.

All is perfect... until I realize my feelings for Zander are no longer an act.

What will I do when our arrangement comes to an end?

https://geni.us/AmandaShelleyBooks

Drew: Book One of the Perfectly Independent Series

Of all people, why him?

He didn't EVEN bother introducing himself, just assumed I knew him from his fame on the court.

I nearly died on the spot when our professor announced we were permanent lab partners. Between his arrogance and the constant interruption from basketball groupies, there's no way I'll survive this semester.

Sure, he's hotter than anyone I've ever seen in a science lab with his sexy blue eyes, cute dimple, and muscles for days - but I can't afford *his* kind of distractions.

Okay. Deep breath.

I can do this.

After all, it's only one semester.

Just when I think my self-control is in check, he does something to show me that he isn't the egotistical, self-centered jerk I thought he was.

How can his stupid smile suddenly make my mind melt, heart race, and palms sweat?

If I take this chance on Drew, will my perfectly laid out plans disappear?

https://geni.us/AmandaShelleyBooks

Vince: Book Two of the Perfectly Independent Series

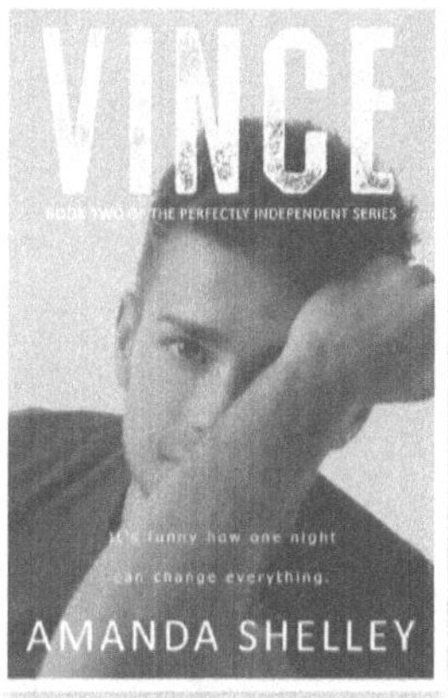

It's funny how one night can change everything.

As a bartender near campus, I'm certain I've heard it all. Rarely a shift passes without some guy taking his best shot, hoping I'll end my self-proclaimed dating diet.

Of course, this is exactly how I meet Vince.

Except, he isn't the one running his mouth.

No, he simply shuts down his idiotic friend, then stops my heart with the simplest of smiles and walks away.

Just when I force myself to forget him, he bumps into me on campus.

Our connection is consuming, and my world is knocked off kilter. It's far beyond physical attraction. He's smart, sexy, and feels like—home?

Wait, that can't be right...

Whatever it is, Vince has me breaking my rules to spend time with him.

My entire life I've prepared for meeting the wrong guys.

What the hell should I do when I find the right one?

https://geni.us/AmandaShelleyBooks

Damien: Book Three of the Perfectly Independent Series

Beautiful girls are not hard to find at Columbia River University.

The coeds on campus are great to look at but I was over that scene after graduation three years ago.

These days, outside of being part of the largest civil engineering job on campus, all I'm searching for is a decent meal and some peace and quiet. It's why I'm happy to have found what I consider a hidden gem in the diner I frequent.

All I need to do is finish this job and move on to the next by year's end.

Should be easy enough. Only when Vanessa walks up with a sexy smile and a mouth full of sass, she does more than take my order. She completely takes my breath away.

Next thing I know, I'm here every morning, making every excuse to dine with this intriguing woman. Not only is she smart and sexy, but she's laser focused on reaching the goals she's set for herself.

The more I get to know her, the more I'm convinced she's the one. I just have to find a way to get her to deviate from her perfectly laid plans and take a chance on me.

https://geni.us/AmandaShelleyBooks

The Vegas Pitch

This pitch could make or break my career.

Not only will it set a personal record for the biggest account I've ever landed, but it could set my newfound company three years ahead of schedule for expansion.

Thank god I've got Nate Bellinger on my team.

Even though I had my reservations hiring the sexiest man I've ever laid eyes on – he more than meets my expectations with his hard work and determination. Together, we've formed a solid team and play off each other perfectly.

As we wait for the final verdict, I begrudgingly take Nate up on his offer for a night on the town. After all, this is Vegas and I need to let the chips fall where they may.

Imagine my surprise when I wake up the next morning to find we've not only won the campaign, but I'm apparently married to the man I've only ever let myself fantasize about.

The kicker of it all – he has no intentions of letting me go.

But what will it mean once we leave Vegas?

https://amandashelley.com/books-by-amanda-shelley-2/

The Summer Dare

Leave it to Nana to think of everything.

After a grueling semester, I'm ready for a peaceful summer in Seaside with my sisters.

Imagine my surprise, when I'm woken by the screeching sound of a saw coming through my wall, the first official morning of break.

Not only did I come flying out of bed swinging, but I gave Ryan, the unsuspecting carpenter the surprise of his life, when I came wielding my killer coat hanger and all.

Too bad, I was only in a tank and undies and it wasn't nearly as effective as I'd hoped.

Of course, he insists he's only doing his job. Since it's Nana's last request to care for us, I can't refuse.

However, I won't let a tall, pesky, sexy as sin, know-it-all get in my way of my summer plans. I pretend I ignore him – that is until my youngest sister pokes her nose in my business and throws down a dare I can't back down from.

Kiss the next single guy who walks up to the bonfire – or explain to my sisters why I get riled up over the contractor.

When Ryan suddenly appears, I know I'm screwed in more ways than one.

Not only will my sisters learn my secret, but from the determined look on Ryan's face, I'm afraid he's eager to reveal it to the world as well.

What have I gotten myself into?

As I walk toward him, one thing is certain – this summer dare will either make or break me.

https://geni.us/AmandaShelleyBooks

The Summer Ultimatum

Watching my sister fall in love last summer gave me something I hadn't expected—hope. It gave me hope that there might be someone out there for me and hope that I might get past my misguided fears and finally let someone in.

With my help, Ryan's planning the most epic proposal. I just have to get the know-it-all musician I work with to fall in line to make it work.

Jax is wicked smart, extremely talented, and sexy as sin. But he can't see the forest for the trees when it comes to his potential. He'd rather keep playing in dive bars along the coast than take a real shot at success.

When the Seaside festival has a music competition, I present Jax with an ultimatum that will either make or break both our careers.

I've laid it all on the line, but can he?

https://geni.us/AmandaShelleyBooks

The Summer Proposal

My sisters are dropping like flies.

They're falling in love and having the time of their lives.

Don't get me wrong, I'm ecstatic for them. I love seeing them happy.

But I'm not ready for that type of commitment.

I can't even keep a plant alive, let alone find someone worthy of getting past a third date.

As the only sister done with school and single as a pringle, I have to do something fast, or I'll be my matchmaking aunt's next victim.

When Jax's drummer joins him for the summer and needs some help with his image, I make him a deal he can't refuse.

All is perfect—until I realize my summer proposal has one minor flaw.

Our relationship may be a sham, but there's nothing fake about my feelings for Finn.

https://geni.us/AmandaShelleyBooks

The Summer Arrangement

One, two, three—it's all down to me.

As the youngest and only single Lancaster, I'm eager to spend my summer in Seaside, Oregon, with my sisters. It's something I've looked forward to all year, and I'm determined to make every minute count. After all, I've only got one year before I graduate from college and have to adult for real.

However, if I want to graduate debt free, I need to work. I have a lead on the perfect summer job with the nanny agency I've spent the last three summers catering to.

I just have to win over an adorable three-year-old and convince her single dad I'm the right one for the job.

Simple enough, right?

Except when I show up at his door, I'm shocked to find he's the guy I hooked up with a few times last semester.

This cannot be happening.

I need this job. There's too much on the line to walk away. Maybe we can put the past behind us and make some sort of summer arrangement?

https://geni.us/AmandaShelleyBooks

The Summer I Found Home

Being a pilot is all I've ever known.

I served my country and I'm damn proud of my career.

But sacrifices were made, especially when it came to family.

I've missed first steps, first days of school, and first dates to name a few.

My kids grew up. They're having families of their own.

Was it worth it?

When an opportunity brings me to Seaside, I jump feet first no questions asked.

It means experiencing all those firsts with my grandkids.

With family as my focus and my guard down, I don't even see Faye coming.

She's a force to be reckoned with and has me holding on for dear life.

I thought our ship had sailed, but now that I'm home for good—I just might get more than one second chance.

arrangement?

https://amandashelley.com/books-by-amanda-shelley-2/

Collide: A Sweet Romance

Falling head over heels was the last thing I expected.

Literally.

Coffee is everywhere – and more than my ego is bruised.

When the handsome stranger I plowed into calls me by name, mortification sinks in.

He rushes off to class. I run home to change, hoping to forget the whole incident.

If only I could be so lucky.

I quickly find it's a small world and Gavin Wallace is completely unavoidable. Everywhere I turn he's there. In my classes. Hanging with my friends.

I've got his full attention and I have to admit, I like it a lot more than I should.

https://geni.us/AmandaShelleyBooks